The Fireraisers

The Fireraisers

Detective Watters Mysteries Book 1

Malcolm Archibald

FOR CATHY

Contents

PROLOGUE
WASHINGTON, UNITED
STATES: APRIL 1862

Silhouetted against the window, the man was rangy with narrow shoulders and a head that seemed too large for his body. Allowing his companions to settle, he stepped forward to the table. The room crackled with tension, barely relieved by the birdsong that sweetened the humid air. The rangy man adjusted the fit of his coat and placed his tall hat on the polished table.

When the birdsong ceased, the only sound in the room was the remorseless ticking of a long-case clock. The rangy man cleared his throat before he began to speak.

'We are gathered here to discuss the possibility that our enemy could find a new ally.' The rangy man looked around the gathering, analysing the resourcefulness of each person in turn. Everybody met his eyes in full approval, with most nodding to reinforce their determination. One man produced a Bible, which he placed in front of him. Gleaming through the window, a beam of sunlight settled on the gold cross on the cover of the Book.

The rangy man continued. 'We all know that the struggle has already cost the lives of tens of thousands of men as well as millions of our dollars. We are engaged in a war which is tearing the Union apart, and we cannot afford to oppose more than one foe at a time. We also know that there has been talk of Great Britain joining the struggle on the opposing side.' He halted, cracking the knuckles of his great hands together as the men shifted uncomfortably in their chairs. A cloud blotted the sun, removing the light from the cross.

The rangy man took a deep breath. 'If the forces of Great Britain join those of the South, we will be facing a possible invasion from Canada, as well as the inevitable sea blockade and raids along the coast.' He permitted himself a small smile. 'We all know why this building is called the White House.'

There was a murmur of agreement from the room. Everybody present was aware of the War of 1812 when a British force had burned Washington. The Capitol Building had to be painted white to mask the scars. One man fidgeted in his seat as if he had been personally responsible for that decades-old disaster.

The rangy man spoke again. 'It is therefore imperative that we keep Great Britain out of the war. To that end, we will enhance the interests of all who support our noble cause and work against all those who oppose us.'

One of the men at the table lit a cigar, puffing aromatic smoke around the room. Others followed his example. When a red-haired man offered the speaker a cheroot, he shook his shaggy head.

'I propose that we use whatever methods we deem necessary to ensure Britannia pokes neither her trident nor her long nose into our domestic affairs. *Whatever* methods.' Again, he met the eyes of the assembled company. Not a single man flinched.

The bird sang again loudly. One of the men sought permission from the speaker then stepped to the open window and pulled it shut. He looked outside, noting the blue-uniformed guards that paraded in the hot sun and the flag that hung limply from its pole. 'Sir, when can we start?'

'Immediately.' The rangy man spoke softly. 'I will send each of you to a British city where agents of the Confederacy may seek to work against us.' Producing a sheaf of folded and sealed documents from within his coat, the rangy man handed one to each man in the room. 'You will all go to the destination written on the front of your document and do your duty for the Union. Inside, you will find two lists of names and addresses. The first gives details of those who may sympathise with us; the second gives details of those who may work against us. For instance, Mr F., you will work in Manchester, which is experiencing a great deal of distress because of the cotton famine. Mr H., you already know Dundee with its connections to both North and South. Each of you gentlemen has all been assigned to equally important destinations. That is all, gentlemen. *Any* methods, remember: the future of this great nation is at stake.'

One by one, the men left the room, all pausing to shake the hand of the speaker before stepping out of the building and into their waiting carriages. Only when they were gone did the speaker slump into a chair. He placed his head in his hands.

'And may God grant you strength and wisdom,' he said, 'for this country is dissolving in tears and blood.' For a second, he remained in that position then slowly stood, opened the window again, and listened to the call of the bird.

CHAPTER ONE
DUNDEE, SCOTLAND:
SEPTEMBER 1862

'Sergeant Watters!'

'Yes, sir?' Watters looked up from his desk.

Superintendent Mackay stood at the doorway. 'There's trouble in Brown's Street. Take a couple of constables and sort it out.'

'Is that not a job for a man in uniform, sir?'

Mackay nodded. 'If I had one available, I would send one. I have you, so I'll send you.'

Sighing, Watters carefully put away his pen with its new Waverley nib, stood up, and reached for his low-crowned hat. 'Do you have any idea what sort of trouble, sir?'

'There's a crowd gathering outside a burning mill,' Mackay said. 'Take Scuddamore and Duff; they're fresh on duty.'

'Send them after me, sir.' Watters lifted his cane, smacked the lead-loaded end against the palm of his hand, and headed for the stairs. 'Tell them to hurry!' He took the stairs two at a time, pausing momentarily at the landing to have a practise golf swing.

Sergeant Murdoch looked up from the newspaper he had been reading at the Duty Desk. 'Where are you off to, George?'

'Brown's Street.' Watters lifted his cane in salute. 'It's either murder and mayhem or a missing dog; I don't know what yet.'

'Probably murder and mayhem because of a missing dog,' Sergeant Murdoch said. 'You know what Dundee's like!'

Watters grinned. 'That's entirely possible, Willie.'

'See if that missing Honourable Peter Turnbull is at the back of it.' Murdoch pointed to a paragraph in his paper. 'So far, he's been seen in Paris, Cape Town, and America. He may as well be in Dundee as well. That fellow certainly gets around.'

'He's not my case,' Watters said. 'I've much more important things to worry about than missing gamblers. I have a crowd of people in Brown's Street.'

Murdoch shook his head. 'That sounds like a major case, George. Take care.' He returned to his newspaper and the missing Peter Turnbull.

Watters heard the babble of noise the instant he walked into the narrow, stone chasm that was Brown's Street. On both sides, cliff-like mill walls soared sheer from the pavement. Smoke was clouding from the mill on the right with scores of people congregated around the two fire engines that were parked on the road outside. Most of the crowd worked in the mill, hard-grafting, tired-eyed women.

'Dundee police!' Watters parted the crowd with his voice. 'Move aside, please.'

'You're no bluebottle,' a gaunt-faced woman challenged him. 'Whaur's your uniform, eh?'

'I'm Sergeant Watters of the Dundee Police.' Watters pushed past as a fireman appeared at the main entrance to the building. 'What's happened here? Is anybody hurt?'

'Nobody hurt, Sergeant Watters.' The fireman tipped back his brass helmet with the embossed DFB, "Dundee Fire Brigade," partly obscured by smuts of soot. He surveyed the damage to Matthew Beaumont's Brown's Street Weaving Manufactory and Mill. 'But it's made a fine mess of the building.'

Water slithered slowly down the cobbled street, carrying the crisped leaves of autumn plus fragments of charred wood. Watters peered through the blue smoke that hung acrid and heavy, trapped by the high-walled buildings. The chimneys of neighbouring mills added to the smog as the now-idle workers of Beaumont's Mill clustered round, pressurising the firemen for information. Through the chatter of the mill hands, Watters could hear the unending clatter of neighbouring mill machinery; the noise seeming to repeat one phrase: 'more pro*fit*, more pro*fit*, more pro*fit*.'

Well, Watters thought, there will be less profit for Matthew Beaumont until he gets his mill repaired.

'How long are you going to be, for God's sake? You're blocking the road!' With his wagon piled high with bales of raw jute, a carter glared at the fire engines that blocked his passage. He cracked his whip, unsettling the horses but not the equanimity of the imperturbable firemen.

'Any idea what caused it?' Watters watched as the firemen loaded their coiled canvas hoses into their wagons. The matched brown horses flicked their ears against the irritation of smut of soot.

'Our job is to extinguish fires, Sergeant Watters, not to find out how they started.' The senior fireman slammed shut the hinged compartment that held the hoses, checked that the water pump was secure, and clambered onto the engine. 'That's the fire out now, so I'll leave the cleaning up to the mill manager.' Raising his hand in farewell, the senior fireman cracked his whip. The horses jerked the machine away, with the second engine following a few moments later.

'About bloody time,' the carter said, cursing again as a group of women swarmed onto the road in front of him.

'Can we get back to work, Sergeant?' The gaunt-faced woman was at the forefront of the crowd.

Watters ignored the questions as he tried to peer through the charred doorway to the still smoking remains of the mill.

'Will we still get paid? I said will we still get paid?' A shrill-voiced woman followed Watters through the threshold of the mill, plucking at his arm. 'I've got bairns to keep and a man.'

Watters gently removed her hand. 'That's something that I can't answer. You'll have to speak to the mill manager.' Pushing open the door, Watters stepped inside the mill, coughing as smoke engulfed him. The interior was more cramped than he had expected: two storeys of closely-packed machinery that left little space to walk on the floor of stone slabs. The ground was a mess of wet ash with scraps of jute lying on top. Light filtered in from the now-open door and high, multi-paned windows.

'You'd better be careful, Sergeant Watters.' Fairfax was the mill manager, a man of middle height and middle age. 'We don't know what problems the fire has left us with.'

Watters nodded. 'Aye, you're not wrong there, Mr Fairfax. Are fires like this common?' Standing in the centre of the floor, Watters surveyed the mess. The damage was not as extensive as he had first supposed; the fire had swept through around one-third of this floor, putting ten spinning machines out of action.

'Not normally, but that's the second fire in one of Mr Beaumont's mills this week.' Mr Fairfax shook his head. 'Terrible.'

Watters narrowed his eyes. 'Oh? That's unusual. Is there some weakness in Mr Beaumont's mills, perhaps, that makes them more vulnerable to fire?'

Fairfax shook his head. 'Not that I am aware of, Sergeant. There was a spate of such fires in the '40s and '50s, but we tightened up since then. It's more likely to be carelessness from the hands than anything else.' Fairfax spoke with a broad Dundee accent, a man who had educated himself as he worked his way up from a half-timer to mill manager. He was pale faced and shrewd eyed with specks of soot polka dotting his sandy whiskers. 'It could have been oil-soaked waste placed near heat or a man going for a fly smoke who dropped his match in a pile of paper or something similar. I doubt that we will ever know. We can only be grateful that the Lord did not see fit to take any lives.'

Watters stirred the ash with his cane. 'Maybe so, but Mr Beaumont will not be happy to see his profits drop. Do you know where this fire started?'

'Not yet.' Fairfax shook his head.

'I'd like to find out.' Watters looked up as his two constables pushed into the mill. 'You lads, send the mill hands home; they won't be working here today.'

'Or tomorrow neither,' Fairfax said.

The constables nodded and returned outside. Watters knew them as reliable men, although Scuddamore liked his drink and Duff could be hot headed.

'If you'll excuse me, Mr Fairfax, I'll have a look around.' Swinging his cane, Watters stepped over a charred beam as he moved deeper into the mill. The interior of any workplace was sad when the machinery was silent, but when acrid smoke drifted between the looms, the place was particularly forlorn. Watters followed the trail of devastation from the merely scorched to the wholly destroyed, from the ground floor to the storerooms in the basement, where the smoke was at its most dense.

'Down here,' Watters said. 'It started down here.' He poked at the now-sodden remnants of jute bales. 'Mr Beaumont is not going to be a happy man when he sees this shambles.'

Tapping his cane on the ground, Watters looked for anything that might have caused the fire. After fifteen minutes, he frowned and headed back to the working levels. 'Mr Fairfax!'

Fairfax hurried up. 'Yes, Sergeant Watters?'

'You seem to believe that carelessness caused this fire.' Watters was not impressed by the mill manager's actions. Rather than taking control the minute he discovered the fire, Fairfax had allowed the flames to take hold. 'It's a mercy that nobody was killed.'

'I run a tight ship, Sergeant.'

Watters tapped the brim of his hat with his cane. 'I heard about some unpleasant practises at this mill. I heard that the overseers were bullying youngsters, using their belts too freely.'

'Not in my mill.' Fairfax shook his head violently. 'I don't allow any bullyragging in my mill.'

'Good.' Having suitably unsettled Fairfax, Watters listed the improvements he had thought of while down in the basement.

'In future, Mr Fairfax, I suggest that you do not permit smoking within the mill walls nor the use of any naked flames, such as candles or lamps, unless the needs of the business demand it.' Watters paused, knowing he was far overstepping his authority. 'I suggest that you place buckets of sand and water in convenient places, and instruct a responsible member of your workforce in their use. It would also be an idea to order your overseers to watch for any possible hazards and take appropriate action.' Watters paused. 'Plus, given the complaints I have heard, I want you to ensure nobody bullies the youngsters. In return, the youngsters can watch for any fire danger.'

Mr Fairfax nodded. Watters watched him closely. The workers did not seem to dislike him, which was in his favour.

'More important than all these ideas, Mr Fairfax, you should create some procedure whereby all your workers can leave the building safely in the event of a fire. We both know that you were fortunate on this occasion, but such good fortune may not occur a second time.'

Watters saw Fairfax stiffen but rather than return with an angry retort, the mill manager nodded meekly. 'Yes, Sergeant. Will you be giving a report to Mr Beaumont?'

Watters grunted. 'I might. Two fires in Mr Beaumont's mills within a week might be a bit more than a mere accident.'

'Fire-raising?' Fairfax raised his eyebrows.

'It's possible. Have you had occasion to dismiss any of your hands recently? A woman with a grudge is a dangerous animal.'

'No.' Fairfax screwed up his face. 'My hands are happy at their work.'

'Oh?' Watters took a practise golf swing with his cane. 'How happy are they? Are you a hard taskmaster, Mr Fairfax?'

'I told you there is no bullyragging here. My girls are well treated, Sergeant.'

'I hope so, Mr Fairfax; I really hope so.' Watters swung his cane again. 'If you can think of anything or anybody that may have a grudge, let me know. You know where to find me.'

The crowd had dissipated from Brown's Street, leaving Constables Scuddamore and Duff to fight their boredom as they lounged outside the mill gate.

'A shilling says he'll go into the mill even though it's shut.' Duff nodded to the lone jute cart that rumbled over the cobbles, with two small boys hitching a free lift at the back.

'You'll lose your shilling.' Scuddamore leaned against the wall, stifling his yawn. 'I know that carter. Eck Milne's not as daft as you look.'

When the boys shouted obscene insults at the two constables, Duff roared at them to the amusement of the blonde woman who sauntered along the pavement.

'Ignore them, Duff,' Watters advised. 'If you react to every cheeky wee snipe, you'll be chasing your tail all day. Right, you lads can go back to the police office now or on to your beat, if it's your time. Keep away from the publics, Scuddamore. Remember that you're on duty.'

As the constables marched off, the jute cart rattled into a side street, taking its attendant boys with it. Only the woman remained, watching Watters and the still smoking mill at his back.

'That looks unpleasant.' The woman was in her mid-thirties, Watters estimated, with bright eyes in a face that was too weather-tanned to be fashionable and too fresh to belong to a mill hand. She looked on the verge of respectability, a woman whose social status Watters could not quite place, which made him slightly uneasy.

'It was a fire,' Watters said. The woman looked vaguely familiar. He sorted through faces and names in his head, trying to place her. She was not one of his regular customers, therefore neither a prostitute nor a habitual thief. No, Watters shook his head. He did not remember who she was.

'I can see that it was a fire.' The woman's English was perfect but with an unusual accent. She was certainly not from Dundee, but neither did she belong to any other region of Britain. 'Was anybody hurt?'

'Would you like anybody to be hurt?' Watters turned the conversation around.

'Good heavens, no.' The woman's protests were too forceful to be genuine, which further enhanced Watters' suspicions.

'You're not from these parts.' Watters began his process of enquiries that would eventually strip away any pretence from the woman.

'No,' the woman admitted frankly. Her smile was bright. 'I'm from the Mediterranean.'

'You're from the Mediterranean, are you?' Watters filed away the information, wondering at its accuracy. *Who the devil is she, and how do I know her?* 'What brings you to Dundee, Miss? Mrs?'

'Miss Henrietta Borg.' The woman gave an elegant little curtsey. Her bright smile did not fool Watters for a second.

'Miss Borg,' Watters touched his cane to the brim of his hat. 'What brings you to Dundee, Miss Borg?'

'A ship,' Miss Borg gave a little laugh, 'and the fortunes of fate. Do you have a name, sir?'

'Detective Sergeant George Watters.'

'I see.' Miss Borg's eyes widened in what Watters knew was only pretended surprise. 'You're a policeman.'

'I am,' Watters said. 'And now, if you would oblige me with your real name, we could get along much better.' He tapped his cane against his leg.

Miss Borg laughed. 'I see that I can't fool you, Sergeant.' She gave another little curtsey. 'I'll tell you next time. It looks as if you are in demand.' She nodded to the dark brougham that was slowing to a halt beside them.

The brougham's door opened before Watters could reply. 'Sergeant Watters!'

'Yes, Superintendent Mackay?'

'You've worked with nautical crime before, haven't you?'

'Yes, sir, down in London.' Watters guessed that he was not going home yet.

'Jump in, then. You could be useful.' Mackay looked curiously at Miss Borg. 'Or is this lady known to us?'

'No, sir, we were just passing the time of day.' Watters touched the brim of his hat again. 'Good day to you, Miss Borg. I'd advise you to try and keep out of trouble. Women who give false names tend not to fare well in Dundee.'

Miss Borg gave another little curtsey. 'Thank you for the advice, Sergeant Watters. I will bear it in mind.'

Miss Borg accentuated the swing of her hips as she strode into the fast-darkening street. 'That's trouble on two legs,' Watters said. 'We'll hear more of Miss Henrietta Borg, or whatever name she chooses to use.' He frowned as an old memory crept into his mind. 'Nautical crime, indeed; she reminds me of somebody I met on a ship, but it couldn't be. That was ten years ago.' Shaking his head, Watters slid into the brougham. 'What's to do, sir?'

'Murder.' Superintendent Mackay was a man of few words.

CHAPTER TWO
DUNDEE: SEPTEMBER 1862

Lantern light cast flickering shadows across the deck of *Lady of Blackness* as Watters stepped onto the weather-stained planking. 'What's to do?'

'There's a blasted body in my hold; that's what's to do.' The man looked as battered as his ship, with his nose broken and twisted to starboard. The white line of an old scar crossed his barely shaven jaw.

'And who might you be?' Watters asked.

'I might be anybody, but I am Captain Murdo Stevenson. This is my ship.'

'Show us the body please, Captain Stevenson.' Superintendent Mackay did not waste time.

'It's in the hold,' Captain Stevenson said. 'Or rather, it's all over the bloody hold. Follow me, gentlemen.' Leading them to a length of knotted rope that stretched from an open hatch to the dark depths below, Stevenson raised his voice to a bellow. 'Bring me two lanterns!'

Without waiting for the light to arrive, Stevenson swarmed down the rope.

'I'll go next.' Mackay followed with barely less skill than Stevenson had shown. Watters descended last, plunging into a darkness that was relieved when a saturnine seaman lowered a pair of lanterns.

'Here's the body.' Captain Stevenson led them to the furthest corner of the hold, where the bouncing light of the lanterns scared away scurrying rats. 'What's left of it after four months at sea.' He pointed downward at the smeared remnants of a man.

'He's been flattened.' Watters looked down at the corpse. 'It looks like every bone in his body had been broken. What happened?'

Captain Stevenson grunted. 'Ask his maker for I'm blessed if I know. We found him here, squashed beneath hundreds of bales of raw jute.'

'I see.' Watters looked around. 'So we don't know if the jute killed him or if he was already dead when the weight of the cargo crushed him.'

Superintendent Mackay nodded. 'Exactly so. This might be murder or a simple accident. I'll leave you to it, Watters. Give me a report of your findings. Don't waste too much time over it.'

'Yes, sir.' Watters looked upward as Mackay swarmed up the rope. 'Could you arrange for the body to be taken ashore? I'd like the surgeon to have a look at him.'

'I know the procedure, Sergeant,' Mackay spoke over his shoulder. 'And Watters, don't forget that you are on volunteer duty tomorrow afternoon.'

'No, sir, I won't forget.' Watters restrained his oath. He had no enthusiasm for his position as a sergeant in the Eastern Division of Dundee Volunteers, which was a further encroachment into his time. However, with the current apprehension that the French might flex their military muscle at Britain's expense, Watters knew it was his duty to don the Queen's scarlet. Besides which, as his wife Marie reminded him, the money came in handy.

'Has the body been moved, Captain Stevenson?'

'No, Sergeant. It's exactly where we found it.'

'I see.' Watters knelt at the side of the corpse. 'Do you have this unfortunate fellow's name, Captain? Was he a member of your crew?'

'I don't know who he might be,' Stevenson said. 'He was not one of my men.'

With the dead man's pockets stuck together with dried blood, Watters had to cut his way in to prise them apart. He questioned Stevenson as he worked. 'Is it normal for strangers to roam around your ship when she's in dock, Captain?'

'It is not. I have a ship's husband who should prevent any strangers from boarding.' Stevenson did not sound pleased, but whether at the questions or the disruption to his routine that the body caused, Watters was not sure.

'Is your ship's husband still on board?' Watters slipped his hand inside the dead man's trouser pockets. They were empty.

'He lives on board,' Stevenson said.

'I'll speak to him in a few moments.' Watters checked the inside of the dead man's jacket. Also empty. 'How many of a crew do you have?'

'Twenty-four.' Stevenson was abrupt. 'Do you want to speak to them all?'

'Yes, I do. Are they all on board?'

'No.' Stevenson shook his head. 'My lads are either at home, drinking away their wages along Dock Street, or with some bobtail in Couttie's Wynd.'

Watters felt along the waistband of the dead man's trousers. There was no money belt or anything else. 'What is the makeup of your crew? Where are they from?'

Captain Stevenson was evidently annoyed by all of the questions. 'It's a typical south-Spain crew. As well as my Dundonians I have the usual Scowegians, Lascars, North Sea Chinamen, and a couple of Americans avoiding their country's troubles.'

'I want their home addresses,' Watters said.

'You'll have to ask the owners about that,' Stevenson said, 'or the boarding master for I'm blessed if I know.'

Watters grunted again. He should have known it would not be easy.

'Who are the owners?'

'Matthew Beaumont and Company,' Captain Stevenson said. 'It's a wholly owned Beaumont ship.'

'Oh?' Watters looked up. That was two incidents concerning the same company in one day. He did not believe in coincidences. 'Thank you, Captain. I'll have a look around the hold. When I come on deck, please have the ship's husband ready for me.'

'There's nothing to see down here,' Stevenson said.

'I want to know why this poor fellow was here in the first place,' Watters said. 'And I want to know if the cargo was lowered on him while he was sleeping or if he was already dead when the cargo was loaded.'

Stevenson nodded. 'If you let me know when you're finished, I'll fetch the husband and any other of the crew who may turn up.'

Watters lifted the lantern and examined the body. In all the score or so of investigations into suspicious deaths in which he had been involved, the cause of death had been apparent. In this case, bales of jute had crushed the man so that Watters found it impossible to tell if the injuries had been caused before or after death.

'I hope the surgeon can see something I can't see.' He looked at the neck and throat for signs of a knife wound and checked the shirt for the same. 'No, it's up to the surgeon now. Now, my unfortunate fellow, why on earth were you down here?'

Leaving the body where it lay, Watters lifted the lantern and paced around the hold talking to himself. *You've no money. Were you an unlucky stowaway? Your clothes are good quality, too good for a tarry-jack; are you a gentleman down on his luck?*

All the time Watters spoke, he was investigating the hold, looking for anything unusual. He stopped and sniffed at a familiar acrid smell. *What's this?* Crouching down, he rubbed his hand along the rough planking of the deck, feeling the coarse grains under his fingers.

Watters pursed his lips. *I see.* He scooped up a pinch of the grains and folded them inside his handkerchief. *I see, but I don't understand.* Lifting the lantern, he carried it carefully to the centre of the hold before taking out his notebook and pencil. After writing a few notes, he returned to his scrutiny of the hold, eventually lifting a couple of items. He examined them before putting them in his pocket. *There is more to this case than a drunken man falling into the hold or a brawl gone too far. We have something of interest here.*

'I'm coming up, Captain!'

Captain Stevenson stood at the break of the poop with a surprisingly elderly man at his side.

'You'll be the ship's husband,' Watters said.

The elderly man nodded. 'That's right, sir.' His voice was hoarse.

Watters poised his pencil. 'I'm not a sir. I am Sergeant Watters of the Dundee Police. What is your name?'

'James Thoms, sir, but everybody calls me Piper.'

'Right, Piper, tell me about that body in the hold.'

'I don't know anything about it, sir, not until we unloaded the cargo and found it.' Piper's hands fiddled with the ends of his coarse canvas shirt.

'Where was the vessel loaded, Piper?'

'Calcutta, sir.'

'Call me Sergeant. Who was in charge of the loading?'

'Mr Henderson, sir, the mate.'

That made sense. The master was in overall command, decided on the course and made the big decisions, while the mate was in charge of the day-to-day running of the vessel. 'I'll speak to Mr Henderson later. Did you see anybody come on board this vessel when you were in Calcutta?'

'No, sir. Nobody came aboard except the crew and the dock workers who loaded the cargo.'

'Sergeant, not sir. Do you think the deceased was one of the dockers?'

'No, sir, Sergeant.' Beads of sweat formed on Piper's forehead. 'The dock workers were all Lascars, sir. That is natives of Hindustan.'

'Of course,' Watters nodded. 'You could not watch everything all the time.'

'No, sir.' Piper looked guilty as if Watters expected him to remain awake and alert twenty-four hours a day. The nervous sweat was dripping from his face.

'Did you delegate anybody to take over when you were off duty?'

Piper nodded vigorously. 'Mr Henderson took over, sir.' He looked pleased to pass the responsibility to the mate.

'Did you check the hold before the loading began?'

'No, sir. There was no need.' Piper glanced at Captain Stevenson as if to confirm his words. 'Nobody ever goes down there.'

Watters wrote in his notebook. 'Thank you, Mr Thoms, and thank you, Captain Stevenson. I'll leave you in peace now. If you can think of anything, please let me know. Send a note to the Police Office on West Bell Street.' Watters checked his watch. Marie would be wondering where he had got to.

As he walked out of the dock, past the Royal Arch, Watters saw the woman silhouetted against the bright glow of a gin palace window. Henrietta Borg was in animated conversation with a man in a bowler hat with a feather thrust through the band.

'Miss Borg!' Watters lifted his cane in salutation and hurried forward. A boisterous crowd of seamen and prostitutes exploded from the public house around Borg, and then she was gone. Had she been watching *Lady of Blackness*? Had she been watching him? Or was her presence here merely another of these coincidences in which Watters did not believe? Swinging his cane at an imaginary golf ball, Watters thought that this case might be interesting.

CHAPTER THREE
POLICE OFFICE: WEST BELL STREET, DUNDEE

Superintendent Mackay looked up as Watters entered the office. 'Have you brought your report, Sergeant?'

'Yes, sir.' Watters handed over a small sheaf of papers.

Mackay surveyed the documents with distaste. 'Give me a brief run-down, Sergeant. Please tell me the death was an accident, and we can forget the whole thing.'

Watters remained standing a foot from Mackay's desk. 'I don't think it was an accident, sir. Some factors make me suspicious.'

'You are a cynical and suspicious man, Watters. That's what makes you such a good policeman. That is why I approved your request for a transfer from Scotland Yard.'

'Yes, sir. Thank you.' Praise from Mackay had to be handled carefully. It was usually a precursor to some unpleasant duty.

'Give me the details.' Mackay leaned back in his seat with his clear Highland eyes fixed on Watters. His fingers slowly tapped on the desk.

'The first thing was the position of the body, sir. It was spread-eagled with the left leg at an unnatural angle, as if the man had fallen down the hatch.'

'Perhaps he did.'

'No, sir,' Watters shook his head. 'If the fellow had fallen, he would have been directly under the opening, or at most only a couple of feet away. The body was a good five feet from the edge of the hatch, nearly touching the bulkhead; that's the internal wall of the ship, sir.'

'I know what a bulkhead is, Watters.'

'Yes, sir. I think that somebody pushed the poor fellow over the edge, knocked him out, or killed him when he was inside the hold.'

Mackay sighed. 'That poses two more questions, Sergeant. Why was he inside the hold, and why did somebody wish to kill him?' Mackay's fingers increased the speed of their drumming.

'Yes, sir,' Watters said. 'I might have a clue as to why he was inside the hold.'

'Tell me.'

'I found this on the deck of the hold.' Watters unfolded his hand-kerchief and allowed the powder to form a neat little pile on Mackay's otherwise pristine desk.

Mackay poked at it curiously. 'That is gunpowder.'

'Yes, sir. Also, there was this.' Watters placed two lengths of fuse beside the gunpowder.

Mackay sighed and leaned back in his chair. 'Give me your theory, Sergeant, if you please.'

'I can only think of one. Somebody was trying to place an explosive charge to sink the ship.'

'I tend to concur.' Mackay's fingers were now beating a tattoo on the desk. 'The question is: Why? Why sink a jute ship?'

'That I could not say, sir.' Watters hesitated. 'If it happened at sea, I would suspect an attempt to scuttle the vessel for insurance money, but not in port and not with explosives. That would be too obvious. Besides which, Mr Beaumont is a respectable businessman with no need to do such a thing. His company appears to be one of the healthiest in Dundee.'

Mackay nodded. 'Carry on, Watters. You have given this some thought.'

'I don't know if the dead man was placing the gunpowder and fuse or if he found somebody with the explosives and was killed for his trouble.'

'It's a bit of a conundrum then,' Mackay said. 'What is your opinion?'

'I would suspect the former. If our man was killed preventing an attack on the ship, I can think of no reason his murderer did not continue with his plan.' Watters consulted his notebook. 'I have spoken to the shipmaster and ship's husband, and I have a list of the crew with the addresses of any local men.'

'You'll be interviewing them, I expect?'

'Yes, sir, and there's more.'

'Oh, there would be with you involved, Watters.' Mackay sounded weary. 'What else, Sergeant?'

'Matthew Beaumont owned the ship, sir. He also owned the mill on Brown's Street that was on fire, and that was his second fire within a few days.'

Mackay's fingers recommenced their tapping. 'It's a long way from Calcutta to Dundee, Sergeant, unless you are suggesting an international attack on Mr Beaumont?'

'I'm not suggesting anything yet. I think it's a bit queer, that's all.'

'Well, Watters, you keep an eye on Mr Beaumont's affairs just in case.' Mackay's fingers continued their assault on the desk. 'And solve this murder for me.'

'Could I have a couple of men, sir? I have a lot of people to question.'

'Take Scuddamore and Duff,' Mackay said. 'They can work in plain clothes if that helps. The budget will have to cope with paying the enhanced wages of two more criminal officers.' Mackay leaned back again frowning. 'I don't like this, Watters. Mr Beaumont is one of our most prominent merchants. If somebody is attacking his business for some reason, I want to know why. Alternatively, you could be making a mountain out of two different molehills.'

'Yes, sir.'

Mackay sighed and stood up. 'All right, Watters. Question the crew of *Lady of Blackness* and look closely into Beaumont's business interests. See if there is anything that could provoke such a reaction.'

'I'll do that, sir.'

Mackay reached for his hat. 'I'll go over to Mr Beaumont's home at Mount Pleasant right now. He won't like this. You may know that his elder daughter is due to be married in a few days.'

'So I believe, sir.' Watters gave a wry smile. 'My wife has kept me in touch with every detail.' Charlotte Beaumont's wedding was one of the major subjects in the society columns of the *Dundee Advertiser.*

'I can imagine. I'll apprise Mr Beaumont of our interest in his situation and advise him that one of our men will be present at the wedding for security.'

'I see, sir.'

'That will be you, Watters.'

'I am not the best man for the job, sir!' Watters said in something like alarm. 'I'm not a social animal.'

'Then ask Mrs Watters for advice.' Mackay sounded vaguely amused. 'She will keep you in touch with every detail.'

* * *

'So what do we have?' Sitting behind his desk, Watters addressed his two constables. 'We have a dead man in the hold of a ship with no identification, no money, and no possessions.' He looked at the blank faces opposite. 'We suspect the fellow was murdered. We have evidence that somebody, either the victim or an unknown party, intended to start a fire in the hold of that vessel. Mr Matthew Beaumont owned the ship, *Lady of Blackness*, as well as two Dundee mills in which some unknown party also started a fire.'

Scuddamore screwed up his face in his effort to think. 'Was the murder not committed before the ship left Calcutta, Sergeant?'

'It must have been,' Watters said. 'The victim was underneath the jute.'

'There can't be a connection then,' Scuddamore said. 'Calcutta is thousands of miles away.'

'Matthew Beaumont is the connection,' Watters reminded patiently. 'I want the crew interviewed.' he produced the crew list he got from the shipping office with the names and home addresses of each man of *Lady of Blackness*. 'There are twenty-four names there. I'll take Mr Henderson, the mate, and the first eleven men. You two gentlemen work together and question the others.'

'They're not all from Dundee, Sergeant,' Duff pointed out.

'Take the Dundee men first,' Watters said, 'and then try the publics, crimps, and cheap lodging houses for the rest.'

'What are we asking, Sergeant?' Scuddamore scanned the list.

'Ask what they know about the murder. Ask if they know the dead man. Ask if they saw anything unusual; get some notes of their movements.'

'They're seamen, Sergeant,' Scuddamore said. 'They'll all be drunk.'

'All the more likely to talk then,' Watters said with far more confidence than he felt. Seamen could be notoriously truculent when faced with authority, while seamen with a drink in them might react badly. However, that was all part of the policeman's bargain.

'It will take a long time, Sergeant,' Scuddamore said.

'Best get started then,' Watters dismissed him.

It took two full days to track down and question the first eighteen of the crew. Two days of knocking at doors and facing suspicious men. Two days of squeezing answers out of reluctant sailors. Two days of talking to men across the battered tables of public houses. Two days of recording similar responses, of frustration, dead-ends, and insults.

'Go to hell, bluebottle bastards.'

'I don't know anything.'

'I helped load the jute. I never saw nobody in the hold.'

'I done what Mr Henderson told me to do. Nothing else. Now bugger off.'

'We're not getting anywhere,' Scuddamore said. 'If any of these seamen knew anything, they would not tell us anyway.'

'We've still got six men to find,' Watters reminded. 'You're the drinking expert, Scuddamore. Where's the most popular place for seamen this year?'

'The Bird,' Scuddamore said at once. 'That's a public down the Dockie, Sergeant. Its name is the Albatross, but it's known as the Big Bird or just the Bird.'

'We'll go there tonight,' Watters said. 'You're meant to be criminal officers, so wear civilian clothes. If you arrive in uniform, the clientele will either riot or run out the back.' His mouth twisted in a mirthless grin. 'I'll send one of my informants in there ahead of us to prepare the way.'

The Albatross crouched unpretentiously on Dock Street with its single window facing onto the spars of the massed shipping in the docks. Watters shoved open the door and slouched through the haze of tobacco smoke to the bar. Most of the drinkers were either seamen or seamen's women with a smattering of dock workers. A man with thinning red hair glanced up, met Watters's eye for a significant second, and looked away again. He sat at a circular table, shuffled his feet, and took a sip at his whisky.

With a pint of Ballingall beer in his hand, Watters leaned against the bar and watched Scuddamore take up position beside the front door, while Duff carried his whisky to the door that gave access to the lane in the rear. Once he was satisfied he had covered both exits, Watters put down his tankard and leapt on top of the bar.

Only a few of the Bird's customers bothered to look up; drunken escapades were a frequent occurrence in the pub.

'I am Sergeant George Watters of Dundee Police!' Watters shouted. 'I'm looking for the crew of *Lady of Blackness*!'

There was an immediate trickle toward the exits until Duff and Scuddamore stepped forward.

Watters tried again. 'Is there anybody here from *Lady of Blackness*?'

A thin-faced woman glared at him. 'Mind your own business, bluebottle bastard!'

The man with thinning hair caught Watters's eye, placed his hand on the table, closed it into a fist, and then extended a single finger toward the table nearest to the window.

'I'm looking for the following men,' Watters read out the list, 'Petersen, Hughson, Rex, Banerjee, Ghosh, and Jones.' As he read, he watched his informant, who tapped his finger on the table at the name Rex.

Watters could see that the two Lascars, Ghosh and Banerjee, were not present. He concentrated on the table that his informant had indicated. 'I only wish to ask a few questions,' he said. 'Nobody is in any trouble.'

'So you say,' a woman in a gaudy crinoline shouted. Red and green ribbons decorated her hair. 'You're just after a man to blame for that murder.'

One of the seamen at the table nearest the window shook his head, sliding slightly further down in his seat. Watters nodded. *That's my man.* 'You!' He pointed with his cane. 'What's your name?'

Watters's bark was so sudden that the man responded purely by instinct. 'John Rex, sir.'

'Are there any of your shipmates here, Rex?' Watters continued before Rex could recover his equanimity.

'No, sir,' Rex looked wildly towards the door as if contemplating a quick escape. Duff moved his burly form further forward.

'I've just a few questions, Rex.' Watters jumped from the counter, holding his cane ready to repel any attack.

'You're no' taking him to any bloody police office.' Rex's female companion put a sinewy arm around him. 'I'll no' let you.'

'We can ask him in the back room here.' Watters decided not to risk a riot. 'You can come too.'

With Duff and Scuddamore remaining nearby in case of a rescue attempt, Watters escorted Rex and his woman into the back room. Lined with kegs of spirits and casks of beer, the room only had sufficient space for the three of them, particularly as the woman wore a full crinoline to counter her narrow, frowning face.

'You know about the murder on *Lady of Blackness*,' Watters said.

'The whole of Dundee knows about it,' the woman said as Rex gave a reluctant nod.

'Who are you?'

'I'm Annie McBurnie.' The woman sounded surprised that Watters had to ask.

'I'm going to ask you, Mr Rex, the same questions as we have asked your shipmates.' Watters tried to reassure the seaman. 'I am not accusing you of anything, and I do not suspect you of anything.' Yet.

'I don't know anything,' Rex said at once.

Watters let that pass. 'Do you know the man whose body we found in *Lady of Blackness*?'

Rex shook his head. 'No, sir.'

'Did you see anybody on the ship that had no business there?'

'No, sir. I only saw the crew and the dock workers.'

Watters leaned closer to the shaking seaman. 'What are you scared of, Mr Rex? Did you kill the unfortunate fellow?'

'No, sir! I never killed nobody.'

'Do you know who did?'

Rex glanced at McBurnie before shaking his head. 'No, sir.'

Watters pounced on Rex's hesitation and the slight alteration in his tone. 'You don't know,' he crouched beside the seaman, 'but you think you *might* know.'

Again, Rex glanced at McBurnie, who pushed her face towards Watters.

'You leave him alone,' she said. 'He already told you that he didn't know.'

Watters moderated his voice. He knew that if the crowd in the public bar thought he was brow-beating one of their colleagues, they could trample over his two constables and break the door down. 'You're right, Annie. So he did. Tell you what, let's have a drink instead. On the house.'

With the walls of the room lined with barrels and kegs, it was not hard to find something to drink. Avoiding the garish labels of the kill-me-deadly concoctions, Watters poked at the upper shelves until he found a five-gallon keg. 'That will do.'

'What's that?' McBurnie was instantly suspicious.

'Smuggled whisky,' Watters said, 'straight from the glens, pure peat reek and the nectar of the gods.' He prised open the bung, lifted the keg to his lips, and pretended to drink. 'Here, Mr Rex, have a wee taste.'

Rex took a drink. 'That's the real stuff.' He handed the keg to McBurnie who tilted her head back as she swallowed.

Watters watched, fully aware that the illicit whisky was more potent than any of the watered-down spirits the pub sold over the counter. Again, he pretended to drink before passing the keg around.

'Now, let's get back to business,' Watters said. 'Who do you *think* might have killed that poor fellow, Mr Rex?'

Rex stopped with the keg at his lips and colourless whisky dribbling down his chin. His eyes were slightly out of focus. 'I can't tell you,' he said.

'If you don't,' Watters spoke quietly, 'you'll be withholding evidence. I could arrest you for that and hold you until you speak.'

'You wouldnae dare,' McBurnie said. 'The boys out there would tear your head off.'

'I would dare,' Watters said. 'I could hold you for aiding and abetting and stealing drink from a public house.' He pointed to the whisky.

'You're a bastard, Watters.'

'I already know that,' Watters said. 'Now, Mr Rex here will tell me something I don't know or,' he pulled the handcuffs from his pocket, 'you'll both be leaving here wearing these.'

'It's nothing to do with Annie.' Rex tried to push McBurnie behind him only for her wide crinolines to jam between two full kegs.

Watters shrugged. 'She'll only get three months or so.'

'I'll kill you, bluebottle!' McBurnie showed her teeth.

'She'll get six months now that she has threatened a police officer.' Watters tightened his grip on his cane. 'Is that what you want, Mr Rex? Do you want to put your girl into jail for six months by protecting a man who might be a murderer?'

'No.' Rex glanced at McBurnie. 'Jones. Look for Richard Jones.'

'He's one of the crew we have not yet located,' Watters said. 'Why him? What makes you think he is involved?'

Rex shuffled uneasily. 'If I tell you, will you let Annie go free?'

'You have my word.' Watters knew that no court in the country would use such slender evidence as he could provide to convict McBurnie.

'I can't really explain it.' Now that Rex was committed, he seemed determined to do his best. 'Jones was not *right*, Sergeant. He sounded like a seaman and knew his way around the ship all right, sir, but he just didn't ring true.'

Watters took notes. 'Could you say anything more specific, Mr Rex?'

Rex took another unconscious swig of the whisky and screwed up his face with the effort of thought. 'No, sir. Well, maybe, aye. His language was more like a Royal Navy man than a real seaman, and even then, it was not quite right. It's like he was trying too hard, sort of. He kept mentioning battles from the past and kings and queens and things.'

Watters noted that down. 'Thank you, Mr Rex. Only one more thing, and you are free to go. Could you give me a description of Richard Jones?'

Rex drank more of the free whisky. 'Why, no, sir. There is nothing to describe. He was just ordinary. He looked like everyone else.'

'Was he tall? Short? Broad? Thin?'

Rex shrugged. 'Neither, sir. He was about average in everything. He was a grey man; nothing stands out at all.' He frowned. 'He might have been French, sir.'

'French?' Watters raised his eyebrows. 'What the devil makes you think he might have been French?'

'I dunno.' Rex shrugged again. 'He was trying too hard, saying things like foreigners would think we said. God save the Queen and that.'

'Thank you, Mr Rex. Have you seen this patriotically anonymous gentleman since *Lady of Blackness* docked?'

Rex shook his head.

'Did he mention anywhere he might go when he came ashore?'

Again, Rex shook his head. 'He spoke about drinking the town dry, sir, and finding a baggage; that's a prostitute, sir.'

'Normal sailor talk,' Watters said. 'All right, Mr Rex, thank you.' Watters closed his notebook. 'You have been a great help.' He opened the door to find Scuddamore and Duff still standing sentinel. The clientele of the pub looked up without interest as Rex and McBurnie sidled out.

'What next, Sergeant?' Scuddamore asked.

'Now we scour the town for a man of average height, average size, and average build with an average face,' Watters said.

Duff stamped his feet on the ground. 'That should be easy, then. Do we have anything else to go on?'

'Yes, he doesn't look quite right; he says God save the Queen, and he might be French.'

Scuddamore looked around the room. 'Can we start here, Sergeant? None of these men looks quite right.'

Watters grinned. 'I appreciate your sarcasm, Scuddamore; we have a difficult job before us. Luckily, we have you on our side. You start searching tomorrow, public by public, boarding house by boarding house, and brothel by brothel. Have fun.' Watters nearly enjoyed the dismay on Scuddamore's face, until he remembered he had a wedding to attend.

CHAPTER FOUR
PITCORBIE ESTATE, FORFARSHIRE: SEPTEMBER 1862

Watters tugged at his starched collar, fidgeted uncomfortably, and wished he could at least look at his watch to see how much longer he had to endure this torture. His natural dislike of weddings was not improved when he did not know the participants.

'I could stand outside the building, sir,' Watters had suggested.

Mackay had shaken his head. 'I've spoken to Mr Beaumont. You're down as a friend of the family and an usher.'

'Yes, sir.' Watters knew that as a police sergeant, he could be working in the most noxious of alleys one day and guarding the queen the next. He accepted that was part of the job, but he did not have to enjoy it.

Watters looked up as the organist began the music and Charlotte Beaumont appeared. From the long veil that concealed her face to the bouquet of orange blossom in her white-gloved hands, past the frilled white dress that enhanced her trim waist, then flounced out to hide the flat white shoes, Charlotte looked as pristine as a bride should.

For a second, Watters nearly smiled for the gloves, from Henry Adams of Dundee, had been his present to her, which Marie had chosen with care.

'You're going to a wedding,' Marie had said. 'You have to give the bride something.'

'I'm not a guest! I'm on duty.'

'I'll choose a suitable present,' Marie told him. 'You guard the guests.'

Watters nodded; there was no advantage in continuing the discussion. Marie had made her mind up.

The instant the ancient church doors creaked open, the bells began to ring. The great and the good of Dundee were present, together with relatives from both families. Watters saw a hundred eyes examining Charlotte as she walked down the aisle supported by her father and followed by her bridesmaids.

Watters concentrated on the guests, searching for potential troublemakers. There was Sir John Ogilvy of Baldovan House, the local Member of Parliament, resplendent in the scarlet of the Volunteers. There was David Jobson, Provost of Dundee, together with his frowning wife. There was Bailie George Ower, sitting stiffly at attention in a soberly cut suit, and beside him was William Foggie, the Hospital Manager. Fidgeting on the nearest pew to the aisle was Charlotte's personal friend, Mrs Foreman of the Dundee Abolition Association. None of these people was likely to cause any trouble, murder stray seamen, or set fire to mills.

George Beaumont's business associates clumped together in a solid block of Dundonian respectability, some looking as uncomfortable as Watters. The Cox clan, whose huge Lochee works was already among the largest jute factories in the world, spoke quietly with the linen and sailcloth dynasty of the Baxters. Patrick Anderson, the Director of the Dundee Banking Company, winked at Charlotte. He had been a family friend for years, as had George Welch, manager of the Tay Whale-Fishing Company. Watters slid his gaze over them. None of these dynamic and respectable gentlemen or their ladies would be any threat to the wedding.

There were others whom Watters did not recognise but knew only by the business cards he had collected at the door. The Earl of Panmure or Joseph Holderby, the United States Consul, were unlikely to be associated with fire-raisers or murderers. Dismissing them, Watters examined the others whose names he strove to remember.

When Charlotte nearly stumbled, Amy, her sister and maid of honour, encouraged her with a hand on the small of her back. Recovering, Charlotte looked up the length of the aisle where the old maids clustered to touch her gown for luck, and the groom's relatives studied her to see what sort of woman was entering their family. For an instant, Watters met the eyes of William Caskie, the man who was about to marry Charlotte, and then he looked away. The groom did not interest him.

Watters glanced upward. Despite the autumn sunshine, candles were necessary to penetrate the gloom of the church, their light flickering off the profusion of late flowers that Amy Beaumont and the groom's sister Elizabeth Caskie had spent hours arranging.

Watters shifted on the pew. He would have brought his revolver until Marie said that would be sacrilege, so instead, he had his cumbersome baton under his jacket. He heard the subdued murmur as the congregation tensed in anticipation for the climax of the ceremony. Watters shook his head, remembering that Marie had ordered him to observe the women's clothes and tell her every detail. He swept his eyes across the gathered women. *What the devil do I know about women's fashions?*

He turned around as the church door opened.

'Excuse me, sir? You seem to be an usher.' The man who had entered indicated the white ribbon on Watters's shoulder. He was about forty years old, five-foot-eight tall, dark haired, and sallow featured with a fine set of whiskers. His clothes were immaculate, yet it was the smooth drawl with which he spoke that drew Watters's attention combined with the sheer elegance of manner. 'I am sorry to be late, but where do you recommend that I sit?'

'Could I have your name, sir?' Watters consulted the list with which the Beaumonts had issued him. Mrs Mary Caskie, the groom's mother, together with Beaumont and Charlotte, had spent hours compiling guest lists.

'James Dunwoody Bulloch.' The man said each word distinctly as if the name should mean something. He smoothed a hand over his side whiskers.

'I'm afraid that you're not on my list, sir.' Watters was barely aware of the minister's voice droning behind him.

'I am a business associate of Mr William Caskie.' When Bulloch smiled, his face looked ten years younger. 'Perhaps the groom was not consulted when the bride issued the invitations.'

'Perhaps not.' Watters deliberately moved to block Bulloch's view of the interior of the church. He kept his voice level. 'However, sir, I am afraid I cannot permit you to enter unless you are on the guest list.'

Bulloch raised an elegant eyebrow and swung the cane that he carried. His smile did not falter, but he allowed his eyes to survey the rows of packed pews. 'You have some distinguished men here,' he said, 'and some fine-looking women.'

'Indeed we have.' Watters refused to be drawn. 'And I am certain that you are equally distinguished, but with the greatest respect, I must ask you to leave.'

Charlotte's voice sounded across the otherwise hushed church, 'I do,' cool and clear and low.

When Watters nodded towards the door, Bulloch reached into his waistcoat pocket and produced his card, which he held up. 'And you have Mr Joseph Holderby too, I see. Perhaps there was a good reason for William not to invite me.' He proffered the card. 'Please present this to Mr William Caskie, sir, and inform him that I did attempt to attend his wedding.'

'I shall do that, Mr Bulloch.' Watters placed the oblong piece of pasteboard in the pocket of his waistcoat. 'I apologise for my inflexibility, but I have instructions.'

'Which you are carrying out admirably, I am sure.' Bulloch spoke with just a hint of irony. He bowed from the waist. 'Your servant, sir.' Withdrawing with a languid grace that Watters could only admire, he walked through a crowd of spectators to a waiting gig. Watters quietly closed the church door.

Removing the business card, Watters glanced at it. James Dunwoody Bulloch it said with little else except the name of his city, Richmond, Virginia. Watters grunted. It was as well he had not allowed Bulloch entry. Having a representative from both the Federal and Confederate sides of the American conflict could have proved uncomfortable for the wedding party.

The congregation was singing as Mrs Mary Caskie led the procession out of the church. She looked neither to the right nor left but moved with the same precision as she seemed to do everything. Mr Beaumont was next, and then Charlotte, with one hand resting lightly on the arm of her husband. Although the veil covered Charlotte's face, Watters was sure he saw a hint of moisture in her eyes. He nodded to the groom.

'Congratulations, sir. You have a fine bride there.'

William Caskie nodded, with the little imperial beard highlighting his powerful chin. 'Thank you for your approval, Mr...' he hesitated then shrugged and stepped outside the church door, his tight lavender trousers emphasising muscular legs.

William Caskie placed the top hat back on his head, took a deep breath of the autumn air, lifted Charlotte clean off her feet, swept back her veil and kissed her soundly. It was the first time that Watters had seen Charlotte close up, and he realised that she was much the plainer of the Beaumont sisters despite her elegance of carriage.

'Three cheers for Mr William and Mrs Charlotte Caskie!' It might have been the head gardener that raised the cry, but the assembled crowd joined in lustily to the apparent embarrassment of Charlotte, who looked like fainting until William tightened his arm around her waist.

'Come along, Charlotte! We're man and wife now; don't let me down.'

At a nod from Watters, two of the crowd threw showers of rice, with some oats for good measure, and raised more cheers for the lucky couple. Mrs Mary Caskie nodded her approval as Watters signalled to the driver to bring the wedding carriage closer. The dark-green bodywork had a gold trim, with high, yellow wheels that crunched smoothly across the gravel. The traces had been specially extended to allow an extra pair of horses, so four matching whites pawed at the gravel.

'A fancy machine, Watters,' Mrs Mary Caskie commented.

'That's Sergeant Watters, ma'am,' Watters said. 'Mr Beaumont had Mr Lewis Mackenzie build the coach especially for the wedding. It is his wedding present.'

'So I believe.' Mrs Mary Caskie's flower-topped bonnet swayed as she nodded. 'I hope it will not be an unnecessary expense.'

'I'm sure the happy couple will find a use for a carriage, ma'am.'

When the driver opened the door, William Caskie handed his new wife into the leather-padded interior and drew himself after her. Shouting their destination to the driver, he waved to the crowd before slamming shut the door.

Beaumont waved back, whispered something to Amy, and sauntered across to Mrs Mary Caskie.

'That was an excellent ceremony, Mrs Caskie, without a hitch. Let us hope the wedding breakfast is as trouble free.'

'Complete nonsense, Mr Beaumont.' Mrs Mary Caskie shook her head. 'All this fuss for a marriage. Of what practical use is a white dress? When will Miss Charlotte ever wear such a creation again? In my time, we wore sensible clothes that would last for years, but ever since Her Majesty married in white, all young girls think they should too. Stuff and nonsense!' She straightened her bonnet. 'Come along, Mr Beaumont, we at least are of an age when we are not afraid to walk. Give me your arm, sir!'

Pitcorbie Parish Church stood only a hundred yards outside the stone wall that marked the policies of Caskie's Pitcorbie House. Mrs

Mary Caskie had insisted that everybody walk from the church to the wedding breakfast within the house but made allowances for her son and his new bride. Now, she led by example, striding through the ornate wrought-iron gates with the lodge housekeeper bowing as they passed. Watters kept to the rear of the party, ensuring that all the guests survived the walk safely and no unwanted villagers or hangers-on entered the house. He grunted as he saw a man at the edge of a belt of woodland standing apart from the guests.

'Do you know that man, sir?' Watters asked Beaumont.

'I do not, Sergeant Watters.' Beaumont peered into the dim of the late afternoon.

'Then with your permission, I will investigate.' Watters smiled to relieve any fear. 'It's probably perfectly innocent.' Lifting his cane, he strode toward the woodland, increasing his pace as the man slid back between the trees. 'Halloa! You there!'

Tree boughs swung behind the man as he turned to run. Watters followed, wincing as a flexible bough smacked across his face. 'Dundee Police! Stop!'

The man increased his pace, ducking beneath the branches, jinking around the tree trunks, and glancing over his shoulder as Watters gradually decreased the distance between them. When the fugitive reached the tall stone wall that marked the edge of Pitcorbie's policies, Watters leapt the final few feet.

'Stand there!'

The fugitive threw himself onto the wall, and for one moment, Watters had a clear view of his face. Young, with luxuriant red whiskers, he looked more scared than dangerous, and then he slipped over the far side of the wall. By the time Watters scaled the wall, the fugitive had vanished into the rapidly encroaching darkness.

'He sported red whiskers,' Watters noted in his notebook. 'But so does every fifth man in Dundee.' He snapped his book shut. *He could have been anything from a poacher to a well-wisher. Or a potential fireraiser.*

By the time Watters returned to the front door of Pitcorbie House, hard-working servants had removed Charlotte's carriage to the stable block, and the sound of feasting was already evident.

'I presume that you were not required?' The taller of Mrs Mary Caskie's two footmen looked down his long nose at Watters. 'There were no armed Russians or mutinous Indian sepoys attempting to disrupt the wedding?'

'Not yet,' Watters agreed, 'only a large-mouthed servant.' Pushing past both men, he followed the sound of revelry to the wedding breakfast in the grand hall. Mr Beaumont must have spent a fortune on the flowers, with every column boasting a floral garland, the long table an arboretum of roses, and even the crystal chandeliers be-flowered. The table for the bridal party, set at right angles to the other, was hidden beneath orange blossoms and roses. Nor had Beaumont stinted on food, with the table piled high with every delicacy that Watters could conceive, and much that he did not recognise.

'Did you catch him, Sergeant?' Beaumont spoke from the side of his mouth as he watched his daughter and her husband.

'No, sir. I chased him away.'

'Well done, Sergeant.' Beaumont moved on.

Charlotte stood in one corner of the hall, arm in arm with her husband. As the principal bridesmaid, pretty Amy was in her element, talking twenty to the dozen as she reminded her sister of the names of people that she had known for years.

After eating, the guests drifted to the great hall for the dancing. Pressed against the wall, Watters watched for the trouble that he hoped would not come. He patrolled from the door to each curtained window, scanning each face for the return of the red-whiskered man, occasionally visiting the hall to check the servants were alert.

'Oh la, Mr Watters, are they not energetic?' Mrs Foreman flapped a fan in front of her face as she spoke. 'Is it not enchanting to see so many young people enjoying themselves?'

Watters forced a smile. 'Indeed it is, Mrs Foreman.'

'I believe that you are a friend of the family, Mr Watters.' Mrs Foreman was about forty with intense brown eyes and a smile that hovered at the edges of her thin lips.

'I am honoured by the association, Mrs Foreman.'

'Yet I have never met you,' Mrs Foreman said, 'and none of the other guests are paying you the least bit of attention.'

'I am rather a quiet man,' Watters said.

'You are not from Dundee, are you?' Mrs Foreman peered into Watters's face as if she was accusing him of a major crime.

'Not originally,' Watters admitted.

Mrs Foreman leaned closer and dropped her voice to a conspiratorial whisper. 'Nor am I. I'm from Perth. Us strangers should stick together, don't you know?'

Watters managed another weak smile as he watched the servants glide in and out of the room and wished he had time to review their backgrounds.

'Well, Mr Watters, I feel neglected, while you are alone. Can you think of a solution to both our predicaments?' Mrs Foreman's smile transformed her face into something quite attractive.

Watters looked around the room, hoping for an escape that was not there. He was trapped. 'Shall we join in the dancing, Mrs Foreman?'

'Why, Mr Watters, what an excellent idea.' Mrs Foreman gave an elegant curtsey and accompanied Watters to the dance floor.

'I am not much of a dancer, I'm afraid.' Watters excused himself in advance, in case he should trample on Mrs Foreman's feet.

'Oh, Mr Watters, neither am I.' Mrs Foreman proved her words by raking her boot down Watters's shin.

Watters disguised his wince with a deaths-head grin. 'I hope that Mr Foreman will not disapprove of you dancing with me.'

Mrs Foreman shook her head. 'Mr Foreman has been gone this last four years,' she said, taking control of the dance and nearly whirling Watters off his feet. One of her hands strayed until her fingertips rested on his right buttock. 'Are you a married man, Mr Watters?'

'I am, Mrs Foreman.' Watters was acutely aware of the position of Mrs Foreman's hand.

'Oh, that is such a pity.' Mrs Foreman shook her head. 'And you are such a handsome fellow.' Her hand patted lightly.

'Mrs Watters might not agree to that,' Watters said.

'I am sure that you are both very well matched.' Mrs Foreman broke off as the music ended. She led Watters back to the seats. 'There is nothing as happy as a well-matched marriage, although I cannot see Mrs Watters here.'

'She is not here,' Watters said.

'In that case, you must make do with me.' Mrs Foreman laid her gloved hand on Watters's arm. 'And I will glory in your company. Do you think that the happy couple is well matched?'

'They seem happy enough,' Watters said.

'I do not think they are well matched at all.' Mrs Foreman leaned closer to Watters and dropped her voice to impart her vital information. 'I think it is a marriage of convenience to patch up Mr Beaumont and Mr Caskie's business rivalries.'

Watters refrained from the temptation to write that in his notebook. 'What makes you think that, Mrs Foreman?' He gave a slightly lop-sided smile. 'Women are much better at working out such things than men.'

'Well,' Mrs Foreman settled down to enjoy her gossip, 'Mr Beaumont and the Caskies have been business rivals for years. When old Mr Caskie died, and that was mysterious, don't you know? When old Mr Caskie died, young William Caskie took over the family business and suddenly became interested in Charlotte.'

'How did Mr Caskie die, and why was it mysterious?' Mrs Foreman's words had aroused Watters's professional interest.

Mrs Foreman leaned even closer to Watters so her breath was hot on his face. She put a hand on his thigh for support. 'I think it was poison.' She patted his thigh, nodding for emphasis. 'One minute, Mr Caskie was right as a thrupenny bit, and the next, he was dead. Now,' she sat back with a look of triumph on her face, 'you tell me that was natural, Mr Watters, and I'll tell you that the sea is blue claret.'

'I did not realise there was any suspicion.' Watters looked up as the urbane figure of Sir John Ogilvy strolled up to him.

'Do you have a moment, Sergeant Watters?'

'Sergeant Watters?' Mrs Foreman placed a hand over her mouth. 'Are you in the Army?'

'No, Mrs Foreman.' Watters smiled, knowing that people did not like a policeman. 'I am a detective sergeant in the Dundee Police.'

'Oh.' Mrs Foreman's eyes widened. 'Oh, how positively delicious.'

'Excuse me, please, Mrs Foreman.' Watters stood, bowed, and stepped away. 'Yes, Sir John.'

Dressed in the full regimentals of the Dundee Rifle Volunteer Corps, Sir John Ogilvy saluted Watters with his glass of brandy and water. 'Mr Beaumont informs me that you served in the Army?'

'No, sir. I was in the Royal Marines.'

'Rank?' Ogilvy demanded. As a local landowner as well as a Member of Parliament and head of half a dozen committees and charities, Ogilvy was used to instant obedience. Watters let him wait for a moment as he watched Charlotte walk to her new husband. She did not look as if the marriage was misaligned.

'I was a sergeant, sir.' Light from the chandelier gleamed on Charlotte's wedding ring. She smiled upwards as William took her arm.

'She will make a perfect wife, I imagine.' Ogilvy had also been watching Charlotte. 'William is a lucky man. You have experience in training men then.'

Watters nodded. 'Some, sir.'

'I know that you are already a sergeant in my regiment.' Ogilvy stepped back as a press of dancers clattered across the room with a laughing Miss Amy in the forefront. 'I would like Mr Mackay to grant you more time with my Volunteers. I do not trust the French. With much of our attention on events across the Atlantic, it would be like them to stab us in the back.'

'I don't know about the French, sir,' Watters said, 'but my work keeps me fairly busy.'

Ogilvy nodded. 'So I hear, Watters.'

'Yes, sir.' Watters rescued a brace of brandy glasses from a passing footman, automatically passed one to Ogilvy, and cradled the second in his hand. He refused to be intimidated by this powerful man.

Sir John accepted the brandy as if it was his right. 'I will ask Superintendent Mackay to give you some more time. There's not just the American business; who knows what might happen with Garibaldi. Europe is in a fearful mess just now.'

'I agree, sir.' Watters had been keeping an eye on the papers. The *Courier and Argus* was full of news from the war in America and the captivity of the Italian patriot Garibaldi. 'Perhaps Mr Bismarck can keep Europe stable. His proposed army reforms may have the French watching their northern border rather than bothering us.'

Ogilvy looked surprised that a mere sergeant was aware of international affairs. He eyed Watters over the rim of the brandy glass. 'Perhaps so indeed, Watters. I can see that you are a man who bears watching.' He took a sip. 'I shall certainly speak with Superintendent Mackay about you, sir. Mark my words.'

'Sergeant Watters!' Amy, bereft of all dignity and with her eyes bright with excitement, tugged on Watters's sleeve. 'Mrs Foreman sent me to find you! She said that she needed you to partner her on the dance floor!' All curls and excitement, Amy bobbed a small curtsey to Ogilvy. 'Pray forgive me, Sir John, but Mrs Foreman requires the sergeant.'

Ogilvy bowed slightly. 'Who am I to stand in the way of Mrs Foreman? She may have Sergeant Watters with my compliments, Miss Amy. Off you go, Watters. We can't keep the ladies waiting, can we?'

CHAPTER FIVE
BROUGHTY FERRY, BY
DUNDEE: SEPTEMBER 1862

'Right, you scruffy bunch of misfits!' Watters greeted the line of Volunteers as they stood on the broad beach of Broughty.

Having been glad to leave the Royal Marines, Watters had swithered about joining the Volunteers, but his sense of duty had compelled him to return to the military. 'Besides,' Marie had said, 'you look smart in scarlet.'

'So you think you want to be soldiers, do you? You think you can face French Zouaves or Russian Cossacks?' Watters paced slowly along the length of the line, staring intently into each face. Most were eager teenagers who hoped to improve their social life, with a sprinkling of mature men, only one of whom stared stolidly back. Watters noted him as a potential troublemaker and walked on.

'Let's see how good you all are then.' He appreciated the genuine attempts of the Volunteers to stand at attention, except for the troublemaker, who seemed to deliberately slump. 'As soldiers, you have to fight, you have to endure hardship, and you have to march.' Watters glanced at the men's ill-fitting boots. 'If you can't march, you will collapse, and the Frenchies will take their bayonets and cut you from groin to throat.'

The low winter sun cast long shadows from the walls of Broughty Castle, where the artillery garrison watched with amusement as Watters harangued his men. Lieutenant Ramsay, busily supervising the cleaning of the spanking new rifled 32-pounder Armstrongs that sat to the east of the castle, smiled in sympathy when Watters clutched his forehead at the Volunteers' attempts at marching.

'March, boys, march! It's simple; first put your left foot forward, then your right, then your left again!' Watters swore in mock despair as the men clustered together, falling over one another in their efforts to keep in step. 'Great God in heaven, don't you know your left from your right?' Watters acknowledged the grins with a shake of his head.

Most of these men were respectable artisans or the sons of shop owners or small farmers. There was no need to bully them into shape or treat them like the ill-or-uneducated gutter scruffs that made up a sizeable portion of the British Army.

'Right then,' Watters pointed to the nearest man. 'You—what's your name?'

The man stiffened to what he evidently believed was attention and grinned. 'Varthley, sir.'

'Right, Varthley, you look fairly intelligent. Step in front of the rest, and we'll demonstrate how to march.' He pointed to the jeering artillerymen on the castle wall. 'Don't worry about them; they had to learn too.'

Using Varthley as a model, Watters demonstrated the length of stride and how to swing the arms in time. 'Let's try again, shall we? Left, right! Left! Keep these arms swinging lads—we're soldiers, not artillerymen!' As he hoped, that raised another smile, and Watters led them along the shifting sands, with the creeping surf to their right and a handful of fishermen to their left. Fisher children kept pace with his Volunteers, laughing and making jokes at the recruits' expense. Half a dozen fishwives appeared and blasted the children into obedience, while the crew of a beached coaster lounged over the tilted bulwark, passing a bottle back and forth.

Watters marched the Volunteers from the shadow of the castle wall, along the beach to the village of Monifieth, bellowing to keep them in step. When the Volunteers flagged with the effort of working in soft sand, Watters marched them back. Only then did he unlock the rifles from their safety racks within the castle walls.

'Congratulations, Varthley. You are now an acting, unpaid corporal. Now help me hand out these rifles to the men.' Watters accepted the thanks of Varthley for his promotion to the most overworked and thankless rank in the British Army then allowed him to pass the rifles. Handling rifles would make the Volunteers feel like real soldiers, so he allowed them a few minutes to become accustomed to their weapons. He studied each man as they lifted the rifle. The troublemaker, Tulloch by name, did not seem as delighted as the others nor as nervous of his rifle.

'Right, lads! Stand easy now.' Watters waited until they had lined up in front of him to the accompaniment of cat-calls from the castle garrison. He lifted up one of the rifles. 'This is a Minie rifle. It weighs ten pounds, nine ounces and fires a conical hollow-based bullet about seven-tenths of an inch in diameter. As you see,' he pointed to the lock, 'it has a percussion lock, which gives the rifle a great advantage over the musket. Why is that, Tulloch?'

'It can fire in the damp,' Tulloch answered automatically, as Watters had intended.

'Precisely. A percussion cap rarely misfires, unlike the old style muskets. What other advantage has the rifle, Tulloch?'

When there was no reply, Watters moved closer, until he stood barely a foot away from the man, who overtopped him by a good two inches. 'Have you forgotten, Tulloch? Have you forgotten all your training?'

'You haven't told us, Sergeant,' Tulloch replied, with his fellow Volunteers murmuring support.

'Silence!' Watters adopted his sergeant's voice. 'I'm asking you, Tulloch, if you have forgotten your training! I've been watching you, Tulloch, and I know all about you. You're no recruit but a trained soldier, Tulloch, are you not?'

This was the moment of fate when Watters had to impose his personality on his platoon. He had to subdue Tulloch and be seen to do so, or these men would never fully accept his authority. In that event, discipline would be fragile, so if ever a real emergency arose, they would question his orders rather than obeying without thought, leading to unnecessary hesitation, possible defeat, and certain casualties.

There was silence on the beach, broken only by the passing whistle of a brace of oystercatchers and the raucous scream of a herring gull.

'Which regiment, Tulloch? If that's your real name. Time served, are you? Or maybe you're a deserter?'

Watters allowed the accusation to hang in the air for a minute, knowing that the suggestion of desertion was a threat of years in the military prison at Greenlaw. He glared into Tulloch's eyes until the man nodded.

'Time served, Sergeant. Forty second; Crimea and Mutiny.'

'Good man!' Watters relaxed into a smile. He held out his hand in a gesture of conciliation. 'We need a second corporal, and who better than a man of the Forty-twa, the famous Black Watch?'

Watters felt the atmosphere lift, as he had intended, and knew that he had gained command of these men. He continued his explanation of the merits and faults of the Minie rifle, ordered Tulloch to demonstrate the best firing positions, and ended with an overview.

'You now know that rifles are more accurate than muskets, and percussion caps lessen the chances of a misfire. You know that the Enfield rifle is now issued to our line infantry, but this Minie was excellent in the Crimea and a step up from the smooth-bore Brown Bess. The Minie bullet has three angular grooves filled with tallow for lubrication, and it fits into rifled grooves inside the barrel of the weapon. It is small enough to slip easily down the barrel, but when the powder charge explodes against the cone in the base of the bullet, the grooves expand to tighten the fit which, together with the spin created by the rifling, increases the accuracy.' Watters stopped to see the impact of his words.

Most of the men were listening, but a few looked dazed at the deluge of information. 'The Minie can kill at nine hundred yards and with the eighteen-inch bayonet fitted can also kill at two yards. You will be trained killers.' He saw Varthley finger the lock of his rifle.

'Right! Enough theory. Now, we'll actually fire the thing, eh? See how it feels to be a real soldier!' Watters knew that the thrill of firing a rifle would more than compensate for all the painful tedium of learning. By morning, the men would remember only a quarter what he had said, but constant repetition would drive the essential facts into their heads. They would be full of themselves for having fired a rifle, which would keep their enthusiasm alive.

When the echoes of the rifles were still echoing across the Tay, Watters addressed his men. 'All right, gentlemen. I know that you want to remain friendly with your kind sergeant, so I will give you all another little job to do. I am looking for a man named Jones. He is a seaman from *Lady of Blackness*, and he is missing. If any of you hear anything about him, it is your duty to tell me all you know.'

Two rows of blank faces stared at him. Watters allowed the request to sink in.

'All right, clean your rifles, replace them in the racks, and dismiss.'

* * *

'So why did you come back to the ranks, Peter?' They sat in the Royal Arch in Broughty, Watters, Tulloch, and Varthley, sharing a quiet pipe and a glass or two of Fowlers Ale.

Tulloch shrugged. 'There are no jobs for men such as me, Sergeant. I was bored doing nothing, and I might meet somebody that can offer me work. You know what it's like when you've been a soldier; nobody wants to know you.'

Watters nodded. 'Very well.' He wondered if Tulloch would consider the police as a career. The man was morose but seemed handy enough. 'How about you, Billy?'

Varthley was younger, slim, with fair hair and intense blue eyes. Alone of all the Volunteers, he had insisted on washing immediately after training. He studied Watters for a few seconds before replying. 'I want the training, Sergeant Watters. I want to be taught how to fight.'

'Oh?' Tulloch glowered over the rim of his glass. 'If you want to fight, why not join the real army? You'll get all the fighting you need there—India, China, Africa, Russia. You'll fight in every God-forsaken cesspit in the world with the bloody British Army.'

'I only want to fight for good causes,' Varthley explained, his eyes earnest over the rim of his glass. 'Once I am fully trained, I intend to ship across the Atlantic and join the armies of freedom.' His voice rose slightly. 'I want to help eradicate the evil of slavery from the world, and this is my first step.'

Tulloch raised his eyebrows. 'Eradicate the evils of slavery? You? God save us all, man, you've still got crib marks on your arse.' He took a noisy swallow from his glass. Watters winced; if Marie had been born a man, she might have done the same as Varthley. For a second, he imagined Marie in the blue uniform of the United States Army. *God forbid.*

'Don't you agree, Sergeant Watters? You must agree that slavery is a cardinal sin!' Placing his glass on the scarred wooden top of the table, Varthley stared unblinkingly into Watters's face.

Watters nodded. 'I don't agree with any form of slavery, Billy. Not the Negro slavery in America or the slavery of enclosing children in factories or the slavery of poverty.' He stopped then for his Chartist ideas were not always accepted. Superintendent Mackay and the respectable folk of Dundee were no friends of such radical thought.

'Sergeant Watters!' Varthley touched his arm while Tulloch sneered into his glass. 'You are one of us! I thought that I saw the light of truth in your face. Join us, Sergeant; help us free the poor black slaves in America.'

Watters withdrew. 'I already have a position, Billy. I am a police officer and a Sergeant of Volunteers.'

'The slaves won't thank you for their freedom.' Tulloch finished his glass and stood up, preparing to leave. 'Get yourself a good woman,

Billy; that's your sort.' He nodded to Watters. 'See you at the next parade, Sergeant.'

'Philistine! I don't deserve a lass yet, not with so many wrongs to right.' Varthley spoke softly, 'But Sergeant Watters, we need men like you.'

'Wait, now.' Watters held up a hand. 'You speak of "us" and "we." Who is us?'

'We are the Dundee and Forfarshire Anti-slavery Alliance!' Varthley spoke as if he expected Watters to recognise the name.

'Ah.' Watters nodded. It was exactly the sort of organisation of which Marie would have approved. 'I'm curious to know where I should fit in, Billy.'

'You have military experience, so you can train us even before we get to America. Imagine, Sergeant Watters, what a fully trained body of men could do with you to lead us!'

'I'm leading nobody.' Watters quenched the youth's enthusiasm. 'If the Frenchies or the Russians invade, I'll fight them, but apart from that, I'm for the quiet life in Dundee, sleeping in my own bed and drinking Dundee beer in a Dundee pub.' Watters grinned. 'Besides, from what I've heard, America has tens of thousands of trained soldiers, all busily slaughtering each other. One more small band would not make much difference.' Swallowing the last of his beer, he slid the glass along the counter. 'I'll give you one piece of advice. Don't put yourself in the way of trouble, lad, for there is always plenty of trouble in the world looking for you.'

'We cannot just leave the world to its evils, Sergeant Watters.' Varthley sounded so sincere that Watters nearly patted his shoulder. Instead, he smiled.

'Join the police, Varthley, if you want to fight evil. And now, I'll bid you good night.'

* * *

'Tell me what you've found out.' Watters sat at his desk as Scuddamore and Duff stood in front of him.

'Nothing much, Sergeant,' Duff said. 'We interviewed the two Lascar seamen.'

'And?' Watters raised his eyebrows.

'They say they don't know anything, Sergeant.' Duff consulted his notebook. 'The fellow Ghosh was the most talkative; the other fellow could hardly speak English. Ghosh has been sailing with Beaumont's ships for three years now. He said that he always gets treated decent and the food is edible.'

'Did he see anything useful?' Watters asked.

'He said he didn't, Sergeant.'

'How about you, Scuddamore?'

'I've been looking for this fellow Jones, Sergeant. I've gone through all the publics,' Scuddamore read out a list of the Dundee public houses, 'and the usual houses of ill-repute without any luck. I spoke to all the seamen of *Lady of Blackness* that we could find and asked about Jones. They all gave the same sort of answer. They worked with Jones, they liked him well enough, but nothing stood out. They thought he was from Wales, some said Cardiff.'

'I was told he was foreign, maybe from France.' Watters grunted. 'Well, that's a little bit more.' He looked up. 'Right, gentlemen, Jones remains our chief, indeed our only, suspect for the Calcutta murder. It may have been nothing to do with him of course. It could even have been a local man with a grudge. I checked with the shipping company for details, but Jones signed on in Calcutta. Mr Mackay telegraphed the shipping agents in Calcutta; they have him as Richard Jones, nothing else.'

'He's a bloody ghost,' Scuddamore gave his considered opinion.

'Keep looking,' Watters said. 'We have a description of sorts. I've telegraphed the police at all the main British seaports with instruction to look out for him, plus all the harbour masters who have a telegraph connection and the major shipping lines.'

'Do you think we'll catch him, Sergeant?' Duff asked.

'I can't say. Most small shipping companies would take a stray seaman without questions, whatever name he chooses to use,' Watters said. 'Now, I have other items that may be of interest. There was an unknown man at young Miss Beaumont's wedding reception.'

'Did you get a description?'

Watters shook his head. 'I glimpsed him in fading light at a distance. I can tell you he was a youngish man with a splendid set of red whiskers.'

'It might have been Jones,' Scuddamore said.

'That thought crossed my mind,' Watters agreed, 'although I can't think why. If the murderer in Calcutta killed a man who was trying to destroy *Lady of Blackness*, then he may have been friendly to Mr Beaumont. If so, why hide and run away?'

Scuddamore and Duff looked as blank as Watters felt.

'I'll leave you to think about that,' Watters said. 'I have more information, which might be very important or mere gossip. I heard that the Caskies were business rivals with Mr Beaumont, and the recent marriage may not have been a love match, although I have no evidence either way.'

Scuddamore frowned. 'What are you suggesting, Sergeant?'

'I'm not suggesting anything, Scuddamore. I am ordering you to investigate the Caskies. Check William Caskie in particular, the young man who sits on the Caskie throne. Duff, I want you to find out particulars of the late Mr Caskie's death. See if there was even a hint of anything suspicious about it.'

'Do you think—' Scuddamore began.

'I don't think anything,' Watters said. 'All we are doing is gathering facts. While you two are checking on the Caskies, I am going to talk to Mr Beaumont again.' He reached for his hat. 'One more thing, check the Caskies for any connection with France. The French seem to be mentioned a lot just now.'

CHAPTER SIX
SEPTEMBER 1862, DUNDEE

The newly installed gas lighting hissed quietly in the background, giving an unusually bright glow that Watters found strangely disturbing. 'Are you sure that these precautions are necessary, Sergeant Watters? They seem quite extreme and will cut into my profit.' Beaumont studied the paper that Watters had handed to him. 'Guards at every door of the factory and hourly patrols for the mills would mean extra hands, which would incur more wages to pay.'

'I am aware of the expense, sir,' Watters agreed, 'but that's two attacks on your mills within a week, plus a murder and possible fire-raising on one of your ships. There was also that red-whiskered fellow at your daughter's wedding. It would be foolish not to take precautions.'

They were in the drawing room at Mount Pleasant House, with the fire throwing warmth toward them and Morag the maid clearing away the remains of a light tea. Cattanach, Beaumont's clerk, stood at Beaumont's side, his face expressionless and his shoulders bowed in fawning servility. In the opposite corner, Amy Beaumont and Elizabeth Caskie discussed the latest fashions over their embroidery. Their voices intruded on the silence as Beaumont read through Watters's list again.

'White muslin is so fashionable, Elizabeth.' Amy plied her needle with speed, intending to complete her work faster than her friend.

'No, no, Amy, it is clear muslin that is the thing nowadays, or perhaps ratlatane, but not Indian cotton stuff in which the poor people disport themselves. Look in the window of Neil's of Reform Street; they have all the latest fashions straight from London, I declare.'

'Oh, Elizabeth! I wouldn't be seen abroad in Indian cotton! The very idea!' Amy put the back of her hand to her forehead as if she would swoon at the thought.

Watters hid his smile. He wondered if the histrionics were intended for his benefit or if they were fashionable for teenage girls.

'And talking about Neil's, did you see that delicious ball robe that they had displayed? And the blue Louisa crepe bonnet? Oh, Elizabeth, I could have died to have worn it!'

'Blue, Amy? Not quite my colour. No, no, grey is more seemly. Grey crepe grooved and adorned with fresh vernal roses. I saw an absolute gem of a bonnet in that same shop. All decorated with ribbon and field flame and finished with a muslin burnous. Quite lovely.' Elizabeth paused for a second as Amy leaned forward in agreement. 'Of course, Charlotte will have the very best of Paris fashions now, with William's good friends over there.'

'Oh, Elizabeth,' Amy touched her arm, 'I will be surprised if poor William has much time to spend with Charlotte, the number of letters you write to him.' She laughed, covering her mouth with her fan. 'Scribble, scribble, scribble, all day long.'

'He has time to write back,' Elizabeth said, with her tone slightly tart, 'so I am sure he will have time for his new bride.' Leaning forward, she whispered something that made Amy giggle, and they resumed their embroidering.

Watters paid more attention, wondering if he could learn anything about William Caskie. *Did William Caskie have friends in France? Here is that French connection again.*

Beaumont put down the list. 'Precautions against what, Sergeant Watters? Do you seriously believe that somebody has a grudge against me?'

'That is a possibility, sir,' Watters said.

'One of my business rivals, you mean?' Prosperity had given Beaumont a pronounced paunch without detracting from the sharpness that had made him one of Dundee's leading businessmen. He examined Watters's proposal again, querying every entry. 'I don't believe that is the case, Sergeant Watters. The business community in Dundee is not of that ilk. Mr Cox is a gentleman of the finest water, as are the Baxters. No, no, you must be mistaken. I have given this matter some thought, and I believe it is a coincidence. Only that.'

'Perhaps so, sir.' Watters thought it would be tactful to give ground. 'And I sincerely hope that you are correct. But in case you are not, we must ensure that your people are aware of the dangers of fire. As you see, I have suggested that you disallow any smoking with the men handing in their pipes and tobacco when they enter the mill.'

'Oh, this is too much, Sergeant Watters! Damn it all, man; I have a business to run, and now you expect me to nursemaid my staff? It won't do, Sergeant. It won't do at all!' Beaumont threw the papers to the floor, which caused Amy to look up in pretended alarm. She rose from her seat in a whisper of petticoats and rushed across the room.

'Papa! Don't fret yourself so!' Adjusting her crinoline, she knelt at his side. 'You're just upset because Charlotte is away. I am sure Sergeant Watters would not suggest anything to do you harm, would you, Sergeant Watters?' Her hazel eyes laughed at Watters.

'We are discussing business, Amy, my dear.' Beaumont's voice changed when he spoke to his daughter. 'It is a minor disagreement, nothing more. Come, Amy, leave this sort of thing to the men. We understand it so much better. You remain with your sewing and piano lessons.'

'Yes, Papa.' Amy agreed so readily that Watters knew she was about to ask a favour. When Beaumont met his eye and winked, Watters realised that her father also understood his daughter. The crusty businessman had revealed his tender side. 'Papa?' Amy pressed herself against her father and smiled into his eyes, the elfin face as innocent as any child.

'Yes, Amy?' Mr Beaumont asked.

'May I crave an indulgence, Papa?'

'Another, Amy?' Mr Beaumont looked over to Watters in mock despair but could not hide the affection that crinkled the corners of his eyes. 'What do you require of me this time?'

'I only require your permission, Papa, and perhaps a little something from your wallet.' When Amy widened her eyes in such a manner, she would have melted the heart of a gargoyle.

'More from my wallet? Amy, you are set to ruin me! Only last week you accompanied Elizabeth to Alyth on the railway at five shillings each for tickets!'

'Yes, Papa, and what a time we had! It was as fine an autumn day as you ever saw.' Amy widened her eyes even further to emphasise the wonder of that occasion. 'Papa, the waterfall at Reekie Lynn was so majestic! We had to picnic there and be thrilled by the splendid sight!' She lowered her head, eyes closing. 'I was so grateful to you for allowing that indulgence, Papa.'

'We both were grateful, Mr Beaumont.' Elizabeth slid gracefully over to add her weight to Amy's request. 'It was such an adventure.' She was not as tall as Amy and adopted a superior air that spoke of her twelve months advantage in age. 'But Mr Beaumont, you will never know what Mama said when she heard we were travelling on the railway, quite unescorted.'

'No, Elizabeth, what did your mother say?'

Elizabeth giggled and then composed herself as a young lady ought. 'Mama gave us both a long hat pin and told us to be sure and place in between our teeth the second that the train entered a tunnel! She said that some men would take advantage of us and attempt to steal a kiss!'

'Mmm,' Beaumont shook his head, 'perhaps I should ask Sergeant Watters to accompany you in future.'

Both girls threw an anxious glance at Watters, who ensured that his face remained without expression. He guessed that they were quite happy to travel unescorted, despite, or possibly because of, the threat from any unknown kiss-stealer.

Beaumont nodded. 'Just so. And just two days since you were at the Corn Exchange Hall to see some performing artiste?'

'She was a female Blondin! Quite remarkable. Papa, she wheeled a loaded barrel across a rope that extended from the stage of the hall quite to the ceiling.' Amy opened her mouth in wonder. 'She did not tumble off once!'

'Not quite the pastimes I would prefer for you, Amy.'

Watters said nothing. He and Marie had sat at the back of the audience. Amy was correct; the female Blondin had been an outstanding acrobat.

'So now what favour do you wish, Amy?' Beaumont asked. 'You seem to have quite exhausted the attractions of Dundee.'

'Elizabeth and I would like to visit the pleasure gardens in Newport, Papa. They are only five minutes from the landing stage, and all the fashionable world of Dundee visit. There is a pavilion for teas and strolls among the lawns with delightful views of the river.' Amy waited hopefully, while Beaumont pretended to consider.

'All right then, Amy, but you take care on the passage. I'm not sure that all this to-ing and fro-ing is good for a girl.'

'Yes, Papa.' Amy agreed dutifully until her fingers closed on the two silver crowns that Beaumont extracted from his wallet. 'We are not going until tomorrow forenoon.'

'I will accept your proposals about the fires, Watters.' With Amy out of the room, Beaumont dropped the formal "Sergeant." 'In future, I will build, or purchase, only fireproof, iron- framed factories. I'll order my managers to go through each of my premises, ensure that the managers, and even the mill girls, understand the seriousness of fire hazard. I will ensure the hands leave nothing combustible lying around and the mill managers place buckets of water handy.' He glanced at the door, presumably to make sure that Amy was not listening. 'I can't think that the unfortunate death on *Lady of Blackness* was anything to do with my company. Are you any further forward with your investigations?'

'Not much, sir,' Watters admitted. 'We are still searching for this fellow Jones.'

'A lone seaman can vanish quickly,' Beaumont agreed.

'Before I forget, sir, I would like to congratulate you on your elder daughter's wedding.' Watters started his gentle probing. 'Mr Caskie seems an eminently respectable gentleman.'

'I would like to think so.' Beaumont was immediately suspicious. 'I presume you mean in contrast to his father.'

'Was Mr Caskie senior less than respectable?' Watters turned the question.

'What Mr Caskie was no longer matters,' Beaumont said. 'Let's not speak ill of the dead.' Beaumont's geniality had all but vanished. 'I will say this, Watters, Caskie senior and I did not see eye-to-eye about very much.'

'I hope that you rub along better with the present William Caskie,' Watters said, 'especially now that you are family.'

Beaumont stood up. 'William is a different man from his father in every way. He is astute at business and honest in his dealings. I hope you are not suggesting that he is behind the fires in my factories.'

'I am suggesting nothing, sir,' Watters said.

'Good.' Beaumont nodded. 'William Caskie is family, and I take my family extremely seriously. Now, Sergeant, I am sure we both have duties to perform.'

'I'm sure we do, sir.' Watters lifted his hat and cane. 'Please remember what I said about the factories. It may save your business both money and lives.'

There were more than 120 factory chimneys in Dundee, from the tall, brick constructions whose ornamental summits spoke of urban pride to the old, squat, smoke-blackened structures that belched out black fumes barely ten feet above the tenement roofs. Some chimneys leaned drunkenly to one side; others seemed as solid as the law, but all hinted of the prosperity that had made one section of Dundee society among the wealthiest in Scotland.

Watters's Chartist leanings came to the surface when he contemplated Dundee's industry. It was because of the factories beneath these chimneys that middle- and upper-class Dundonians could saunter along Reform Street or the High Street, gazing at the splendid shops, or buy the solidly comfortable houses of West Ferry or the Perth Road. The owners ran pony-chaises and travelled first class in the railways, while the workers worked a sixty-hour week of ceaseless labour to earn their keep and precious little else.

Watters spent the next day asking mill managers about recent fires. There had been no spike in alarms elsewhere in the city; only Beaumont's mills had been affected. In the evenings, Watters toured the docks and public houses asking for Richard Jones with no success at all.

'What have you found out about Beaumont?' Watters sat at his desk in the police office with his two constables standing in front of him.

Scuddamore spoke first. 'Beaumont owns five factories and mills through Dundee, but unlike the Cox and Baxter families, they are not concentrated in any single area. Two are near the Scouringburn, one in Lochee, one is on Brown's Street, and one is off the Dens Road.'

That much Watters knew already. He drummed his fingers on his desk, realised he was aping Mackay, and immediately stopped. 'And Caskie?'

'The elder Caskie was a bitter man,' Scuddamore said at once. 'Nobody liked him. His foremen drove the hands hard, and he undercut his rivals by paying low wages.'

'How did he get hands for his mills if he paid badly?'

'He recruited in Ireland,' Scuddamore said. 'The poor girls didn't know what they were coming to until it was too late.'

'And the younger Caskie?'

'William Caskie raised the wages as soon as he took over the company,' Scuddamore said. 'He has business interests in France; something to do with shipping, I believe.'

Watters noted that down. 'France again,' he said. 'I know that William Caskie has taken his new bride over there. Did you make out a list of the hands who Beaumont's mills have released recently?'

'Yes, sir,' Duff said. 'There are only three. Two young girls, one aged fourteen who fell asleep at her work, one seventeen-year-old who swore at the supervisor, and a forty-year-old man with a history of drunkenness.' Duff looked up. 'He was named Alexander Mitchell; you might know him.'

'I know the name,' Watters said. 'I arrested an Alexander Mitchell three months ago for a drunken assault on a prostitute. I'm surprised that Mr Beaumont even employed him. Scuddamore, bring him in for questioning, and Duff, you talk to the young girls. I doubt they are involved, but it's best to make sure.'

'There is one more thing, Sergeant.' Duff consulted his notebook. 'The day after *Lady of Blackness* sailed from Calcutta, one of Caskie's ships, *Godiva,* also sailed. She arrived in Dundee six days earlier than *Lady.*'

Watters lifted his head. 'Did you get her crew list?'

'Yes, Sergeant. All Caskie's vessels have log books that include a list of the crew. I took a copy.'

'Good man.' Watters glanced at the list that Duff gave him. 'Round them up and question them. I'll speak to the master and mates.'

Police detective work was like that, Watters thought as he knocked on Captain Bremner's door. From the outside, it looked glamorous and exciting, waging war against crime, protecting the respectable from rogues and blackguards, but most of it was routine and tedious. For every fifty men and women that he questioned, perhaps two would be guilty of some crime, and mostly, it was petty theft or drunkenness.

Captain Bremner of *Godiva* was young, vigorous, and helpful. He listened to Watters's questions and responded directly.

'Yes, I was aware of *Lady of Blackness* berthed alongside, and yes, I knew of the rivalry between the two companies.' He grinned at that. 'Old Mr Caskie always paid us a bonus if we beat a Beaumont ship to port.'

'Are you aware that there was a murder on board *Lady of Blackness?*'

'I am.' Bremner nodded.

Watters instinctively liked this man. 'Are you aware there was an attempt to set fire to *Lady of Blackness*?'

'I heard the rumours,' Bremner said at once. 'The police found gunpowder and fuses in the hold next to the body.'

'I'll come straight to the point, Captain Bremner. We think it is possible that somebody working for Mr Caskie may have wanted to damage or sink *Lady of Blackness*.'

Bremner was equally direct. 'Why would he want to do that? *Godiva* is a much faster ship built to young Mr Caskie's French design. *Lady of Blackness* is the oldest and slowest of the Beaumont fleet; she is no threat to *Godiva* or any of the Caskie ships.'

French design? 'The two companies are business rivals,' Watters prompted. 'Perhaps somebody wished to remove the competition.'

Bremner shook his head. 'No, Sergeant. I am a shipmaster, not a merchant, but as far as I can see, business is sufficiently brisk to ensure profit for everybody.'

'Do you think it is possible that a member of your crew may have killed the victim?'

Bremner screwed up his face as he considered his reply. 'Seamen have been known to brawl, Sergeant, particularly after a drink or two, and the crews of different ships sometimes fall out on shore. I won't say that did not happen, but I can't see why one of my men should have boarded *Lady of Blackness*. There would be no reason for it.'

'Can you vouch for your hands, Captain?'

Again, Bremner screwed up his face. 'No, Sergeant. They were a decent enough bunch, the usual mixture of experienced Sou' Spainers, Lascars, men looking for a passage home, and keen youngsters.'

'Were they the same men you had on the outward passage?'

'Mostly,' Bremner said. 'We always lose a few men in Calcutta, some Lascars return home, and some men don't leave the brothels in time. We contact one of the crimps—that's the boarding masters—and make up the numbers that way. I use three-fingered Ned normally.'

Watters nodded. That was a fair answer. Boarding masters, or crimps, were the usual port-of-call for shipmasters desperate to get crew. The boarding master or his women would welcome any stray seaman into his den, offer them drink, food, and female company for as long as their wages lasted. The moment the money ran out, the boarding master would hand the seaman over to any shipmaster that paid the required amount.

'We do what we have to do,' Captain Bremner said.

Watters's liking for this uncomplicated seaman intensified. 'Thank you, Captain. You have been very helpful.'

What had he learned? He now knew that William Caskie had no pressing commercial reason to attack Beaumont's ship in Calcutta. Was there a personal reason? He would have to dig deeper. He had also confirmed William Caskie's French connection. It was not much of a step forward after a full day's labour, but it was something.

CHAPTER SEVEN
DUNDEE: SEPTEMBER 1862

Doctor Musgrave looked up as Watters entered the chill chamber. 'You'll be here about the body.'

'I am.' Watters looked around the mortuary. It was clean and smelled of soap with three oil-filled lanterns casting a gentle light.

'Your man was too badly damaged for me to ascertain the exact cause of death.' Doctor Musgrave smiled through his beard. 'I'm sorry, Sergeant; I know that is not what you wish to hear.'

'No, Doctor,' Watters said. 'Can you tell me anything that might help my enquiries?'

'Not much.' The doctor lifted a thin sheaf of notes from a shelf and leafed through them. 'This unhappy fellow was five-foot-eleven, well made, brown-haired, and about thirty years old. He was muscular enough but with soft hands.' The doctor lifted the body's arms and ran his fingers over the palm of the hand. 'You see? There are no calluses; your victim was no seaman.'

'No seaman? I wonder what he was doing on board a ship then.'

'That is hardly my province, Sergeant Watters.' Doctor Musgrave replaced the hand.

'I know that, Doctor. Do you have a list of his injuries?'

'Yes.' The doctor turned over the pages in his notes and read out a long list of broken, splintered, and crushed bones. 'And finally, one deep and very narrow puncture wound in his neck that might have been caused by a loose spike in one of the bales.'

Watters stored that information away for future reference. 'Thank you, Doctor.' He glanced at the fragmented human mess that lay face up on the marble slab. 'Do you have his clothes? I'd like to examine them.'

'The pockets were empty,' the doctor said.

'Yes, Doctor. Do you have them, please?'

As Watters had already discovered, the man's clothes were of good quality but well used. 'It's as if he was once a wealthy, or at least a comfortably-off, man who has fallen on hard times,' Watters said.

Doctor Musgrave nodded without interest. 'Hard times indeed.'

'Thank you, Doctor.' Watters nodded. 'That's one more mystery in this very mysterious case. Lifting the sleeves of the man's shirt and jacket to his nose, Watters sniffed. 'Gunpowder,' he said. 'I found gunpowder on the deck of the hold, so now I know this unfortunate fellow put it there, or at least was involved in some way.'

Again the doctor expressed supreme indifference.

Watters checked the lining of the jacket, feeling nothing. Using his penknife, he slit the lining and turned the material inside out. 'Empty,' he said. 'Sometimes professional thieves conceal items inside the lining, or the odd coin or personal belonging slips through a hole in the pocket. Not in this case. There is nothing here. This fellow has nothing to help identify him.'

'Is that not usual if he's been robbed?' Doctor Musgrave asked.

'Maybe that's all it was, Doctor,' Watters said. 'Maybe this was a simple case of robbery, and the gunpowder was coincidental.' He looked up with his lip curled in a half-smile. 'Except that I don't believe in coincidences, especially in cases of murder.'

'You have work to do, Sergeant.'

'I have. Could you have these forwarded to the police office, please?'

'I'm a doctor, not a letter carrier,' Doctor Musgrave said. 'If you want them, send a man to collect them.'

Watters nodded, knowing that the doctor was correct. 'I'll send one of my criminal officers,' he said. 'Now, Doctor Musgrave, I have another question to ask you. Do you remember the manner of Mr Caskie's demise?'

Doctor Musgrave frowned. 'Yes, I remember Mr Caskie's death,' he said. 'It was a terrible thing; a man struck down in his prime.'

Watters held Musgrave's gaze. 'Was there anything suspicious about the death, Doctor?'

'Suspicious?' Doctor Musgrave's frown deepened. 'No, there was nothing suspicious. The poor fellow's heart gave out on him, probably due to nervous exhaustion. These businessmen have a terrible life with all the burden of responsibility they carry.'

Watters thought of Mount Pleasant and the luxurious Pitcorbie Estate. 'They must suffer dreadfully,' he said. 'Did you perform an autopsy?'

'An autopsy on Mr Caskie? Indeed no, there was no need for such a thing.'

Watters grunted. 'Was there no suspicion at all of foul play? No suggestion of poison perhaps?'

'Absolutely none!' Doctor Musgrave shook his head. 'Mr Caskie was a respectable and much-loved businessman, one of Dundee's finest.'

'Thank you, Doctor.' Watters lifted his hat; he would make no progress here. He stepped into the street, took a deep breath of the smoky atmosphere, and coughed. Now he had more complications, more questions, and no answers. The dead man had soft hands and quality clothing. He might have been a gentleman down on his luck or an office clerk who played with gunpowder. Taking a practise golf swing with his cane, Watters tried to make sense of everything. The murder victim had certainly not been a seaman with a grudge. Lining up a stone, Watters hit it against the wall and frowned. He sighed, realised that two women were watching him with expressions of curiosity, straightened up, and marched away with as much dignity as he could muster. His golf would have to wait until he had solved this case.

* * *

The roads in Dundee seemed busier than usual as Watters travelled to Lochee to interview Mr Milne, the mate of *Godiva*. Coal carts clattered at every junction, a string of Cameron's wagons pulling away from Thomas Moodie's hotel at Hood's Close, beside the Murraygate, and jute carts everywhere, with pieces of the brittle material breaking off and littering the streets. Beaumont had told him that the war in America was good for business, with the Union army demanding as many jute horse blankets, sandbags, and gun covers as Dundee could ship out. Watters had heard one of the Baxter clan describing his factory as "better than a gold mine" and had raised his eyebrows at the profit figures that were quoted. With so much wealth being generated, he thought, the mill owners could perhaps pay their hands a decent wage.

By the time Watters reached Lochee, two miles outside Dundee proper, the onset of darkness seemed to increase the unceasing racket from the mills. Nodding to the Lamplighter, who was just beginning his evening work, Watters fumbled in his pocket for his pipe, stuffed down tobacco with his thumb, and swore when he realised that he did not have a match.

Watters did not know Lochee well. He looked around for a shop he could buy a match. He found fleshers, bakers, general stores, and even a music teacher but no match seller.

'Blasted Lochee,' Watters said as his craving for tobacco increased. 'Normally, I am plagued by wee lassies selling the damned things, and when I want one, there are none to be seen.'

Watters stomped down the street, coughing as the reek of the sewage-choked Lochee Burn caught the back of his throat. He waved a hand to try to clear the smoky atmosphere. There were mills everywhere, with East or Burnside Mill, Pitalpin Mill, Cox's huge Camperdown Linen Works, West Mill, and Beaumont's own Bon Vista Mill. Like Dundee, Lochee was noisy with carters carrying their loads of jute, others with building materials, lime, and the essential coal for the steam-powered works, while the railway trains also rattled past, spreading smoke smuts into the air.

At last, Watters saw a shop standing snug at a corner of the High Street with gold lettering across the window announcing *Foote's To-bacconist: quality tobacco and cigars.*

'A packet of Lucifers, please.' Watters threw a copper half-penny down on the shop counter.

The shopkeeper shook his head. 'Sorry. We've sold out.'

'Sold out of Lucifers?' Watters wondered what sort of shop could sell out of such an essential commodity. He shrugged; with so many mill workers in the area, maybe they needed the solace of tobacco. 'A box of Palmer's Vesuvians then.' He did not really like these matches, which were too quick burning and unpredictable for pipe smokers, but beggars could not be choosers; he desperately needed a smoke.

The shopkeeper shook his head. 'Sorry again. None left.' He was a tall, calm-faced man with a bald head that shone under the smoky lantern.

Watters grunted and left without another word. He wondered if the drizzle had driven the match sellers off the street, entered another to-bacconist, to be told the same sad tale. 'Sorry, mate. I've just sold my entire stock, not an hour since.'

'What was it? A mad rush by the quarry workers?' Watters was not in the best of temper, and being deprived of his tobacco made him worse. 'What sort of place is this Lochee anyway?'

'It's the sort of place where people work hard for a living and don't ask stupid questions!' The shopkeeper was clearly not a man to be easily subdued. 'No, one fellow bought all my matches.'

'All of them?' Watters shook his head incredulously. 'In God's name, why?'

The shopkeeper shrugged. 'How should I know? Maybe he collects them. Maybe he wants to sell them on the streets. Maybe he's scared that he runs out. Who cares?'

Watters started. 'Or maybe he wants to start a fire.' He hesitated for a second, thinking of the mysterious blazes in Mr Beaumont's mills. 'Did he say anything to you? Anything at all?'

'Of course, he did. He said: "give me all the matches you have." What do you think he was, a bloody mute?'

'No, I didn't think that. What was this fellow like? Tall, short, fat, thin?'

'He was like a customer.' The shopkeeper leaned closer. 'Look, are you going to buy anything or just ask questions? I've got a business to run.'

'I'll come back later.' Watters was already leaving as he spoke. 'When do you shut?'

'Midnight and not a second later!' The shopkeeper shook his head and wiped his hands on his already stained apron as his door banged shut. Watters hurried away; Mr Milne's interview would have to wait. A man buying hundreds of matches might mean danger for Mr Beaumont.

One of the smallest mills in Dundee, Beaumont's Bon Vista was a converted water-powered mill hard by the Lochee Burn. Watters heard the refrain of the machinery before he reached the plain, near-windowless walls. More profit, more profit, more profit. Again and again, the looms repeated the same phrase, more profit, more profit, so that Watters wondered how the workers endured the ceaseless racket yet still retained their concentration.

There was an enclosing wall of massive sandstone pierced by iron gates, which were swung wide open to permit the passage of the jute wagons. Those coming in carried bales of raw jute straight from the ships in the dock. Those leaving carried sandbags and sacking, wagon covers, and rough canvas for half of Britain and most of the developing world. Mr Beaumont would have these items loaded onto ships for the war in the United States and the expanding colonies of Australia, Canada, and South Africa.

Watters dashed into the Bon Vista. 'Where's the manager?'

The watchman barely looked up. 'Through the door and up the stairs, mate.'

Watters glanced at the man and pushed into the mill where the bustle was worse. Rows of cop winders in the spinning department kept their heads down as they worked. Their hair was tied up to keep loose strands from falling into the fast-moving machinery, their hands busy as young children darted beneath the machines to retrieve any loose pieces of material. The noise was deafening with moving belts spiralling at an appalling rate amidst the constant grind and rattle of the machines. Yet all the time, the exhausted-looking women spoke in high-pitched, nearly nasal accents that could be heard even above the noise.

Watters flinched at this reality of Beaumont's wealth. The labours of these women created the fortune that had built Mount Pleasant House and allowed Miss Amy to indulge herself in pleasure trips to Reekie Linn and Newport. The sweat and toil of these children made the profit that paid for straw bonnets and the most fashionable clothes from London.

More *profit*. More *profit*.

'Hi! Who are you?' An overseer approached Watters. Stocky and bold, he pushed past the women. 'Who said you could come in here?'

Well done, Watters thought and said, 'I am Sergeant Watters of the Dundee Police. Where is your manager?'

The overseer's manner changed at once. 'The manager is this way, Sergeant.' He led Watters up a flight of wooden steps to the upper level, where the mill's offices provided a view of the shop floor.

The manager was a Mr Cosgrove, weary-eyed, smart in a dark jacket, and with hair long enough to be fashionable in an earlier age. He greeted Watters squarely but listened with growing concern as Watters explained his suspicions.

'Fire-raising in my mill?' Cosgrove looked down at his workers. 'We must evacuate. I'll get the girls out at once. I won't risk any of them getting hurt.'

'But Mr Cosgrove,' one of his assistants protested, 'we'll lose money. We might jeopardise the orders.'

'I'd rather jeopardise the orders than risk the lives of my people.'

'If you'll excuse me for saying, Mr Cosgrove, I have another suggestion.' Watters knew that a police sergeant had no authority to give orders to a mill manager, but he hoped that Mr Cosgrove would listen to what he said. 'Rather than send the women outside, could you not use them? Nobody knows the mill better than you do, but these women will know their own areas well enough. They could help search for anything suspicious, such as a pile of matches.'

Cosgrove shook his head. 'Some would panic, and panicking workers amidst moving machinery?' He paused to allow Watters time to picture the results. 'I won't hazard my hands. The women furthest from the door will be released first,' he looked at Watters and hardened his voice, 'with no loss of pay. The overseers and managers will search the premises. And Sergeant Watters,' the friendly approach was gone, 'you had better be correct. This is a competitive industry, and Mr Beaumont will not appreciate a drop in profits. He will be only too happy to inform Superintendent Mackay if your warning has lost him income.'

The women grumbled as they filed out, some because they did not understand 'what all the fuss was about,' others because they 'wanted to finish their shift,' but most because complaining was virtually the only entertainment that they had. Not until the women had clattered into the smoky rain outside did Cosgrove begin the search. He was systematic, dividing his mill into areas and sending each man to scour the section that he knew best.

Cosgrove glanced at his watch. 'Thank the Lord it's Saturday,' he said. 'Early finishing; the girls would be lousing in an hour anyway. We're not losing too much working time.'

Watters could only follow the searchers as they peered in dark corners and swung lanterns to illuminate the normally hidden spaces beneath machinery. There was something almost uncanny about the emptying mill, with sounds echoing and the slow ticking of machinery as it cooled down. The smell of jute permeated everything, together with hot oil and the perspiration of fifty female bodies.

'Anything?' Watters was unsure whether he wanted to be proved right or to find that he was mistaken and Mr Beaumont was not the target of some unknown arsonist.

'Not yet.' Cosgrove shook a tired head. 'We've only the yard to check now and the loading bays where the jute arrives.'

Watters followed. He must be sure that everything was done correctly, for if there were another fire at this mill, he would now be held responsible. If there was anything wrong, he had to locate it.

The loading bay was a gloomy place, thick with the smell of jute. There were machinery parts stored in obscure corners, kegs of whale oil, spare leather belts for the weaving shop, and coiled rope for attaching bales of jute to the flat carts.

'Aye, Sergeant Watters,' the stocky overseer said, 'this is where it all happens. This is the most important part of the mill.'

'This is where the carters have access.' Watters looked around. 'So this is probably the place where a visitor would plant his combustibles. I want everybody down here, Mr Cosgrove, and I want every corner searched. Every corner! If there is anything wrong, it will be here.'

Watters could sense the resentful glares of the overseers behind his back as he drove them on. 'Come on, lads! This is not just extra work; this could be your livelihood or even your lives!'

'There had better be overtime for this,' one thin-faced man grumbled. 'We're well past lousing time.'

Ignoring the moans, Cosgrove signalled to Watters. 'We're nearly done, Sergeant Watters. Only the boiler room now, where the coal is stored.'

Watters nodded. 'Lead on, Mr Cosgrove!'

Knowing his mill, it did not take Cosgrove long to search out the most likely places for a fire to start. 'Sergeant Watters! Here!' Cosgrove lifted a strong hand. 'Look at this!'

Somebody had emptied hundreds of matches into two wooden boxes. Each box had been soaked in whale oil and then placed beneath the massive piles of coal that waited to be shovelled into the boilers.

'This is our reserve supply,' Mr Cosgrove said. 'We won't be using this unless all the other coal is gone.' He shook his head. 'Anyway, they won't cause a fire like that.' He looked to Watters for an explanation.

'Indeed not,' Watters agreed. 'But I'll wager whoever put them there will return tonight and set light to them.' He looked at the coal, which seemed to rise forever into the gloom of the building. 'How much of this stuff do you use, for goodness sake?'

'This was a water-powered mill, Sergeant, until Mr Beaumont converted it only a few years back. He uses one large chimney so that the smoke is high above the buildings. You'll have heard about the Smoke Act, of course?'

Watters nodded. Mr Beaumont had complained about the Government Act that ordered as little smoke as possible in the belief that it was harmful. As if smoke could hurt anybody.

'Yes? Well, this mill chimney has sixteen boilers, each with two furnaces. They work for sixty hours a week, from six on Monday morning until three on Saturday afternoon. That is the same hours as the girls work, of course, and in that time, the boilers consume 200 tons of coal.'

'Does the coal arrive by wagon?'

'Yes, we have a constant stream of coal wagons bringing it in.'

'Do you have a single supplier? Or do you use multiple suppliers?' Watters looked around the boiler room. 'Are the cart drivers employed by Mr Beaumont or merely contractors?' He wondered how many people had access to this mill. Between mill girls and carters, engineers and coal carriers, it seemed that half of Dundee could come and go as they pleased.

Cosgrove shook his head. 'The carters are contracted. The ships bring coal from Tayport, or the Tyne, and carters carry it here. We have our regulars, but if somebody offers it cheap, we'll take their offer. We can hardly get enough coal.'

'So I see.' Watters shook his head, trying to imagine a fire amidst all this fuel. With the coal and combustible whale oil together with the inevitable mill waste, the building was an invitation to any fire-raiser.

'But who would do this? Why would anybody wish to burn down a mill?' Cosgrove wondered.

'That is something I would like to know,' Watters said. 'We believe it might be a business rival or somebody with a grudge against Mr Beaumont.'

Cosgrove looked genuinely surprised. 'Why that should be I cannot imagine. Mr Beaumont is the kindest man imaginable, charitable to a fault and paternalistic to a degree. Why, Mr Watters, only last year he allowed my mill girls a day trip to Broughty Ferry by rail and paid for it himself! Out of the profits of this mill! And every Christmas, he has the mill managers and some of the staff to his house for lunch. Surely nobody would dislike Mr Beaumont.'

Watters nodded. What Mr Cosgrove said made sense. He had never heard anybody say a bad word against Beaumont. Within the limits of profit, he was a conscientious employer who cared for his workers. The seamen on his ships were as well fed as any British sailor, while his factory workers enjoyed wage levels that equalled anybody in the industry. Even his business rivals seemed to respect him.

'There must be some other reason for the attacks, Mr Cosgrove, but we'll find out what later.' Watters thought for a moment. 'Dismiss the men. Tell the watchman to have an early night. I will remain here and wait for the fire-raiser.'

Marie will hate me being away on a Saturday night, but it can't be helped. As long as I'm with her for the church tomorrow.

'I'll do as you wish,' Mr Cosgrove said at once. 'I'll see the wife will find you some food. It could be a long night.'

Mrs Cosgrove did better, sending along great hunks of bread and cheese to sustain Watters in his vigil.

'Thank you.' Watters settled into the darkest corner of the loading bay to watch the spot where the matches had been left. It was a dismal wait, listening to the churning of the nearby Lochee Burn and the drunken yells of a few revellers, but by eleven, the night was quiet, with only the patter of rain against the windows. Twice Watters heard movement, but the first alarm was the gatekeeper's wife trudging to her outside toilet, and the second was a squabble among the resident rats. Apart from that, the night was uneventful.

When the dark gradually faded, Watters knew that his night had been wasted. Scribbling a short note in the pocketbook that he carried, he stretched his legs with a walk to Lochee High Street, handed the note to a beat constable, and resumed his position within the loading bay. It was entirely possible that the fire-raiser had been scared off, but Watters was determined not to leave his post until he was quite satisfied. Settling down, he allowed the hours to pass.

Marie will know I am working. She won't like it, but she will understand. It's Sunday, the mill is empty, a perfect day for a fire-raiser to come. I will be here, waiting.

At about noon, the gatekeeper's wife brought him another welcome hunk of bread and cheese. He thanked her, wishing that Duff or Scuddamore would relieve him, closed his eyes, and failed to fight off his fatigue.

'Sergeant Watters?' Scuddamore looked as if he had been running hard. He loosened the buttons beneath the leather stock at his neck before he spoke. 'Mr Mackay sends his respects, Sergeant, and says I have to take over from you here.' Scuddamore lowered his voice. 'Mackay says you've to go to Beaumont's house at Mount Pleasant. Miss Amy Beaumont has been attacked.'

CHAPTER EIGHT
MOUNT PLEASANT HOUSE:
SEPTEMBER 1862

'Sergeant Watters!' Mr Beaumont grasped Watters's hand. 'Thank God you've come, man. It's Amy!'

Beaumont was dishevelled, with no tie at his neck and his waistcoat incorrectly buttoned. He held a bandana handkerchief in his hand, which he alternately squeezed and wrapped around his knuckles.

'Is she badly hurt?' Watters asked. 'Where is she?' Watters instinctively fingered his neck for there was a great spate of garrotting attacks across the country. It was common practice for a pair of assailants to approach their victim from behind, and while one slipped a noose around his or her neck, the other would bludgeon them into submission.

'I sent her to her bed, Mr Watters, as soon as she arrived, and she lies there still, all a-swoon; I shouldn't wonder. Oh dear Lord, I wish her mother was still here!'

'May I see her?' Watters hesitated for only a second. 'Morag can remain in the room at the same time.'

'Morag? What has my maid to do with this?' Beaumont looked confused for a second until he realised that Watters was asking to visit his daughter in her bedroom. 'Oh, of course.' He gave Watters one

The Fireraisers

hard glance then shook his head. 'I trust you, Sergeant, of course, I do. Dammit, man, you're a married man and a police detective!'

Beaumont led Watters up the stairs to Amy's bedroom, tapped gently on the door, and turned the floral-decorated china handle. He peeped in. 'Amy, here's Sergeant Watters to see you. Are you fit and decent?'

'Yes, Father.' Amy's voice was weak. 'Send him in.'

Amy lay beneath a pile of covers with her head propped on three pillows. Her dishevelled hair covered half her face. She looked up as her father and Watters entered. 'Oh, Sergeant Watters, I'm so glad that you've come.'

A confusion of clothing covered the only chair in the room, so Watters knelt awkwardly beside the bed. He noticed the smelling salts on the bedside table and the crumpled cloak that lay discarded on the floor. 'Can you speak, Amy?'

'Yes.' Amy struggled to sit up. When Watters put out a hand to help her, she gripped his arm. 'It was quite exciting really, Sergeant Watters, but a bit scary.'

'Exciting!' Beaumont exploded the word. 'Exciting! You could have been killed! My God, Watters, I'll never let her out of my sight again! I'll never forgive myself, allowing her to traipse around the countryside unescorted.'

'Father, don't distress yourself so!' Amy said. 'Nobody got hurt, and it was only one man.'

Watters waited until she was settled. 'Tell me exactly what happened, Miss Beaumont. Start from the beginning. Don't leave anything out.'

'Well.' Amy patted the outside of the coverlet with her hands, smiled to Watters, and straightened her hair so it fashionably covered the left side of her face. 'Goodness, I must look a mess. Could you pass over my hairbrush, Father, and a mirror?'

'Later. Tell us what happened now, Amy.'

'All right.' Amy contented herself by clawing her fingers through her hair. 'Well, after church, Elizabeth and I caught the Newport Ferry;

74

the river was a little choppy, and the weather was damp, so we had to shelter a bit, but that was all right. I thought Elizabeth would be a better sailor than me, with all her travelling experience, but she was not.' Amy looked pleased with the frailty of her friend.

'And then?' Mr Beaumont was a patient father, but there was a slight edge in his voice as he prompted Amy.

'I'm coming to it, Father!' Amy threw him a cross look before continuing. 'We went to the pleasure gardens to admire the views. We both had a cup of tea and some delicious cakes, but then we walked to the far side of the village so that Elizabeth could show off her new parasol. That was when we saw the man watching us.'

'What sort of man?' Watters asked. 'Could you describe him, please?'

'Oh, I don't know; he was just a man. He was not tall, quite handsome in a weak-faced way, if a little, well, *common.*' Amy shrugged. 'He was just a man, really.'

'And then?' Beaumont looked towards Watters. 'Did he touch you? Threaten you? Or anything else?'

Amy's eyes opened slightly wider, and her mouth began to tremble. When Watters saw the marks where she had been biting her lips, he reasoned that Amy's casualness was only a front. He saw the tracks of fresh tears down her face and knew she had either been genuinely frightened or was a superb actress.

'I know this must be hard, Miss Beaumont, but we're here now. Please tell us everything that you can remember, and I'll do all that I can to make things better. Now, tell me what happened?'

Amy began to cry; great tears rolled slowly down her face to drip from the end of her elfin chin. She dashed them away with her right hand, apologising for her 'silliness' until Beaumont wiped her face with his neckerchief.

'Come now, Amy. I'm not angry with you. Please tell me. Tell your old father, who loves you dearly.'

Taking a deep breath, Amy looked away. 'We were just walking, looking at the view up the Firth, and Elizabeth was twirling her parasol when a man appeared from the shrubbery.' She hesitated for a second and looked at Watters. Her eyes filled again, so her father leaned forward. He gently dabbed her tears with his handkerchief. 'There, I'm all silly again.'

'Nonsense. You take your time,' Watters said.

'He came right up to me, and said, "Are you Beaumont's young lass?" '

Watters said nothing.

Amy continued. 'I said, "Yes, that's me," and smiled to him. I smiled nicely, Father; I did not do anything to make him angry.' Amy looked worried.

'I believe you, Amy.' Beaumont touched her shoulder. 'Carry on now, Amy. What did the man do next?'

'Well, he walked toward us, and suddenly, he sort of lunged. Like this!' Amy jerked forward in bed, her hair flopping loose and her hand reaching out. 'He grabbed at me, swearing. Oh, Father, his language was horrible! Then he slapped me.'

Watters kept all expression from his face. 'Did he indeed? He slapped you?'

'Yes. Here.' There were more tears as Amy pushed back her hair to reveal a red mark on the left side of her face. 'He said, "Creatures like you should not be allowed to walk, not when your father is encouraging so much suffering in the world!" Then he ran away.'

Now Amy began to cry in earnest, deep sobs that shook her entire body so that Beaumont roughly pushed Watters aside and took her in his arms.

Watters waited until Beaumont had comforted her. Only after a full ten minutes did he again kneel at the side of the bed. 'I know that this is hard, Miss Beaumont, but try to describe the man that attacked you. Tell me everything that you can: face, height, speech, anything.'

'There was nothing, Mr Watters. He was so ordinary.'

'Height?'

'About the same as you.'

'He was about five-foot-eleven, then. Build? Was he fat, thin, normal?'

Amy shook her head. 'I don't know. Normal, maybe thinner than you.' She fought another bout of tears. 'Except, he smelled strange. Like a woman.'

'Like a woman? What do you mean?' Beaumont stared at Watters. 'Could it have been a woman in disguise?'

'No, nothing like that. He had a man's voice and face. But he smelled,' Amy struggled to remember, 'clean. He smelled of soap. Not of tobacco and leather, like you both do. He was soapy.'

'He smelled of soap.' Watters rose slowly. 'And he said that Mr Beaumont was encouraging suffering.'

Amy nodded.

'I won't keep you long now, Amy. This man, could you tell me everything you remember about him. Any little detail would help. Take your time.'

'Yes, Sergeant.' Amy looked at her father as if for inspiration. 'He was not old. Not really old.'

Watters nodded. 'About fifty, then, would you say? Or about forty? Or maybe the same age as your father?'

'Oh, no!' Amy shook her head, looking like a dog emerging from a puddle. 'He was nothing like as old as Father. He was maybe twenty-eight or thirty at most.'

'About ten years older than you then, Miss Beaumont.' Watters wrote the details in his notebook. 'What colour was his hair, would you say?'

'Dirty,' Amy shook her head. 'I would be ashamed to have hair like that.'

'I am sure you would be,' Mr Beaumont said, 'but that was not what the sergeant asked.'

'Blond,' Amy said at once, shaking her head. 'I don't like blond-haired men. I hope my husband is tall and dark and...' she looked at her father, flushed, and closed her mouth.

Watters frowned. 'Late twenties to thirty, blond-haired, and smelling of soap, you say?'

'Yes, Sergeant Watters.'

'Thank you, Miss Beaumont.' Watters stood up. 'I am not sure I understand this man's comments about you, Mr Beaumont. Amy told us that he said, "Creatures like you should not be allowed to walk, not when your father is encouraging so much suffering in the world." Do you have any idea what he might be referring to?'

Beaumont screwed up his face. 'I cannot think of anything, Sergeant Watters.'

'Do you think it may be because you are trading with the Confederate States of America, the Slave States?' Watters prompted.

'I am a merchant,' Beaumont said. 'I trade for profit. I don't know anything about slavery.'

'Of course not, sir. Thank you.' Watters snapped shut his notebook. 'Thank you, Amy, you have been a great help.'

Beaumont followed Watters out of Amy's bedroom. 'I think you know who this blackguard is, Watters?'

'I believe I might,' Watters said. 'I am not sure. If I am right, I am going to make sure that he does not bother Amy, or any other young girl, again.' Watters came to a sudden decision. 'Mr Beaumont, I have some arrangements to make. Could you keep Amy indoors for the next day or so?' He waited until Beaumont nodded before continuing.

'Good. Tell Amy that I will send in a policeman to speak to her again. Until then, keep your servants alert for strangers. Don't allow anybody into Mount Pleasant unless you know them well.' Lifting his hat, Watters marched out of the house, fighting his tiredness.

CHAPTER NINE
LOCHEE: SEPTEMBER 1862

'Anything happened?' Watters asked as he returned to the Bon Vista mill. He felt better after taking a detour to speak to Marie. He had eaten, shaved, and picked up his revolver.

Scuddamore tried to hide his pipe as he stood up from his chair. 'No, Sergeant. It's as quiet as the grave here.'

'I'll take over again,' Watters said. 'Go back to your normal duty.'

'Yes, Sergeant.' Scuddamore hurried away.

Ignoring the pipe smoke that Scuddamore had left in his wake, Watters sank onto the chair. He checked his watch; the hours were slowly ticking past. Night again fell, accompanied by a light, chilling rain.

This attack on Amy was a worrying new development. If the murder on *Lady of Blackness*, the attempts at fire-raising, and the assault on Amy were related, then somebody undoubtedly was pursuing a feud against Beaumont. Waiting for the fire-raiser was insufferably tedious, but it might provide the key to the entire case. Watters considered that if he were lucky, the fire-raiser might also be the murderer. He checked his watch. It was nearly three in the morning, the hour when people were at their lowest ebb.

Watters heard the slight click somewhere in the dark. Had that been a rat? Or had it been the mill cat chasing a mouse? Or had the rising wind knocked something against one of the windows? Gripping his cane more tightly, Watters felt the reassuring weight of the revolver inside his coat.

Come on in; I'm waiting for you.

The click sounded again, followed quickly by a thin beam of light. Watters nodded; somebody had entered the mill with a bull's eye lantern fitted with a shutter. The shutter could be moved to regulate the light the lantern emitted. Watters kept still, allowing the intruder free range. He watched the light play along the heaps of coal and the immaculate machinery until it paused on the broken match-heads.

Time to move.

Rising quietly from his chair, Watters took two steps forward, halting when he heard the murmur of voices.

There was more than one intruder. That could make things awkward. Flexing his grip on his cane, Watters took another three steps. The rasp of a Lucifer was followed by the sudden flare of a match. Wavering orange-yellow light reflected on the grimy faces of two boys.

'Stop right there!' Watters shouted. He saw the flame fall as the nearest boy dropped his match. The lantern light swung round to focus on Watters's face. 'Dundee Police!'

The second boy swore. 'Run! It's a bluebottle!' He dropped the lantern, which rolled onto its side, casting its thin beam of light across the floor.

'Not so fast, you little blackguards!' Watters strode forward, cursing as he saw a burst of flame from the pile of match-heads. Taking a running kick, he scattered the combustibles across the floor and stamped out the fire. By the time he looked up, the two boys had fled, each in a different direction.

'Not so fast!' Chasing after the nearer of the two, Watters grabbed a handful of the boy's shirt. 'Got you, you little devil!'

The boy wriggled free, leaving Watters with his shirt as a prize. Swearing, Watters lunged forward, taking hold of the boy's greasy hair. The boy yelled, struggling in Watters's grip.

'Now where's your friend.' Dragging his foully protesting prize behind him, Watters was in time to see the second boy clamber swiftly up the inside of the door to a tiny fanlight and wriggle half-way through. Swinging his cane, Watters caught the boy a smarting cut across his backside. The boy yelped shrilly as he vanished outside.

You'll remember that, my fine little fellow. I wish I could have given you more.

Retaining his grip on the first boy's hair, Watters lifted him bodily off the ground. 'Right, my lad,' he said. 'You're coming to the police office with me, and you're going to do a lot of talking.'

'I never done nothing!' The boy wriggled, both hands holding his hair. 'I never done nothing.'

* * *

'What's that you have there, Watters?' Sergeant Anstruther was tall and blond with a scar across his chin.

'A young fire-raiser,' Watters said.

'A fire-raiser, is he?' Anstruther shook his head. 'You've spent two nights and half the police resources, and all you can catch is a ten-year-old boy? I could pick up half a dozen young tykes down the Overgate within half an hour.'

'Oh, he's more than just a fire-raising little tyke.' Watters gave the boy a none-too-gentle shake. 'He's the key that's going to unlock my whole case. Come on, my lad, and we'll have a talk. We have a fine cell just waiting for you.'

The cells were stark, clean, and cold, with a tiny, barred window set high in the wall and a peep-hole in the door. Watters bundled the boy inside.

'Is that the fire-raiser?' Duff had followed Watters to the cells.

'This is he,' Watters confirmed.

'He doesn't look like much.' Duff banged the cell door shut.

Watters released the boy, who crawled onto the plank bed and sat there with his arms folded across his knees. His big eyes were half-pleading and half-defiant.

'Seven years transportation they get for fire-raising.' Duff planted his back against the door. 'Seven years in Australia with the snakes and tigers and murderers. Do you think he'll survive that, Sergeant?'

'Not for a minute,' Watters said. 'They eat little blackguards like him over there. They skin them alive and eat them raw.' He forced what he hoped was an unfeeling laugh. 'What's your name, boy?'

The boy looked from Watters to Duff and back. He said nothing.

Duff laughed. 'He's another of the suddenly silent ones,' he said. 'Are you going to torture him, Sergeant? The rack or red-hot iron?'

Watters grunted. 'We'll try asking him nicely first. What's your name, boy? I won't ask you a third time.'

'Willie.' The boy looked as if he was trying to burrow into the brick wall behind him.

'Right, Willie.' Watters stood over him. 'What's your last name?'

Willie shrugged. 'Dunno,' he said. 'I'm just Willie. A'body calls me Willie.'

'What's your father's name?' Duff asked.

'Dunno,' Willie said. 'I never met him.'

'Your ma, then. What's her last name?'

'Dunno. I never met her.' Willie's head was down as he mumbled his replies.

Watters killed his instinctive stab of sympathy. 'Right then, Willie. We know you were going to start a fire in the mill. Why?'

Willie shook his head. 'Dunno.'

'Come here, you.' Duff took a single stride into the cell, grabbed hold of Willie's ankles, and lifted him upside down. 'Let's have a look.' He shook the boy back and forward until two silver half-crowns fell from his pockets. 'Now where did a wee tyke like you get five shillings? Don't tell me you earned it.'

'Set him down.' Watters picked up the silver coins. 'Answer the constable, Willie. I don't believe that you set these matches and planned to burn down the mill all on your own.' He jingled the coins. 'I'll keep these.'

'They're mine!' Willie made an ineffectual grab for the coins. 'Give me them back!'

Watters tossed the coins in the air and caught them again. 'I'll tell you what I think, little Willie no-name. I think that somebody paid you five shillings to go into the mill and start a fire. Is that right?' He showed the silver coins again.

'Yes.' Willie held out his hand. 'Now gimme.'

'What was he like?'

'What was who like?' Willie made another ineffectual grab for the coins.

'The man who paid you to start a fire,' Watters said patiently.

'What man?' Willie was gaining a little confidence. 'You ken nothing, you.'

'You watch your lip, you cheeky little bugger.' Duff stepped forward. 'You need a thick ear!'

'If it wasn't a man, it must have been a woman. Was it a woman?' Watters put out a hand to stop Duff from grabbing Willie again. 'Did a woman pay you to start a fire, Willie?'

Willie nodded. 'Aye. Now give me my money.'

'Not quite yet, Willie.' Watters sat on the edge of the bed. 'What was the woman like, Willie?'

'She was all right.' Willie grinned. 'Not bad looking for an old woman.'

'What was her name?' Watters asked.

'She never told me. She was a foreigner, though.'

'A foreigner? Are you sure?' Watters glanced at Duff.

'Of course, I'm sure,' Willie said. 'I'm no' a daftie! She came up to me at the bottom of the Wellgate Steps and asked if I wanted to make ten shillings. I said aye, and she sez go into old Beaumont's Mill and set fire to it. How do I dae that, I said, and she sez that there would be a pile of matches and oil ready and all I had to do was set fire to it and run.'

'You said ten shillings,' Watters said. 'There's only five shillings here.'

'She said she would give me the rest later. I was to meet her on the Wellgate Steps.'

'When?'

'Eight o' clock on Wednesday night.' Willie said.

'Seven years transportation,' Watters said as he stepped out of the cell. 'That's what you'll get if you lied to me.'

'What will happen to him?' Duff asked when Watters closed and locked the cell door.

'If he's got no parents to look after him, the magistrate will give him sixty days in jail and then send him to an industrial school until he's sixteen,' Watters said.

'Poor wee bugger,' Duff said.

'Maybe,' Watters agreed. 'But he'll be fed and watered and clothed and washed. The school will teach him a trade and give him a chance in life. If he continues to live on the streets, I reckon he will end up transported or worse.'

Duff nodded. 'How about this foreign woman?'

For a moment, Watters thought of Henrietta Borg and her bowler-hatted companion.

'We're going to wait at the Wellgate Steps with young Willie on Wednesday. I have a notion I know who she might be.' Watters checked his watch. 'Now, Duff, I have to get home. Marie is already fuming at me.' He grinned. 'Besides, I need some sleep.'

* * *

'You want permission to what?' Mackay stared at Watters across the width of the desk.

'I want permission to have Mr Caskie's body exhumed for a post-mortem,' Watters repeated.

'Why?'

'There is a suggestion he was murdered.' Watters explained what Mrs Foreman had told him.

Mackay shook his head. 'No, Watters. I am not allowing such a desecration on the suppositions of a foolish woman.'

Watters had expected nothing else. 'As you wish, sir. I would be obliged if you would give the idea some thought.'

'Your job is to see if the murder on *Lady of Blackness* links to the fire-raising at Mr Beaumont's mills, not to delve into the death of a respectable businessman. Please remember that. If you wish another case, Sergeant Anstruther is more than capable of continuing your investigation. I need a sergeant to close down all the shebeens in town. If I take you off the *Lady of Blackness* case, you will be free.'

'Yes, sir.' Watters realised the gloves had come off. 'It was only a thought.'

'It was a foolish thought, Watters. Now get about your duty.'

'Yes, sir.' Watters stepped outside. So far, his attempts at investigating Mr Caskie senior's death had failed as dismally as his investigations into the murder on *Lady of Blackness*. He would keep the possibility of foul play in mind but concentrate on his primary duty.

* * *

'Right, gentlemen!' Watters addressed his platoon. He had sent a runner to round up a dozen picked men for an impromptu pre-dawn parade on the hard sands beside Broughty Castle. He glanced over them, from Tulloch with the cynical glower to fair-haired MacPherson from Badenoch who had enrolled in the Volunteers because he thought it the right thing to do. 'We are one man missing.'

The Volunteers stared at him, not yet disciplined enough to remain expressionless. 'We are going on a wee march through Dundee to pay a call on our missing man. Corporal Tulloch!'

'Sergeant.' Tulloch stepped forward, his face set hard.

Watters spoke quietly to him for a few minutes. 'Have you got that?'

Tulloch nodded. 'Aye. I've got that.'

Watters led them from the Broughty sands to the eastern suburbs of Dundee. Carts already crowded the road plus an occasional carriage and a horseman or two out for exercise, but Watters stopped for nobody and nothing. After the forced march, the men were flagging when they reached the new Gas Works at Peep o' Day. Watters turned into the narrow close that led to Foundry Lane. It was now seven on the dark autumn morning, with the air crisp and the sun a dull gleam behind the gas works. Checking the address with his pocketbook, Watters stopped outside a tenement flat.

'Right, lads. It's time for a sing-song.' The Volunteers looked at him in confusion.

'You heard the sergeant!' Tulloch reinforced the order with all the power of his lungs. 'Sing! *Bonnie Dundee!*' None of the inhabitants of the close looked out. They had more important concerns than the actions of a bunch of eccentrics playing at soldiers.

The words were well known, for Walter Scott's poetry was recited throughout the civilised world, from the dirtiest Dundee close to Balmoral Castle itself.

The tenements here were stone built, each with a single entrance door that led to a common passage, from which four or more doors opened to the individual houses. Entering the first passage, Watters approached the nearest door, lifted his fist, and hammered. The sound echoed hollowly along the passage. He knocked again, and when the door cracked open, booted it wide.

'Varthley! Come out here!'

Without waiting for a reply, Watters thrust inside. The single room had scrubbed wooden floorboards, a pile of books, and a table with yellowing newspapers in place of a table-cloth. Clothes were piled neatly on a hard-backed chair. Naked as a new-born baby, Varthley retreated to his bed, goggling up as Watters thundered in. 'What? What's this, Sergeant?'

'Sergeant be buggered! Come out of that, you bastard!' Reaching out, Watters grabbed Varthley's hair and hauled him upright.

'What's the matter?' Yelling, Varthley clawed at Watters's hand. 'What's this? Sergeant Watters? What is it?'

Before Varthley could cover himself with the single thin blanket, Watters dragged him through the narrow close to the street outside, where the Volunteers were still singing.

> '*Come fill up my cup, come fill up my can*
> *Come saddle my horses, and call up your men;*
> *Come open the West Port and let me gang free*
> *And its room for the bonnets o Bonnie Dundee.*'

While one hand covered his nakedness, Varthley used the other to try to tear Watters's hand away from his hair. 'What have I done?'

'What have you done?' Watters kicked him in the shin. 'Ask Amy Beaumont! Ask Elizabeth Caskie! Mr Beaumont encouraging suffering, is he?'

Watters signalled to his gaping Volunteers, 'Form a circle around us, boys. Face outward and keep singing.' Releasing Varthley, Watters produced his revolver from inside his tunic. The pocket Tranter Dragoon had a .32 calibre bullet and a manageable four-and-a-half-inch barrel. He cocked the weapon. 'Kneel, Varthley. Kneel before your peers and tell me what it was all about.'

The singing faltered until Tulloch snarled at the Volunteers, then they picked up again:

> '*The bells are rung backward, the drums they are beat;*
> *But the Provost, douce man, said, "Just e'en let him be,*
> *The Gude Town is weel quit of that Deil of Dundee*'

Varthley stiffened. When he looked up, there was a light in his pale eyes. 'You won't do anything, not in front of so many people.' He tried to rise until Watters shoved him back down.

'Kneel. Or I'll blow your kneecaps off!' Watters leaned closer and hissed in Varthley's ear. 'Amy Beaumont is only a child.'

'Her father is helping the slave keepers!' Varthley retorted. 'Beaumont must be made to suffer until he alters his ways!'

Watters closed his eyes. Varthley's words had removed his shadow of doubt.

'Sing louder!' Watters ordered as the Volunteers' voices again faded. They were more interested in the drama beside them than in a song that told of an ancient dynastic dispute. 'Say goodbye, Varthley.' Watters rammed the barrel of his revolver into Varthley's mouth. Again, the singing faltered until Watters glared at the men.

'There are hills beyond Pentland, and lands beyond Forth;
If there's Lords in the Lowlands, there's chiefs in the North.'

Varthley was trembling, shifting his head from side to side as Watters spoke, 'This is a percussion revolver with a single, double-action trigger. You attacked a young girl who was doing you no harm.' He squeezed the trigger as even Tulloch stopped singing.

The click was clearly audible as the hammer fell on an empty chamber. Varthley collapsed, sobbing in fear.

The music faltered and faded to silence.

'What's all this, then? Singing in a public street?' Middle-aged Sergeant Murdoch was as experienced as the two constables who accompanied him. 'I brought the drunk's cart like you said, George.' He indicated the wooden handcart, which the Dundee police used to transport drunks to the cells.

'This blackguard,' Watters kicked the naked and sobbing Varthley, 'attacked Miss Amy Beaumont, Mr Beaumont's younger daughter. I was about to ask him why.'

Sergeant Murdoch jerked a thumb to his men. They grabbed Varthley and threw him none-too-gently on top of the cart where they tied him with lengths of rope. 'We'll take care of him, Sergeant Watters; don't you worry.' Murdoch watched dispassionately as a constable covered Varthley with a blanket. 'I'll ask him why.'

'Beaumont is a friend of the slave keepers.' Varthley recovered a little of his spirit. 'He must be stopped by any means.'

Murdoch was broad in the shoulder and face. He signalled to his men, who began to wheel Varthley away, the cart rattling over the uneven cobbles. 'I'll know by nightfall, George.'

'I'll accompany you, Willie.' Watters replaced his pistol in its holster. 'Corporal Tulloch can march the Volunteers back to Broughty.' He nodded. 'Thank you for your help, men. Dismiss at the castle walls.'

When they reached the police office, Watters placed Varthley in the coldest of the cells, still naked.

'Do you think he'll tell us anything?' Murdoch asked.

'I hope so,' Watters said. 'He's only a pawn. He doesn't have the brains to set up anything. Either he or young Willie could lead us to whoever is behind this.'

Murdoch wrapped a massive hand around his mug of tea. 'I don't hold much with men that slap women around. I've got three sisters and two daughters.' He curled his left hand into a massive fist. 'If anybody touched one of them...'

'Varthley's an idealist,' Watters interrupted. 'He wants to cure the world of all its ills. It would be easy to convince a man like that to do anything to further his cause. The big question is why target the Beaumonts? If we can find out that, we are a step forward in finding out who is behind all this nonsense.' Watters took a sip at his tea, added more sugar, sipped again, and added more.

'Any ideas, George?'

'I have a vague unease about a French connection,' Watters said. 'This William Caskie fellow has dealings with France. It also seems that Varthley believes that Beaumont is trading with the slave states of America. Varthley is very intense in his crusade against slavery.'

'That's in Varthley's favour, then.' Murdoch took out his watch. 'He's been stewing down there for a couple of hours. Maybe he's ready to talk to us.'

Watters nodded. 'Let's give him a call. Better for him to talk to us and lead us to whoever is pulling his strings than for him to take all the blame.'

'He won't get much for a simple slap,' Murdoch said, 'more's the pity.'

'If it was a mill hand he slapped, or a shop worker, I'd agree,' Watters said. 'For slapping the daughter of one of Dundee's leading businessmen, it might be a bit different. We both know that social position matters.'

Murdoch drained his mug. 'We might use that.' He caressed his fists. 'Come on George.'

'I don't like bully-ragging prisoners,' Watters said.

'Nor do I, but if it saves lives.' Murdoch shrugged. 'Think of the young girls caught in a burning mill. That might help.' He stood up, sighing. 'Off we go then. Try to look heartless.'

'Well now.' Watters stood over Varthley who crouched against the wall with his arms crossed over his knees. 'I want to know why you attacked Amy Beaumont.'

'I already told you,' Varthley said. 'Her father is dealing with the slave owners.'

'So you attack a young girl.' Murdoch closed his fists. 'You attacked a girl who is the same age as my younger daughter.'

Watters looked up as somebody knocked at the cell door. 'Not now!'

Duff looked in. 'Sorry, Sergeant. Could I have a word, please?'

'Are you deaf, man? I said not now!'

'Yes, Sergeant.' Duff had the grace to look uncomfortable. 'It's about the case, Sergeant.' He glanced meaningfully at Varthley.

Watters sighed and stepped out of the cell. 'This had better be important, Duff, or you'll be on permanent night duty on Dock Street.'

'When we searched Varthley's house like you said, Sergeant, we found this.' Duff held up two golden sovereigns. 'Varthley's a mill hand. He doesn't make enough to pay the rent, hardly.'

Watters tested one of the coins. 'This feels genuine. Is Varthley a thief?'

'There is no record of him being a thief, Sergeant.'

'Thank you, Duff. You were right to interrupt me.' Watters returned to the cell. The situation was so similar to that of young Willie that he already guessed the outcome.

'Two golden boys, Varthley.' Watters kicked Varthley on the leg. 'That's what we found in your house. Two golden boys. You're a thief as well as a cowardly blackguard. From where did you steal them?'

Varthley looked up. 'I never stole them, Sergeant.'

'Oh?' Watters did not have to force his look of scepticism. 'Tell me that you saved up from your wages. You earn 17/6 a week; your rent is 8/-. That leaves 9/6. My constables checked your local shops. You pay about 7/- for food; that leaves 2/6 for tobacco, clothes, and drink. Not much left for savings.'

'A man and a woman gave me the sovs.'

'Oh?' Watters laughed. *A man and a woman; how many people were involved in this case?* 'These people just came up to you, did they? "Here, Varthley," they said. "Here are two golden boys. Away and burn down a mill." That does not sound likely, does it?'

Varthley looked away.

'All right. Theft it is. Two sovereigns should earn you a good few years' penal servitude. Added to the cowardly assault on Miss Beaumont...' Watters shook his head. 'I doubt you'll be the same man when you come out. Solitary confinement, bread and water, and the turnkeys will let everybody know that you maltreated a young girl.'

'They came to the anti-slavery meeting,' Varthley gabbled. 'They said that we could fight for the good cause over here as well as over in the United States.'

'Keep talking,' Watters said.

'They said that Beaumont was involved with the slave states, and we could do our bit by scaring him off.'

'So you decided to attack a young girl.'

Varthley looked away. 'They told me to.'

'All right, Varthley, describe these mysterious couple to me. In detail.'

Varthley looked up. 'Can I get some clothes, please, Sergeant?'

'Maybe. If I believe what you tell me.' The pattern was repeating itself.

'The man was just average,' Varthley said. 'He wore a long coat all the time.'

'Dark hair? Fair hair?'

'He wore a hat. He had queer teeth, though, with a gap in the front.'

Watters had expected to hear of a man with a bowler hat. 'He was an average man with a gap in his teeth; that will earn you a pair of socks. You'll have to do better to get fully dressed, Varthley. What kind of hat?'

'One of these big wide ones, Sergeant. A wide-awake.'

'That's better. Did the man have a name? How did he introduce himself? Did he say why he was so keen to attack Mr Beaumont?'

'No.' Varthley looked confused at so many questions. 'He never gave a name; he just said that Beaumont was helping the slave owners.'

'Did he have you set fire to the mills as well?' Watters threw that question suddenly.

Varthley shook his head. 'No, Sergeant, I never did that.'

'Did he say why he was so concerned that he could afford to give away two golden boys?'

Varthley shook his head. 'No, Sergeant. I never asked; I supposed it was because he was American.'

'American?' Watters stared at Varthley. 'You never mentioned that before. Are you sure?'

'Yes,' Varthley said.

Watters glanced at Murdoch, who nodded. Coupled with Beaumont's trading with slave states, an American involvement was a worrying development. This affair went far beyond a simple assault or fire-raising.

'And the woman?'

'I never saw her clearly, Sergeant. She stayed behind the man. She came to my house later with the money and told me what to say, but I never saw her clearly. She stood in the doorway in the shadows.'

'Was she American too?'

Varthley shook his head. 'No, Sergeant.'

'Tall? Short?'

'She was quite tall,' Varthley said. 'She spoke strange though. Not local.'

'Was she foreign?'

'I don't know, Sergeant.' Varthley looked away. 'I don't know any more, Sergeant. I was going to use the two sovs to further the cause.'

'I'm sure you were.' Watters raised his voice. 'Bring this man some clothes!' He nodded. 'I don't like you, Varthley; I don't like men who hit young women. However, we might need you, so I'll be straight with you. If you co-operate with me, I'll help you all I can.'

For the first time, Watters saw a glimmer of hope in Varthley's face. 'Yes, Sergeant. What do you want me to do?'

'Anything I ask you to.' Watters looked up as the cell door opened and Duff looked in.

'I don't know his size, Sergeant, but these might do.' Duff threw across a bundle of clothing.

'There we are, Varthley.' Watters stepped to the cell door. 'Don't go away now. I may have work for you.' He slammed shut the door.

As much of the work of the police depended on information from men such as Varthley, Watters knew he might drop most of the possible charges and stick to the assault on Amy. More important was the fact that an American and a possibly foreign woman were at the back of the attacks. He had made some worrying progress.

'Are you all right, Sergeant?' Duff asked.

'I'm taking a few moments to think,' Watters said. 'Varthley's way out of his depth. I don't think he knows much more.'

'Scuddamore and I investigated him further.' Duff's grin was pure evil. 'We found out who his friends are. The Dundee and Forfarshire Anti-slavery Alliance is a very interesting group that raises money for the Abolitionists in the United States.'

'That's a worthy cause,' Watters said. 'My wife would completely approve.'

'Wait, Sergeant.' Duff held up his hand. 'I've got more.'

'Carry on.'

'There are six in the group.' Duff read out the names.

Watters nodded. 'They're all local with Scottish names. No Americans or other foreigners.'

'No, Sergeant.'

Watters nodded. 'Let's see if Mr Mackay allows us to have a wee word with these allied people. They might know more about this American and his mysterious female friend.'

CHAPTER TEN
DUNDEE: OCTOBER 1862

'An American and a foreign woman?' Superintendent Mackay stepped up from behind his desk to pace back and forth in his office. 'That brings an international dimension to things, Watters.'

'Yes, sir,' Watters said. 'If we can find these two, we can probably clear the whole thing up. I'm not sure about the Calcutta murder, though. We are still looking for Richard Jones.'

'I'll alert the entire force,' Mackay said. 'There can't be very many Americans running loose in Dundee. There are plenty of foreign women though, dammit.'

'The American might not be in Dundee. He may be based in Glasgow or Edinburgh or even Aberdeen.' Watters paused to allow Mackay time to think. 'My first thought was for James Bulloch, the fellow from the Southern states who came to Charlotte Beaumont's wedding and claimed to know William Caskie.'

'I know that name.' Mackay stopped and stared at Watters. 'Bulloch. He works for the Confederate States.'

'Yes, sir. I found out about him. He buys ships for the Confederate Navy. However, the description that Varthley gave did not fit.' Watters shook his head. 'Also, it would make no sense for Bulloch to target the Beaumont family if they trade with the Confederate States.'

'If the American in question even existed,' Mackay said. 'We only have Varthley's word to go on. The man may not even be American. If so, it is more likely he came from the Northern States than the Southern.'

'I agree, sir.'

'Our first call will be the United States Consulate,' Mackay continued. 'I'll speak to Holderby, the vice-consul here. He's receptive to sense.'

'Yes, sir. He seemed a decent enough fellow when I met him at the wedding.' Watters waited for a moment. 'I believe I might be able to find the foreign woman.'

Mackay returned to his desk. 'Keep me informed of everything you do, Sergeant. Just be careful not to create any international ill feelings. We have just come through one delicate incident with the United States; we don't want another.'

'Yes, sir.' Watters paused again. 'I don't believe that the foreign woman is American, sir. Do you recall that I met a woman the day of the murder on *Lady of Blackness*?'

'I don't recollect anything of the sort.' Mackay was already shuffling papers on his desk.

'She called herself Henrietta Borg, sir. She told me she was from the Mediterranean.' Watters tried to phrase his words to capture Mackay's imagination. 'France has a Mediterranean coastline, and Mr William Caskie has French connections.'

Mackay's fingers danced a polka on the desk. 'Be very careful, Watters. Don't do anything until you are certain. You seem to be chasing shadows just now with your tomfool ideas about Mr Caskie senior's death and stray French women.' He looked up from his papers. 'You can't go imagining that every woman you see is French.'

'I didn't say that, sir. I feel that there is something wrong with this Henrietta Borg woman, and I'm certain that Borg is a false name.'

Mackay's fingers stilled. 'Don't act until you are certain, Watters. That's all I have to say on the matter.'

'There is also Varthley's abolitionist group, the Dundee and For-farshire Anti-Slavery Alliance,' Watters said. 'I'd like your permission to pick them up on suspicion.'

'On suspicion of what?' Mackay asked. 'On suspicion of trying to help these poor fellows in chains? Do you have any evidence that they have tampered with Mr Beaumont's mills?'

'No, sir,' Watters said. 'May I speak to them?'

'You can speak but nothing else,' Mackay said. 'Don't spread your-self too thin, Watters. Sergeant Anstruther is keen to take over the case.'

'I'm sure he is, sir.'

* * *

Rain swept the Wellgate Steps, forming puddles that grew to drip down the steps one by one. With his hands thrust deep into the pock-ets of his great coat, Watters stood in the semi-recessed doorway of a shop, blinking at the water that wept from the brim of his hat. He looked up the steps where Duff huddled into a green greatcoat trying to look innocent. Scuddamore and young Willie sat in the comparative comfort of a hired Hackney carriage, waiting for eight o'clock.

Watters checked the time. Five minutes short of the hour. Snapping shut his watch case, he replaced the watch in his waistcoat pocket and continued his survey. The wind strengthened, blasting sharp rain across the steps. Two women hurried past, one carrying a paper bag full of her daily shopping with the paper already dissolving in the wet.

Duff lifted his hand slightly, signalling to Watters that a lone woman was coming. Watters tilted his hat to ensure that the brim concealed more of his face, swearing at the resulting cascade of rainwater.

The woman appeared at the head of the steps, walking with her head held high despite the weather. Watters nodded in satisfaction as he recognised her right away. 'Right, Henrietta Borg. Now we'll see who you really are.'

From the corner of his eye, Watters saw the Hackney door open and Scuddamore step outside. As Scuddamore reached back, Willie slipped under his outstretched hand, jinked left and right, and ran, head down and feet kicking up spray from the puddles.

Blasted boy!

Watters swore again. 'Catch him, Scuddamore! Duff, take the woman!'

'That woman! Stop where you are!' Duff launched himself from the doorway, slipped on the top step, and nearly fell. As he tried to recover, Watters emerged from his doorway, cane in hand.

'You there! Borg!'

'Murder!' Borg gave the nationally recognised yell for help. 'Murder! I'm being attacked!' Pushing aside the staggering Duff, Borg leapt back up the steps to the Wellgate, lifted her skirt, and ran.

''You bloody idiot!' Watters snarled at Duff. 'Catch that woman!' Borg was quickly disappearing along the street.

'Stop!' Watters ran in Borg's wake. *Man but you're a scud, Borg*! Watters lengthened his stride, splashing through puddles and ignoring the stares of other pedestrians.

Borg neither hesitated nor looked around. She ran in a straight line shouting, 'Murder! Help!'

With his coat flapping around his shins and his hat blown off his head, Watters finally got close enough to Borg to launch himself in a flying dive. Grabbing hold of Borg around the waist, he brought her to the ground.

'Hey!' A man shouted. 'You leave that woman alone!'

'Aye, leave her alone.' The voices were rough yet concerned. Somebody landed a hard kick on Watters's thigh. 'Let her go, you blackguard!'

Others joined the kicking man, pulling roughly at Watters, trying to help Borg to her feet as indignant voices, male and female, joined in.

'Get the police!'

'Bugger the police, give him a doing! Treating a poor woman like that. Look at the mess he's made of her clothes!'

'Police!' Duff arrived, panting with exertion. 'Dundee Police!'

'About time you got here.' The first man landed another kick on Watters. 'This bugger,' he kicked again, 'jumped on that poor woman.' Another kick.

'If you don't stop kicking that man, I'll arrest you for assaulting a police officer,' Duff said. 'That's Sergeant Watters of the Dundee Police. The woman is a suspect in a murder enquiry.'

'Murder!' A woman repeated. 'She's too respectable for to be a murderer!'

As Watters pulled himself up, Borg looked anything but respectable. Soaking from head to foot, with her hair a tangled explosion and the laces of her left boot trailing on the ground, Henrietta Borg tried to straighten her clothes. 'I have no idea what you are talking about.' She sounded genuinely angry.

'We'll discuss that at the police office.' Watters attempted to regain his dignity after rolling about on the filthy road.

'Oh, Sergeant Watters,' Mrs Foreman was amongst the crowd. 'Have you caught a murderer? Was it that woman who poisoned Mr Caskie?' She peered across at Borg. 'Oh, doesn't she look wild! You are so clever, Sergeant Watters.'

'I didn't poison anybody,' Henrietta Borg said.

'We don't know if she is guilty of anything yet, Mrs Foreman,' Watters said. 'We are only suspicious.'

'Get back now.' Duff pushed the spectators away. 'There's nothing to see here! Get off to your homes.'

Borg said no more as Watters and Duff escorted her to the police office. Only when she sat down at Watters's desk did she ask why she had been arrested.

She listened intently as Watters mentioned the fire-raising and Willie. 'I know nothing about either of these things.' She sounded faintly amused despite her now-bedraggled appearance. 'Why should I wish to start a fire in a mill or pay a small boy to do so?'

'That is something we intend to find out,' Watters said.

'I'll be interested to find out how I turned into an arsonist and why,' Borg replied. 'I presume you will pay to get my clothes cleaned?'

'Where have I seen you before?' Watters asked the direct question.

'Brown's Street,' Borg said.

'Before that?' Watters sat opposite her.

Borg smiled, took a mirror from inside her coat, and began to straighten her hair. 'I get around, Sergeant Watters.'

'Here's young Willie now,' Duff said with some satisfaction. 'That's your goose cooked, missus.'

Scuddamore looked tired and dishevelled as he dragged Willie along behind him. 'Right, you little blackguard, tell us that's the woman, or I'll kick your backside black and blue.'

'What woman?' Willie looked at Borg with complete disinterest. 'Who's that?'

'Is that not the woman who owes you five shillings?' Scuddamore asked.

'Nuh.' Willie shook his head. 'I never seen her before in my life.'

'Don't lie to me!'

'I don't think he's lying,' Borg said. 'I've never seen him either.'

'I'm warning you, you wee rascal!' Scuddamore lifted a hand as if to strike Willie, who cowered away.

Watters shook his head. 'None of that, Scuddamore.'

'May I leave now?' Borg asked with a smile. 'I have somebody to meet.' She stood up. 'I'll send you the bill for having my clothes washed, Sergeant Watters.'

Watters's frustration mounted as he watched Borg leave. He thought he had found a lead in this case only to slam against a dead end. His only success had been with Varthley.

'Right, gentlemen,' Watters lifted his much-battered hat. 'We have the Dundee and Forfarshire Anti-slavery Alliance to interview. Let's salvage something from this shambles.'

'Mr Mackay won't approve,' Scuddamore said.

'Blast Superintendent Mackay,' Watters said. 'We'll do this my way.' Now that he was committed, he dismissed his usual caution. 'We'll hire two growlers and pick up the whole bunch of the Alliance. If they're in custody, they can't burn anything, and we'll question them closely to find out about this foreign woman and the American.'

'Mr Mackay...' Scuddamore began.

'Mr Mackay is not invited,' Watters said. 'Go and hire two hansoms, Scuddamore. We're leaving within the hour.'

Despite their grandiose name, the members of the Dundee and Forfarshire Anti-slavery Alliance were concentrated in three streets on the eastern side of the town where Dundee merged with West Ferry.

'Nice part of the world.' Duff looked around at the walled gardens that surrounded each large house.

'Yes.' Watters did not wish to waste time with small talk as he glanced over the list of members. 'Robert Stanton, Peter Kelly, Jillian Ware, Lorraine Middleton ... Hopefully, one of these two women is our foreign woman.'

'Jillian Ware and Lorraine Middleton,' Duff said. 'They don't sound very foreign to me.'

'Perhaps they married a Scotsman,' Watters said. 'We'll round them up and question them. Scuddamore, you stay with the carriages. Duff, we'll take Robert Stanton first. You go to the back door in case he tries to escape.'

Darkness had long fallen, and with no street lamps in the area, the only illumination came from the house lights. A rising wind flicked tree branches back and forth, spilling the last of their leaves, although Watters was glad to note the rain had eased to an occasional spatter.

A single candle burned in an upstairs window when Watters knocked on the door.

'Who's there?' The voice was loud and masculine.

'Sergeant George Watters of the Dundee Police.'

'What do you want?'

'Open the door!' Watters knocked again, louder than before.

As the door opened, Watters barged in. 'Are you Robert Stanton?'

The man was about thirty, already plump with prosperity, and wearing a long, embroidered nightshirt. 'Yes, that's me.'

'Are you a member of the Dundee and Forfarshire Anti-slavery Alliance?'

'Yes.' Stanton's sallow face coloured. 'Why?'

'We have reason to believe that one or more of the members of your society have been involved in fire-raising, issuing threats, and possibly murder.' Watters felt some cruel satisfaction when Stanton looked as if he was going to faint.

'Murder?' Stanton sat down on an ornately carved chair that was situated behind his front door.

'You may be charged with the murder of a seaman and attempted murder by means of setting fire to mills and factories, thereby endangering the lives of the workers and those who live in neighbouring properties.' Watters produced a set of handcuffs. 'Shall I need these?'

'Oh dear Lord, no, please.' Stanton's voice was little more than a whisper.

'Get yourself dressed and come with me,' Watters said.

None of the six Alliance members offered any resistance, although both women protested in undoubtedly Scottish accents. One man ducked his head as he passed Watters.

'What's that fellow's name?' Watters asked.

'Peter Kelly,' Scuddamore answered at once.

'I know you!' Watters grabbed Kelly's hair and yanked his head back. A pale face surmounted by red whiskers stared up at him. 'You were the fellow at the Beaumont wedding. I'll speak to you later.'

Within the hour, Watters deposited all six into the rapidly filling cells of the police office. 'That was easy enough,' he said. 'Now we'll leave them for a while.' Watters grinned. 'For the first time in this case, I feel that we're making progress, gentlemen. Now, all we need is one of the women to admit to being the foreign woman who hired Willie, and we're home and dry.'

'That still leaves the American,' Scuddamore reminded.

'Let's press them on the American,' Watters decided. 'We'll interview Jillian Ware and Lorraine Middleton first, in case one of them is our foreign woman. Kelly can wait.'

'They sounded very Scottish to me,' Duff said.

Scuddamore laughed. 'Aye, but you wouldn't know a Scotswoman from a collie dug. You've never met a woman except to arrest her.'

'Give them half an hour and bring up Ware.' Watters ignored the by-play. 'In the meantime, we all have paperwork to do.' He lifted his pen.

'You have no right to imprison me.' Jillian Ware was intense of eye as she sat erect on the hard chair in the interview room. 'I am not one of your mill workers or prostitutes. My father is a solicitor.' Watters guessed her age at about twenty-two.

Ignoring Ware's bluster, Watters sat opposite her. 'Do you know a young boy named Willie?'

When Ware shook her head, Watters nodded to Scuddamore, who brought over a much scrubbed and newly-clothed Willie.

'Is that the woman who owes you five shilling?' Scuddamore asked.

'No,' Willie said. 'It's nothing like her.'

'Show him Middleton as well.' Watters felt that fate was closing that window of hope.

'I demand you release me,' Ware nearly shouted.

'Why did your group set fire to Mr Beaumont's mills?' Watters asked the direct question.

Ware lifted her chin in sudden defiance. 'I am not ashamed of that act,' she said. 'I am proud that our association struck a blow for the freedom of the slaves in the Southern States.'

'I see.' Watters was not used to his suspects immediately admitting their guilt. 'How many mills did you set fire to?'

Ware rose from her seat and lifted a hand in the air. 'We set two of the monster's mills ablaze. We will continue to fight against those men who willingly support slavery by trading with the slave states.'

Duff pushed her down with a painful thump.

'Well,' Watters said. 'You'll have to do it from a prison cell then for by wilfully fire-raising, you put the lives of scores of men, women, and children at risk, as well as damaging private property.'

'No jury will convict us when they hear our reasons,' Ware said.

'I would not be too sure of that.' Watters recognised that Ware's convictions were as strong as Varthley's had been. 'Is the unfortunate fellow who died on *Lady of Blackness* anything to do with your organisation?'

Ware looked confused and then shook her head. 'We did not kill him.'

'All right.' Watters believed her. 'Has your organisation ever operated outside Dundee?'

'No.'

'Do you have any association with India?'

'No.' Ware looked directly at Watters.

'Take her away,' Watters said. 'Charge her with fire-raising.'

Watters had been a policeman for long enough to know that Ware was not lying. She was pursuing a just cause but with the wrong methods. Watters looked up as Scuddamore brought back Willie.

'No luck, Sergeant,' Scuddamore said.

'Youse cannae find her, can you?' Willie scoffed. 'You're no good are you?'

'Come with me, you wee scoundrel.' Scuddamore dragged Willie away.

'Bring in Kelly.' Watters wondered if Willie was right.

Kelly was white-faced and trembling as Duff thumped him down on the hard chair. Watters stared at him for a long three minutes without saying a word. When tears appeared in Kelly's eyes, Watters passed over a sheet of paper and a pen and ink.

'We are going to charge you with fire-raising,' Watters said. 'We might also charge you with intimidating or attempting to intimidate Charlotte Beaumont and being connected with the murder of an unknown seaman in *Lady of Blackness*.'

'Murder?' Kelly had an educated voice. 'I did not murder anybody!'

'Who put you up to the fire-raising?' Watters asked.

'I don't know his name,' Kelly said. 'He came to our meeting with a woman.'

'Describe them both.'

Kelly's descriptions matched that of Varthley. 'They told us not to do anything until they gave us equipment, but we got our own.'

'Equipment? What sort of equipment?' Watters pounced on the word.

'I don't know.' Kelly shrugged. 'That's all the man said.'

'All right, what were you doing at the wedding of Charlotte Beaumont?'

Kelly looked away. 'Nothing.'

'That's true. You were doing nothing because I saw you. What would you have been doing if I had not seen you?'

'I wanted to see them,' Kelly spoke slowly. 'I wanted to see what these slave-supporting monsters looked like.'

'What did they look like?' Watters was genuinely curious.

Kelly shook his head. 'I don't know,' he said. 'I thought I would see the evil in them, but they looked just like everybody else.'

'You can't tell wickedness,' Watters agreed. 'You look like a sensible young man, yet here you are, involved in fire-raising and murder.'

Kelly looked up, eyes wide. 'I already told you that I did not murder anybody.'

Watters held Kelly's gaze for a long minute. 'I believe you.' He tapped the paper and pen. 'Write down all you have told me, with every detail of your organisation.' He signalled to Duff. 'Take over here, Duff.'

Back at his own desk, Watters sighed. Although he had arrested the group who had started the fires and the man who had intruded on the Beaumont wedding, he felt nagging unease. He was no further forward in the case of the murder on *Lady of Blackness*. This case was like a game of chess, except he was trying to checkmate both the king and queen. All he had managed to do was remove some of his opponent's pawns. Unfortunately, he did not know who his opponent was or what his or her final objective might be. The only sure thing was that this case was not yet closed.

CHAPTER ELEVEN
DUNDEE: OCTOBER 1862

When Watters entered the drawing room, Amy was sitting sewing, pale-faced but composed. Mr Beaumont stepped closer to his daughter when Watters told them he had arrested and interviewed both Varthley and Kelly.

Beaumont squeezed Amy's hand. 'So this creature Varthley was not acting alone?'

'Indeed not, Mr Beaumont. It seems he was part of a group that called themselves the Dundee and Forfarshire Anti-slavery Alliance. There were only six of them, and they believe that you are trading with the Confederate States of America.'

Watters waited for a comment before continuing. He did not know all of Beaumont's commercial interests but was quite sure that he would trade with the Devil if it meant turning a profit.

'I have done that,' Beaumont agreed calmly. 'I have bought cotton in Charleston, South Carolina and sold jute products to the South as well as the North.' He shrugged. 'That's business, but I haven't sent a ship to the South for upwards of a year now. What with the Federal blockade and so on, the level of profit is just not worth the risk.' He gave a wry smile.

Watters glanced at Amy. 'This group have been targeting you, sir. They were also involved in setting fire to your factories.'

'Have they, by God!' Beaumont looked up angrily.

'Indeed.' Watters did not give details of the interrogation process or the mysterious American and woman. 'We have every single member of the group in custody, Mr Beaumont.' Watters nodded to Amy. 'We are holding them very secure, so there is nothing for you to worry about, Miss Beaumont. We have charged the group with fire-raising. I don't expect they will see the outside of a jail for many years.'

'Thank God.' Beaumont held out his hand to Watters. 'You have relieved me of a great deal of anxiety, Mr Watters, and I cannot thank you enough.'

'It was my duty, sir.'

'We heard what you did to Varthley, Mr Watters.' Amy put a small hand on his arm. 'You dragged him, all unclothed, from his house.' She giggled. Her eyes were huge as she considered the scene. 'All unclothed! Then you threatened to shoot him. Tell me, Mr Watters, would you have done the same for your lady wife?'

Watters held her eyes. 'I would, Miss Amy.' That was true. He would have done exactly the same if Varthley had attacked Marie, except that he would have used a loaded gun and blown the man's head off. The thought of anybody attacking Marie made his blood run cold.

* * *

'Sergeant,' Scuddamore hurried up the moment Watters returned to the police office, 'do you remember that jacket you brought back from the dead house?'

'The deceased's clothing,' Watters corrected.

'Yes, Sergeant. Well, the jacket has a unique style.'

'Is it?' As a married man, Watters had no spare money for stylish clothing. He bought for practicality and wore what was hard-wearing.

'Yes, Sarge.'

'Sergeant.'

'Sorry, yes, Sergeant. You can't buy a jacket like that in this country; it's an American style made in New York.' Scuddamore sounded quite excited.

Watters nodded. 'That could be interesting. Our dead man could be an American, or he could have visited New York at some time in the past.' That might tie in with the mysterious American. It might also be connected to Beaumont's association with the Confederate states, although New York was in the North.

'Thousands of seamen visit New York,' Scuddamore said. 'He could be a seaman.'

'Would that coat be expensive?' Watters asked.

'Yes, it's good quality.'

'Then we can discount an ordinary seaman then, with their starvation wages. Our dead fellow might have been an officer, perhaps even a ship's master.' Watters sighed. 'Or he could have had nothing to do with the sea at all. He had soft hands, as I recall. We are back to the same question, was the dead man connected in some way to the fires in Dundee?'

Scuddamore shrugged. 'I doubt we'll ever know, Sergeant. Our flat corpse was in Calcutta, thousands of miles away, and our only tangible link is Jones, who's disappeared.'

'America.' Watters said. 'That must be our connection. It's Beaumont's trade with America. We have a dead man with an American jacket while an unknown American throws golden boys around at local idiots who think they can end slavery in America by burning down mills in Dundee.' Watters looked up as Duff appeared.

'Sorry to disturb you, Sergeant. The old man wants you.'

'Try that again, Duff.'

'Superintendent Mackay sends his regards, Sergeant, and asks if you could attend him at your earliest convenience to keep him informed of the latest developments.' Duff drew himself to attention. 'I think he means now, Sergeant.'

'I am sure he does.' Watters pushed himself upright. 'Scuddamore will keep *you* informed of the latest developments, Duff.' He sighed. Pursuing a case was sufficiently tricky without Superintendent Mackay interrupting him every few minutes. 'We'll get together later and work out what's best to do.'

'Sergeant Watters,' Mackay had listened to Watters report without any visible emotion, 'I had hoped that rounding up that gang of scoundrels would have closed this case, but your American link spoiled that idea, and now we have a further complication.'

Watters nodded. 'What would that be, sir?'

'When Mr Beaumont returned home last night, he found that an intruder had been in his house.'

'Did he, sir?' Watters wished that Mackay would just get to the point rather than talking around the subject.

'Not only that,' Mackay said, 'the intruder invaded Mr Beaumont's bedroom and left a tailor's dummy in the bed, covered in a shroud as if ready for burial.'

Watters nodded. 'That's unpleasant.'

Who would have done that? The mysterious woman or the American? It can't have been my abolitionists as they are all locked up.

'Exceedingly so,' Mackay said. 'It is as ugly a threat as I have met in my career, Watters. I have posted men at Mount Pleasant. I advised Mr Beaumont to live elsewhere, but he said he would be damned if he'll bow to threats of that nature.'

Watters felt a glimmer of respect for Beaumont. 'He's a brave man.'

'Yes, brave but foolish. However, Mr Beaumont does not wish to expose his younger daughter to the same danger.'

Watters nodded. 'He seems exceedingly attached to her, sir.'

'Mr Beaumont mentioned your previous work with his daughter.' Mackay leaned back in his chair. 'He was impressed with the speed you acted with Varthley.'

'Is that so, sir?' Watters wondered what pill Mackay was preparing beneath the sugary compliments.

'It is so, Watters. Mr Beaumont asked specifically that you act as guardian to his family, Watters.'

There's the pill. How bitter will it be? 'What does that mean, sir?'

'It means that you will take Amy Beaumont away from Mount Pleasant House and guard her until this whole sorry business is concluded.' Mackay drummed his fingers on the desk. 'I know it's not your usual type of duty, but Mr Beaumont is one of our most influential citizens. I hope you will treat his trust as an honour.'

Watters fought his dismay. 'I'm a detective sir, not a nursemaid! I have a case to solve.'

'Not any longer, Sergeant Watters. I will put Sergeant Anstruther on the case. As from now, you are the bodyguard for Beaumont's younger daughter.'

'Anstruther is a thorough policeman, sir, but not a detective. He'd be better looking after Beaumont's family. Anyway, I know the case far better than Anstruther does.'

'Mr Beaumont asked for you, Watters, and what Mr Beaumont wants, he gets, including our full cooperation.' Mackay's face closed into a frown. 'A few days ago, you chased down and arrested a completely innocent woman merely because she was foreign. I can't recall Sergeant Anstruther making such a mistake.'

Watters nodded. He could not argue with that fact. He altered his attack. 'There's my wife, sir. If I am to look after the Beaumont girl, she will be alone.'

'I'll instruct the duty constable to keep an eye on her.'

'Yes, sir.' Fighting his frustration, Watters bowed to the inevitable. 'Where do you wish me to take Miss Amy?'

'You will be aware that Mr Beaumont has considerable properties scattered around Dundee.'

'Yes, sir.'

'His estate is quite large but not compact. It includes the lands immediately around Mount Pleasant House, with holdings elsewhere, including property at the fishing village of Nesshaven. Do you know it?'

'Not well, sir. I've never been there.'

'Nesshaven is a tiny place only a few miles north of Broughty Ferry.' Mackay looked up. 'Ness House is not as large or as luxurious as Mount Pleasant.'

'I am sure it is a beautiful property, sir, compared to where Mr Beaumont's workers exist.'

Mackay shook his head. 'I was doing some digging myself, Watters, and between you and me, Patrick Anderson, the director of the Dundee Bank, believes that Beaumont has some financial problems.'

'Does he, sir?' Watters had seen much genuine hardship in his time and knew that the majority of people in Dundee existed in one- or two-roomed homes in unsavoury tenements. Financial problems for such as Beaumont probably meant that he had to drink only one bottle of wine at a sitting rather than two.

Mackay sensed Watters's cynicism. His mouth set in a hard line. 'Report to Mount Pleasant as soon as you can, Watters.'

'Yes, sir. And the case? The murder and the fire-raising?' Watters tried one last time.

'I am sure Sergeant Anstruther will keep you apprised of all that happens. That's all. Dismissed.'

Watters closed the door firmly. Was that the end of his involvement in the case? Was he now relegated to babysitting duties while Sergeant Anstruther did the real work? Watters shook his head. *I'll be damned if that will happen.* Running upstairs, he thrust into the duty room.

'Scuddamore! Come here! I need a word!'

CHAPTER TWELVE
NESSHAVEN: OCTOBER 1862

'In you go!' Surging grey waves thundered onto the beach, exploding in a roar of surf that engulfed the small group of fisher folk. When the next swell came, it nearly submerged the women but only splashed the men that sat on their shoulders. Spindrift rose high, splattering the tall masts as the men clambered into the boats, grabbing at gunwales for support.

'Push!'

Freed of their masculine burden, the women bent to their next task, putting their shoulders to the rough wood of the hulls and shoving the boat into the sea. Twice waves thundered in, completely covering the women, but they persevered, slithering on the bands of shingle between the sand until the boats were tossing on the choppy water. The women staggered back, rubbing sore shoulders and easing the strain on their backs. When they reached the beach, the youngest fell onto all fours gasping. An elderly matron helped her up. They stood for a moment, wringing the worst of the water from their long blue gowns as they watched the boats row out to sea, but when the fishermen raised their sails, the women slowly returned to their homes. Only the youngest turned to ensure that the boats were safely past the ridge of rocks known as the Sisters.

Watching from the driving seat of the gig, Watters shook his head but said nothing. Dressed in his hard-wearing, brown tweed suit, he had collected Amy Beaumont from Mount Pleasant at dawn that morning.

'I don't like the idea of Amy being alone in that draughty house at Nesshaven,' Beaumont had said.

'There will be servants,' Watters said. 'And I'll be there.'

'Girls need female company,' Beaumont said. 'I sent for Elizabeth Caskie to keep her company.' He smiled. 'I'm sure you won't mind having two young people rather than one.'

'It's probably easier that way.' Watters tried to hide his increasing dismay.

'Good man.' Beaumont's smile could not mask the concern in his eyes. 'Take care of her, Watters.'

'I will, sir,' Watters promised. Suddenly, this job assumed new importance. Rather than trying to solve a crime that had already happened, he had the duty of protecting a young life. 'She's safe with me.'

'I hope so. Take my spare chariot, Watters. I have it ready for you.'

The drive to Nesshaven, with two not-quite-awake, grumpy young women, had been trying, but now the girls were taking more of an interest in life.

'You see what I mean?' Amy spoke to Watters as if he were to blame for all the ills of mankind. 'These fisher people are not like us. We'd be better at home.'

'You're safer out here.' Watters rapped the reins against the flank of the horse, driving it over the ford of the Corbie Burn. They splashed onto the muddy track that was the only way in or out of the village and rolled on until Watters pulled to a stop outside the single-storied building that claimed to be the lodge for Ness House.

'You ladies sit here for a few moments while I speak to the gate-keeper.'

'Can't we at least leave the chariot, Sergeant?' Amy asked. 'We do not require a chaperone to walk a few dozen steps.' Her voice was cold, her eyes narrow and unforgiving. 'My father had no business sending you here with me.'

'He is merely looking after you. As I am.' Watters understood Amy well enough not to tamely submit. 'Remember what happened in Newport.'

'Yes, Sergeant Watters,' Amy said.

The gatekeeper was short and surly with red-grey, mutton-chop whiskers.

'I am bringing these ladies to Ness House.' Watters tapped his cane against the man's barrel chest. 'I don't want anybody else arriving at the house except tradesmen you know personally.'

'Who might you be?' The gatekeeper did not look the sort of man to be easily intimidated.

'I am Sergeant George Watters of the Dundee Police.'

'You're a Dundee bluebottle? The Dundee Police have no authority here.'

'They have now.' Watters tapped harder. 'If anybody else comes close to this lodge or lingers outside or, God help them, comes into the grounds, stop them or tell me.'

The gatekeeper gave a greasy sneer. 'Then what?'

'Then I will deal with them,' Watters said.

The gatekeeper glowered at Watters through a fringe of matted hair, contemplated spitting a stream of tobacco juice onto the ground, looked into Watters hard blue eyes, changed his mind, and swallowed noisily. 'Yes, Sergeant.'

'Good man. What's your name?'

'Ragina. Raymond Ragina, ex petty-officer, HMS *Glasgow*.'

'Well, ex-petty-officer Raymond Ragina, you have your orders.'

Ness House was an early eighteenth-century anachronism, out of place in this modern world of gas lights and plate glass. All three servants lined up outside the arched front door. The manservant gave a curt bow, while the maids swept in curtseys that would have done credit to a far more gracious age.

Watters eyed the house and wondered how his pampered charges would view it.

'It's tiny.' Amy was evidently determined to find fault with everything. She looked coolly at the servants. 'Only three?'

'It's lovely,' Elizabeth said. 'Can I explore it, Sergeant?'

'I'll look around first,' Watters said. 'You two stay here.' If he had to act as a nursemaid, he would do the best job he could.

The interior of the house was as old-fashioned as the exterior, with draughty, ill-fitting windows, creaking floorboards, and furniture and décor that would have been out of date some thirty years previously. However, the window shutters closed snugly, both front and back doors were complete with sturdy bolts and heavy locks, and the attic was as secure as could reasonably be expected in a house some hundred and fifty years old.

'All right, ladies.' With his inspection complete, Watters ushered the girls inside. 'Explore and make yourselves at home. The servants have been wonderfully busy ensuring your rooms are comfortable.'

'Thank you, Sergeant Watters.' Elizabeth gave a brief curtsey while Amy stormed into the house as if by right.

'You servants,' Watters called them together and explained the position. 'If you hear or see anything or anybody you even think might not belong, I want you to let me know immediately.'

'Yes, Sergeant.' The servants seemed an intelligent trio.

'Particularly foreigners,' Watters said. 'I am searching for an American man, a foreign woman, and an ordinary looking sailor who might call himself Jones.'

The housekeeper, an elderly woman with shrewd eyes, shook her head. 'There haven't been any strangers visiting this house for months,' she said. 'Not since Mr Beaumont bought it. We'll let you know.'

'Thank you. Now, ladies and gentleman,' Watters always thought it politic, as well as good manners, to treat servants with respect. They knew more than they admitted and usually more than the master and mistress of the house would like. 'I'm letting the girls have today to get used to the house. I'll take them into Nesshaven tomorrow. Please look out for them.' He lowered his voice as if imparting a confidence. 'Young Amy is a bit upset at being sent here. Go easy on her.'

When they smiled, Watters knew that they were on his side. His few words had gained him three extra pairs of eyes and ears.

* * *

Watters paused to light his pipe before strolling along the main street of the village. There were about twenty cottages, each one with its gable end to the sea, and there were small boats pulled up in the alleyway between every single-storey building. Each house had its pile of fishing gear outside, from the ripp-baskets that would hold fish the women would sell around the countryside to the triangular hake on which fish were dried. Despite the early hour, the street was busy with women sitting on stools busily cleaning unused bait and pieces of marine waste from seemingly endless lines of hooks. All looked up suspiciously when Watters and the girls passed, although some children ran inside the house to peer through small-paned windows.

'I don't think they get many strangers here,' Watters said.

'They're looking at us.' Elizabeth edged closer to him. 'Do you think they know who we are?'

'I'm sure they do,' Watters said. 'Gossip passes through these small places like fire through dry grass.' He nodded to an old, bearded man who was busy mending a net.

'Good morning.' Watters lifted his cane in salute.

The man nodded, wordless.

'It's a grand day,' Watters tried again.

'Aye.' The man continued with his net-mending.

'Do you get many strangers here?' Watters asked.

'Too bloody many.' The man looked up briefly.

'Have you had any recently?'

'Aye, there's one asking me damned fool questions right now and standing in my light so I can't get any work done.'

Watters stepped quickly aside.

'Good morning to you, Miss Beaumont.' The man spoke directly to Amy. 'Now could you and Miss Caskie kindly take the bluebottle away?'

'They do know who we are.' Elizabeth sounded pleased to be recognised.

Local lore in Nesshaven claimed Norse ancestry for the fisher folk, although the Picts had been here long before that time. Men from the village were said to have taken part in the battle of Barry when King Malcolm II turned the burn red with Danish blood. Since those glory days, times had been hard for Nesshaven. Reduced to serfdom by the local landlord, the fishermen had suffered poverty in their isolated village.

'There's nothing here,' Amy said. 'No shops, no style, no anything.' She looked along the coast of the grey-white surf. 'I wish I was back in the Ferry.'

'It's lovely,' Elizabeth said. 'It's so different from the city with its smoky chimneys or from Paris with its crowds of people. I shall certainly tell William all about it in my next letter.'

'Charlotte is in Paris now,' Amy said. 'How lucky she is.'

'When were you in Paris, Miss Elizabeth?' Watters asked.

'Last year,' Elizabeth said. 'William had some business there, and Mama said I should go to broaden my education.' She smiled. 'William was very put out that he had to take his younger sister with him. We met the most charming Frenchman, Jean-Baptiste. He was so handsome with a neat little beard and such exquisite manners.'

Watters gave his most endearing smile. 'Do you know what business this French gentleman had with William?'

'Jean-Baptiste was absolutely adorable,' Elizabeth said. 'I don't know what his business was. Something to do with ships or guns or trade, I imagine. That's all that William thinks about, ships and guns and trade. Oh, God, he is so tedious! Not like Jean-Baptiste or that Belgian fellow, Joseph.'

'Which Belgian fellow was that?'

Elizabeth was evidently pleased with this attention. 'His name was Joseph something. It began with an M. Monty? Montigny! That was it: Montigny.'

Watters took a deep breath. 'Joseph Montigny,' he repeated. 'Was the very charming Frenchman named Jean-Baptiste Verchere de Reffye?'

'Yes!' Elizabeth nearly jumped in the air. 'That's the man! Do you know him?'

'I know the name,' Watters said, 'but we've never met.'

Watters stilled his sudden desire to leave the girls and race back to Dundee. Joseph Montigny was a leading Belgian arms manufacturer, while Jean-Baptiste Verchere de Reffye was rumoured to be developing a machine that could fire bullets ten times faster than a rifle. Watters could think of no good reason for a Dundee jute merchant to associate with foreign arms manufacturers. He would have to send this new information to Scuddamore and Duff, perhaps even to Anstruther, dammit! Watters curbed his impatience. His interest in the Beaumont case was not over; he felt as if it had taken a new direction.

They stood on the beach where the Corbie Burn gurgled into the sea, watching the grey-white breakers smash onto the fangs of the Sisters rocks. An upturned boat acted as a fishing storehouse, with its crudely carved door flailing in the breeze.

Watters looked around, assessing any possible dangers for his charges. Out to sea, a smirr of rain smeared the horizon, concealing the distant white pillar of the Bell Rock Lighthouse. To the west, the rocky headland of Buddon Ness marked the boundary between the German Ocean and the Firth of Tay, while a hundred yards to the East, the beach ended in a rising ridge of dark cliffs. About a mile offshore, the shapes of boats could be dimly seen, clustered together as if seeking solace. Much nearer, surf growled on the rocky ridge of the Sisters. Watters swung his cane. The fisher folk would undoubtedly know of any foreign vessels coming here, and with only one bad road in and out of the village, Amy was as safe here as anywhere in the land.

'Can you hear that?' Amy asked. 'What is it?'

Herring gulls screamed mournfully overhead, but it was another sound that intrigued Amy, a low moaning that seemed to come from the sea itself.

'Seals,' Watters said. 'They must be out there on the rocks.'

'I don't like seals.' Amy seemed determined to dislike everything about Nesshaven. 'They sound like Frankenstein's monster.'

'You've never heard Frankenstein's monster,' Elizabeth said. 'Anyway, you told me last week that you like all animals.'

'I've changed my mind, Elizabeth Caskie.' Amy turned her head away. 'I don't like seals one bit.'

Watters sighed. Dealing with teenaged girls was far more trying than hunting murderers and fire-raisers.

'I've had enough of Nesshaven,' Amy announced. 'I want to go back to the house.'

'We've only been half an hour,' Watters began to protest until he realised that he would have a better chance of contacting the police office from Ness House. 'As you wish, Miss Amy.' When he saw her smug smile of triumph, he was suddenly glad Amy was Beaumont's daughter and not his. 'Back to the gig, ladies.'

Watters took the reins, shouted 'Ho!' and prepared to manoeuvre along the street, but a press of women and children barred his path. It seemed that the entire population of the village had left their homes to hurry down to the beach. Women were hastily drawing shawls over their heads or running with a hand covering their mouth. The young woman who had fallen on the beach was visibly weeping.

'The boats must be back,' Amy spoke loudly above the rising wind. 'We can watch them come in. At least that will provide a few minute's diversion in this miserable place.'

'The women seem a mite agitated.' Watters flicked the reins, easing the gig onto the upper beach, stopping only when the wheels began to sink in the sand. He sighed; why was it that when he wanted to hurry, the world conspired to slow him down?

The majority of the women had gathered at the edge of the sea with some wading thigh deep into the now crashing waves. As Amy had said, the boats were returning, steering around the surf-white rocks of the Sisters. Most were under sail, but some used oars alone, looking like nautical centipedes as they alternatively disappeared into the trough of the waves or mounted the crest. The fishermen's voices sounded in the wind, sometimes clear, at other times distorted.

'Listen! They're singing!' Amy climbed agilely from the gig. 'But look at the women!'

Although the women were pointing and shouting, the wind carried away their voices. Behind the main fishing fleet, a single boat was apparently in difficulties. A scrap of ragged canvas flapped madly where its sail should have been, while its oars rose and fell unevenly. As Watters watched, it came level with the Sisters, but when a backwash caught it, the boat staggered. A rogue wave broke silver-white over the gunwales.

'Oh, Johnnie!' a woman screamed as the boat lurched to one side with the four men on board grabbing the gunwales for support. When one of the oars slipped free, the sea hurled it onto the Sisters, where it snapped audibly. A man rose to his feet, waving until the backlash from the rocks capsized the boat and threw baskets of fish, gear, and crew into the water.

'The rocks! The Sisters!' The cry was universal as women watched, screaming at this tragedy unfolding only seventy yards from shore.

'Sergeant!' Amy rocked the gig as she jumped up and down. 'Sergeant Watters!'

Watters saw the sea frothing viciously around the upturned keel of the boat. He saw the black heads and waving arms of the men as they struggled to avoid being dashed onto the wicked fangs of the Sisters. He heard the sucking thunder of the sea and smelled the tang of salt.

'Sergeant Watters! Can't we do something?'

The ridge of the Sisters extended from the headland half a mile into the sea. It undulated in height so that in places it lay just beneath the waves, and in others, it rose six or ten feet above, acting as a barrier that protected Nesshaven from the worst of the weather but also as a dangerous obstacle at the entrance to the bay. Even while the crew

Malcolm Archibald

of the capsized boat struggled in the waves, Watters wondered if he could take a rope along the ridge. When a wave exploded against the rock with a vibration that shook the ground, Watters knew that it was impossible. The sea would claim him as it had so many others.

'We'll need a line!' He indicated the boat storehouse.

Amy understood at once. 'You can't swim in that!'

'No choice.' Watters was moving as he spoke, running clumsily across the shifting sand. Wrenching aside the drunken door, he peered inside. The smell of wet canvas and hemp hit him like a fist, but he hauled the nearest coil of rope outside.

'Jesus!' The blasphemy was heartfelt as the length of rope crumbled in his hand, rotted beyond repair. The next was no better, so Watters had to dive deep into the darkness of the storehouse, even as Amy peered anxiously in behind him, her teenage tantrums forgotten as the real person shone through.

'You must be careful, Sergeant Watters!'

There was a litter of spars and oars, a collection of creels, then finally a neatly coiled line sufficiently strong to bear his weight. Grabbing it, Watters backed out of the shed, nearly knocking Amy down in his hurry. He threw off his coat and, hopping on one leg, removed his boots.

'I'll tie this around my waist!' Watters held up the line. He had to shout over the noise of the squall, while the women and children stared out to sea. Watters did not object when Amy helped, her face tight with concentration as she looped the line around him. 'Tie the other end to the gig.' Watters hesitated for a second, then realising that he could not expect Amy to tie a secure knot, he did it himself.

'Good luck, Sergeant Watters.' Amy's words followed Watters as he waded into the surf.

The power of the first wave all but unbalanced Watters with its swift undertow. Lifting his feet, he allowed the tide to pull him out before striking out over arm for the stranded men. Within a minute, he had lost sight of the bobbing heads, relying on instinct to guide him forward.

Seventy yards, Watters told himself, thrusting forward. *Only seventy yards*, but already he felt the chill biting into him, while the rope dragged him backwards and chafed at his waist. Lifting his head, he saw only the sea, hissing in a nightmare of spindrift and spume, with grey-white waves breaking all around. Something was floating nearby, a piece of wood, perhaps from the stricken boat, and then the sea sucked him under. Watters struck out again, gasping as salt water surged into his lungs.

Another stroke, another ducking, then Watters enjoyed a brief lull as he lay in the trough between two growling waves. Taking a deep breath, he rested on a rising wave. He saw a boat bobbing madly on the sea with a man only three yards distant, waving feebly. Watters lunged forward, but a fluke of the current drove him away and under; when he emerged, the man was gone. The boat swept past, men pointing beside him, their mouths open as they yelled words that were lost in the roar of the sea.

Then there was only grey water and a confusion of spume, a seagull circling overhead, its beak gaping open, and the rope tearing at his skin. Watters struck on, cursing the obstinacy that had forced him out here. One moment he saw a rising grey sea, and then the man was in front of him, his eyes wide in despair mingled with a sudden dawning of hope.

'Hold on!' Watters's first clutch caught only the sea, but his second seized a handful of hair as the man sunk again. Watters hauled upward, swearing as the man struggled, kicking out mightily. 'Keep still, you blackguard! Stop wriggling!'

Panicking, the man could not hear, so Watters cracked a short punch to the point of his jaw. Shocked or unconscious, the man began to sink, dragging Watters down with him. The roaring of water in Watters's ears was unforgettable, terrifying. He kicked upward in near-panic until he manoeuvred the prostrate man onto his back to begin the long haul back to land.

The tide had helped Watters on his way out. Now it worked against him, dragging him toward the seething horror of the Sisters, where the sea exploded in spume that rose fifteen, twenty, twenty-five feet into the air. Swimming one-handed with the other holding his burden secure, Watters could make little headway until the line around his waist began to tighten further. As he felt it pulling him back to land, he swam all the harder.

'Drive on now!' Watters heard Amy's young voice through the cacophony of the storm and felt rough sand scraping beneath him. Retching with the seawater that he had swallowed, he lay still.

'Sergeant Watters?' Elizabeth was at his side. Watters looked up. Amy had backed the gig into the sea and was now driving it up the beach, with the line drawing him clear of the water.

'Hold, now!' Amy's voice was clear and commanding, and then she ran down toward him as he floundered in the shallows. 'Sergeant! You saved someone!'

Turning onto his side, Watters spewed out vast quantities of water before he tried to reply. 'Aye. Just one.' His voice was hoarse, his throat and chest burning. He saw Amy's face hovering over him, smiling through hazel eyes, then she moved to the man that Watters had rescued.

'Is he dead?' There was concern in her voice.

'No. I had to knock him out.' Watters watched as an elderly man turned the survivor onto his side, using his arms as an efficient pump. Suddenly aware that there was a crowd of women and children around him, Watters clambered to his feet. 'How many were in the boat?'

'Four,' one of the women said. She hugged a shawl to her shoulders. 'Bessie's Tom made it back himself, you saved Curly John, but we cannae see Dumpy.'

Watters was aware that the fishing community possessed only a limited number of surnames, so affixed tee-names, or nicknames, to identify each other. 'That's only three,' he pointed out. 'You said there were four in the boat.'

'Aye,' the woman looked at him without expression. 'There's the Buckie as well. He's waiting on the Sisters.'

'Waiting?' Watters looked out to sea. He could see the shape of a man on the Sisters, half hidden behind the bursting spray. 'Waiting for what?'

'He's waiting for the sea to claim him or for you to bring him back.' The woman was about twenty-five with clear skin and eyes. 'Would you? He's my man.'

Even as he pumped Curly John dry, the old man spoke. 'Fishermen can't swim,' he explained. 'They've never learned.' His voice was flat. He did not suggest that Watters try to rescue the Buckie but waited patiently for his decision.

Watters felt sick at the thought of going back in the sea. He looked at the heavy leather boots with iron-shod soles of the man he had rescued and thought it was no wonder the fishermen could not swim. These boots would drag anybody down.

'Do you think he can hold on until the tide is fully ebbed?' Watters already knew the answer. If the man slipped or weakened further, the tide would pull him out to sea with no chance of survival. *I have to go out there again.* 'Could you back the gig as far as possible into the sea, Amy?'

'Yes.' There was no hesitation.

Brave girl. 'Come on then.'

'Please take care, Sergeant.' Elizabeth touched his arm.

'I will,' Watters promised.

Amy was as good as her word. She drove until the gig wheels were under water and waves surged along the side of the horse, and only then did Watters again plunge into the sea. He was tired now and allowed the tide to drag him out, just kicking enough to keep his head above water. The Sisters seemed very far away, and the line around his waist was rubbing at already open wounds. Again there were the waves, rising, curling, tossing him around in a mad frenzy, but this time, Watters had a definite objective in view.

The rocks were ahead, looking even uglier now that he was close. Black fanged, streaked with seaweed, spangled with whelks and mussels, they alternatively appeared and vanished as the waves surged, exploded, and receded. The Buckie sat on the rock, eyes closed and mouth open as he struggled to breath.

'Buckie! Move toward me!' Watters swore as a wave smashed him against the rock, drawing blood from his left shoulder. 'Move, man!'

The Buckie opened his eyes, staring at him without moving. Another wave lifted Watters and threw him against the Sisters, dragging him across the sharp rock, tearing his shirt and trousers and forcing him under the water. There was a moment of blackness, that terrifying roaring in his ears, and then the sea threw Watters up again, smashing his head agonisingly against a spur. Reaching out, Watters clung on, swearing as he saw his blood easing from a dozen scrapes and cuts.

'Come on, man! Come to me! I'll save you! Otherwise, we'll both drown here!'

The Buckie's eyes were wide, his mouth working, and Watters realised that he was singing a psalm.

'Buckie!' Sudden anger surged through Watters. He dragged himself onto the rock, slipping on the seaweed. He staggered as a wave splintered at his feet, grabbed the Buckie by his jacket, and held his shoulders.

Buckie only stared as Watters shouted above the thunder of the waves. 'Your boots! Take them off!'

When Buckie shook his head, too shocked to move, Watters began to haul at the thigh length leather boots. 'They'll pull you right under!' Dragging both boots off the unresisting fisherman, Watters threw them into the sea. 'Now come on!' Watters could feel the rope biting into his waist. The salt water was stinging his various scrapes.

'It's God's will,' the Buckie began, so Watters manipulated him from the rock.

'Hold onto me! Kick for the shore!'

Watters felt the familiar sick fear as the waves rose above him, the same terrible thunder in his ears, but at least the Buckie had learned how to kick his legs. Watters felt his strength ebbing as the fisherman's weight dragged on his shoulders. He would be all right if he kept fighting, kept struggling. *Move, kick, use my arms, ignore the pain, move kick, use my arms, ignore the pain* ... The world was only salt water and sudden spells of agonising air.

Watters reached the beach in a sudden welter of noise and light. The fisherwomen had remained, watching in a tense silence that somehow highlighted the sinister suck and crash of the sea. There were fishermen too, most moving to help, others waiting in hope. Watters lay with the sand rough beneath his face and the surf exploding around him.

Let me die here. I can move no further.

'Up you get.' Rough hands grabbed Watters by the shoulders; gruff voices sounded in his ears. 'You're safe now.'

Watters spewed seawater. He heard a familiar voice among the crowd. 'Let me have him. That's my husband.' He looked up. Marie was there, giving orders, taking control. He closed his eyes. Everything would be all right now; Marie was there.

CHAPTER THIRTEEN
NESSHAVEN: OCTOBER 1862

Watters recalled nothing of his journey from the beach to Ness House, but he knew that Marie helped carry him from the chaise to the dining room, where the warmth of the fire relaxed him as much as the bite of raw whisky that persistent hands pressed past his lips.

'I must examine him.' Marie gave firm orders. 'Put him on the table.'

Watters felt strong hands lift him gently onto the table. He saw strands of blonde hair wisping across Marie's concerned eyes; he felt her capable hands on his head. 'You're covered in blood, George. I'll have to look.' There was a pause, during which he heard her voice as a low murmur. 'We'll need your shirt off.'

Watters allowed Marie to manoeuvre him, and then the bite of kill-me-deadly whisky on his wounds made him gasp, but Marie's eyes were critical and kind.

'Plenty scrapes here, George. They're ugly enough but shallow and not dangerous. They go right around your waist where the rope burned and down your side.' Marie paused. 'We'll need your trousers off too.' She raised her head. 'Could you all please leave? Except you.' She pointed to the manservant. 'You can stay. I might need you. What's your name?'

'Andrew,' the man said.

'I want to stay too,' Amy said.

Marie's voice cracked. 'Leave! This is between my husband and me.'
Marie lifted Watters's hips and eased down his trousers. She soothed
him with quiet words as she examined his cuts, and then turned him
onto his face to see how extensive they were. 'This will sting a little,'
Marie said as she smeared the whisky from thigh to flank, cleaning
each scrape with a thoroughness that in other circumstances would
have made Watters yelp. 'Lie still now.' Marie's voice was gentle as
she worked the spirit into a long cut that extended from his hip down
his left thigh. Watters could feel Marie's breath hot on his body as he
instinctively tensed.

'No major damage,' she said at last, and when she brought her attention back to his face, her eyes were pure blue. 'Your clothes are wet.
I brought dry clothing for you.' She watched him, smiling. 'That was
a brave thing that you did, George.'

Watters shook his head. 'It had to be done.' He would probably never
admit how frightened he was or how near he had been to panic. He lay
still for a moment, revelling in her attention before he forced himself
to rise from the table. 'Marie. We'll have to get you home. It's late.'

Marie shook her head. 'I'm not leaving you here.'

'I'm on duty,' Watters said. 'This is Mr Beaumont's house.'

Marie nodded. 'I am well aware of that.'

'It may be dangerous.'

Marie swept a hand to indicate his battered body. 'So I see.'

'I mean it might be dangerous for you.'

'You'll look after me,' Marie said, 'and I'll help you look after the
girls.'

'It's not only the American to worry about.' Watters knew that he
had already lost the argument. 'There is the seaman Jones, the foreign
woman, and I have no idea who or what else.'

'I'm staying with you,' Marie said with a smile. 'So just accept that.'

'In that case,' Watters bowed to the inevitable, 'could you check the
girls for me? It's not proper that I should look into their bedrooms, and
they've had a bit of a busy day.' He hesitated, dressing slowly as his injuries stiffened. 'I must send a note to Scuddamore at the police office.'

'Andrew will take it,' Marie decided for him. 'You aren't going any-where tonight. Write a note, and Andrew will get to Broughty and send a telegraph from the post office.'

Watters nodded, bowing to superior authority.

There was a tap on the door. 'Oh, Sergeant Watters.' Elizabeth poked her head into the room. 'What a lot I have to tell William in my next letter.'

'Get to your bed!' Marie snarled and winked at Watters. 'You've been letting these girls away with murder. That will change now that I'm here; I'm telling you.'

* * *

As dawn grey-streaked the horizon, Watters limped around the grounds, checking that each shuttered window was still secure, look-ing for scuff marks or footprints that might indicate a prowler, asking the unshaven gatekeeper if there had been any movement during the night.

'Two foxes and a deer. Nothing else.' Ragina shook his head. 'I heard you were swimming yesterday.'

Watters nodded.

'That won't be forgotten.' Ragina bit on a hunk of tobacco. 'You'll have heard about that foreign boat that's cruising offshore.'

'No.' Watters shook his head. 'The fishermen are a bit close-mouthed.'

'Aye, they don't like strangers. The customs men check the nets too much and don't trust them in case they're smuggling in duty-free.' Ragina turned away, reached behind his door, and tossed over an empty bottle. 'You said you were looking for strangers. What do you make of this?'

Watters lifted the bottle. 'That's an interesting shape; I've never seen one like that before.' He sniffed the neck. 'What was in it? Gin?'

'Gin,' Ragina confirmed, 'from a stranger boat.'

'Did foul weather force her in?'

'Nothing like,' Ragina said. 'She turned up a few weeks ago, cruising the coast and selling gin to the fishermen.'

'Is that usual along this coast?'

Ragina shook his head. 'It's the first I've heard of it up here. It's common off the English East Coast.' He grunted. 'I was down that way with the Royal Navy before we went to the Med.'

'HMS *Glasgow*, you said?'

'That's right. The Navy kicked me out after I got wounded at the Battle of Navarino back in '27.'

The Battle of Navarino. The name jarred in Watters's head, although he was not sure why. There was something about Navarino that should be important to him.

'Anyway, you were asking about strangers,' Ragina said. 'I thought it might help to know about the foreign boat.'

'Thank you.' Watters was not sure if the information was of any use to him. 'Why did you not tell me this earlier?'

Ragina shrugged. 'When you first came, you were just a Dundee bluebottle,' he said. 'Now, you're the man that saved Curly John and the Buckie.'

Watters nodded his understanding. He had proved himself.

'There's another thing that might interest you.' Now that Ragina had started to speak, he seemed determined to make up for lost time. 'This foreign vessel has a woman in charge.'

Watters stiffened; a foreign vessel, a woman in charge, and the Battle of Navarino. *That was the connection: Isabella Navarino.* He thought back to his first case as a young criminal officer with Scotland Yard. A group of daring fraudsters had sailed a stolen ship around the world, taking on cargos without paying. One of the principals in the case had been a female ship's captain named Isabella Navarino, so called because she had been born on HMS *Genoa* during the battle of Navarino.

'Are you all right, Sergeant? You have gone very quiet.'

'Thank you, Mr Ragina.' Watters touched the brim of his hat. 'You have been extremely helpful.'

Henrietta Borg *was* Isabella Navarino. Although Isabella Navarino might not have been the foreign woman who bribed children to become fire-raisers, Watters knew that she was no blushing innocent. That was something else to notify the police office about. Watters grunted; his trip to Nesshaven had proved more worthwhile than he had thought.

Watters lined up a patch of nettles and swung his cane. He had gathered quite a lot of information over the past few weeks. Now he had to place it all in order and see what sort of picture it created. At present, nothing made sense. He desperately needed a round of golf to clear his head, but that was not possible.

Striding around the grounds of Ness House, Watters examined the various pieces of the puzzle. He had a dead man who may or may not have been an American. He had a series of fires in Mr Beaumont's mills, with no real idea who had instigated them. He had a female gin-dealing ship's captain wandering around Dundee under an assumed name. He had threats to Mr Beaumont, probably because of his past involvement with the Confederate States of America. He had a missing suspect who may or may not be named Jones. He had an unidentified foreign female who bribed little boys to set fire to mills. He had an equally unknown American and possibly the same woman who paid a naïve abolitionist to attack Mr Beaumont's daughter. He had a vague possibility of murder with Mr Caskie senior's death. He had stories that William Caskie junior had dealings with France, possibly through armaments. There was no apparent link except a loose affinity with the war in the United States and perhaps with France.

That was the debit side. On the credit side, he had arrested a small group of misguided people who had been duped into criminal fire-raising. Once again, the chess analogy came into Watters's mind, but who was the king, and even more importantly, who was moving the pieces?

Watters shook his head. The pieces of this puzzle were too fragmented to make any sense. He would have to keep worrying away, putting small scraps of information together in the hope of creating a coherent picture. In the meantime, he had a girl to keep safe. Watters swung his cane in frustration. He needed to get onto a golf course.

When Watters returned to the house, Marie was waiting for him.

'Why did Mr Mackay send you out here?' Marie challenged him across the breakfast table.

'To look after Amy,' Watters said.

'There's more to it than that,' Marie pressed him. 'This is a complex case. There is a murder, and there is fire-raising.' She held Watters's gaze. 'How many murder cases does Mr Mackay give to a sergeant?'

Watters frowned. 'There are not many murders in Dundee.'

'That's not what I asked,' Marie said. 'How many murder cases does Mr Mackay give to a sergeant?'

'None,' Watters said. 'An inspector normally gets the murders.'

'Exactly so,' Marie said. 'Why give this particular case to a sergeant and then take you off the case when you begin to make progress?'

'I don't feel as if I am making progress,' Watters said.

'You are.' Marie stopped any further protests. 'You got Varthley and Kelly and their gang into jail and then what? Mr Mackay gives the case to Anstruther.' She rolled her eyes. 'Anstruther of all people! A man who can hardly lace his boots without help. No, George, there is something very wrong here.'

'What do you think?'

'I think that for some reason, Mr Mackay does not want this case solved. He knows more than he's saying and did not expect you to find anything.'

'It's political,' Watters said. 'Mackay can't tell me everything.'

'Exactly,' Marie agreed. 'It's political. That's why Mackay is trying to keep clear of it. Politicians are a dirty, underhanded, double-dealing set.' She leaned closer to him across the table. 'You have two choices here, George. Your first choice is you can do your duty, look after these young ones while Anstruther bumbles through and finds nothing.'

'Or?' Watters already guessed what Marie was about to say.

'Or you do your utmost to solve the thing to prove to Mr Mackay that you are a better detective than Anstruther or a hundred

Anstruthers.' Marie sat back smiling. 'You can show Mr Mackay that he was wrong to treat you in this manner.'

'Solving the case is what I have been trying to do,' Watters said.

Marie smiled. 'I thought so. I did not marry a man who would give up merely because Mr Mackay is shy of probing anything political.'

'Mr Mackay might not have a choice,' Watters said. 'He has had interviews with Sir John Ogilvy, the MP, and Holderby, the US Ambassador lately. One or both of them might have warned him to steer clear.'

'Has anybody warned you to steer clear?'

'Worse.' Watters shook his head. 'Mackay more or less ordered me to walk away.'

'Well, that's that then.' Marie sat back in triumph. 'He's scared you might solve it and find answers he does not want to be revealed.'

Watters sighed. 'We have what may be a small clue.' He placed Ragina's bottle on the table.

'Gin, is it?' Marie sniffed at the mouth of the bottle. 'I thought some of these fishermen were drunk yesterday. I smelled it on their breath, even through the seawater. No wonder they capsized their boat.'

'I am not here on a moral crusade,' Watters said. 'The fishermen's drinking habits are nothing to do with me.'

'Maybe they have,' Marie said. 'Why would somebody sell gin to fishermen?'

'To make money.' Watters explained about Isabella Navarino and the stranger boat.

'So it's a business thing then.' Marie's eyes were sharp with interest.

'Yes.' Watters wondered where Marie was headed.

'What's the first rule of business?' Marie continued.

'I couldn't even begin to guess.' At one point in his life, Watters had believed the contemporary wisdom that women were incapable of understanding such matters as politics or business. Then he had met Marie.

'I could guess,' Marie said. 'I would say that the first rule is to make money, as you already said, so why is the vessel here?'

'What do you mean?' Watters allowed Marie to pursue her course.
'This is a minor fishing area. Except when the herring shoals are on
the coast, there are only a few dozen boats out at most.' Marie raised
her eyebrows. 'That vessel selling gin won't make much of a profit
off Nesshaven. Her captain would be far better looking for custom off
Aberdeen or in the Forth or the Dogger Bank.'

Watters caught on. 'There must be another reason for the strange
boat being here, then. The gin selling is only a cover.'

'That's what I think,' Marie said. 'But you're the detective; I'm only
a weak-minded woman.' Marie mocked her statement with a smile.

'So I am told.' Watters walked to the window and looked over the
policies of the house. 'I'd like to have a look at that gin-seller.'

'What's her captain's name again?' Marie asked.

'Isabella Navarino,' Watters said, 'although she calls herself Henrietta Borg.'

'She sounds foreign too.' Marie was instantly disapproving. 'You say
you've already met her in Dundee. Maybe you can ask her in the town.'

'She would deny any wrong-doing,' Watters said. 'I'll have to meet
her at sea.'

Marie nodded. 'Maybe one of the fishermen could help; after all,
you saved two fishermen's lives.'

Watters shook his head. 'In such a close-knit community as
Nesshaven, I'm as much a stranger to them as any women with a foreign name. Besides, they only have small boats. They would have to
leave a crewman behind to accommodate me. No, I would need to hire
a boat from somewhere and maybe a man to help crew her.'

'Do that,' Marie said.

CHAPTER FOURTEEN
BROUGHTY FERRY:
OCTOBER 1862

'I build boats from keel to mast, or convert older vessels.' Mr James Gall was a time-served craftsman in his late thirties, with arms like hawsers and a lugubrious expression on his face. 'I don't hire out boats, Sergeant Watters.'

'It's a one-off,' Watters said. 'I won't be gone for more than a day.'

Gall grunted and smoothed his hand over the keel of an upturned dinghy. 'The thing is, Sergeant, I don't know you. If this were official police business, you would requisition it through the proper channels; you're not doing that.'

'It's legal.' Watters felt his anger rising. 'You'll be paid in cash, up front.' He hoped that his pay could cover the cost.

'So what's the occasion?' Gall sat on the upturned boat and cast a critical eye over his workforce who were busily hammering and planing. 'A fishing trip is it? I thought you policemen were busy failing to solve this murder on *Lady of Blackness*, the fires on Beaumont's mills, that missing gambler, and these illicit shebeens all over the place.'

'It's connected.' Watters did not wish to give too much away.

'I see.' James Gall transferred a wad of tobacco from one side of his mouth to the other. 'You're still working on Big Man Beaumont's case, then? Aye, I'm already building him half a dozen boats for that new ship of his.'

'What ship is that?' It was the first Watters had heard about a new ship for Beaumont.

Gall stood up to inspect a fishing boat, running an experienced eye along a row of wooden strakes that appeared to Watters like human ribs. 'The Big Man's having Rogers build him something special up in that new covered yard of theirs. Rogers copied that idea from Alexander Stephens, anyway.' Gall shrugged. 'As soon as *Scotia* was launched, Rogers transferred all the men onto this other vessel. At it night and day they are, hammering and cutting at the steel plate.' Gall ejected a brown stream of tobacco onto the ground at Watters's feet. 'The ship's about completed, I hear, and in record time. It must be costing Beaumont a fortune.' He looked up, eyes shrewd. 'Rogers only put in the enclosed yard when this work started. He said it was to shelter the workers, but I hae my doots about that.'

'Oh? Why do you think it was put in?'

'To hide what they're doing, of course. Keep away prying eyes from seeing Rogers's new shipbuilding techniques.' Gall shrugged. 'The workies talk, though, when they're in drink. They think they're building a ship for some foreigner.' He grunted. 'I've heard that it's for the Emperor of China or the Emperor of France or some other fancy potentate, but I don't know if that's true.'

Watters shrugged. 'I have no idea about that,' he admitted. He knew Rogers, of course, a company only eight years old but already one of the largest shipbuilding yards in Dundee. Mr Rogers also owned the Stannergate Foundry, which gave him a distinct advantage in building iron and steel ships. Rogers had followed Gourlays to bring the compound steam engine to the Tay, and now Rogers was building something special for Beaumont. Watters grunted; perhaps Mr Beaumont was genuinely having financial difficulties if he was building a new steel ship on top of Charlotte's wedding and Amy's extravagances.

'Listen, Mr Gall. Could I hire a boat from you, or not?'

'Maybe.' Gall gave a twisted smile. 'Seeing as Mr Beaumont is a customer and you're investigating his case, I might think about it. Come back tomorrow, and we'll see.'

'I'll do that.' Lifting his cane in acknowledgement, Watters was about to leave when a thought struck him. 'You say Mr Beaumont's new ship is for a foreigner and not for him?'

'Aye, so the workies say.'

'Thank you. How many boats are you making for this new vessel?'

'Six. I'm building two boats of five-and-thirty feet and four of two-and-twenty,' Gall said. 'Your Mr Beaumont was specific in his requirements. He wants them strong and fast, with double strakes in the bow, rather like a blubber boat for breaking the ice.'

'I see. So you are not building ordinary ship's boats then?'

'Nothing like.' Gall returned to his work.

Watters swung his cane as he left Gall's yard. He would really have to get onto the golf course soon. Beaumont's actions were intriguing. Having a new ship built for a foreign buyer was very unusual. Why did the foreigner not come directly to Rogers' Yard? Why the secrecy? Something was wrong here, something was very wrong. Watters swung his cane again, beheading a bunch of dried thistles so the seeds scattered along the side of the road. *I'll have a wee look at this covered yard of Mr Rogers's and see exactly what Mr Beaumont is having built in there. It might relate to the case, and it might not, but at this frustrating stage of my investigation, I'll try anything.*

With that decision made, Watters was in a better frame of mind. Progress could be made in a variety of different ways.

* * *

Clouds scurried across a scimitar moon as the rising wind clattered a loose piece of equipment somewhere within Rogers' Yard. Watters waited in the densest of the shadows, waiting for the night-watchman to complete his rounds and retire to the shelter of his wooden shack.

'If old Mackay hears about this, we'll lose our jobs and our pensions.' Scuddamore pulled his jacket closer to his shivering body. Like Watters, he was dressed in dark, close-fitting clothing.

'Just say that I ordered you to come.' Watters adjusted his soft woollen cap. 'Anyway, we'll be in and out inside ten minutes. Mr Mackay will never find out.'

'Why do you need me anyway?'

'You're my lookout.' Watters saw the watchman sit on his bench and poke life into his brazier. The red glow looked extremely inviting. When the watchman put a frying pan on the heat, the aroma of bacon drifted towards them.

'Look at that lucky bugger,' Scuddamore said. 'He's sitting eating and getting paid for it, while we're out in the cold and chancing our jobs for the sake of a man who makes more money in one week than we do in a year.'

Watters waited until the watchman was fully occupied before leading Scuddamore across to the ten-foot tall outside wall of Rogers' Yard. He threw a heavy blanket over the broken glass that defended the top.

'Your Marie won't like her best blanket being ripped,' Scuddamore said.

'That one cost me tuppence in a pawnshop.' Watters pulled himself up the wall and rolled over the far side. Scuddamore followed a few seconds later.

'There's the covered shed.' Watters nodded to a huge, barn-like shape that dominated the eastern half of the yard. 'I'll go first. You follow.'

Scuddamore's breathing was ragged with nerves. He glanced over his shoulder. 'We'd better not get caught.'

'The watchman's too busy eating to bother about us.'

The yard had a ghostly feel in the faint moonlight with unknown objects casting weird shadows while unseen mice scurried around spars and baulks of timber. Ignoring everything except his objective, Watters ran from shadow to shadow until he reached the covered shed.

It was logical to head for the end nearest the Tay, where the ship would be launched. The doors were as high as a three-storey tenement and firmly closed with four iron bars slotted in place, each equipped with two padlocks.

Watters swore. 'I hadn't expected that. What the devil is Beaumont hiding in here?' He glanced around. 'That will slow us down.'

'Can you pick the locks?' Scuddamore asked.

'Yes.' Pulling the bag from his back, Watters extracted his packet of lock picks. 'This job has its benefits. I took these from a cracksman I arrested in London. They've served me well for years.'

'That could come in handy,' Scuddamore said. 'When Mr Mackay kicks us both out of the force, you can start a new career as a thief.'

'We'll have less of your lip, Scuddamore. You keep watch for me.'

The padlocks were large with a simple mechanism. Watters opened the first within a minute, and with the technique mastered, the others took half that time. The iron bars were next, each one weighing ten or twelve pounds. He placed them quietly on the ground and tried the door. It creaked at his first touch.

'Opening that door will alert the watchman,' Scuddamore said.

'We'll wait for a gust of wind,' Watters decided. 'The noise of rattling will hide everything.'

They crouched by the door with the padlocks and iron bars at their feet. A pair of seagulls passed overhead, screaming, while somewhere in the Seagate, a drunk began to sing. The sudden gust of wind nearly took Watters by surprise.

'Come on, Scuddamore!' He eased the door a fraction open, sufficient to slide inside, with Scuddamore at his back. Darkness closed around them, laden with the aroma of oil and an earthy smell Watters could not place.

'Lights!' Scuddamore said. 'I can't see a bloody thing!'

Reaching into his bag once more, Watters hauled out a bull's eye lantern and a box of Lucifers. Pulling the door closed behind him, he struggled to light a match, swearing under his breath.

'Come on, come on, come on,' Scuddamore muttered.

Watters scratched a Lucifer, with the tiny light flickering as he put it to the wick of the lantern.

Adjusting the shield so the lamp produced a thin beam of light, he aimed it into the interior of the shed just as he heard the snarl.

'Oh, you devil!' Scuddamore's yell echoed around the shed. 'Dogs!'

Watters saw them leap up, three mastiffs with rows of sharp teeth in open jaws. He threw the lantern at the nearest, decided that remaining was not an option and turned for the door. Scuddamore beat him to it by a head and then both were running across the yard with the dogs howling at their heels.

Watters yelled as a dog sank its teeth into his calf. He kicked out, swearing, heard the dog yelp, and ran on, limping. Scuddamore was a good three yards ahead of him as they approached the wall.

'Hey! Stop!' The watchman lumbered in their wake, shouting and waving his arms. 'Stop, thief!'

'Come on, Sergeant!' Scuddamore was on top of the wall, waiting. 'Jesus! He's got a gun!'

Watters had time for only a brief glance over his shoulder. The dogs were slavering a few feet behind, and the watchman had stopped. In his left hand he held an old-fashioned lantern, and in his right, he held an equally antique pistol, with a bore that seemed as wide as a cannon. Then the dog leapt on Watters.

The first bite had been little more than a nip. This time, the mastiff got a grip of Watters's thigh and held on, snarling. Watters yelled, staggering under the weight of the beast.

'Sergeant!' Scuddamore called. 'Hurry up! The old bugger's going to fire!'

The shot sounded as a deafening roar that scared a dozen seagulls into a screaming frenzy. The sound shocked the mastiff into releasing its grip, giving Watters the chance to throw himself up the wall. He fell over the other side, where Scuddamore was already waiting.

'Run!' Scuddamore said and ran off into the distance. Cursing, and with his left leg on fire, Watters limped after him. *What is so secret about that ship that Beaumont needed mastiffs and an armed man to*

*guard it? And even more important, what will Marie say when I come
back with my leg bleeding and my trousers in tatters?*

CHAPTER FIFTEEN
NESSHAVEN: OCTOBER 1862

James Gall had come up trumps with a solid, if slow, vessel with a short foredeck and single mast.

'Her name is *Grace*, and she's as seaworthy as you'll get,' Gall had said, 'even for a landsman to take out.'

'I'll take care of her,' Watters promised.

'You're limping,' Gall said. 'You might not be fit to sail.'

'I'll get local help,' Watters said.

'You'll be lucky.' Gall did not pursue the conversation. 'Ten shillings a day.'

'That's very steep,' Watters said. 'Two and sixpence and you're still cheating me.'

'Seven and six and that's my final offer. What if you steal it? Or capsize?'

'I'm a police officer,' Watters reminded.

'That's what I mean. What if you steal my boat?'

'Three shillings and you're lucky to get that much,' Watters said.

Now, *Grace* was sitting a few miles south of the Bell Rock Lighthouse, rising and falling on the swell. Marie and the girls were huddled amidships, swathed in layers of extra clothing, while Watters had pressed Ragina into coming along to act as crew and steersman.

'You know the local conditions,' Watters said and grudgingly agreed to pay his crewman for his services.

Now they were out on the sea with the wind whipping spindrift from the wave crests and seagulls screeching in a raucous chorus. Holding a pawnshop-purchased telescope to his eye, Watters balanced against the uneven motion of the boat to examine the distant fishing boats.

'Can you see anything?' Marie asked.

'Aye. The lads are fishing. Longlining for mackerel by the look of it, and not doing too badly either. They must have struck on a shoal there.' Watters passed the telescope to Ragina. 'See what you make of them.'

Ragina raised the telescope and nodded. 'That's your sort, boys! No, not like that! You're making a right haggis of that, you useless buttons!' He shook his head. 'I think these boys have already been at the gin. Look at the way they're handling that line!' Shaking his head, he focussed again. 'Now that's what we've come here for. Here she comes round the Inchcape! See that, Sergeant Watters? If that's not a coper, I don't know what is!'

'A what?' Amy asked.

'A coper.' Watters took back the telescope, extended it to its fullest extent and balanced on the foredeck of the madly swaying boat. 'There's a brig coming from the lee of the Inchcape, right enough. She's wearing no colours, but I'd wager that she's foreign built.'

Amy looked up curiously. 'Is that important, Sergeant Watters?'

'It might be.' Watters passed back the telescope and settled down between the thwarts.

Ragina nodded. 'Aye, she's a Dutchy, sure as death. They control the coper trade from Dunkirk to the Dogger and all points north. Dutchy, and that's the end of it.'

'Coper? Could somebody tell me what a coper might be?' Amy did not flinch as a wave splintered on the prow, spattering her with spindrift.

'Amy asked you a question.' Marie poked at Watters's sore leg until he replied.

'Copers are seagoing dealers in gin or other spirits, Miss Amy. Sometimes fishermen call them grog-ships or the Devil's floating parlours. They come out of the Dutch ports, often at night, and sell their stuff at sea. Their main customers are fishing boats, but as my lady wife has already reminded me, it's unusual for them to come this far north. Normally they infest the Dogger Bank, where the English trawler fleets work.' Watters adjusted the sail a fraction to keep *Grace's* head toward the wind.

'So why are they here?' Marie directed the question at Ragina. 'Is there a reason?'

Ragina shrugged. 'Maybe they're searching for new custom, Mrs Watters. Fishermen like the copers, but the stuff they sell is often rotgut, kill-me-deadly firewater, the roughest of rough poison. I've heard of entire crews of English trawlers falling overboard drunk or just dying on deck. The Dogger Bank is notorious for fishing up dead bodies, and these copers are the cause of many of them. They're bad news.'

Mari fidgeted, looking at the girls. 'Can't the Royal Navy do anything about them? Chase them away?'

'Not normally,' Ragina said. 'They usually operate outside the three-mile limit.'

'How about the deaths? Can't they be blamed for that?'

'Seamen don't have the same laws as on land. Nobody has to even report a death on a fishing boat, not unless there's damage to gear as well. Fishermen's lives are worth that,' Ragina snapped his fingers, 'or maybe a bit less.'

A rogue wave battered *Grace* sideways. Marie took hold of Amy. 'Are you girls all right?'

'This is exciting.' Amy seemed to be enjoying herself. 'Are you going to arrest the Dutchy, Sergeant Watters?'

'No, I can't,' Watters said. He frowned. 'I was wrong. That's no Dutchy. If that boat's not French, then I'm a Chinaman.'

'A Frenchie, Sergeant?' Amy said. 'What's a Frenchie doing here?'

'I wish I knew what she's doing here.' Watters had spent at least one night a week training up his Volunteers in case of a French landing. He had seen the Armstrongs of Broughty Castle exercised in case a French fleet should sail up the Tay, and now, here was a French vessel openly trading a few miles off the Scottish coast. He frowned, remembering William Caskie's dealings with the Continental arms manufacturers. Was this vessel a spy? Surely not. Watters shook his head; he was never a man to believe the rumours spread by the lurid press, and he was not about to start now.

'She's selling grog by the looks of it.' Watters focussed on the two-masted foreign vessel around which the fishing boats were clustered. 'Maybe she's just smuggling.'

'Maybe she is.' Marie replied. 'Do you want to sail closer and challenge her?'

'Not with you and the girls on board,' Watters said, 'but I will be alerting Mr Mackay and the customs officer at Dundee. I think I've seen enough here.' He ordered Ragina to return *Grace* to Broughty Ferry. 'I'll get Scuddamore and Duff to stand guard over the girls.'

'I'll stay with them too,' Marie said.

'I know you will.'

'Sergeant Watters.' Once they were on course for Broughty, Ragina had requisitioned the telescope. Now he had it focussed on the quarterdeck of the French vessel. 'There's that woman I told you about.'

'Look after the boat.' Watters took back the telescope to concentrate on the coper. Dressed in a seaman's white trousers and blue jacket, with a cap struggling to hold her flowing hair in place, Isabella Navarino stood on the raised quarterdeck of the brig. On one side of Navarino stood the man with the feathered bowler; on the other side was William Caskie.

Watters took a deep breath. *What the devil is Caskie doing out here?*

'Are you all right, George? May I see?' Marie knew her husband too well.

'I'm fine, thank you.' Watters lowered the telescope. He could not allow Amy or Elizabeth to see William Caskie. 'I'm just a little surprised to see a woman as master of a ship.'

Marie shook her head. 'I know,' she said. 'Women have a habit of surprising men. That's not what's bothering you, George.'

'I'll tell you later.' Watters kept his head down. He did not wish Caskie to recognise him or the girls. 'Take us back as fast as Christ will let you, Ragina.' He felt Marie's stare. She knew he only blasphemed when he was worried.

* * *

It was indicative of Watters's state of mind that he accepted Murdoch's invitation to a game of billiards in Russell's Royal Hotel the next evening and then played badly. Since it had been refurbished a decade before, Russell's on Union Street boasted the finest billiards room in Scotland, but Watters failed to recapture any of the skill he had possessed as a young man. He could only watch as Murdoch rattled the balls home.

'You're not concentrating, George.' Murdoch placed his cue against the table, leaned against the polished wooden panels of the wall and ordered another round of whisky-and-water. 'What's on your mind? Those fishermen buying all that foreign gin?' He grinned, dismissing the matter as unimportant.

'Not so much,' Watters said. He cued, hit his mark, and watched the ball spin nowhere. 'But that French coper was a bit worrying. I warned the customs officer, and I told the Navy too.'

'Oh?' Murdoch potted his ball, cued for another, and stopped. 'What did you tell them? There's a French brig off the Inchcape Rock? I wager they did not thank you for the information, or do you think that the French are going to land in the Tay? Louis Napoleon III will lead ten thousand French soldiers, fresh from Mexico into Dundee, to rape and spoil and plunder?'

'Why is William Caskie on a French ship when he should be on honeymoon?' Watters watched the balls run true for Tulloch. 'And this woman, Isabella Navarino, is trouble. The first time I met her, she was mixed up with a stolen ship. How did Caskie get involved with her?'

'Blessed if I know,' Murdoch said. 'That's not your job, George. You're a Dundee policeman. Your job is to investigate crime in Dundee, not sail the seven seas after Frenchmen and whatnots. In fact, your present job is to nursemaid young Amy Beaumont.'

'There's more.' Watters watched as Murdoch potted three balls in quick succession. 'I've heard that Rogers is building a ship for a foreign buyer, either the Emperor of China or Napoleon of France, so I'm told.'

'Oh? Good. More work for the lads.' Murdoch looked over his shoulder. 'The Emperor of China and Napoleon ideas are only covers, of course. They're fictitious names to hide the real buyer. Why so glum, Rab; would you rather we were like Lancashire, with thousands of men idle and the factory chimneys quiet?'

'French ship offshore with Dundee businessmen on board, a foreign ship being built in Dundee, Volunteers drilling at Broughty Ferry...' Watters closed his eyes.

'And?' Murdoch had not clawed his way to a Dundee police sergeant without knowing how to read men. 'What else, George?'

'Beaumont, Willie. Jimmy Gall, the boat builder, tells me Beaumont is having this ship built at Rogers's for the foreign buyer.'

'Then your answer's as plain as a drunken prostitute at a Free Kirk sermon, Dode. Ask Beaumont straight. He's a businessman, not an idiot. I doubt that he would build a ship for the French, no matter how much money was involved. You can't trust these Frogs. Remember the last Napoleon Bonaparte? They're a bad lot.' Murdoch cleared the table with a rapid display of skill that left Watters in despair. 'This night's costing you a fortune, George. Another game?'

'Better not.' Watters paid his dues. At a sixpence a game, he was losing a quarter of a day's pay with every two games that Murdoch won. 'You're in form today, Willie. But keep your ears open for me, will you? In case there are any strangers in town.'

'This is a nautical town, George. There are hundreds of strangers!' Murdoch laughed. 'Aye, I know what you mean. I'll watch out for anything suspicious. More importantly, I'll ask the better half too; Ruthie never misses a trick, sharp as a needle, my girl!'

* * *

'I believe these are yours, Watters.' Mackay passed over the wallet of lock picks. He sat silently, waiting for Watters to comment.

'Yes, they are, sir. Where were they found?'

'In the covered shed at Rogers' Yard,' Mackay said. 'It seems that somebody broke in. Perhaps they were trying to steal a ship.'

'That's been done before, sir.' Watters placed the wallet in his pocket.

'Not by you, I hope. Did you find anything interesting?' Mackay's Caithness accent was pronounced as he leaned forward.

'I did not have time, sir.' There was no point in lying to Mackay. 'As soon as I got into the shed, three dogs attacked me.'

'I heard the watchman fired a shot as well,' Mackay said dryly. 'He boasted that he chased away a whole band of desperadoes, half a dozen at least.'

'It was dark, sir. He would not see clearly.'

Mackay grunted. 'I don't approve of my officers acting outwith the law, Watters, however noble their intentions. Why were you there?' His fingers drummed on the table as Watters told him about Beaumont financing the ship for a foreign owner, William Caskie's conversation with the French and Belgian arms manufacturers, and Caskie's presence on the French coper.

'Who was Caskie meeting?' Mackay's question was direct.

'I don't know, sir,' Watters admitted.

'You found nothing in Rogers' Yard.'

'No, sir. The workmen believe the ship is being built for either the Emperor of China or of France.'

'We know the China idea is nonsense,' Mackay dismissed the suggestion out of hand. 'I am not happy about this business at all, Watters. I sent you to guard young Amy, not to play tomfool games in a ship-building yard or go pleasure boating.'

'Yes, sir.' Watters lifted his head. 'I wish to solve this case, sir, even if others may not.'

'And what the deuce does that mean?' Mackay's face turned an angry red.

Watters avoided a direct answer. He needed to keep his position. 'I believe that there are people in Dundee who are not being as helpful as they should, with Mr Beaumont possibly among that number. I think there is a political angle here with either France or one or other of the American powers involved.'

Mackay's frown deepened. 'You are a sergeant of police, Watters, not a politician or a diplomat.' His fingers rapped urgently on the desk and then stilled as he closed his hand into a fist. 'Your duty is to ensure the safety of Amy Beaumont. Sergeant Anstruther is now pursuing the supposed murder on *Lady of Blackness*. If you happen to chance upon anything political, bring it to me. I will notify Sir John Ogilvy and let him deal with the government side of things. We will stick to what we know.' Mackay's index finger recommenced the tapping. 'Do you understand, Watters?'

'Yes, sir,' Watters agreed.

'Good.' Mackay relaxed a little. 'Now that's cleared up, I can tell you that Sergeant Anstruther is no further forward with the murder case or the fire-raising. He would be happy to hand the case back to you.'

'Yes, sir.' Watters nodded. 'My men, Duff and Scuddamore, have interviewed the people of the Dundee and Forfarshire Anti-slavery Alliance again and again without learning any more. They don't know the identities of the man and woman who paid them.'

Mackay nodded. 'Are you convinced that they are guilty of fire-raising?'

'Yes, sir. They admit freely that they set the fires in the factories; they seem quite proud of it.'

'Why?'

'The same reason as before, sir; they say that Beaumont is dealing with the Confederate states, the slave states.' Watters shook his head. 'Mr Beaumont told me that he stopped trading with the South over a year ago.'

Mackay sighed. 'These Alliance people are blasted idiots. They've endangered the lives of scores of mill workers because a couple of foreigners told lies about a Dundee businessman. Now they'll spend months or maybe years in prison.'

'As you say, sir, they are blasted idiots.' Watters had no sympathy for people who pushed forward their ideas at the expense of innocent people. 'They could easily have been murderers as well.'

'Have you found that fellow Jones yet?'

'No, sir.' Tempted to remind Mackay that he had been babysitting Amy Beaumont in Ness House, Watters thought it politic to keep his tongue still.

'Do you have any fresh ideas, Watters?'

'Jones could be on board any ship sailing from any port in Britain under a different name.'

Mackay grunted. 'Keep searching. He could be the key to the whole thing. What's your next move?'

'I am moving in six directions at the same time, sir. I have the mysterious American, the even more mysterious foreign woman, the French coper, the ship being built at Rogers' Yard, Richard Jones and Captain Isabella Navarino.' Watters forced a smile. 'If you could spare another couple of men...'

'We're overstretched as it is,' Mackay interrupted. 'Indeed I'm thinking about pulling Duff and Scuddamore into other duties. Since you arrested the Dundee and Forfarshire Anti-slavery Alliance, there have been no further arson attempts or attacks on the Beaumont household. I'm beginning to think the foreign woman and the American are figments of that group's imagination.'

'There was the mannequin in Beaumont's bed, sir...'

'I'm wondering if we all overreacted to a child's joke. Probably one of the younger daughter's friends.' Mackay dismissed the incident with a wave of his hand. 'I can't see you solving the Calcutta business now, Watters. As you say, your man Jones will probably have already shipped out.'

Watters shook his head. 'I don't agree, sir. I don't think we've reached the bottom of this case yet.'

Mackay's fingers began to drum once more. 'What do you have in mind?'

'I'm still stuck in Ness House with young Amy, sir, but I've ordered Scuddamore and Duff to watch Rogers' Yard for any foreigner, particularly any French-looking foreigner.' Watters grinned. 'Not that I know how to tell a Frenchman from anybody else.'

Mackay stood up. 'You can leave Ness House, Watters. Mr Beaumont wants his daughter back. Apparently, Mr Beaumont's elder daughter is returning home tomorrow, and he would like you to bring Amy back to greet her sister. Mr Beaumont also thinks the threat is gone now if it ever existed.'

Watters thought about Isabella Navarino and the French vessel. 'Yes, sir.' He headed for the door.

'Watters,' Mackay called him back. 'I'll give you one week. You have seven more days to find something positive, and then I will call a halt to this case. That is all.'

Seven days. Watters felt as though Marie was correct, and Mackay was moving him from pillar to post so that he could not delve too deeply into the *Lady of Blackness* murder.

CHAPTER SIXTEEN
MOUNT PLEASANT:
NOVEMBER 1862

Watters had never seen Mount Pleasant so illuminated before. Every tree on the curved driveway was decorated with a lantern, while torches flared at the entrance gates and the main door. Carriages massed in front of the house, outside the stable block, and filled the courtyard. Most of the coaches were modern, with dark paint gleaming under the lights, but Watters saw a pair of open chaises that were entirely unsuitable for night-time travel in a Scottish autumn, a light, low-wheeled calash, and even an ancient cabriolet, with its spokes painted in alternate red and yellow to contrast with the black leather hood. The woman who creaked out of the cabriolet looked as ancient as the vehicle, but she refused assistance to mount the stairs, and she tapped her ivory fan against the footman's chest while exchanging pleasantries.

A harassed driver cracked his whip over the head of a latecomer. 'Move that damned chariot! You're blocking the driveway!' Then he noticed the angry look from the dismounting guests and touched a hand to the brim of his hat. 'Begging your pardon for the language, ma'am!'

'I should think so indeed!' Elizabeth Caskie reproved him, looking every inch her twenty-two years as she picked her way through the horse droppings. 'I've never heard the like!' More dignified than many women twice her age, Elizabeth ascended the stairs with a flick of her crinoline.

With many of the servants being hired for the day, Watters asked details from Morag.

'It seems to be getting more common nowadays, Sergeant Watters. Each businessman has to outdo the other with fancy balls and what-nots. Mr Beaumont has to keep up with the rest, so he allowed Amy to arrange this one.' Watters remembered Amy and Elizabeth writing scores of letters. He also recalled that Beaumont was said to have financial problems.

Morag raised her eyes. 'Oh, for the old days when we could just jog along happily without all this tomfoolery! And the servants! Mr Beaumont had to bring them in just for the evening. Goodness knows what sort of people they are. Not respectable at all, these ones, and maidservants that don't want to wear their cap!'

'I'm sure you'll cope, Morag,' Watters sympathised.

'Cope? Oh, I'll cope all right, but I just wonder when we'll get to bed tonight. And how much silver will be left in the house when it's all done! Here! You!' Morag raised her voice to admonish a young servant who was mangling the cloak of a guest. 'That's no way to handle a gentleman's clothes! Give it here before I box your lug for you!' She shook her head to Watters. 'Honestly, they've no idea! Give me your coat and hat, Sergeant, and then you'd better get along to see Mr Beaumont. He's up in his study, keeping well out of the way!'

Watters nodded. 'I'll get up to him in a moment. Do you have a list of the servants that I can see? I must check them over.'

'Oh,' Morag frowned, stopped to berate a young girl for her clumsiness, and delved in a drawer. 'Here, Sergeant, names and references, or what they call references nowadays.'

'Thank you. I'll look these over when I have seen Mr Beaumont.' Escaping from the hubbub below, Watters mounted the stairs to Beaumont's study, with its portraits of his daughters and late wife on one wall and the bookcases on another. The window overlooked the Tay, where glittering lights told of ships moored in the Roads, smeared now by a slow-falling drizzle.

'Ah, Sergeant. Are the girls all right?' Beaumont looked up from a pile of papers. 'I'll be down to greet the guests in a moment.' His smile was weary. 'I'm afraid I am not the best of hosts.'

'The girls are safe and happy,' Watters said. 'They stopped at Pitcorbie House to change on the journey.'

'Good, good.' Beaumont looked distracted. 'Amy arranged this damned ball to welcome Charlotte home and invited all sorts of people.' He shook his head. 'Elizabeth thought to invite some of her friends too. I gave permission, but it's damned inconvenient.'

Watters raised an eyebrow. In his opinion, Amy was milking her father of everything she could get purely to impress Elizabeth.

Beaumont continued, 'I allowed Amy to make whatever arrangements she saw fit and forgot clean about the thing until today, and I have a business meeting planned with Mr Holderby.'

Watters raised an inquisitive eyebrow. 'The American vice-consul?'

'We have business matters to discuss.'

'Yes, Mr Beaumont.' If Beaumont were trading with the Southern States, he would hardly be likely to meet Holderby, Watters reasoned. After all, Holderby was at Charlotte's wedding, while Bulloch, the Confederate's agent for purchasing shipping, knew William Caskie, not Beaumont. Watters knew that nothing quite made sense here. There were still too many pieces missing to form a true pattern.

Watters had seldom heard such a noise as filled Mount Pleasant House. Every one of the hundred guests seemed intent on outdoing the others in loud speech and laughter. He saw Holderby at once, a tall, slender figure who watched from a corner of the great hall, bowing to the ladies with tremendous dignity. Taking up a position in the corner, hard against one of the Doric columns that supported the domed ceiling, Watters sighed. He had intended ensuring Amy and Elizabeth were safe, then leaving quickly, but with Holderby present, together with a dozen unknown servants, he thought it better to remain.

The guests clustered in groups around the buffet meal that Amy had arranged, with the men discussing business while the women compared fashions, literature, servants, and men. Watters looked up with interest when William Caskie arrived with Charlotte on his arm. He eased closer to listen when they passed.

'You said you would be here all day!' Charlotte's whisper was forceful, but William countered with a quick jerk on her arm.

'Something came up. Business! I have to meet somebody.'

'William! I hardly saw you in Paris. At least I thought I would see some of you at home. You are meant to be my husband after all!'

Then the couple swept past. Watters saw Beaumont descend from the upper levels, smiling with the effortless grace of a perfect gentleman.

'Mr Beaumont.' Watters moved through the press of guests, wishing that he had time to at least change before mingling with such a crowd. He had worn the same clothes all day and was ridiculously underdressed for the occasion. 'If you try and stay with Mr Holderby, I will attempt to sheepdog the others. Perhaps Mr Caskie could help?' Watters wondered if William Caskie's meeting was with Isabella Navarino or one of the foreign gun manufacturers.

Beaumont nodded. 'I would not count on William. He seems to be having a little trouble with Charlotte at present.' Beaumont shook his head. 'God save us all from headstrong women, Watters! I'll stay with Holderby, as you suggest.' He glanced over his shoulder. 'Where the devil is Cattanach? Have you seen my clerk, Watters?'

'No, sir. If I do, I'll send him to you.'

At that second, Watters had another man on his mind. He did not know what made him turn; he only knew that the man standing in the doorway was dangerous. There was something about the way he carried himself, an aura of awareness, like a hunting cat or a prizefighter as he entered the ring. The man saw Watters at the same time and instinctively put a hand inside his jacket.

Watters recognised that movement. The man had been reaching for a weapon. Forcing a smile, Watters stepped forward. He had seen this man before, except on each previous occasion, he had been wearing a bowler hat with a feather tucked into the hatband.

'Good evening, sir.' Watters held out his hand. 'I am Sergeant George Watters of the Dundee Police.' There was no harm in letting the man know with whom he was dealing.

'Good evening.' The man took his hand from his jacket. His grip was firm. 'Walter Drummond.'

'I've seen you around Dundee.' Watters pushed his advantage. 'You're a friend of Henrietta Borg.'

Drummond looked confused. 'I am afraid I don't know anybody of that name.' His accent was North American; Watters guessed from one of the Southern States.

'You might know her as Isabella Navarino.'

'I know that name well enough,' Drummond agreed at once.

'May I ask why you are here?' Watters prepared to block Drummond if he reached for his weapon. Having a man from the Southern States in the same room as the United States vice-consul could lead to significant complications for Mr Beaumont.

'I have business with Mr Caskie.' Drummond smiled. 'He is waiting for me across there,' he nodded behind Watters, 'talking with his new wife.'

Charlotte was still engaged in a heated discussion with William, punctuated by the occasional quick smile as she greeted the guests.

'I'll come with you.' Watters saw Beaumont shaking hands with Holderby. 'I'll wish the happy couple all the best.' Keeping between Drummond and Holderby, Watters walked across to Charlotte and William Caskie.

'Ah, Drummond,' William extended his hand.

'You have the most charming of wives.' Drummond's bow would have graced the finest salon in Paris. 'I have something for you.' He put his hand inside his jacket in that old, familiar gesture that had

Watters preparing to leap on him. However, rather than a weapon, Drummond produced a long paper with an ornate seal.

'I wish you the most possible happiness for the future, Mr and Mrs Caskie.' Drummond handed the sealed paper to Charlotte, who immediately ripped it open.

Charlotte looked up, smiling. 'So much! Oh, Mister Drummond! I can nearly forgive you for robbing me of my husband.'

'I'll only detain your husband for an hour or so,' Drummond said. 'After that, he is all yours.' He bowed again, smiling. 'I do not understand how he can bear to tear himself away from such a charming wife merely for business.'

Charlotte bowed. 'You are too kind, sir. I willingly relinquish my husband to such an eloquent and generous man.'

Watters stepped back and watched as Drummond and William Caskie retired to another room. He saw Charlotte open the document again to re-read whatever sum of money Drummond had handed her.

'Miss Amy! Miss Elizabeth!' Watters called the girls over. 'I require you both to do me a major service.' He lowered his voice conspiratorially. 'I want you to watch for a man coming downstairs and engage him in conversation. While one of you holds his attention, I wish the other to fetch me immediately.'

'Is he a handsome gentleman?' Amy asked, wide-eyed with innocence.

'More importantly, is he an eligible gentleman?' Elizabeth patted her hair into even more immaculate place.

'He is both handsome and intelligent. I cannot answer for his eligibility,' Watters told them. 'Although, dressed like that,' he allowed his eyes to briefly flick onto the low neckline of Elizabeth's dress, 'you could charm a gargoyle from its stance.'

Both girls giggled with Amy pretending to be shocked and Elizabeth tapping her ivory fan against Watters's arm. 'Where is this gentleman, Sergeant Watters? And why do you want us to charm him?'

Watters smiled. 'I wish you to charm him to help your father, Miss Amy, and to ensure he does not meet the United States' consul, who is your father's guest.' He gave them precise instructions. 'I hope your intervention is not necessary.'

'I hope it is.' Elizabeth was laughing. 'A handsome gentleman to enchant?' She wiggled her hips in a manner that Watters knew would shock her respectable mother. 'I am sure I can manage that, Sergeant.'

It was an hour before Beaumont appeared with Holderby. 'Gentlemen! Mr Holderby!' Watters approached the American consul with his hand outstretched. 'It's a pleasure to meet you again!'

'Why, thank you, sir.' Holderby looked his surprise at Beaumont, who watched Watters through narrowed eyes.

'I am Sergeant Watters of the Dundee Police,' Watters reminded him with a lowered voice. 'I must warn you that we have another of your countrymen present. His name is Walter Drummond, although I am not sure from where he comes but certainly somewhere in the South.'

'I was not aware that we had such a guest,' Beaumont admitted.

'Sergeant Watters!' Amy panted up. 'Elizabeth is with that American gentleman!'

'Thank you, Amy. I will be along directly.'

'I wish to meet this Mr Drummond,' Holderby said.

'Is that wise, sir?' Beaumont asked.

Holderby looked at Watters. 'I wish to meet Mr Walter Drummond.'

Watters raised an eyebrow. 'Come with me, sir, and I will introduce you.' He was unsure what the correct diplomatic procedure was for enemies meeting at a private house, but his philosophy was to keep things in the open. Violence and resentment smouldered in secret places rather than in the light of day.

Guiding Holderby through the press of highly dressed women and evening-suited men, Watters marched straight to where Drummond was backed against the wall, pretending interest in Elizabeth's tales of the wonders of Paris.

Elizabeth changed her subject matter as Watters approached. 'Did you realise, sir, that a lady's waist is ideally twenty-two inches round?' When Drummond shook his head in assumed fascination, Elizabeth tapped his arm with her fan. 'While a gentleman's arm is twenty-two inches long! Is nature not admirable to arrange things in such a manner?'

'Nature is indeed wonderful,' Drummond agreed.

'Mr Drummond and Miss Caskie!' Watters was aware of Beaumont and Holderby two paces behind him. 'I am afraid I must interrupt this most interesting conversation.'

Elizabeth gave a little curtsey, smiling to Amy as she slipped quietly away.

'Mr Drummond,' Watters said. 'I would like to introduce a good friend of your host. May I introduce Mr Holderby, the Vice Consul of the United States of America? And Mr Holderby, this is Mr Walter Drummond.'

Unsure what to expect, Watters was surprised when both men shook hands with perfect politeness, although he was aware of the underlying tension. 'I know that your nation is experiencing certain difficulties at present.'

'Difficulties!' Holderby gave a small smile. 'There's a damned war going on!'

'So I believe.' Watters conceded the point. 'But that war is being fought on American soil. I think it best that in this house, you should meet in friendship, or at least in the spirit of neutrality.'

'Neutrality it is,' Holderby said at once. 'I have no intention of embarrassing my host, who is a good friend of the United States.' *That was well emphasised*, Watters thought.

'Excellent.' Watters did not relax. 'I would like to assure you both, gentlemen, that Mr Beaumont did not draw up the guest list, or this unfortunate situation would never have arisen.' He could feel Beaumont's glare switch from him to Amy, who was beginning to look discomfited. He saw William Caskie hovering in the background.

'Can I assume that Mr Beaumont's household will not be disturbed in any way?' Watters allowed an edge to creep into his voice. He did not want to threaten these gentlemen, but he was prepared to use as much force as necessary to ensure the peace of Mount Pleasant.

'Mr Beaumont's house has always made me welcome,' Holderby said, 'and I would never abuse his hospitality. I cannot, however, speak for my fellow countryman.'

Drummond bowed, first to Beaumont, then to Watters, and lastly, and fleetingly, to Holderby. 'The culture of the South, gentlemen, is the apex of civilisation. We are the true descendants of the knights of chivalry. With our unique heritage, we are trained in culture from infancy.'

'Your unique heritage, sir, includes trading in human flesh and keeping innocent men and women in bondage!' For all his professions of neutrality, Holderby was inclined to be verbally aggressive.

'My dear, sir.' Drummond tried to move beside Holderby to find that Watters was there first. 'Our Lord approved of slavery, and repeatedly exhorted slaves to know their place and obey their masters.' Drummond's hand twitched, but Watters was leaning against his left side. He could feel the hard bulge where the pistol was.

Drummond bowed again, this time to Amy. 'No gentleman from the South would ever disturb the peace of his host and especially not when we have the company of such beauty. I was told that the fairest roses grew in England, but now I remind myself that Scotland has her own variety.'

'Thank you!' Elizabeth gave a curtsey, and as Drummond bowed in return, Watters used the opportunity to deftly thrust his hand inside Drummond's jacket and remove a long-barrelled Colt from its shoulder holster.

'I shall take care of this for you, Mr Drummond. That way you will be able to dance with more freedom.'

Before Drummond could reply, William Caskie appeared with Charlotte at his side. 'Mr Drummond! I see that you have met my father-in-law.' He glanced at Watters, and his tone chilled, 'and his pet bulldog.' Caskie ushered Drummond away, leaving Watters holding the Colt.

'Was that altogether wise, Watters?' Beaumont eyed the pistol.

'I believe so, Mr Beaumont.' Watters tucked the Colt into the waistband of his trousers. 'I will take care of this. Both visiting gentlemen know about the other, and we have asked them to respect your neutrality. I would doubt that there will be any trouble now.'

'Very good, Mr Watters. However, your methods are sometimes a little too direct for my taste.' Beaumont relaxed a little. 'You have my apologies, Mr Holderby, for any embarrassment I have caused.'

'No need, sir. I asked to meet this Drummond fellow. Your man, Watters, seems to have the measure of these gentlemen of the Secesh government.' Holderby nodded briefly to Watters, a smile at the corners of his mouth. 'I will say, without intending to cause offence, that Sergeant Watters's dress sense leaves a lot to be desired.'

Amy and Elizabeth both giggled at that, with Amy nudging Watters with her fan.

'I'll be speaking to you later, Amy.' Beaumont's voice was as stern as Watters had ever heard. 'This situation could have been extremely damaging.' He looked across to Holderby, who shook his long head.

'Nonsense, Mr Beaumont. I'm sure that the young lady meant no harm. These things happen, do they not? So let us just enjoy the night.' His bow took in both Elizabeth and Amy. 'Mr Drummond and I will merely avoid each other's company.'

'I'll watch Drummond,' Watters said quietly. 'He seems to be a bit of a loose cannon.'

Mrs Mary Caskie sailed across, tutted at the demeanour of the servants, took Elizabeth aside for a disapproving word about her too-revealing dress, and smiled politely to Holderby and Drummond simultaneously. *The Americans are not the only people who have mastered the art of polite diplomacy,* Watters thought as Mrs Mary Caskie found herself a chair. Elizabeth, not in the slightest disconcerted by her mother's disapproval, joined Amy.

Watters moved to a position against the wall where he could watch both Drummond and Holderby. He started as Elizabeth slapped Amy across the face.

'Miss Elizabeth!' He strode forward, fearing that a general row was about to break out, but Amy was not concerned. Stepping to a mirror that hung prominently on the wall, she examined her cheek.

'Not yet, Elizabeth. Do it again, harder!'

'But I don't want to hurt you, Amy.'

'Do it!'

Elizabeth did so so that Amy gasped, then again checked the mirror, smiling at the red blush that marked her cheek. 'Now the other one—I want a high colour!'

Once Amy was satisfied, she struck Elizabeth with some force until both girls had bright cheeks, to which they added by biting their lips until they were swollen and as red as their faces.

'Oh, what we suffer for fashion and beliefs!' Amy laughed to Watters. 'Some ladies swear that a slight pinch on the cheek will add blush, but that colour soon wears off. Others, from,' she dropped her voice a little, 'from *lower down* the social scale, actually wear *makeup*, but that's not suitable for Ladies! We must make do.' She twirled around, allowing her crinoline to rise from the floor and reveal her multi-layered petticoats. 'What do you think, Sergeant Watters? I look much more attractive than Charlotte! And now she's fallen out with William again, so she's off to sulk in her boudoir while we enjoy the dancing!'

The Dundee Philharmonic Society provided music with their violins and the piano drowning out all sound except the rhythmic batter of feet on the wooden floor.

'Oh, just look at Isabell Grant!' Amy's voice sounded high through a break in the music. 'That's never a silk dress; it's alpaca, or I'm a canary in a cage!'

'Some canary, you! Elizabeth was panting at her side. 'With that red-and-blue dress that your father does not yet know he has to pay for! But see the look that Isabell is giving you! You're in the black books now!'

Drummond proved to be an expert dancer, matching anybody in the waltz, despite Mrs Mary Caskie's objection to such an 'indecent display, with such voluptuous intertwining of the limbs. Such violent embraces and canterings! To think that my daughter should be a witness to such an exposition!'

'You surprise me, Mrs Caskie, for I hear that Her Majesty is something of an expert, and your daughter appears to be following the example of her queen.' Mr Beaumont winked to Watters as he offered an arm for Mrs Caskie, who tutted then accepted.

Elizabeth laughed as Drummond twirled her round with great speed. 'My, Mr Drummond, I feel as safe as the Bank in your arms and as happy as a cricket! La, do you have any sons of my age?'

'Is that a reminder of my advancing years, Miss Elizabeth?' Drummond frowned as he realised that Watters was watching him closely. 'Do not fear, Mr Watters. I will not upset the equanimity of my host.'

The music whirled them away for a few moments. Watters waited until they returned before continuing the conversation. 'I trust in your word, sir; now, when you have a moment, could you inform me why you grace this city with your presence?'

The orchestra came to a finale, the dance partners bowed to each other, and Drummond released Elizabeth into the arms of an eager young elegant. Watters strolled across and repeated the question.

Drummond gave a slow bow. 'Business, Sergeant Watters, business, and no gentleman should inquire into the business of another.'

'I am afraid that my job does not submit to gentlemanly behaviour,' Watters said. 'So I must ask again what *business* you have in Dundee.'

'Mr Drummond's business is with me.' William Caskie appeared at Watters's shoulder. 'I assure you that it is not connected with your case. Neither Mr Drummond nor I were in Calcutta when that unfortunate fellow was murdered, and neither of us has been starting fires in Mr Beaumont's premises.'

'Thank you, Mr Caskie.' Watters knew he could progress no further at present. 'I will take your word as a gentleman that neither your business nor that of Mr Drummond affects my case.' He stood back as Holderby and Amy strolled past, smiling at some private joke.

The music started again, a polka that was sufficiently loud to drown out their conversation. Watters saw Drummond looking past him where Amy was dancing with Holderby. The United States vice-consul had accompanied Amy through the quadrille, leading like an expert, but had failed miserably in the intricate steps of the minuet.

'Are you not dancing, sir?' Drummond altered the angle of the conversation. 'The ladies are well worth the energy!' His smile seemed genuine. 'Come, sir, put politics aside for a while and concentrate on the finer things of life: wine, music, and some of the fairest creatures that it ever has been my pleasure to observe.'

Drummond was such a charming man that Watters could not help but meet his bow. 'Perhaps you are right, Mr Drummond. Both Miss Elizabeth Caskie and Miss Amy Beaumont would grace the finest houses in the land, while Miss Isabell Grant is not at all far behind, whatever Elizabeth thinks of her dress!'

Both men laughed, Drummond signalled to a servant, removed a brace of brandy-and-waters from his silver tray, and presented one to Watters. 'Your health, sir, and the health of our host, Mr Beaumont!'

The drink was welcome, and when the music changed to a slow waltz, Watters moved to the side to allow more space on the suddenly crowded dance floor. Mr Beaumont swept past with Mrs Mary Caskie in his arms.

'They make a fine couple.' The voice was unexpected. Mrs Foreman appeared beside Watters. 'Don't you think?'

'I had not thought at all,' Watters said.

'Oh, but they do,' Mrs Foreman said. 'They make a fine, if a mismatched, couple. There's poor Mr Beaumont who still mourns his wife, and Mrs Caskie, the woman who wore black for less than a month when her husband died.' She tapped Watters's leg with her fan. 'I see you are not dressed for the dance, Sergeant Watters.'

'I am not,' Watters confirmed.

Mrs Foreman sighed. 'That is a pity. I think we would make a fine couple as well; we are better matched than poor Mr Beaumont and Mrs Caskie. I do hope he knows what he is doing. I would not wish him to be the next husband that she buries.'

'There are far superior dancers to me in this room,' Watters said.

'Perhaps there are superior dancers, Sergeant Watters, but less interesting people.' Mrs Foreman teased Watters by flicking open her fan and peering at him over the top. 'I think I shall join you.' She sat at his side, accepted the glass Watters extracted from a passing servant, and sipped delicately. 'How are your enquiries progressing, Sergeant? That is the right word is it not? Enquiries?'

'It is,' Watters said. He was not sure if he liked Mrs Foreman or not. She certainly seemed to like him. 'We're making progress,' he said. 'Slow and steady.'

Mrs Foreman's eyes widened. 'Have you arrested the murderers?'

'Not yet,' Watters said. 'We did arrest a group of fire-raisers. Murderers? Do you think there is more than one?'

Mrs Foreman nodded. 'Yes, indeed, Sergeant Watters. There is the murderer of Mr Caskie and the murderer of that unfortunate man in the boat.'

'Ah,' Watters said. 'We have not yet had the good fortune to make an arrest.'

'Never mind.' Mrs Foreman patted Watters's thigh. 'Don't give up hope. If you want to talk things over, I am sure I have some ideas that may interest you.'

'Thank you.' Watters forced a smile. Sometimes he would prefer to be hunting a pickpocket through the most noxious closes in Dundee than trying to manoeuvre the social niceties of the supposed elite.

Beaumont eased up, bowing to Mrs Foreman. 'I must ask for Sergeant Watters's attention, Mrs Forman. It is duty, I'm afraid.'

'Oh,' duty must come first.' Mrs Foreman eyed Watters archly over her fan. 'Pray don't mind me, Mr Beaumont.'

'Sergeant Watters, I know that I have asked you to be relieved from looking after Amy. I am afraid I have one more task for you if Superintendent Mackay agrees.'

Watters took a deep breath. He had hoped to return to normal policing. 'Of course, Mr Beaumont.'

Beaumont smiled. 'It is only a simple shopping trip, Sergeant.'

CHAPTER SEVENTEEN
DUNDEE: NOVEMBER 1862

Standing at the corner where High Street met Reform Street, Watters slanted his low-crowned hat over one eye. The new Sharps revolver was a comforting weight inside the pocket of his coat. He preferred his old faithful Tranter, but Mr Beaumont had presented him with the Sharps as a personal gift for dealing with Varthley, so it would feel impolite to use anything else. It was a new design, being patented in 1859, with four barrels that slid forward with each shot, and at only four-and-a-half inches long was easily concealed. He was not too happy about the lack of a trigger guard, but his trials in the courtyard of Broughty Castle impressed him with the accuracy of the pistol at close range.

Watters swung his cane, lifted his hat at Amy as she and Elizabeth Caskie sauntered past, laden with a basketful of unnecessary purchases, and watched them stroll along the elegant Georgian terrace of Reform Street. He shook his head as the combined width of their crinolines forced other pedestrians from the pavement into the horse-muck of the road. Trust Amy to use all her charm as she smiled her thanks to each be-spattered gentleman. Elizabeth wore a fashionable, loose red jacket that showed support for Garibaldi, the Italian patriot, although Watters thought the man little better than a bandit.

Watters grunted as Elizabeth hurried past the ready-made clothing at J P Smiths; she would never dream of buying anything ready-made, so Amy had to follow her example. They lingered far longer outside the display window of W. Neill's where the latest London fashions were on show, but Elizabeth guided Amy into Henderson Brothers, who boasted a new stock of satin hats by Ashton. Watters shook his head; he could see more of Mr Beaumont's hard-earned money being spent in that shop.

More critical to the case, however, were the far more considerable sums Mr Beaumont was spending on that mysterious ship in Rogers' Yard. Three more times Watters had tried to gain admission to the yard, and three times the watchman had fended him off, saying that without an actual crime to investigate, Watters had no excuse to enter. His attempts to gain information from Mr Beaumont had failed, so he was left frustrated. Every hour that passed decreased the time he had to solve the case, and here he was, still babysitting children.

One unwelcome possibility nagged at Watters's mind. Was it possible that Mr Beaumont was lying to him and playing a double game? Watters's informants had told him that Bulloch, the man who purchased ships for the Confederate Navy, was back in Dundee, while Beaumont was secretly building a ship for a mysterious foreign buyer. Was Beaumont in league with the Southern States? That would certainly give a reason for the abolitionists to target him, as well as casting serious doubts on his morality and gentlemanly ethics.

'Sergeant,' Duff must have stood on his toes to pass the height test for the Dundee Police, although his breadth of shoulders was equal to the tallest of men. In his civilian clothes, he looked more like a middleweight prize-fighter than a police officer.

'Don't say that too loudly in public,' Watters said.

'Sorry Sergeant.' Duff did not moderate his voice. 'Remember that you told me to watch Rogers' Yard for anything strange?'

'I remember,' Watters said patiently.

'I saw a strange, foreign gentleman coming out of Rogers' Yard,' Duff said. 'I followed him until he went into Russell's Royal Hotel on Union Street.'

Progress! 'Thank you, Duff.' Watters nodded down the street. 'I'll leave you to watch Miss Amy and Miss Elizabeth. What was this strange, foreign gentleman like?'

'He was a tall fellow with fancy clothing and a foreign-looking moustache.' Duff hesitated. 'I know all the local businessmen, and he wasn't one of them.'

'Thank you. Watch the ladies.'

Twirling his cane, Watters tried to look like a man without a care in the world as he sauntered towards Russell's Hotel. A casual knock at the clerk's desk and the exchange of a shilling for five minutes with the hotel register allowed him to peruse the names.

'Emmanuel Smith, merchant, London.

'Otto Frankel, flax merchant, Hamburg.

'Captain David James MacPherson, shipmaster, Inverness.

'Alain Dumas, traveller.'

Of the four visitors, three could be instantly discounted. Emmanuel Smith and David MacPherson were obviously British subjects, while Otto Frankel would presumably be visiting one of the German companies based in Dundee, either Jaffe Brothers or Moore and Weinberg. That left Alain Dumas, a name which Watters thought sounded French, and a man who had conveniently left out his address. *There is that French connection again. Perhaps this affair is about France after all and not America.* For a further sixpence, the clerk gave Watters a brief description. 'A tall man, very elegantly dressed, with a flowery weskit and check trousers. He spoke with an unusual accent too.'

'Do you recall anything that Mr Dumas said, sir?'

The clerk spread his hands until Watters rattled the coins in his pocket. 'Mr Dumas said he had not got time to spare as he wanted another trip around the town.'

Watters rattled his silver again. 'What sort of trip?'

'That I could not tell you, Sergeant.' The clerk's smile suggested that he had more information.

Watters put another shilling on the table and slammed his hand on top. 'You could not tell me, but I wager you know somebody who could.'

The clerk's gaze did not waver from Watters's hand. 'Yes, Sergeant. Mr Dumas asked for our cab again.'

'And?' Watters moved his hand sufficiently for the gleam of silver to show between his fingers.

'We have an arrangement with a Hackney driver,' the clerk said. 'He parks outside the hotel, and we send him customers. You see, that way, we provide a service for our clients. Mr Dumas was out all morning and came back to...'

Watters was outside the hotel before the clerk finished speaking. 'Halloa, you!' He hailed the driver of the Hackney that waited outside.

'Yes, sir?' The driver was younger than Watters had expected, a freckle-faced, tousled-haired rogue with a ready smile.

'Have you had a busy morning?' Watters asked. 'I hear that you dropped off that French fellow.'

'French was he?' The cabbie seemed eager to talk. 'I knew he was some kind of foreigner. He had me all over the place.'

Watters passed over the shilling the desk clerk had eyed so avariciously. 'I wager he asked you to show him the Royal Arch and the docks. Foreign visitors like that sort of thing.'

The cabbie accepted the coin and touched a hand to the brim of his hat. 'Why, thank you, sir. You're wrong though. He was a decent enough chap for a foreigner, good tipper, but he's not had me at the Arch. He had me out to the Ferry and the big hooses, and then he wanted me to take him to Rogers' Yard.'

'Which big houses?' Watters thought that he already knew the answer.

'Mount Pleasant; you know, Big Man Beaumont's, by West Ferry?'

'I know it,' Watters agreed. He felt a mixture of despair and elation. Mr Beaumont was indeed involved with this Frenchman. *Did anybody tell the truth in this modern age?*

'Aye? Well, the gentleman that the foreign fellae hoped to find was not there, so he had me drive out again, away out to Pitcorbie House and back by the docks.' The cabbie shook his head. 'You should have seen the traffic at the docks! A convoy of coal wagons was jammed in that narrow entrance to the docks. What with the Camperdown Dock not being opened yet, all these lighters unloading in the Tay, and the traffic here building up all the time, it's a nightmare driving a growler in this town. Time the council did something about it, I say.'

'You're right.' Watters could not have cared less about the traffic congestion in Dundee, but the news that Dumas had followed Beaumont to Pitcorbie was vastly interesting.

The cabbie was still speaking, 'Now I've got to pick up that French fellow again at Rogers' Yard in an hour, bring him back here, and then get back out to the Ferry this evening for some other fellae!' The cabbie's mock disgust ended in an abrupt grin. 'Good money, though, sir. He's paying me 2/- the hour, so your tip is an extra. The bairns will eat well this Sunday!'

Watters tipped the cabbie another shilling, wondered what Marie would say about this profligate expenditure of their money, and handed sixpence to the hotel clerk.

'I hinted at a shilling,' Watters said to the clerk. 'The other sixpence is waiting if you follow my instructions.' Telling the clerk what he wanted, Watters strolled upstairs. He knew that Amy and Elizabeth were safe with Duff. If Dumas was coming back to Russell's, it was best to wait here and see what he was like.

Settling himself in the hotel's smoking room, Watters lifted a newspaper. The content seemed never to alter. There was news of the war in America, Garibaldi, the French exploits in Mexico, and an unseasonal cricket match between the Albert and Broughty Ferry Cricket Clubs. Watters scanned columns about police raids on shebeens, the Jessie McLachlan murder trial, the search for the Honourable Peter

Turnbull, who had disappeared leaving colossal gambling debts, and the United States Navy boarding the British steamship *Gladiator.*

'*Gladiator!*' The name echoed Watters's thoughts. He glanced up to see two tall men standing with their backs to him. One answered the description of Dumas, with checked trousers beneath a thigh-length coat, but rather than Mr Beaumont, the other was William Caskie. The two sank languidly into the deep armchairs that were set on either side of the comforting fire, sipped at brandy-and-water, and drew deeply on long cheroots.

'That affair of *Gladiator,*' William Caskie repeated, 'has rather put the cat among the pigeons. It reminded us all exactly what sort of government we are dealing with.'

Watters hurriedly re-read the article. It seemed that Commander Wilkes of the United States Navy had sent a Thomas Stevens to board the British steamer *Gladiator* off the coast of Bermuda. Only when the escorting Royal Navy warship, HMS *Desperate,* had cleared for action had the American backed off. It was the latest in a series of incidents that had seen United States warships clash with British ships on the high seas, but one in which cutlasses had been rather vigorously rattled.

'Which is why we must act together in this struggle.' Dumas was all profile as he waved his cheroot in emphasis, but his accent was from the Confederate States of America rather than France. 'Britain needs cotton; we have cotton. Your people in Lancashire are starving without our trade!' Dumas leaned forward to add weight to his points. 'Why, sir, you could have a civil war in your country under the pressure of distress and unemployment, and all because you choose to remain neutral in this affair. An affair, I need not remind you, in which one antagonist remains your friend, while the other attacks your ships on the high seas.'

Watters shrunk deeper behind the broad wings of his armchair, burying his head further into the newspaper.

'I could not agree more,' William stroked the small imperial that decorated his upper chin, 'which is why I am building *Alexander MacGillivray* even as we talk.'

I am building? I? Watters presumed that *Alexander MacGillivray* was a ship. Was every businessman in Dundee having vessels built this season? Or was *Alexander MacGillivray* the vessel at Rogers' Yard?

Watters listened as William Caskie continued. 'Until recently, the Federal Navy was poor; there was no real difficulty for blockade-runners to evade their patrols. But now, the Federals have more vessels and are becoming more professional, so your ships also have to improve.'

Watters realised that there was an ornate mirror on the wall to his left. He had only to shift sideways to obtain a view of Dumas and Caskie.

Mr Dumas stirred uncomfortably in his seat but still managed to blow a perfect smoke ring that shivered in the air before dissipating. 'You may be correct, Mr Caskie. I'll grant that the blockade of the Southern ports is tighter now than hitherto.'

'Indeed. However, Mr Bulloch, who I know intimately, has been working hard to rectify the deficiency. He has ordered vessels built in both France and with John Laird on the Mersey. Correct?' When Caskie raised his glass to signify that he required a refill, a flunkey hastened to his side. At that moment, Caskie looked every inch the businessman.

Dumas appeared even more uncomfortable than he had a minute before. He leaned closer to Caskie. 'You are discussing things that should not be voiced abroad, sir. We know that there are Federal agents in this city. They could be in this room even now.'

'Nonsense.' Lifting himself up, Caskie glanced around the room. Watters shrunk behind his newspaper. 'There are no other Americans in this room, Mr Dumas. I know the cut of their clothes, by God!' He settled down again. 'All of Britain knows about Mr Bulloch's connection with Frazer, Trenholm and Co of Liverpool and his efforts to raise a Confederate Navy. Many of us applaud him. We know of his success in running the blockade with *Fingal*. We know he purchased *Alabama* and *Florida*.' Caskie permitted himself a small laugh. 'That is the ships, not the states. We all know that every yard on the Clyde is busy building blockade runners for the Confederates.' Caskie rattled off a dozen names, counting each on the long fingers of his left hand. 'There is *Rothesay Castle, Falcon, Flamingo, Ptarmigan,* and *Evelyn*. There are few secrets among businessmen, Mr Dumas, whatever governments may believe.'

Caskie sipped at his drink. 'We also know that Bulloch hopes to build a powerful squadron that can challenge the Federal Navy toe-to-toe, or yardarm-to-yardarm.' He allowed himself another brief laugh while he stroked his imperial. 'We are well aware that Bulloch hopes to build a fleet of ironclad rams that would reduce the Federal vessels to matchwood. Is that not so?'

Dumas placed his brandy onto the mahogany-wood table with enough force for the contents to spill. 'Mr Caskie! These are state matters. They should not be discussed here!'

Caskie gave a lazy kick to a log that hung out of the fireplace. A shower of sparks fluttered upwards. 'As you wish, Mr Dumas. These new rams will not be completed until at least May of next year, and they will indeed be formidable. However, Mr Rogers assures me that my vessel will be finished in a matter of days.' He leaned closer. 'And will perform better than either Laird's or the French vessels.'

Mr Rogers? Watters nodded. The mysterious ship at Rogers' Yard was indeed *Alexander MacGillivray* then, with William Caskie involved in the building. One piece of the puzzle clicked into place. But where did Beaumont fit in?

'How will your ship perform, sir?' Despite his evident discomfort, Dumas gave a small smile. 'I would like to know more about this famous warship of yours, but pray, sir, moderate your tone.'

Watters turned a page noisily and lay back, pretending to settle into sleep.

It appeared that Dumas was not inclined to tell Caskie that he had already viewed his vessel. Did he not trust his business associate?

'*Alexander MacGillivray* combines the best of both worlds,' William Caskie boasted. 'The finest Southern naval designers drew up her plans, which were then improved by Rogers's own men. She is iron built by Scottish engineers, who are undoubtedly the most advanced in the world, and she is faster and more manoeuvrable than any warship currently afloat.'

'You laud her greatly, Mr Caskie, but please explain further.'

Watters heard the alteration in William's voice as he began to describe his ship. 'She is long and narrow for speed with bows like a clipper but with the addition of a ram. Her masts are cut low to prevent her being sighted at sea, with the simplest of rigging, as we use in the Dundee whaling industry. She has a turtledeck forward to shrug off any waves that break on her. And her engines! You know that Dundee leads the world in marine engineering, with our whaling ships breaking the ice...' Caskie laughed again, louder, in admiration of his own play of words, 'in modern machinery. The Clyde pioneered the marine compound engine, where steam passes through first a high-pressure and then a low-pressure cylinder, but Dundee has improved on even the Clyde's methods.'

'Tell me more.' Dumas leaned forward on his chair with a notebook in his hand. 'Tell me of the advantages this engine has.'

Watters wished he could also take notes. He hoped he could remember the gist of the conversation.

'Ah!' Caskie placed his brandy glass on the fireplace. 'The compound engine can reduce the rate of coal a vessel uses by around a third. Think of that! A steamship that can operate on long-haul routes or a warship that hardly needs to refuel! I'll give you an example...' it was clear that Caskie was embarking on a favourite topic as he quoted facts and figures, all of which Dumas carefully noted down. '...and there was *Bogota*, who had consumed 38 hundredweight of coal every hour, but with a compound engine, reduced that to 19 hundredweight. Randolph Elder, another Clydeside firm, is poised to supply the Royal Navy with these compound engines, so that says everything.'

Dumas finished scribbling notes, replaced his notebook in his pocket, and rose from his seat. Watters tried to shrink further into his newspaper, trying to disguise the sudden hammering of his heart, but Dumas was merely stretching his legs before settling back down again.

'Are these vessels fast, Mr Caskie? Federal warships are among the fastest in the world, able to sail at ten, twelve, even fifteen knots!'

'*Condor* and *Ptarmigan* sailed at 20 knots. Proven.' Caskie kept his face immobile for a minute, and then his enthusiasm returned. 'And *Alexander MacGillivray* has twin screws. Twin screws!' Caskie waited for some reaction by Dumas but explained further when the Confederate said nothing.

'With twin screws, we can put one screw forward and one aft, turn her on a tanner; we'll run rings around anything that floats. You can use *Alexander MacGillivray* for an Admiral's command for she can race from point to point. You could use her as a blockade runner, or a warship, once you equip her with armaments.' William Caskie laughed again and stroked his imperial in self-congratulation. 'I have that in hand, of course.'

Watters remembered Caskie's meetings with the French and Belgian armament manufacturers. The pieces were falling together one after the other without helping him find his murderer or the people behind the fire-raising. One huge piece was still lacking: where did Beaumont fit in?

After a half hour, the two men rose and strolled casually toward the billiard room.

Watters gave them another five minutes before he left the hotel. For the remainder of that evening, he walked around Dundee, swinging his cane and allowing the day's events to settle in his mind so that he could make sense of them. He knew now that the ship was being built for the Confederate States of America rather than for France and that William Caskie was heavily involved.

As Watters walked the streets, he pondered all the aspects. With Britain neutral in the American Civil War, William Caskie had no business interfering by building the Confederates a ship, particularly a warship. Neutrality laws were strict, and if Britain came down too heavily on either side, there was the risk of war with the other. Great Britain had recently come through two major wars; she would be foolish to enter another. There was also the dangerous possibility of a European power attacking Britain while she was involved across the Atlantic; twice before Britain had fought the youthful United States while simultaneously facing half of Europe.

Watters knew well that Napoleon III had renewed his alliance with Russia in 1860. It was fear of a Russian fleet combining with the French Navy out of Cherbourg to invade Britain that had encouraged the creation of the Volunteers and the refurbishment of coastal forts such as that at Broughty. An alliance of France, Russia, and the United States would be formidable indeed.

Watters swung his cane as he followed his line of thought. If Britain's involvement ended in defeat for the North, then that nation would undoubtedly gather her strength and seek revenge. An invasion along the long, vulnerable border with Canada was always likely, which meant that Britain would have to increase her minuscule garrison there, thus weakening her defences at home or in India. The Russians, smarting after their defeat at Sebastopol, would benefit. Watters shuddered to think of hordes of Cossacks thundering through the Khyber Pass, uniting with the Pashtun tribes and others who remained unhappy with British rule.

Overall, it was a dangerous game that William Caskie was playing, with higher stakes than perhaps he realised. And more crucial to Watters, where did Mr Beaumont fit in, and was all this international dealing related to the fires in his mills and the murder in Calcutta?

CHAPTER EIGHTEEN
DUNDEE: NOVEMBER 1862

'I would have a word, sir.' Watters held his hat under his arm as he stood in Beaumont's study.

'Of course, Sergeant.' Beaumont put down his pen and looked up. The portrait of the late Mrs Beaumont smiled down upon him. 'You did better than I thought with that Confederate fellow, Sergeant.' He shook his head. 'You may be assured that I let Amy know I was out of temper with her.'

Watters took a deep breath. 'I wouldn't be too hard on Miss Amy. I suspect that Miss Elizabeth Caskie had a hand in choosing the guests. Her brother, Mr William Caskie, appears to be quite close to the Confederate gentlemen.' He stepped back slightly, ignoring the anonymous Cattanach, who handed Beaumont a document. 'I believe that Mr William has shipping business with them.'

Beaumont looked suddenly wary as he read the document. He signed it with a flourish. 'Possibly, Sergeant Watters, but in business, a man must abide by the law and deliver whatever he has promised despite any political complications that turn up.' When he looked at Watters, there was no smile on his face. 'A man must keep business separate from his family concerns.' He sighed. 'Damn it, man, we know each other well enough by now.'

Beaumont dismissed Cattanach and sent the servants to bed before lighting the candles in his room. He settled in his favourite chair beside the fire. 'We can relax a bit now, Watters. What is it you wish to ask me? More about that damned murder in Calcutta?'

'It may be related, sir.' Watters remained standing. 'It is about a vessel named *Alexander MacGillivray* presently building at Rogers' Yard.'

Beaumont's face lost all expression. 'What about it, Watters?'

'I have heard rumours that your company may be involved in this vessel. Is that correct?' Watters held Beaumont's stony stare.

'That's business,' Beaumont said.

'If this vessel is intended for the Southern States, sir, it may be the reason that somebody is attempting to *damage* your business.' Watters tapped his cane on the floor. 'I would like you to be honest with me so I can assess the danger to you.' Watters paused for a moment. 'And I can assess the danger to your family. Neither of us wishes any harm to come to Miss Amy or Mrs Charlotte Caskie.'

As Watters had intended, Beaumont looked away. 'Sit down, Sergeant. Before I begin, I want you to swear that you will not repeat what I am about to tell you. Understand?' Standing up, Beaumont opened a cupboard and took out a decanter and two glasses.

'That would depend on the legality of the matter, sir.' Watters accepted the brandy-and-water that Beaumont poured for him.

Beaumont grunted. 'I don't know your feelings about this American affair, but I am in the business of making a profit. Morals must take second place.'

Watters said nothing.

Beaumont sipped at his drink. 'You must understand that I have hundreds of families depending on my companies for a livelihood. Men who are not in business do not understand how precarious the margin is between success and failure, profit and loss. There is no place for idealism in the marketplace.'

Watters wondered if Beaumont was trying to persuade himself more than anything else. 'I am a policeman, Mr Beaumont. My job is to uphold the law, not to judge people for their morality or political beliefs.'

'As you say.' Beaumont looked at Watters over the top of his glass. 'I trust in your honesty, Sergeant Watters. Now, I'm not sure how much of this affair you already know, so I will start at the beginning. Please bear with me.'

Watters placed his glass on a small table and took out his notebook. 'I will only write down matters pertinent to the case, sir, and nothing personal.'

'Thank you,' Beaumont said. 'You are fully aware that my elder daughter, Charlotte, was recently married to William Caskie. You do not know that the Caskie family are not as wealthy as they appear. They are not an ancient family, Mr Watters. The grandfather was a merchant in India around the turn of the century.'

'I see, sir.'

'Well, Grandfather Caskie returned to Scotland with a fortune; he was what people term a nabob and bought property in the area. Pitcorbie is an ancient house, so he bought history too. However, his sons spent lavishly, so that by the time William came along, the Caskies of Pitcorbie were on their uppers.'

'Yet you let him marry your daughter, sir.' Watters knew that he should not make such a personal comment.

Beaumont sipped at his brandy. 'I knew that the family was strapped for cash, but I did not know that they were virtual paupers, damnit! I'd never have agreed to the match else.'

'Yes, sir.' Watters pondered that kindly, affable Mr Beaumont, as pleasant and companionable a man as it was possible to meet, had agreed to his daughter's marriage without checking out the groom nearly as carefully as he would examine a business deal. 'Did Charlotte agree to the marriage?'

Beaumont looked up sharply. 'What the devil has that got to do with it? Charlotte knew that her marriage would add lustre to our name by connecting us to a landed family. It was her duty to get married, and that's all there is to it.'

'I see, sir.' Watters began to see that all was not gold under Beaumont's urbane charm.

Beaumont's complexion mottled. He placed his brandy down and leaned closer to Watters. 'Let's face it, Watters, my Charlotte is a fine woman, but she is hardly a prime catch. Amy is a peach, but Charlotte is—a bit plain, shall we say?'

Watters grunted. 'It is not my place to compare the attributes of your daughters, sir.'

'I am proud of them both, Sergeant Watters.' Beaumont was smiling again. 'However, neither my pride nor their good qualities are the subject of this conversation. Mr William Caskie is.'

Watters nodded. 'Yes, sir.'

'Now, William is a proud man. He wishes to raise himself, and his family, from the precipice of poverty. Quite naturally, he is using the opportunity of this American war to make money, and how better than to exploit the skills that Dundee has to offer? When he asked me for a loan at a moderate rate of interest, naturally, I did not at first agree. I thought that he was building a ship for the French government. But when I heard he was building a blockade-runner, well, where's the harm in sailing food into a beleaguered town? So I agreed and allowed my name to be used in case Mr Rogers was wary of William's embarrassed situation. It's a work of charity in its own way, feeding the starving.'

'A blockade-runner, sir?' Watters approached the subject with some caution. 'I thought Rogers was building a warship.'

'*Alexander MacGillivray* is to be a blockade-runner, Watters. The Confederate government is prepared to pay a quite sizeable sum of money for such a vessel. Oh, I know that they have been buying up all the surplus ships that the Mersey and the Clyde have to offer, and even vessels from Dublin, but William's vessel is something special, I hear.' Beaumont stifled a yawn and stood up. 'So there you have it. That's not so bad, eh? William is doing his best to care for his family by engaging in legitimate business while helping hungry people at the same time.'

Watters stood up and wondered if he should tell Beaumont what he had overheard in the Royal Hotel. *Best not to. Yet.* 'Thank you for letting me into your confidence, sir.'

'Nonsense. You did a good job in keeping the peace between these squabbling Americans.' Beaumont tilted his head to one side as if examining him. 'Well, you'd better get back to your duty.' He chattered cheerfully as he ushered Watters to the door of his office. 'Good night to you now.'

* * *

Superintendent Mackay listened as Watters related his discoveries. 'You say that Mr William Caskie is having an ironclad built in Dundee for the Confederate States of America with Mr Beaumont footing the bill. That would explain Mr Beaumont's current financial constraints.'

'Yes, sir,' Watters said. 'I don't think that Mr Rogers is aware of the intended destination. Caskie sold him some tomfool story about the ship being destined for the Emperor of China.'

'You have already told me that,' Mackay said. 'Last time you were here, you believed the ship was for French owners. Now you believe it is for the Confederates. Have you any proof, Watters?'

'I overheard a conversation, sir.' Watters gave details.

'Hmm.' Mackay's fingers began their drumming on the desk. 'No court in the land would take heed of that evidence, Sergeant, as you are aware. Nor is Mr Caskie doing anything illegal. No. We cannot act on it.' Mackay made his decision. 'There is nothing there that advances our case of the murder on *Lady of Blackness*.'

'It may give a reason for the attacks on Mr Beaumont, sir,' Watters explained, 'if some anti-slavery group thinks he is advancing the cause of the South.' He waited a moment for Mackay to consider his words. 'Mr Caskie's actions may even create some interference from the Federal government.'

'What?' Mackay's fingers stilled, and he looked up frowning. 'No, no, Watters. I doubt there will be anything of that significance. The United States has too much to worry about to be concerned with one Scottish merchant. Forget this blasted metal ship.'

'As you wish, sir,' Watters agreed, fully aware that he would continue to follow any lead that may help solve the case.

Mackay sighed, with his fingers drumming the *pas de charge*. 'I will agree that there's some damned awkward double dealing going on here, Watters.' He leaned forward over his desk. 'French boats and American agents and diplomats and God knows what else.'

Watters waited for Mackay to get to his point.

Mackay forced his fingers into stillness. 'Remind me, Watters, what is the case? You were ordered to find a murderer and to stop the fireraising in Mr Beaumont's mills. You succeeded in the latter and have tried every avenue with the former. I also sent you to protect Beaumont and his family from possible danger. You were with the family for some days, and Mr Beaumont said that although nothing transpired, you were instrumental in keeping the peace in a possibly delicate situation. However, I think we can safely agree that Mr Beaumont is correct when he says that any danger has passed.'

'I am not sure I agree, sir. I am still unsure why Mr Beaumont was targeted or by who. There is also the matter of the mannequin in his bed.'

'Forget the mannequin; some childish prank, no doubt. As the fireraising has stopped, we can be fairly sure it was by that abolitionist group.' Mackay shook his head. 'Now as for that French vessel, you think she is a coper and working with William Caskie. I am not so sure. I am coming around to your French theory. I think she might be here to spy on our shipping.'

'If she is, sir, all she can spy on is the Nesshaven fishermen.'

'Go out and have a look.'

'With respect, sir, I am a policeman, not a spy. Surely that's the Navy's job.'

'With respect, Sergeant Watters, I have given you an order.' Mackay tried to smile. 'I do not know if your vessel is engaged in espionage, Watters, but if the Navy hauls up an innocent French vessel, then it's a diplomatic incident. If an overzealous Dundee policeman examines her, people will shake their heads and then forget it.'

'Yes, sir,' Watters said. 'Will the time I take out at sea be included in the four days I have left to solve the murder on *Lady of Blackness*?'

'Don't be damned impertinent, Watters!' Mackay's hands clenched into fists. 'I've given you your orders; it's your duty to carry them out.'

'Yes, sir.' Watters reached for his hat. 'I'll need to hire a boat. May I draw some funds to cover the cost?'

* * *

A pair of oystercatchers piped Watters clear of the beach, their calls somehow reassuring above the crash of the surf. Both birds circled the boat, their black and white plumage contrasting with the orange bill and legs.

With her name *Joyce* painted in simple black letters on her white hull, the boat was smaller than *Grace*, with a single mast and a pair of oars. Hoisting the lug sail, Watters concentrated on the tiller, hitting the waves at an angle so they broke on the bows and dashed aside. Keeping well clear of the surge around the Sisters, he caught the land breeze to steer out to sea. The Nesshaven fleet always fished the same two areas, either near My Lord's Bank, two miles to the north and within sight of the growing village of Carnoustie, or ten miles out in the lee of the Inchcape Rock. Watters knew by experience that the gin coper did not come close inshore, so the fleet would be off the Inchcape, where the Bell Rock Lighthouse thrust itself from the sea.

Spindrift pattered inboard, streaking the foredeck with salt as *Joyce* cleared the Sisters. Watters touched the New Testament that Marie had insisted on giving him.

'I worry about you,' Marie had said. 'Take this with you.'

'You know I'm not particularly religious,' Watters reminded.

'I am, though,' Marie said. 'Please take it.'

Now, strangely, Watters was glad to feel its bulk in his breast pocket.

'You manage the sail, Ragina!' Watters called above the crash of the sea and the whine of wind through the rigging. He eased the tiller a little as the wind shifted a few points to the north. He watched Ragina fight to adjust the sail.

'I hope you bluebottles are going to pay me for this,' Ragina grumbled.

'So do I,' Watters said, 'because as sure as God, I can't afford it.'

The land was far behind them now, with the waves rising sharply, not the great greybeards of the North Atlantic or the horrifying mountains of Cape Horn, but short, steep, and ugly. Watters ignored the seagulls that circled the boat, constantly calling in their quest for food. He could see sails rising on the horizon, but visibility was restricted at the level of this small boat. The oystercatchers had deserted them.

'Are those our boats?'

'I'm not sure!' Ragina said. 'They might belong to Arbroath or Broughty, even Easthaven or Westhaven. I won't know until we're closer.'

The sea was rising faster than Watters had expected, and he eyed the bank of dark cloud that was rising to the northeast. 'I don't like the look of that!'

'Nor do I,' Ragina said. 'We might be better returning to harbour.'

'I have my duty to do,' Watters said.

'You can't do any duty if you're drowned.' Ragina altered the angle of the sail.

Watching the run of the sea, Watters gradually eased the boat around as waves slapped against their starboard bow, splashing inside. Purple-black clouds were racing over the horizon, already concealing the pencil-thin finger of the Bell Rock Lighthouse. The sea was changing, with the waves higher and longer, tipped with hissing beards of foam. Watters could not see the fishing boat sails, while belts of driving rain even obscured the land.

'You were right, Ragina. We should have turned back.'

'Too late now, Sergeant. We'll have to ride the squall,' Ragina shouted.

Watters abandoned all thought of reaching the Nesshaven fleet as the waves raised *Joyce*, shook her like a cat playing with a mouse, and tossed her back into a trough of the waves. The wind veered, coming from the north, then the east, hammering walls of chill water against their hull. Sudden darkness descended as the squall closed and rain scythed horizontally.

'We're being driven back!' Ragina said.

Watters nodded. He could hear a rhythmic pounding, and somewhere ahead was a high ridge of white.

'The Sisters! We're being driven onto the Sisters!'

A sight that had been ugly from the land was terrifying at sea. From here, the Sisters formed a long, wickedly-fanged barrier of rocks across which the sea surged and broke in mast-high spray.

'We'll have to get out to sea until the weather breaks!' Ragina worked the sail, fighting the taut canvas to try to head them away from the rocks.

Watters swore as the sea struck them broadside on, half filling the boat as he steered her away from the Sisters. For a long moment *Joyce* hovered a few yards from the rocks, and then a backlash forced her further away. The wind altered again. It blasted from the land, strengthening until the sail filled and the rigging strummed with the strain.

Watters felt the muscles in his arms ache as he wrestled the tiller, pushing against the weight of wind and sea. With the wind still veering, Watters eased the bows further east, out to sea, away from one danger and straight for the froth-crested rollers that hissed toward him.

The wind was gusting, alternatively filling and leaving the sail, but Watters still headed out to sea, aware that these German Ocean squalls often had a nasty kick in the tail. *The more distance we put between the boat and the coastal rocks the better.* The rumble of thunder came as a shock, the near-simultaneous flash of lightning startled him, and then the world collapsed.

There was sudden, intense, stuffy darkness combined with a stench of burning and a tingling sensation that made Watters's hair bristle. He swore loudly, thrashing his arms to free himself of whatever seemed to be smothering him.

'You're all right!' That was Ragina's surprisingly calm voice. He hauled away the sodden canvas sail.

Watters looked around. The mast had broken, bringing the sail on top of him. He swore again. They were adrift on the German Ocean with the cliffs of Forfarshire a mile away and the wind veering wickedly. The mast hung half over the side, attached by a tangle of loose ropes and canvas.

'Come on, Sergeant,' Ragina said. 'Let's get this shipshape.'

They cleared the raffle from the boat, cutting the loose ropes, lifting what remained of the mast and rolling it into the sea. The residue drifted quickly away, leaving them with a splintered, blackened stump about five feet high.

'Now we row back to Nesshaven.' Watters tried to sound optimistic as he searched for the oars.

'No, we don't,' Ragina said. 'The sea's taken one of the oars. We'll have to scull.'

'Damn!' It was many years Watters had last sculled, and his muscles and hands were soft, but there was no choice as he stood in the stern with the cold numbing his face. 'We'll take spells each. I'll go first.'

'We're caught in a rip-current,' Ragina said. 'It's taking us out fast, so we'll have to work hard to get back to land.'

Watters sculled, cursing, feeling the oar rasp the skin from the palms of his hands as his back and thigh muscles screamed with the unaccustomed effort.

After half an hour, they changed places. Ragina now held the single remaining oar. Their combined strength was not enough to fight the combination of the fast rip-current and the ebbing tide, so they were drawn further out into the wild waters of the German Ocean.

'It will be dark soon,' Ragina said.

Watters did not reply. There was no point in stating the obvious. He looked up, hoping for a sight of a sail, but saw only the waves. Although the storm had abated, there was still a mist on the sea, limiting visibility to less than a quarter of a mile.

Eyeing the waves, head bowed, they worked through the night, fighting the pain, with Watters feeling despair settle on him, hoping for the tide to turn.

'Listen! What's that?'

There was a regular thumping, combined with a faster splashing sound that Watters recognised at once. 'It's a paddle steamer. That's the sound of the walking beam and the smack of the paddles hitting the sea.'

'It's getting louder! It's coming this way!' Ragina waved both hands. 'Here! Over here!'

The noise increased until the splashing was a definite churning, and Watters began to worry that the steamer might run them down. He joined Ragina in waving and yelling as the sound rose to a crescendo, then the shape of a ship loomed from the mist, its starboard paddle threshing the sea only twenty yards away as smoke from its funnel formed an ugly fan astern.

'Steamer, ahoy!' Watters yelled.

The steamer continued, with the wake of its passing rocking the small boat, and it disappeared into the mist leaving only disturbed water and the smuts of its smoke.

'There'll be others.' Watters moved to the stern to relieve Ragina at the oar. 'And the tide will turn soon.' Ignoring the screams from tortured muscles, he bent to his work, feeling the pressure of the wood against the fresh blisters on his hands.

By midnight, the mist had closed upon them, blocking stars and moon, so they steered by the compass alone, hoping the tide was helping. With no bandages in *Joyce*, Watters tore off a sleeve from his shirt to cover his raw blisters. They fed on a biscuit, drinking half the flagon of water they had brought with them.

'How far out do you think we are?'

'No idea, but the tide's with us now, so we're moving in the right direction.'

'You said that an hour ago, Sergeant.'

It was the sound that alerted Watters. 'What's that?'

'It's a fog horn,' Ragina said. 'Probably from the Bell Rock Lighthouse.'

Watters said nothing. He continued to scull. There was nothing else he could do.

They heard the foghorn one more time, fainter than before, and then there was silence broken only by the lapping of waves and the harsh gasps of whoever was sculling.

Watters saw the lights but waited until they came close before he stood up and waved, yelling. Although he had no lantern, the vessel obviously had an efficient lookout, for there was an almost immediate alteration in her course.

'Ahoy!' Ragina's voice was hoarse with salt. 'Ship, ahoy!'

The vessel steered close, with men reaching out with boathooks to pull them close. There was the gleam of lanterns, the chatter of conversation, and three wiry seamen thumped onto the boat. Bearded faces smiled upon them; friendly hands raised them over a low bulwark and onto the waist of a two-masted vessel.

'Bring them here.' The voice was familiar, but Watters was too cold and exhausted to say from where. There was the whiff of cheroot smoke, the click of hard heels on the wooden deck, and Walter Drummond smiled down at him.

CHAPTER NINETEEN
GERMAN OCEAN:
NOVEMBER 1862

'Well now.' The Southern drawl was less pleasant as Drummond ran his eyes over Watters. 'This one I know. Sergeant Watters, I believe?' He raised his voice. 'Take them below. Keep them separate.'

Watters had time for a single glance along the deck. He was on a two-masted sailing vessel with a large crew and various canvas covered bundles tied to the deck. The crew looked efficient but spoke in a variety of tongues, from the accents of the Confederate States to French and others that Watters did not recognise. Powerful hands grabbed him and hustled him down a steep companionway that descended into the depths of the vessel. A door opened, and he was thrown into darkness.

Drummond thrust his head in. 'We'll speak later,' he said, nodding. 'And you will tell me why you are here.' His nod carried more of a threat than the long-barrelled Colt that filled the holster at his belt.

'It would be best if you told me why *you* were here,' Watters retaliated as the door slammed shut. He began to examine his surroundings. The coiled rope and canvas told him that he was probably in a cable and sail locker, but one that also contained tar, by the smell. A painful experiment taught him that the deck beams above were far too low for him to stand upright, while he had perhaps three feet of space between the stacked stores. It was then that waves of tiredness hit him. He slumped on the deck, hoping the scurrying rats left him in comparative peace.

The creaking and swaying were unfamiliar when Watters opened his eyes, but the sharp nibble of teeth on his feet brought him back to the present. Starting up, he again banged his head on the deck beams, cursed, slumped down again, and tried to ease the stiffness of cramped limbs and still the shivering that sleeping in wet clothes in an unheated space brought on. He was glad that years of living outdoors had hardened him to heat and cold alike.

With nothing else to do, Watters fell back asleep to be wakened by the crash of the door opening. A lantern gleamed in his eyes and a shadowy figure hauled him out where other men surrounded him speaking in a mixture of languages.

'This way!' With somebody shoving from behind, Watters was soon in the cold daylight of the upper deck.

Drummond was waiting, with the suave Alain Dumas at his side and half a dozen burly seamen behind him. 'I hear that you are Sergeant Watters,' Dumas spoke quietly.

'That's correct. I am Sergeant George Watters of the Dundee Police.'

Dumas glanced at Drummond. 'You're not in Dundee now, Sergeant. I believe that you were searching for gin copers.'

'We were.' Watters ignored the grins of the seamen around.

Dumas raised his voice incredulously, while his seamen began to openly laugh. 'I am not sure whether you are a complete fool or just a liar, Sergeant Watters, but either way, I don't believe you.' He leaned closer. 'Well, congratulations. You are aboard your gin coper.'

Drummond was wearing a seaman's canvas jacket and loose trousers with the feathered bowler hat balanced on the back of his head and a long-barrelled colt revolver thrust through his broad leather belt. 'Welcome aboard *Pluton*, Sergeant.' He was as much as ease on the deck of the brig as he had been in Mr Beaumont's grand house. 'Just do what you're told and things will be easier for you.'

'Where is Ragina, the man who was with me?'

Drummond glanced significantly at the sea. 'Didn't you hear the splash?' His smile was as sinister as anything Watters had ever seen.

Watters felt a cold chill creep up his spine. 'Did you throw him overboard?'

'He was no further use to us once he told us what he thought you were looking for.' Dumas said.

Some of the crew laughed. Others watched Watters, gauging his reaction.

Watters hid his anger. 'I see.' he kept his voice neutral. 'You murdered him.'

The sound of the fiddle called Watters's attention to the mizzenmast. Isabella Navarino sat cross-legged on the cross-trees with the violin to her shoulder and her hair loose around her shoulders. Lifting her bow, she waved to him and slid down the backstay to the deck.

'Good day to you, Sergeant Watters. What brings you out here?'

'Good day to you, Captain Navarino. I'm searching for a gin coper.'

Navarino grinned and tossed back her hair. 'Did you find one?'

'I believe one found us.' Watters felt the fury burning behind his eyes. 'Where is my companion? Mr Ragina was with me, and he appears to have vanished.'

'I heard.' For a moment, Navarino looked angry. 'I would wish that had not happened. I had no part in that affair, Sergeant.'

Dumas stepped closer to Watters. 'I was going to throw you to the fishes too, Sergeant Watters, but Mr Drummond tells me that you are a capable man. You might have found out something that is none of your business.'

Watters said nothing.

'What do you think you know of our operation, Sergeant Watters?' Dumas's voice was soft. 'More important, what have you told your superiors?'

'They know everything.' Watters tried to sound calm. 'You may as well sail back to France, Mr Dumas.'

Dumas nodded. 'I've no time to deal with you now.' He raised his voice. 'Take him away, boys. Don't worry if he gets a little hurt.'

Although Watters tried to defend himself, he fell as a gaggle of seamen fell upon him. Punches and kicks propelled him along the deck until he was pushed down the companionway, saving himself from serious injury only by grasping the rails as he fell. He landed just one telling punch before he was back in the store, where two of the seamen kicked him a fond farewell. Even as he curled into a foetal ball and rode the blows, Watters knew that he could not blame the sailors. Dumas had given them a direct order. All that was little consolation as the last seaman slammed shut the door. The darkness was a welcome friend, while the pressure of Marie's New Testament in his pocket was more comforting than he would have believed.

Time passed slowly in the storeroom as Watters considered what Dumas had said. They had thrown Ragina overboard: cold, brutal murder. He would not forget that. He would pursue Dumas and Drummond, somehow, when he could. Watters put Ragina's death to one side to concentrate on the other questions.

It was evident that Dumas and Drummond were not here to sell gin to Scottish fishermen; they were here on business connected to *Alexander MacGillivray*. Watters tried to sort the disparate pieces in his head. There were two opposing parties in his case. There were William Caskie and his Continental arms manufacturers plus Drummond and Dumas, and there was the mysterious foreign woman who persuaded the abolitionists into fire-raising. Stuck in the middle was Beaumont. Why the devil did these people choose Dundee to fight their sordid little war?

Watters turned ideas over in his head until the thunder of feet informed him that things were happening on deck. Putting his ear to the door, he tried to listen but could not distinguish anything other than confused noise.

The door crashed open. 'You! Out!' A Confederate by his accent, the man was tall and lanky, with bad teeth and ears that could have formed handles, but his eyes were level and his grip firm as he pulled Watters to his feet. 'There's someone to see you.'

'What?' Watters had no need to pretend confusion as the Confederate dragged him back to the upper deck. A large number of men were gathered around the mainmast, far too many to be only the crew of *Pluton.* Some glanced at Watters, others were talking amongst themselves, one was whistling, which immediately marked him as a non-seaman in Watters's eyes, but most were staring at the ship that lay close alongside.

Painted light grey, the newcomer was long and lean. Her prow was cleaver sharp, with a ram at water-level, her profile sleek, from her twin, low cut masts to the two funnels whose emissions smeared the sky, and she was easily three times the length of the brig in which Watters stood.

'Do you like her?' Dumas puffed on a cheroot, his eyes busy. 'That's your nemesis, boy. That's *Alexander MacGillivray*; remember the name because she is about to change history.'

Aching from bruised ribs and limbs, Watters glared through his one good eye. A swelling bruise closed the other. 'Is she? How? By racing the Federal Navy?' He decided to taunt Dumas. 'Mr Holderby knows all about her, even the twin screws. So she's to lead the new Confederate battle fleet, is she? What with? She's no guns!'

Despite his words, Watters privately admitted that Rogers' Yard had done a fine job, as they always did. *Alexander MacGillivray* looked every inch the predator, except for her lack of firepower.

'Not yet,' Dumas said. 'But we'll add those once we complete her fitting out in another port.' The gentlemanly drawl cracked as he leaned closer. 'Your damned British government wants us to win but won't break the neutrality laws. Don't you all understand that together we could whip the Yankees from here to Christmas and back?' Dumas's voice rose an octave. 'With your industrial might, your Royal Navy, and our soldiers, this war would be over in months. You're all afraid of the Yankees in case they take Canada!'

Watters thought of the battered men who had worn the faded scarlet in campaigns from Quebec to the Crimea and Salamanca to Serangipatam. He thought of the stubborn squares at Waterloo and the incredible advance at Minden, the smoke and mist at Inkerman, and the ragged handful who died at Gandamack. 'Afraid?' His laughter mocked Dumas. 'Man, you know little about us and understand less. Afraid!' He laughed again, deliberately taunting the Confederate.

When Dumas hit him, casually, as an abstract gesture that had little meaning, Watters spat blood onto the deck. Isabella Navarino would hate her ship being sullied in that manner. *Good.* He spat again, making sure some of the blood spattered on Dumas's immaculate boots. 'You're a hero with a hundred men at your back, Dumas. I wonder what you'd be like one to one.'

When Dumas stalked away, Drummond touched his shoulder holster. *Was that a threat? Probably.*

Smoke poured from the twin funnels as *Alexander MacGillivray* steered closer and then came to a skilful halt. Crewmen lined the decks of both vessels, with *Pluton* rocking in *Alexander MacGillivray's* wash. When Isabella Navarino snapped a quick order, a boat pushed out to return with two men from the steamship. With *Pluton*'s low freeboard, the men scrambled aboard handily, and the taller of the two looked Watters full in the face.

'What the devil is he doing here?' With his knee-length black coat half open and a top hat balanced on his head, William Caskie looked out of place on *Pluton*, although he stood rock solid despite the lively motion of the brig.

'We picked him up a couple of days ago,' Dumas said. 'He was in a small boat.'

Watters had never seen such a mixture of expressions cross a man's face in such a short space of time. First, there was rage, then doubt, then a hint of relief, followed by fear that was replaced with renewed anger that warned Watters of the blow to come. He ducked beneath it, leaving William Caskie floundering on deck, but Dumas grabbed him until Caskie recovered for a second swipe.

'I have brought you a fine ship,' Caskie said at last.

'And him?' Dumas indicated Watters.

Caskie shrugged. 'Do whatever you like with him. It is of no concern to me.'

'He might have information,' Dumas said.

Caskie threw Watters a look of contempt. 'He's only a sergeant. He knows nothing.'

Watters was not surprised that the second man who had boarded was James Bulloch.

'Good day, Sergeant.' Bulloch gave a small bow. 'You seem to be in an unfortunate position today. Such is the fickle nature of war.'

'I'm not at war,' Watters said.

Bulloch sighed. 'I'm afraid *we* are, Sergeant.' He turned to Dumas. 'He's no danger to us here, Mr Dumas. Just let him watch. He is a minor complication. It is far more important that we get *Alexander MacGillivray* manned and moving for we are far too close to the British coast for my liking. The last thing we need is a confrontation with the Royal Navy.'

'That would be unwelcome,' Dumas agreed.

Watters had already guessed that the huge crew on *Pluton* was intended for *Alexander MacGillivray*. Dumas had presumably used *Pluton* as a mobile base while he kept an eye on progress in the shipyard, returning to some foreign port to collect a crew for the handover. Judging by the dominant language in the mixture of nationalities on board, Dumas had used a French port, which tied in with the ship's appearance. Watters wondered briefly how much of Charlotte's French honeymoon had been pleasure for William and how much business.

The handover was accomplished with impressive professionalism. As *Pluton*'s crew transferred to *Alexander MacGillivray*, the seamen who had brought her this far crossed to *Pluton*, so for half an hour, there was an interchange of sailors, all of whom seemed intent on outdoing the others in shouting cheerful banter. Only William Caskie seemed harassed as he travelled back and forth between the two vessels, giving orders in English and French.

'Open the hatch covers,' Caskie ordered as he stood on *Pluton's* deck. 'Get the merchandise out!'

Watters watched with interest as half a dozen seamen hauled out a score of large cases from *Pluton's* two holds.

'Careful with these, damn you,' Caskie grated as the first case swung perilously close to the mainmast. 'I've paid a lot of money for them!'

'Mr Beaumont's money, I believe, Caskie,' Watters said. 'You're as close as dammit to bankruptcy.' Caskie's glower was very satisfying.

Isabella Navarino manoeuvred *Pluton* so close to *Alexander MacGillivray* that the yardarms of both vessels were nearly touching, making the passage from one to the other so much the easier.

'What's in the cases?' Watters asked.

'That's none of your damned business.' One of the crew reinforced his words with a blow that sent Watters staggering to the deck. 'We should toss you overboard like your friend.'

What would Caskie pick up in France? Remembering Caskie's connections on the Continent, Watters guessed the cases would hold armaments of some kind. The chess-board had been cleared away, and Caskie was playing a much more dangerous game for a purse-starved merchant in a neutral country. Caskie was gambling with Beaumont's money on a high-stakes table.

A handful of uniformed officers assumed charge of *Alexander MacGillivray*, giving a rapid sequence of commands that saw the crates bundled below. More orders sent the hands scurrying to their positions.

'You stay there,' Drummond snarled at Watters. 'You two!' He pointed to the jug-eared seaman and a lanky man with a permanent scowl. 'Take this and watch him. If he tries anything, put a bullet in his belly.' Drummond handed over his Colt.

The jug-eared handled the Colt as if it was an extension of his arm. 'You're a lawman,' he said. 'I don't like lawmen.' He perched on the rail, evidently hoping that Watters would try to escape. His companion crossed his arms and glared, making himself look even uglier than nature had intended.

Once the transfer of crews was complete, the boats carried more bundles and casks, kegs and chests, some of which Watters recognised as bearing the stamp of the French government and he guessed held small arms and ammunition. He saw a brief exchange of documents between William, Dumas, and Bulloch, and then somebody jerked a thumb to him. His two guards dragged him into a small boat.

'You can sail with the Confederates, Watters,' Caskie leaned over the side of *Pluton*, 'or you can shake hands with Davy Jones. You're too much damned trouble to be allowed back in Dundee. The Confederates might keep hold of you until the end of the war, or press gang you into their navy. I don't know.' He shrugged. 'And frankly, I don't care. Good day to you, sir.' Caskie tipped the rim of his hat in a mocking salute and then sauntered along the deck as Watters was ferried across to *Alexander MacGillivray*.

While the crew was as varied a collection of maritime vagabonds as Watters had ever seen, the officer who surveyed him was immaculately dressed in a grey uniform with twin stars on the shoulder. The weak sun gleamed from the double row of brass buttons down his coat.

'I am Commander Black. You appear to be a most unfortunate gentleman,' the officer said. 'But now you can change your luck.'

Force of habit had forced Watters to attention. He said nothing.

Commander Black adjusted the angle of his peaked cap. The sunlight glinted on the gold rim. 'We are about to embark on a cruise to fight against the tyranny of the United States. You are now part of our crew. We pay $12 a month for landsmen, $14 for ordinary seamen, and $18 for trained seamen. If you obey orders and do your duty, you will find life on board pleasant.'

Watters grunted. He had not eaten, shaved, nor washed for days, so his temper was not of the sweetest. 'Obey orders? I am a British subject, not a Confederate seaman. I demand that you put me ashore.'

'Do you wish to volunteer aboard *CSS Alexander MacGillivray*?' Commander Black spoke quietly, man to man. 'If I were you, I'd be grateful to Captain Edwards.' He nodded to a large, bearded officer who had taken over command. 'Mr Dumas wanted to throw you overboard; as a member of Captain Edwards's crew, you'll be fed and treated like a man.'

Watters looked over his shoulder to see *Pluton* heading under all sail for the Scottish coast. From this angle, she was beautiful, heeling over to starboard with the spray rising from her bows. Sunlight picked out the white and blue paint on her stern.

'Well? Come along, sailor!' Commander Black's drawl sharpened.

Already *Pluton* was a quarter of a mile distant, merging with the grey haze that rose from the surface of the sea. Her masts seemed to wave a dismal farewell. Watters watched, knowing that he could do nothing but unwilling to look away. One of the crew, a tow-headed man with broad shoulders, looked over to him, winked, and gave a gap-toothed grin. 'Come on, mate, join the Confederate Navy, good grub, good treatment, and a chance to fight the bloody Yankees.' His words may have come straight from the South, but his accent was more Shoreditch than Savannah.

'Join the Confederate Navy?' The masts of *Pluton* were diminishing with distance, leaving only the rising grey haze and the practicalities of the present. Watters shrugged his shoulders. 'Why not? I've already been a Royal Marine and a policeman. Why not serve in a Confederate man of war?'

'Good man!' Commander Black held out his hand in a gesture that Watters found nearly incredible in a uniformed service. 'You have seagoing experience, you say? That's a rare thing among this bunch. The South has a fine army but a shortage of seamen, so you are doubly welcome.'

Marie will be worried sick. I can't do anything yet, but the first chance I get, I will contact her.

Apart from Marie and Willie Murdoch, there were few Dundonians who might miss him. Police officers were not the most popular people on the planet. It seemed likely that the South would win the war, so a cruise of a few months followed by disbandment after the war was not too bad. Then he would find a ship for Glasgow or Leith or Dundee and be home again. *I have to try to contact Marie.*

'Aye, sir.' Watters threw a salute. 'Let's hunt a few Yankees!' There was no sign of *Pluton*. She had vanished into the haze.

'Come and get your uniform, mate,' the gap-toothed Londoner invited. 'This way!'

The petty officer in charge of clothing was breaking open bales of uniforms to hand out to the crew, who formed a disorderly queue beside Watters. 'Cloth pants – jumper, two pairs of woollen socks, a jacket, and a round, dark, grey cap, a pea jacket, blue flannel underdrawers, undershirt, and a black, silk neckerchief!'

Watters heaped the pile of clothes in his arms, remembering his first few days in the Royal Marines when he had been a raw seventeen-year-old with bright eyes and an idealistic view of the world.

'You'll need fed,' the Londoner chirped. 'Come on mate! I'm Ted Houghton, by the way.'

'George Watters.' Watters held out his hand. 'Good to meet a fellow Briton.'

'Oh, there's a few of us on board,' Ted said. 'I'll introduce you to a couple later.' He grinned again. 'You'll feel at home here in no time.'

Ship's biscuits and French cheese was not the best food Watters had eaten, but sustenance gave him the strength to continue. Ted accompanied him, making cheerful comments as Watters changed from his battered land clothing to his new uniform.

'My wife gave me this.' Rather shame-faced, Watters held up his New Testament.

'Nothing better than the Book.' Ted gestured to Watters's new clothes. 'You're lucky, mate; not many Confederate seamen are so well supplied. You've even got a spare shirt there. You'll have to pay for it, of course. All this will cost you around $100—near six months' pay.'

Watters nodded. At that moment, he did not care if he was paid or not, or whether he fought the Federal Navy, Burmese dacoits, the Russians, or the Grenadier Guards. He just wanted to get news to Marie.

Extending to his waist, the eighteen-button monkey jacket was comfortingly warm. Once he slipped the jacket on, Watters felt less of an outsider in the crew. That was the point of a uniform, he knew. Uniformity helped individuals to fit into the common mass.

With the crew on board, *Alexander MacGillivray* steamed out of British waters and steered westward and south into the German Ocean. Black rated Watters an Ordinary Seaman and handed him a paintbrush and a pot of grey paint. 'Now you can start to earn your pay.'

'Aye, aye, sir.' Watters looked around; he saw only the misty sea.

'Start painting at the bow and work your way astern.' The petty officer was a tall Swede. 'Don't leave any holidays.'

The petty officer swaggered away, shouting, as another man joined Watters.

'Swede sez as we've to paint her.' The man was leathery-skinned, with an egg-bald head and tattoos of mermaids on both forearms. His accent was pure Liverpool.

Shrugging, Watters obeyed, slapping grey paint onto grey iron while the grey sea surged past. One job was like another, one boss like another, one day like another. Do what you are told and like it. When one was at the bottom of the pile, such was the way of the world in every culture.

They painted in companionable silence as *Alexander MacGillivray* thrust through seas as sombre as Watters's thoughts.

'Here we are, mate.' Ted's grin seemed permanent as he perched himself on an iron stanchion. He bit into a hunk of tobacco. 'I see you've met Scouse.'

Scouse offered a hand like a gorilla, although his grip was surprisingly gentle.

'This other blackguard,' Ted nodded to a rangy man who stood behind him, 'is Niner.'

Niner nodded his wind-reddened face while surveying Watters through chillingly cold blue eyes.

'The name Scouse I understand,' Watters said. 'You're from Liverpool.'

Scouse nodded. 'Paradise Street,' he said in a husky croak. 'I worked on the Black Ball line to Boston.'

'Ah, you were a Packet Rat,' Watters said. A packet ship was one that sailed between two ports on a fixed route. The packet ships between Liverpool and Boston had a reputation for speed and brutal seamanship. That made Scouse one of the toughest seamen afloat.

'Niner?' Watters shook his head. 'I can't figure that name out.'

'It's short for Forty Niner,' Niner said. 'I was in the first rush for gold in California.' He snorted. 'Never found a single nugget and ended up at sea.' Niner looked up. 'I should have stayed ashore.' He shrugged. 'It's too bloody late now.'

'So where are we headed?' Watters wanted to know.

'As far as I know, we're sailing to some Prussian port.' Ted gave the answer without hesitation. 'We're getting armed there. Scuttlebutt says we're getting guns by Krupp's, with some of these Prussian needle guns for close work. By the time we're finished, *Alex* will be a match for any ship in the Federal Fleet—too fast for the heavy vessels to catch and too powerful for the smaller ones to fight. It's honour and glory for us and victory for the Confederate States of America!'

Watters looked aloft where *Alexander MacGillivray's* flags flapped in the growing wind. It felt strange to sail under Confederate colours, with the Stars and Bars bold against the dirty sky and the commission pennant streaming from the mainmast. Twice they passed close to merchant vessels, but the captain did not deviate from his course. *Alex* was flush decked and fast, her wake arrow-straight and Captain Edwards alert in the stern. Surprisingly, Edwards also walked the deck, speaking to the men.

'You're that British lawman that decided to join us?' Edwards had a neat grey beard and sharp grey eyes that suited his uniform.

'I didn't have much choice,' Watters said.

Edwards gave a small smile. 'Do any of us have a choice? Fate intervenes. Man proposed but God disposes. Good luck on board.' He nodded and strode on, hands behind his back and eyes busy with the cut of his ship.

'I want these masts raked further aft! We can go faster than this, by God!'

Watters knew that the German Ocean was busy with vessels, from fishing boats to Prussian traders and the ubiquitous British brigs, so he did not look up as one more ship hove into view.

'That's the Royal Navy, damnit.' Ted's London accent grated as he scurried across the deck. 'Best warn the captain.'

Watters stopped painting. 'We're in international waters, aren't we? The Navy can't touch us.'

Ted snorted. 'The Royal Navy can do anything they damn well please, mate. I should know; I served with them for ten bloody years.'

Almost immediately, *Alexander MacGillivray* increased speed. At once, the Royal Naval ship altered course towards them, sails straining before the wind and a bone splendid in her jaws.

'She's gaining.' Ted could not keep the pride from his voice. 'Look at her shift! Her captain's reaching for every puff of this breeze, is he not? I don't recognise her; I don't recognise her at all!'

As the Naval vessel came close, *Alexander MacGillivray* powered forward. Perhaps Captain Edwards had been toying with the Royal Navy to see how close she could get, but now Rogers's ship revealed her true speed.

'That's the way, Captain! Put a fire in her tail!' Ted exulted, but still watched astern, where the Royal Naval ship was dropping toward the horizon. 'She made us change course, though. Captain Edwards will take that bad, I reckon.'

Despite her advantage in speed, *Alexander MacGillivray* seemed unable to shake off the Royal Navy. Every time she returned to her original course, a lookout would shout a warning, and the topmasts of the Royal Navy thrust up from the horizon.

'Persistent bugger, isn't he?' Ted grinned at Watters. 'Typical Navy, stiff-necked, stiff-lipped, and stiff on the seas.' He looked upward as another mast pierced the horizon. 'There's the Navy again!'

'How does she know where we're headed?'

'That's a different ship; there must be a flotilla out, probably an exercise and the commodore got inquisitive! The Navy-boys captains will probably have years of experience in chasing pirates and slavers or whatnot.' Ted grinned. 'They can't fire on us, though, but I'll wager that the Commodore wants to see who and what we are.'

'They're treating us like game on the moor.' Watters looked around. This Royal Naval squadron was driving them, appearing at different points of the compass to usher *Alexander MacGillivray* before them.

'Could be.' Ted shrugged, bit off a hunk from a quid of tobacco before offering the remainder to Watters, who refused. 'No? Tobacco keeps the blood clean.'

By nightfall, it was apparent that the Royal Navy was serious. They seemed to hover just below the horizon, appearing at different angles every time that *Alexander MacGillivray* attempted to alter course. 'Blasted Navy. Ever since Nelson, they think they rule the bloody sea.' Ted had been painting alongside Watters. 'We'll lose them at night, then it's hi-ho for Prussia, and we get our guns. Then we'll show the world and these blasted Yanks. Pay them back for 1812, eh?'

'1812?'

Ted shook his head. 'Don't they teach you any history in Scotland? We was fighting Napoleon Bonaparte, wasn't we? We was trying to save Europe from his tyranny when the bloody Yanks joined in. Took half a dozen ships when our back was turned, then threw up their hands and clamoured for peace as soon as we had Boney licked and we could fight them proper. They wanted Canada, but we burned their White House for them. This time, we'll do more.'

'We? Britain?' Watters pretended confusion, probing to see how much of the international situation Ted understood.

Ted shrugged. 'Sure. Once this ship starts to run amuck, the Yanks will be red raw that a British-built ship caused so much destruction. They'll demand retribution and attack our merchant shipping, so the Navy will sort them out proper this time.'

Watters grunted. 'What about the slaves? Lots of people won't want to fight alongside the slave states.'

'They'll just have to do as they're told, won't they?' Ted's voice hardened. 'Obey lawful authority, same as the rest of us. If they don't like it, then they can lump it for all I care.'

When night fell, *Alexander MacGillivray* showed her riding lights and altered course due south, doused her lights, turned, and headed north. Watters noted that Captain Edwards had her sailing slowly so that the white froth of their wake would not gleam through the dark. Twice the lookout reported seeing the shine of moonlight on canvas, but *Alexander MacGillivray* steamed on in near silence with her sails furled. In common with most of the crew, Watters and Ted were sent below. In the darkness of pre-dawn, they altered course again, but when the first pink-grey streaks lightened the sky, the warship lay right across their path, her guns levelled, and the flag of the United States limp but recognisable on her stern.

'All hands to battle stations!' The order came.

CHAPTER TWENTY
GERMAN OCEAN:
NOVEMBER 1862

'That's not good,' Ted said. 'And us without our main armament.'

'Do we fight?' Watters wondered.

'What with?' Ted asked.

'You men! Stand ready!' Commander Black ordered.

'Ready for what?' Watters asked, without receiving a reply.

'Put about! Full speed!' The order from the quarterdeck was distinct as *Alexander MacGillivray* used her twin screws to turn sharply before the Federal warship could fire. White smoke jetted out, and tall fountains of water rose from the exact spot where *Alexander MacGillivray* had been only minutes before.

'Good shooting,' Ted sounded laconic, 'but she won't catch us.'

The Federal warship fired again, the shots screaming overhead to raise more waterspouts a quarter of a mile away. Commander Black ran aft with a Sharp's rifle, aimed, and fired a single shot before Edwards snarled another order and *Alexander MacGillivray* jinked to port.

Some of the crew cheered when a drift of wind ruffled the Confederate saltire, with the weak, winter sunlight picking out the red, blue, and white.

'Nice flag,' Watters said.

'Nice enough.' Ted looked aloft. 'But it doesn't feel right, somehow, fighting under foreign colours.'

Another salvo crashed close by, raising a tall column of water, which remained upright for a long moment before thundering down on deck. 'Watch my blasted paintwork!' Ted swore and shook a fist toward the pursuing Federal warship. 'Jesus! What's Captain Edwards up to? What's he doing now?'

Alexander MacGillivray veered sharply to starboard, steering right through another salvo that shook the ship and sprayed splinters across the deck.

'That's why.' Watters pointed ahead, where another vessel emerged from the rising sun.

The second ship was low and lean, with side paddles that churned the sea into froth. Her guns immediately opened up. Now *Alexander MacGillivray* had to show her speed as both vessels closed in on her from opposite angles with their guns raising columns of water and spray all around.

The first Federal ship altered shape as she presented her broadside, then she disappeared behind a gush of white smoke. Watters counted the seconds before there was a succession of whines all around, and huge waterspouts rose, rattling the fabric of the ship.

'Bugger!' Watters swore.

'And more than bugger,' Ted said, grinning. 'But the Yank has lost a lot of distance firing her broadside guns like that. She won't make that up again.'

Alexander MacGillivray surged on, Captain Edwards using both screws to make a rapid series of course alterations that seemed to confuse the Federal vessels for their next two volleys were far short.

'We'll do it!' Ted waved his fist defiantly at the nearest Federal vessel.

As if in reply to Ted, the next shot landed a cables-length astern, skipped across the waves, crashed against *Alexander MacGillivray's* counter, and bounced off the steel plate.

Commander Black walked briskly along the deck. 'Break out the arms,' he shouted. 'Mr Dumas, it's time to see if your fancy machines work.'

For the first time since the chase began, Dumas appeared, holding his wide-awake hat and strapping on a pair of long revolvers, which looked more theatrical than useful in this long-range battle.

'You men! Did you not hear me? Do something useful!' Black pointed to Watters.

'Aye, aye, sir,' Watters responded automatically.

As Edwards ordered an erratic course to avoid the Federal fire, Dumas supervised the unpacking of one of the crates that *Pluton* had carried, with Black snarling orders at the men. Watters helped lever up the brass bands that held the wooden planking together, grunting at the familiar, sharp tang of gun oil.

'Get this thing unpacked fast!' Dumas glanced over his shoulder as one of the Federal vessels fired again, with the shot screaming overhead.

A scramble of seamen unloaded various pieces of machinery, all coated in thick, yellow grease.

'Never mind the muck! Lay them on the deck.' Dumas raised his voice to be heard above the constant thunder of the engines, the whine of the wind, and the continuous slap and surge of the sea.

'Captain Edwards will hate this mess on his deck.' Ted gave his gap-toothed grin.

'Stand aside!' Dumas began to piece the machinery together.

Alexander MacGillivray made a hard turn to port, followed by one to starboard, avoiding the next salvo from the Federal vessels by a good three cables' lengths.

'We're getting away,' Ted said. 'Old Captain Edwards has got their measure!'

'What is this thing?' Scouse asked as Dumas continued to fit the pieces together.

'It's a *Montigny mitrailleuse*,' Watters said quietly. *Now I know why William Caskie had been in France.*

'A what?' Scouse stared at Watters. 'A Monty Mitrally? What does it do?'

'It's a machine that fires bullets faster than a dozen rifles at once,' Watters said. 'A very charming Belgian gentleman named Joseph Montigny has been working on it for the past few years.'

Dumas glowered at him. 'Have you ever seen one, Watters?'

'Never,' Watters admitted.

'Well, you're going to be firing one soon. Give me a hand here.'

'What the hell does *mitrailleuse* mean?' Niner asked.

'It means grapeshot shooter,' Watters said. 'Another Belgian fellow invented it back in '51, a fifty-barrelled volley gun. This one is an improvement.'

'This weapon is a prototype,' Dumas was surprisingly forthcoming, 'and one that will help win the war for the South. I've bought thirty examples, each one capable of winning a battle on its own.' He stood up when two of the machines were assembled. The Federal vessels were closer than before. 'As you can see, the weapon is crank operated. You wind that lever and the barrels turn, firing a constant stream of bullets at the enemy. These are revolutionary devices, adapted from the original by a Frenchman named Jean-Baptiste Verchere de Reffye.'

'Another charming fellow.' Watters remembered Amy's words.

'We slide in the magazine plate into the breech like so,' Dumas demonstrated, 'lock it in place with this hinged loading lever at the rear, aim, and turn the crank.' He slapped the breech. 'As you see, there are thirty-seven barrels inside the casing, and when we turn the handle, all the barrels fire. With luck, the operator can fire 150 rounds a minute. With skill, he can fire more.'

Black glared at the greasy, wondering men. 'This thing's damned heavy, so it'll need all of your muscle power to move it. I want one of these machines in the port bow and one in the starboard quarter.'

Seamen were vastly experienced in moving heavy weights with block and tackle, so despite the constant firing from the Federal warships, they had the *mitrailleuse* in position within a few moments.

In the time it had taken Dumas to prepare his wonder weapon, the Federal warships had approached to barely a quarter of a mile, with gun smoke hazing the Stars and Stripes that flew proudly from their mizzens.

On a word from Captain Edwards, *Alexander MacGillivray* slowed further, allowing the Federal warships to close.

'Throw a cover over these machines and lie down,' Edwards shouted. 'Now lower the flag but keep it handy.'

'We're not surrendering!'

Ted's cry swept the ship from stern to stem. 'We're not surrendering to the Yankees.'

As the Confederate flag fluttered down, both Federal ships stopped firing and crept closer. Watters could see the officers grouped in the stern of each, examining *Alexander MacGillivray* through extended telescopes.

'Here they come,' Ted murmured.

Dumas swore. 'I wish we had time to train the men on these damned guns.'

Watters grunted. He was not sure what he wanted; if the Federal ships won, he could be a prisoner of the North for months, and if the Confederates won, he could be forced to fight for them for the same period of time. He could also be killed. Instinctively, he touched his New Testament and wished he could contact Marie.

The Federal ships parted, with one coming to the stern of *Alexander MacGillivray* and the other to the bows. The Federal officer's telescopes scanned the Confederate's deck, focussed on the canvas covered machines, and moved on, wary of a trap.

'They're closing.' Dumas stood in the centre of the deck, allowing himself to be seen as he gave orders to the prone men. 'On my word, rise up, pull the covers from the *mitrailleuse*, and fire at the closest enemy ship. They have boarding parties massed ready. That's your mark.'

Lying on the deck with the canvas cover on top of him and the vibration of the ship beneath, Watters felt the tension rise. *What the devil am I doing here, fighting in another country's civil war that had no interest to me whatever?*

'Ready… Ready… Now!' The instant Dumas shouted the order, the lying men leapt to their feet, dragging away the canvas covers. The Federal vessels were within ten cables' length, efficient-looking ships with the sea breaking in silver spray around their bows. Boarding parties crowded amidships.

'Flag!' Captain Edwards roared. Eager hands hauled the Confederate flag back aloft. For a second, it hung limp, and then a gust of wind opened it to blaze its colours against the leaden northern sky.

'Shoot!' Dumas shouted. 'Shoot the Yankees flat!'

Two Confederate seamen were first to the *mitrailleuse*, aiming and turning the crank even as Dumas said the last word. At that range, they could not miss. Watters saw the bullets spray into the crowd of would-be boarders. He saw some fall, saw a thin film of blood rise from the impact of the bullets on frail human flesh, and heard a chorus of shouts, shrieks, and yells. Then the *mitrailleuse* stopped.

'Reload!' Dumas ordered. 'For God's own sake, reload!'

Clumsy hands worked the machine, but the Federal vessel had halved the distance between them before the *mitrailleuse* fired again. Once more, the bullets spattered along the wooden deck of the Federal ship, and then Captain Edwards shouted, 'Hard aport and full steam ahead. Ram them!'

Alexander MacGillivray surged to port, aiming at the closest of the Federal vessels. The Confederate crew cheered wildly, with the men at the stern *mitrailleuse* loading and firing again, missing their target as both ships manoeuvred on the choppy sea.

'We're going to get away!' somebody shouted.

The explosion came from inside the ship, rocking her to starboard, ripping a hole in the deck and sending a fountain of metal shards upwards. There was immediate pandemonium, a chorus of yells and curses.

'What the devil?' Dumas looked stunned as *Alexander MacGillivray* slewed round with smoke gushing from the gaping hole amidships.

'They've hit us.' Scouse sounded as calm as if he was ordering a round in a Scotland Road public house.

'What's happened? The Federals haven't fired!' Ted looked at Watters. 'What's happened?'

'I'm blessed if I know,' Watters said as the Federals took advantage of the situation to circle away from *Alexander MacGillivray's* ram and unleash a broadside that clattered and clanged against the Confederate vessel's steel sides.

Another explosion sounded from below, tearing an enormous hole in *Alexander MacGillivray's* bow and sending murderous splinters of steel cascading along the deck. Somebody below began to scream, high pitched and hopeless, and the Federal warships fired again. Solid shot hammered against the hull, bouncing back into the water but doing no damage save to increase the confusion on board.

A man ran past Watters, moaning and holding a hand to his shattered face. The jug-eared Confederate lay on the deck, staring stupidly at what remained of his legs. The screaming from below reached a crescendo, stopped, and started again. More shots battered against the Confederate ship, and someone yelled that they surrendered. Commander Black had lifted his Sharps rifle and was firing back, ignoring the carnage all around him. 'I'll show you, Yankee pirates. I'll teach you,' and then he was gone, carried clean away by a cannonball.

More cannonballs crashed and rattled along the deck, more shells exploded, more water erupted alongside, more men screamed, until Watters found himself lying beside the rail, wondering what had happened as red-stained sea water hissed and bubbled past him. There were further explosions, the acrid sting of smoke in Watters's throat, and rapid footsteps on the deck. Someone was shouting 'lower that damned rebel flag,' and a man scrambled aloft to fall as somebody shot him. Watters heard rifle fire, sharper than the previous cannon, the distinctive crack of a revolver, and polished boots tramped beside his face.

'Up, you rebel bastard!' The boots moved as the owner kicked him hard in the ribs. 'Get up, damn your hide!'

Rough hands hauled Watters upright. He stared into the lean face of a young man in the blue uniform of the Federal Navy. 'Join the rest!' Somebody shoved him forward, where he collapsed at the feet of a bunch of smoke-blackened, shocked survivors of *Alexander MacGillivray's* maiden voyage.

'You all right, mate?' Ted sounded concerned as he knelt down. 'You was out for a bit there.'

'We were beating them.' Watters was still dazed. 'We were beating them until there was an explosion inside the ship.'

'Nah.' Ted shook his head. 'I thought that, but it was just the Federal's shells. See the corvette there? Fine looking ship; I wonder if they want any recruits.'

Watters later heard that the Federal corvette was a sister to the new *Tuscarora*, with nine powerful guns including two pivoting eleven-inch columbiads, six broadside cannon, and a rifled Parrot. The corvette did not linger but got steam up, raised her sails, and sailed away as soon as the paddle steamer had the smoking wreck of *Alexander MacGillivray* secure.

The Federal crew were efficient, searching every quarter of their prize, taking note of everything and comparing their prisoners with the crew manifest. A petty officer ran an expert eye over what remained of the Confederate ship before he stepped over to Watters.

'Name?'

Still dazed, Watters could only mumble his name.

'Watters? Who the hell are you?' the petty officer said. 'You're not on the list.'

'A volunteer recruit,' Ted said. 'He just signed on yesterday.'

'Put him with the rest.'

One of the younger Federal officers looked at Watters through narrow eyes as he was hustled away below to be crammed into another storeroom packed with barrels, boxes, and dejected sailors. Some men nursed wounds, from the minor cuts and bruises that were common on board any ship to obscene horrors caused by shellfire. Scouse looked up, shrugged, and looked away. Niner sat in a corner, staring at the ground. In a clear area in the centre of the room, two severely wounded men gasped their way to death.

Watters slumped in a corner between a sobbing Frenchman and a barrel of tar. Some voyage this had been, from *Joyce* to gun-runner to would-be-Confederate warship to Federal paddle steamer all in the space of three days. Rather than solve the murder on *Lady of Blackness*, he would be a prisoner in some festering Federal camp for the foreseeable future.

Ted winked at him. 'All right, mate? Chin up; you're alive, aren't you? Lots of lads aren't so fortunate.'

'You're cheerful enough, anyway.'

'Always the optimist, that's my motto.' Ted handed over a bite of tobacco. 'And why not? What's the use of being downhearted? I've worked the Thames barges, been a hand in a New South Wales convict ship, a bluejacket, and a Confederate seaman. I even worked for the United States once.' He eyed Watters for a second. 'There's not much difference between the lot of them. Hard work and hard knocks, and at the end, a trip down to Davy Jones's Locker.' He chewed vigorously. 'So what does it matter where you are and what you do, eh?'

Watters said nothing. For the past few weeks, he had reacted, rather than acted, allowing others to control his life with the result that he was now a prisoner in a war of which he knew and understood little. 'Bugger it,' he decided. 'I'm going home.'

'Good for you, mate.' Ted was jammed against him, chewing mightily. 'And I hope that she's worth it.'

The thought of Marie worrying about him made Watters's situation worse. 'I have to get back.'

'Too late now, mate. We're heading south, and at some speed, to judge by the racket.'

Watters could hear the different beat of the paddles as they thrashed the water. In this mechanical age, speed was everything, from the frenzy of the mills to this mad dash by a steamship. All of life centred on ever-increasing velocity with no room for thought.

After a few worrying hours, a surly Federal seaman fed them standard Navy rations, which Watters found as bad as he expected. Some of the men lit pipes, threw the spent matches on the deck, and began to grumble. Leaning back, Watters rubbed his face with its three-day accumulation of beard. He closed his eyes; sleep was as important as food to fortify him against the hard times he was sure lay ahead.

Watters did not know what woke him. It might have been a sound, or perhaps it was his policeman's instinct. He only knew that something tore him from dreams filled with the sound of gunfire and the screams of wounded men. He lay still for a moment, unsure where he was or what he should be doing.

Two uniformed seamen had entered the cabin and were standing over Ted. Watters balled his fists, ready to jump to the rescue until he saw Ted rise willingly to leave with the seamen. Scouse and Niner followed only a step behind. They closed the door and locked it quietly behind them.

What was all that about?

With his police instincts thoroughly roused, Watters stepped carefully over the prostrate bodies of his companions to reach the door. He had heard the key turn in the lock but had not heard it withdraw. Kneeling, he peered into the lock, nodding in quiet satisfaction when he saw the key tip blocking the light. He was in a store cabin, not a police cell; the key and lock had been designed to frustrate casual seamen, not a man with his experience of the criminal underworld. If he had brought his tools with him, Watters could have picked the lock in seconds. As it was, he lifted one of the spent matches, split it in two and inserted the ends into the lock.

While his usual tool for this kind of delicate operation was a pair of long-nosed pliers, the split match was better than nothing. The wood was far too lightweight, but Watters persevered, with the smoky, stuffy room bringing beads of sweat to his forehead until the key turned with an audible click. Watters crouched for a long moment, hoping that nobody had heard the sound, although with the creaks and shudders of a moving paddle-steamer that was unlikely. Only when he was sure it was safe did he slowly, cautiously, open the door a crack. He peered outside; there was no sentry. Watters slipped through, closing the door behind him. He was in a long, dark corridor with a single lantern casting dim light as it swayed with the rhythm of the ship.

Now he was outside the storeroom, what should he do? Watters considered his options. His first was to find somewhere to hide in the ship, although he knew every square inch of the warship would be utilised. The second option was to slip over the side and swim for shore. Although Watters was a fair swimmer, the ship might be a hundred miles out to sea, so such a course could be suicidal. His third was the best: if he were fortunate, there would be a dinghy or other small boat. If he were very fortunate, the dinghy would be equipped with water and ship's biscuits.

Listening for the sound of footsteps or voices, Watters walked through the ship until he reached a companionway that stretched upwards. Taking a deep breath, he climbed the steps to a closed, varnished door, listened for voices, heard none, opened the door, and breathed deeply of air mingled with salt and soot.

Watters found himself on a deck smeared with sooty smuts from the smokestack. Cold winter air blasted him, while the constant beat of the paddles thrust the ship onward through grey waves tipped with silver white. Seabirds kept pace with the ship; their wingtips quivering.

Watters glanced along the deck. The officer of the watch stood on the starboard paddle-box, staring through a telescope. The steersman was in the stern, too concentrated on his task to notice a stray seaman wandering around the deck.

Sitting near the steersman, the captain's dinghy invited Watters's closer inspection. If he could get the dinghy into the sea, he might be able to reach land somewhere. It did not matter where it was; anywhere would be better than a Federal prison. Watters slipped closer to the dinghy. He frowned when he realised that professional hands had ensured her lashings were stiff. It was years since Watters had worked with maritime knots, and he was struggling to unfasten them when footsteps sounded.

Swearing softly, he looked up. A young midshipman was marching purposefully along the deck with his arms swinging and his hat squared on his head. A file of marines stepped at his back.

Still cursing, Watters sunk down and crawled away. He neither knew nor cared why the midshipman was leading his marines. He only knew they had interrupted what may be his only chance of escaping.

Opening the nearest door, Watters slid down a companionway to find himself in a small corridor with three plain, unvarnished wooden doors. One had the name 'Captain' embossed on a brass plate.

Where now? Watters glanced urgently around.

The corridor remained thankfully empty with a single shaded lantern swinging with the motion of the ship. Hearing the murmur of voices in the captain's cabin, Watters tried the door opposite, found it locked, and slid inside the cabin next to the captain's.

Watters gasped his relief when he found the room unoccupied. Two cots and a single desk took up most of the space with a pair of sea-chests filling the rest. Watters could hear people moving about in the cabin next door and the distinct murmur of voices. With nowhere else to go, he sat on a cot, aware of the constant churn of the paddles and the swish of the sea against the hull. The voices continued.

'Beaumont.'

The name had been repeated at least three times before the significance dawned on Watters. Squeezing as close to the thin bulkhead as he could, he listened to the voices.

'I don't agree with that at all.'

The reply was muffled, and Watters cursed his earlier inattention.

The first voice sounded again, the New England accent distinct. 'My orders are to drop you off in London and return. No more.'

Again the mumble, but the next words were clear, 'Mount Pleasant.'

The throbbing of the engine combined with the steady thump of the paddles made eavesdropping difficult, so Watters slid outside again and crept to the door of the captain's cabin. There were two voices inside. One belonged to the captain, with the Down East twang nasal and unmistakable. The second was more gentle and slower, perhaps from further west.

'I don't agree with murder, damn it, Mr H., or whatever you call yourself!' That was undoubtedly the captain. 'I don't hold with all this underhand subterfuge, and I don't like being used as a ferryboat for a murderer.'

'You fired on a virtually unarmed ship as part of your duty to the Union,' the gentler voice said. 'I will kill this man to help preserve that same Union.'

Who is to be killed? As Watters moved as close as he could, his boots scraped on the deck. He froze, but in a moving steamship, one more noise made little difference. The conversation continued unchecked.

'We're not at war with Great Britain, Mr H.,' that was the captain's voice, 'but actions such as this would provoke one.'

'It's an example,' the gentle speaker said, and with a start, Watters recognised Ted's voice, although with a different accent. *Ted Houghton and Mr H. are one and the same.* 'I want to send an example to all other British merchants that might help the South. We have already tried to destroy his businesses by fire.'

'You failed, sir,' the captain said.

'I relied on amateurs.' That was Ted. 'I will not make that mistake again. The arson attempts were the work of a local abolitionist group who jumped the gun. They should have waited until I supplied the correct equipment, such as this little device.' There was a pause while the speaker obviously showed something to the captain.

'What is that? A new cigar?' The captain's cynicism was apparent.

'Looks like it, doesn't it?' Ted's voice was bland. 'Our people have been working on this for months. It's small enough to fit inside one's pocket but deadly enough to burn down an entire building. I can open it... see?' There was silence for a moment. 'You notice the two com-partments inside? One has sulphuric acid, the other potash. At present, this thin copper membrane separates them. If I push this little button, just here, the acid is free to eat its way through the copper, leaks into the potash, and boom! The thing heats up amazingly, setting fire to everything it touches.'

There was another silence, and then the captain spoke. 'Damn if that isn't the most devilish thing I ever saw. We're fighting to preserve the Union, not burn down Great Britain. I don't like it at all.'

Ted gave a gruff laugh. 'They work. I planted two in the ammunition stored for these French machine rifles on *Alexander MacGillivray*; otherwise, you would never have caught her.'

'We would have caught her.' The words had stung the captain's professional pride.

Watters grunted: *That explains the mysterious explosions on the Confederate ship. So Ted was an agent for the Federal government. Marie was correct; this whole affair had been political all the time.*

Ted spoke again, 'If the people in Dundee had waited until we provided these little beauties, then Beaumont's factories would have all burned to the ground, he would have been ruined, and there would have been no finance for the rebel ship. Instead, they tried arson with matches and old rags.'

'Your scheme failed,' the captain said.

'One man attacked Beaumont's daughter; the Dundee police took notice and slammed most of the abolitionists in the lockup. Their leader is still free. We can still use her.'

'Their leader' and 'we can still use her?' Who might that be? The women who paid Varthley? It could be no other. Who was she? No wonder I have not cracked this case.

The captain sighed. 'This is a sordid business. Have you tried any other methods of damaging this Beaumont fellow?'

'No.'

No? Watters frowned. *How about trying to sink* Lady of Blackness? *Or are you ashamed that you failed there too, Mr H.? Can your pride not cope with another failure?*

Watters listened with disbelief as these men from a civilised, neutral nation calmly planned the murder of a British businessman. It was true that Beaumont was ruthless in business and his financial backing of William Caskie was morally questionable, but Beaumont was not a political animal. His motives were profit based, not vindictive, and that surely was no reason to have him murdered. For one second, Watters contemplated jumping into the captain's cabin and disposing of both men, but sense chased away the red rage. They might be armed, and anyway, Mr H. would be very capable of looking after himself. It would be better to escape somehow and warn Mr Beaumont and the British authorities.

'Hey! You!' The challenge echoed along the corridor. A young ensign was hurrying towards Watters with his face contorted in anger. 'What the hell are you doing, skulking outside the captain's cabin like that?'

Jumping to his feet, Watters knew he had a quick decision to make. Either he could run further into the bowels of the ship or push past the ensign onto the deck. The ensign was young but looked fit, strong, and angry, while to run deeper into the ship would be only to delay the inevitable.

'Out of my way!' Watters charged forward. The ensign blocked his way, but Watters was the more desperate. After a brief struggle, he knocked the ensign to the ground. Then it was a hurried scramble up to the deck and a quick breath of smut-filled air before searching for sanctuary.

There was none. Watters ran his gaze down the deck: a swivel gun fore and aft, four broadside cannons, a main and mizzen mast, a port and starboard paddle box, and four small boats, each one as securely lashed down as the captain's dinghy. The deck of a Federal paddle steamer did not provide a plethora of places in which to hide. Watters heard footsteps behind him as other seamen joined the ensign.

It was dawn, grey and heavy with the promise of rain. A sudden blast of wind swept across the deck. Watters ran aft, hoping for a miracle that he knew would not transpire. His choice was stark, surrender or jump overboard. If he fought, he would be shot, for these Federal seamen would have no time for escaped Confederate prisoners. Watters hesitated, looked at the leaping waves, and then dived back down the hatch that led below. Hearing the clatter of feet behind him, he kept running.

The layout of this warship was unfamiliar, but the basic plan was the same as the vessels on which Watters had sailed. He had expected there to be more crew then remembered that some would have been sent on board the captured *Alexander MacGillivray*. He ducked low, slid down a steel companionway, and scurried along a dimly lit corridor that throbbed and vibrated with the proximity of the engine.

There were more voices ahead, with footsteps echoing along the corridor and the banging of a door. Watters slid through a small hatch, stifling his gasp as he slithered down into utter blackness. He lay still until his eyes adjusted to the gloom of what he realised was an ammunition locker, surrounded by piles of solid shot. Feet clattered past, somebody's voice echoed in the corridor, but Watters waited for a long five minutes before easing open the door.

The corridor was deserted, with only a single vibrating lantern providing light. Watters slipped free, paused for a second, and hurried aft. He could not hide on board for long, so all he could do was try again to free one of the ship's boats to chance the German Ocean. Removing his shoes, he padded quietly toward a companionway and eased upward toward the deck.

'Hey!' The voice startled him, but he controlled his jangling nerves. He looked around, waving a casual hand to the confused-looking able seaman who had challenged him.

'I'm new on board,' Watters explained and moved onto the deck hoping that the dark concealed the colour of his uniform. The officer on watch was well forward, staring into the night, and this time, there was no midshipman or file of efficient marines.

Once again, Watters shivered in the blast of sea air as he moved toward the captain's dinghy. The cover was well lashed down, but he persevered, cursing that he had neither knife nor marline spike with which to free the ropes. He would have to loosen the davit attachments and hope that a final pull would release both at the same time. Sweat streamed from his face as he wrestled with salt-hardened rope, but he untied one before the shout came.

'That's him! That's the rebel!'

Watters was moving before the last word, running below as feet clattered across the deck. He dived back into the chill damp of the corridors, plunging in any direction as he heard the noise of pursuit. There was another corridor ahead, with a cabin door flapping open. Watters slipped in, trod on a surprisingly carpeted deck, and kicked shut the door. He leant against the bulkhead, trying to control his gasping breath in case it could be heard amidst the clamour of the paddle steamer.

There was a desk bolted to the deck, with two wooden chairs and a collection of charts and nautical books. There was also a sextant, a safe, and a file of official documents marked: *US Navy: For the Eyes of the Captain.* Watters swore; he must be in the captain's day cabin; he had run full circle around the ship.

A quick tug at the door of the safe assured him that it was securely locked, while the official documents referred only to the supposed movements of Confederate vessels, highly crucial to the Federal Navy but of no interest to him. Slowly opening the top drawer of the desk, Watters saw a four-inch-long cylindrical case tucked into the side. He had never seen the like before, and he remembered Ted describing a fire-raising device. Perhaps this was to what he referred? Watters grunted, shoved the metal case into his inside breast pocket, and left the cabin. He had no option; he had to try the dinghy again. Cautiously opening the door to the deck, he stepped onto the pristine timber.

'Rebel!'

There were men behind him now, that ubiquitous midshipman with a group of others. The midshipman shouted. 'Get back here! Back or I shoot, y'hear?'

The crack of a revolver sounded immediately after the midshipman's words, but where the shot went, Watters could not tell. Slithering onto the paddle box, he steeled himself to leap. The sea looked cold and grey. Would the Federals accept his surrender when he had been found spying? That was unlikely. Watters looked back; four men were pounding across the deck, the slender Midshipman, Scouse, Niner, and Ted Houghton holding a revolver. Watters swore when Ted stopped to aim.

Ted fired; the bullet gouged a long splinter from the paddle box. No prisoners, then. Taking a deep breath, Watters leapt into the sea as far astern as he could, hearing the revolver crack a third and fourth time as the water closed over him and the churning maelstrom of the paddle's wake caught him, thrust him under, and tossed him around like a cork.

CHAPTER TWENTY-ONE
GERMAN OCEAN:
DECEMBER 1862

Disorientated by the steamer's wake, Watters could not tell in which direction the surface lay until his head emerged. He spat out seawater, gasping as he kicked to keep afloat. The lights of the paddle steamer gleamed two cables-lengths to his right, fading slowly even as he watched. *The blackguards aren't even going to search for me.*

He had no idea how far the coast was, but the steamer had been travelling south, so if he swam at right angles to her starboard side, he should hit the coast of the United Kingdom sometime. Or drown, more likely, for Commander Pierce was taking care to be well outside the three-mile limit. Watters knew he could either swim or give up, and the latter was not an option. Spitting out another mouthful of the German Ocean, he swam slowly, hoping to retain his strength as long as possible. The water was so cold that already he felt the numbness spreading through his extremities.

After half an hour, Watters rested his arms, treading water to keep afloat as he watched the morning light unveil a panorama of tossing waves in every direction. 'Keep swimming,' he muttered, 'keep swimming.' He thought of Marie, of Amy squealing her delight at the bright windows in Reform Street, and then of Marie again, smiling.

'Move,' Watters said. 'Stay alive, keep moving; fight the pain.'

More waves, but he could see something else, something brown in the distance. Watters was unsure what it was, but he headed in that direction until he felt a terrible force pulling at his legs. He had heard of the wreck of *Birkenhead* when hundreds of British soldiers jumped overboard and were eaten by sharks, and for a second, he froze. Were there sharks in the German Ocean? He kicked out, yelling, and something dragged him into the sea.

Watters panicked, swallowing seawater that burned in his chest as he fought this powerful force that was pulling him underwater, backward, and upside down. So this was death; it seemed so unfair to be killed by some creature only a few miles off the British coast. What would Marie say when she heard if she ever did hear?

The sound of drowning was terrible, a roaring that seemed to rip open his ears, combined with a burning that tore at his lungs and light that burned his eyes as he momentarily broke the surface into fresh air. He heaved, spewing out what seemed like gallons of boiling hot water, retched again, and tried to stand, but something held his hands and feet in a vice. He was plunged back into the water again, covered in hundreds of slippery, slimy things that wriggled as they remorselessly pressed the life out of him, and then he was lifted and dropped, cursing, onto a shifting surface.

'We've got another corpse.' The voice was laconic but the accent English. Watters opened his mouth to speak, only to have something slimy and wriggling force its way between his teeth.

'That's no corpse; he's alive!'

'Well, praise the Lord.'

'He's trying to eat our fish, though.' A hand snatched the fish from Watters's mouth. A broad face loomed over him. 'He don't look like a fisherman.'

'He's got some sort of uniform on. He could be a Frenchy or a Dutchy. Look, he's reaching for his pocket.'

Rough hands pulled Watters free of the net that had entangled him, and bearded men in oilskins knelt at his side. Somebody thrust a bottle in his mouth. Watters drank thirstily of the water.

'Look, Silas, he was reaching for the Holy Book!'

The voices seemed to echo from a great distance off, but they were kindly and concerned. 'A Bible, and it's wrote in English. He's as English as we are, God bless him!'

The fishermen propped Watters on deck with his legs sprawled in front of him and his back to a stout mast. 'Thank you.' He glanced around, noting that he was on a solid looking fishing smack with two masts. It looked and felt very secure compared to the open vessels used by the Nesshaven fishermen.

'He don't sound English.' There was disappointment in the voice. 'He's a foreigner, like enough. Irish maybe.'

'It don't matter what he is. He's Christian; that's all we need to know.'

Watters smiled as the four-strong crew, bearded, brown-faced men, all knelt around him with one praying lustily. They ended with a single verse of a hymn then looked fondly at him as if he were their personal property.

'What's to do, mate? Who are you? How did you come to be here?'

'George Watters. From Scotland, by way of the United States Navy, and I really have to get to Dundee. There's going to be a murder else.'

'He's a Scotchman!' The preacher, who Watters took to be the skipper, looked around at his crew. 'I told you he was as English as we are. Up you get, Scotchy, and we'll get you comfortable. What do you mean, there's a-going to be a murder?'

'It's a long story, but I have to get back to Dundee as quick as I can. How far off the coast are we?'

The fishermen looked at each other with a great shaking of heads. One sucked in his breath, but they waited for the skipper to speak. 'A long way off, mister. We're fishing the Dogger, and we're not due home for months yet.' The skipper thought for a moment, fingering the piece of amber that hung around his neck as a preventative for rheumatism.

'Tell you what, though, we can put you in the cutter. They're due today, and they'll drop you off in London if that's any good to you?'

'The cutter? And London?'

The fisherman explained patiently that they belonged to a fleet of Hull smacks that fished the Dogger all winter, only returning to port in the spring. Once a week, a cutter came out, lifted their catch to carry it to market in London.

'Fine place the Dogger, but cruel for corpses. We're always hauling them up.' The skipper grinned, his blue eyes crinkling with amusement. 'We thought you was a dead 'un at first, but then we find that you're a Scotchman and not dead at all.' He touched the New Testament. 'The good Lord kept you safe.'

'Indeed.' Watters hoped that immersion in seawater had not ruined Marie's New Testament. He also hoped that whatever was in the cylinder had not been damaged.

The Hull fishermen dug deep to help Watters, scrambling through their pockets for what money they had and asking the neighbouring boats in the fleet to help so that when the cutter came, Watters felt quite wealthy. He thanked the fishermen for their generosity, shaking each man by the hand before scrambling aboard the cutter, whose crew accepted his presence with a phlegmatic calm that was entirely English. 'Back to the Smoke, mate?' The skipper asked. 'We'll have you there before you knows it.'

'How long will it take?' Watters asked as he looked around the craft with its vast sails and holds now full of silver fish.

'As quick as Christ will let us,' the skipper said. 'Billingsgate wants its fish fresh, so we don't linger. You better hold onto something, Scotchy, or the wind of our passage will blow you into the sea, else.'

The cutter's crew laughed, hoisting full sails to catch the rising wind.

The cutter skipper was as good as his word, and Watters had never experienced anything quite as exhilarating as racing up the Thames under full sail.

'How fast are we sailing?'

'As fast as we can,' the cutter's captain told him. 'You sit there. We'll have you ashore in half a mo.'

They arrived in the early evening when the respectable were bustling home from work and the denizens of the night were beginning to emerge.

It seemed that half the world's shipping sailed or steamed to this hub of Empire, with every flag represented in the Thames, from the United States to France, Sweden to Austria, as well as the ubiquitous Union flag of Great Britain and a dozen flags and ensigns Watters struggled to recognise. The crowds were immense, all seeming to be hurrying somewhere or talking at the top of their voice in their thin London accents.

Shaking hands with the crew of the cutter, Watters hurried toward the nearest telegraph office. As always in London, the streets were packed with top-hatted businessmen, side by side with the poor and the paupers who crowded around. Watters brushed away the fanning hand of a professional pickpocket, ignored the bold-eyed invitation of a be-feathered prostitute, and winced as the roar of thousands of wheels on millions of cobblestones besieged him. He had considered approaching the local police but realised that they might not listen to him. His story was too complicated and his ragged appearance not calculated to gain respect. Instead, he had decided to send a telegram direct to Beaumont's office. The operator scarcely looked up as Watters took the pencil at the telegraph office to scribble a message on the pad that was provided.

'Take great care. You are in personal danger.' Watters gnawed the already well-chewed end of the pencil before adding a few instructions. He composed another note for Superintendent Mackay and handed both to the telegraph operator, who slowly counted the words to calculate the cost.

'This will cost you a pretty penny.' The operator bent to his machine.

'You won't be sending that.' The voice was educated yet familiar.

Dear God! How did he get here?

Dressed as a respectable businessman with an ornate waistcoat beneath his tailed coat, Ted touched his cane to the brim of his tall hat. 'Well, Sergeant Watters. This is a piece of luck. You do have nine lives, don't you?'

'How the devil...?'

'How the devil did I find you?' Ted gave his gap-toothed grin. 'Pure good luck, my man. I was just passing through, and there you were, large as life.'

Brushing past Watters, Ted leaned casually through the telegraph operator's door. Giving a broad smile, he ripped the pad from operator's hand.

'What? You can't do that!'

Without hesitation, Ted pulled a long knife from inside his jacket and stabbed the telegraph operator through the heart. The operator slumped silently to the ground where his blood formed a spreading red pool. The whole incident had taken less than ten seconds; one moment the operator had been doing his duty, the next he was dead.

Momentarily shocked, Watters could only stare as the murderer cleaned the blood from the blade of his knife.

Ted kept his smile. 'You are a redoubtable sort of fellow, aren't you?' He tossed the knife from hand to hand. 'You have something of ours. I want it back.'

For one second, Watters wondered if he could overpower Ted in a straight fight, and then he saw Niner and Scouse looming in the background. *Run!*

Pushing past Ted, Watters ran, darting in the opposite direction from Niner and Scouse. More intent on escaping the immediate threat than in reaching any particular destination, he did not take note of his direction. There was an instant of hope when he saw a uniformed policeman at the end of a crowded street, but the pursuers were too close behind to chance stopping.

Glancing over his shoulder, Watters ran on. The docks were to his right, the smell of the river as unmistakable as the disreputable quality of the streets. By now, gaslights were flaring on those streets that the authorities deemed should be lit, and Watters found himself running northward, stumbling and gasping up the Ratcliffe Highway. Groups of bare-headed sailors' women shouted to one another as they adjusted the provocatively low cut of their dresses.

'Why the rush, sailor; ain't I good enough fer you?' A heavily painted woman clicked her brass heel on the filthy ground. 'Here! Are the rozzers after you or summat?'

Other women turned to watch as Watters stumbled by, his clothes immediately betraying him as a seafaring man, and so one of their own.

'What ship, sailor? Make your berth with us!' The crimp's face was bright with promise, his intent as vicious as any predator.

Watters ran on, past bright-windowed shops that displayed marine goods, clothing and drink in every variety from porter to jigger gin. Advertisements for Grand Concerts plastered the doors of respectable looking dance-halls with large men standing sentinel outside. Beside them were seedy dram-shops whose fronts were painted with pictures of sailors dancing with buxom women whose living likenesses waited outside to catch the eye and wallet of the passing seamen.

Reeling with exhaustion, Watters leaned against the corner of a public house named the White Swan. He looked back down the Highway. Even amidst the scores of half-drunk revellers, he found his pursuers. Ted was staring directly at him, his respectable clothing marking him as an outsider in this street of seamen, while Scouse looked in one of the brightly lit shop windows, eying the collection of overpriced trinkets. Niner slowed to a casual walk, tall, frowning, and ugly.

'Well, are you going to block the light, sailor, or buy me a drink?' The woman was blonde, with artificial flowers emphasising the swell of her breasts. She thrust her left leg forward so her crinoline skirt rode up her shin. 'This is Paddy's Goose, you know!'

Watters took a deep breath. 'I'd love to buy you a drink.'

The woman was diminutive, with the top of her head reaching Watters's chin. 'In you come then, sailor!'

As his three pursuers spread out and approached, Watters darted inside the pub. Paddy's Goose was well known throughout the maritime world as a haunt for prostitutes and crimps. It was also larger than he had expected, with amiable-looking women of all ages dancing attendance on bronzed seamen. Amidst the raucous banter, nobody gave Watters a second look as the small woman guided him to the bar.

'Mother's ruin,' the woman ordered gin for herself. 'My man will have the same.'

Dropping a shilling on the counter, Watters kept one eye on the doorway.

'This way.' The woman led him to a corner table. 'What ship, sailor?' She was bright-eyed and cheerful rather than seductive, with a snub nose that Watters found strangely alluring. Her sharp, London accent was not unpleasant.

'*Alexander MacGillivray*,' Watters said unthinkingly.

'Don't know that one.' The woman smiled. 'I thought I knew all the ships.'

'From Dundee,' Watters said wryly, 'via the Dogger Bank.'

The woman looked strangely at him. 'Naw,' she said, 'that doesn't ring true, sailor. So what are you?' She eyed his battered Confederate uniform. 'Bluejacket on the run? Unusual uniform if you are.' The blonde automatically arched her back to present her semi-exposed breasts.

'Sharp, aren't you?' Watters slid down his seat as Ted Houghton looked in the pub.

Catching Watters's movement, the blonde stood up to shield him from view. 'You're in some kind of trouble, that's for sure, but not from the Royal Navy, not in that uniform.' She held up a hand. 'Don't tell me, sailor; I don't want to know.' Bending forward to adjust her morocco boots, she eyed Ted and his two companions. 'He's a bad 'un, that's for sure, sailor. Welshed on a loan, have you? Are you looking for a berth till the smoke blows away? Or just for the night?'

Watters shook his head. 'Neither,' he said honestly. 'I'm not staying. I have to get up to Dundee.'

A sudden shadow of disappointment aged the woman. 'A fine man like you too.' She sighed, nearly upsetting the false flowers while deliberately allowing Watters another display of smooth white breasts. 'I'm Katy, in case you're interested, but I can see that you're not. Why do all the good ones never stay?' Her eyes were sad when she surveyed him again. 'Not a proper sailor are you, Jack? Come with me then.' Slipping her arm through his, she led him through the throng to the back of the room then up a narrow flight of stairs. 'Don't be so nervous, Jack; I ain't a-going to eat yer.' She squeezed softly, pressing against him. 'More's the pity, eh?'

Katy led him into a small room with a single bed and a painted chest of drawers. A crucifix hung on the wall, while a narrow window overlooked an unlit alley. 'Out the window, Jack, and sharp. Look, follow me, will you?' Throwing open the sash, Katy unrolled a knotted rope. Winking at him, she slid out in a flurry of petticoats to climb nimbly down the rope. 'You ain't the first man to climb out this window; I'm telling you!'

The alley stank of urine and rats, one of which scurried away before them. A copulating couple did not pause as Watters and Katy scrambled past, and then they were back on the Highway, passing a group of raucous South-Spainers, at one of whom the women Katy blew a kiss and, moving closer, nipped his backside.

'How are you doin', Jack?' She jerked her head toward Watters. 'This is a friend of mine, in trouble with the Law.'

The South-Spainer threw Watters a beery grin and belched. 'Is that so?'

'Sure and it is. So if you see three men following, one in a high hat and fancy weskit, another a rangy looking fellow, and the third bald as a billiard-ball with blood on his sleeve and death in his eyes, say hello from Katy.' She pulled Watters a few steps further on before turning back. 'Oh, and Jack, wait for me in Paddy's will yer? If you want a berth for a night or two.'

'That's Jack,' Katy told Watters as she hurried him along. 'He's one of my regulars. Jack's a good man when he's sober but a prime bastard in drink. He's a drunken sot too.'

Watters knew the terrible reputation that London prostitutes had; he had heard them called the scum of the earth, but this woman, Katy, was she so bad? Katy guided him up the Ratcliffe Highway, stopping every few yards to speak to warn everybody she recognised about the man in the fancy weskit. 'I'll see you safe, Jack,' Katy said. 'The rozzers done me a few times; I'll not see them get an honest man like you. It's not the bluebottles though, is it? What was it? Old woman narking you too much and you didn't stop hitting her? A knifing? A welshed bet? Or maybe just smuggled goods?' Her eyes were mischievous. 'No, don't tell me; I don't want ter know. I do, though, of course I do.'

A sudden outbreak of noise behind them made Katy turn. 'That's one of your friends in trouble,' she said. 'Common enough on the Highway. Come on, Jack.'

There was a knot of well-dressed men outside what Watters thought might have been an opium den and a group of Greek seamen arguing with naked knives, while three tall Scandinavians watched from a distance.

'This is Bloody Bridge over New Gravel-lane,' Katy told him as they paused on a bridge overlooking what seemed like a ditch of stagnant water. 'A friend of mine threw herself over here.' Suddenly sober, Katy paused, pressed her hands together in prayer. 'God rest her soul, but she was dying of the pox anyway.' The devil-may-care grin was back. 'Poxed-up-bitch, we called her, but she started well enough.' Katy shrugged. 'Just bad luck, ain't it, Jack, to end up a whore on the Highway or a Jack-at-sea. Come on, now.'

Katy led him up Cannon Street Road to a prominent church. 'St George's,' Katy said as if the name should mean something to him. 'There was a riot here a few years ago, but the town's quiet now. Nothing happening.' She looked behind her. 'Right, Jack. Your friends have gone; they won't find you here, but it's time you earned your keep.' The friendly eyes were suddenly acute. 'You owe me, mister.'

Watters could not deny the fact.

'Did you think I was helping you from the goodness of my heart?' The acute eyes turned bitter. 'Nah, you have to pay your keep wiv me, Jack-my-lad.'

'You helped me,' Watters said. 'I'll help you.'

'Right then, I'll draw him up, you knock him down, and we'll split the take.'

For a moment, Watters did not understand, and then Katy's grin was back. She removed the flowers, lowered her neckline even further, and thrust out her breasts until they strained at the thin material of her gown. About to object, Watters thought of the men who were following then of Katy's possible reaction if he refused. 'Come on then, Katy!'

The grin widened. 'I thought you was a spunky one, Jack! Don't let me down now!'

It was easier than Watters had imagined. Katy stood beside St George's church with one hand on her hip and a leg thrust provocatively forward, talking to every man that passed. The first three did not reply, the fourth merely grunted, but the fifth was a youngster in evening dress, apparently keen to explore the seedier side of life. Katy helped him advance his education.

'Good evening, sir.' Katy stepped forward. 'You look a likely sort of gentleman. I like a top-drawer man like you.' She slipped her arm inside his in a manner that Watters recognised. 'Indeed I do.' She leaned closer. 'Yes, sir. With a handsome man such as you, I won't charge a penny, no, nor a farthing neither. I'll take you for the fun of the thing!'

Watters watched the youth pass through a variety of emotions, from initial pleasure to terror, lust mingled with avarice, and then a smug acceptance of his own good fortune. He was still smiling when Katy led him to the shadows in the churchyard. Watters hit him, only once, on the back of the head. When the youth crumpled to the ground, Katy looked at Watters with appreciation, 'You've done this before, Jack, I can see,' and began to search the body.

'Good pickings.' She held up a jingling wallet. 'See? Seven sovereigns, ten shillings, and a few coppers.' Her eyes were hard as she put the coins in two separate piles. 'Fair do's eh? Half each and I'll take the extra.' She stepped back as if expecting Watters to snatch the lot, but she smiled when he scooped the smaller amount into his hand.

'Good, then I won't need this.' Katy revealed the long-bladed knife that she had concealed up her sleeve. 'I'll have his clothes too. They'll fetch a pretty penny. Give me a hand here.'

Aware that he could now be transported or sent to penal servitude, Watters helped Katy strip the unfortunate youth. 'All his clothes,' Katy said, 'good quality linen will sell too, and if he's left stark, he'll be less likely to run to the peelers or follow me up the Highway.' She looked down dispassionately at the naked youth. 'He won't be running after floozies again for a while. Well, Jack,' Katy held out her gloved hand, 'we'd better go our separate ways now.' Her accent had changed again, becoming so much more refined that Watters wondered at her antecedents. 'You get back to Dundee, and I'll get rid of this.'

'It's been a pleasure, Katy.' Watters gripped her hand, nodded briefly, and walked away. He did not look back. Katy had her own life to live, he had Mr Beaumont to save, and the youth would be none the worse for learning a little humility. It was better for him to have a sore head than a dose of whatever diseases Katy would be carrying anyway.

CHAPTER TWENTY-TWO
LONDON: DECEMBER 1862

Pushing through a crowd of porters, some wheeling their baggage, others chatting with harassed travellers, Watters looked for his train. He stopped a harassed porter who was manoeuvring a barrow through a cloud of steam, a collection of thieves, morning- suited businessmen, and casual travellers.

'Is this the train for Dundee?'

'That's your sort, mate. Change at York and Edinburgh.' The porter was thin-faced and tired, but his blue uniform was tidy. He put a hand to his cap in a perfunctory salute.

Having calculated exactly what the fare would be, Watters mentally thanked the fishermen for their generosity and the youth for his stupidity. Although a second-class ticket did not allow him upholstery on the wooden seat, at least he had glass in the windows. The lack of cushions was nothing compared to the discomfort of an open boat in the German Ocean, but the worry about Marie suffering at his absence kept him awake the entire jolting ride north. The impending attack on Beaumont was of secondary consideration. At least Ted Houghton and his accomplices were far behind in London, but Watters had no interest in the constant unfolding of the English countryside he passed through. He consulted his Bradshaw Guide three times, hoping to find a connection that would bring him faster to Dundee but without success.

Unless he was actively employed, Watters fretted, but his nervous fidgeting eventually upset the six travellers who shared his compartment so that he had to force himself to sit still despite the energy that itched and burned inside him. There was an exodus at York when he had to wait for an hour to change trains; he found a seat, and the train rattled on to Edinburgh.

When his attempt to telegraph Beaumont failed because the lines were down, Watters spent a cold two hours waiting for his connection to Dundee. Eventually, he squeezed into a crowded train. The guard grunted at him. 'You're lucky to get on, mate. The carriages are full, but you can take your chance. On you get.' The guard ushered him on board, touching his badge with its ornate double crest of Edinburgh and Berwick. Almost immediately he blew his whistle so the train creaked forward in a great cloud of white steam.

Watters settled back on the wooden seat between an unsmiling Edinburgh matron with long pins prominent in her hat and a man in a black coat who was chewing an apple. As the train entered the first of the tunnels that took them out of Edinburgh, Watters tried to concentrate his thoughts on Beaumont. When they emerged into daylight, the matronly woman was removing a hatpin from between her teeth while the man had settled down with a newspaper. They rattled on northward toward Granton and the *Leviathan*, the rail ferry that crossed the Forth.

Despite a rising tide that could have complicated matters, the train passed smoothly across the Forth. Watters watched as a call-boy on the bridge transmitted orders from the ship's master to the engine driver who drove the freight coaches on board the rail ferry. The passengers transferred to *Auld Reekie*, whose paddles churned the Forth impatiently as they boarded.

The passage was only thirty minutes but seemed longer, with Watters wondering if he would have time to telegraph Beaumont while he was in Fife.

'Excuse me,' he asked one of the seamen. 'Is there a telegraph machine at Burntisland?'

The seaman stared at him. 'Maybe, I don't know. Ask at the harbour office.'

Auld Reekie was docking first, so Watters thought he might have time to telegraph while the freight wagons were unloaded. With his hopes rising, he glanced ashore.

Oh, dear God.

Ted Houghton stepped onto the stone quay, still in his tall hat. One hand was inside his coat as he examined the passengers on the ferry.

Of course, Ted will be travelling to Dundee. He is going to murder Beaumont. What a fool I was not to consider that. If Ted is here, Scouse and Niner will be with him. They must have caught the same train as me.

Ted was undoubtedly a professional, so would probably have any telegraph covered. Watters swore and shrunk into the crowd. Burntisland looked bustling enough with the chimneys of factories and tenements for the workers, so there would be a police station here, but what chance would he have of finding it before Ted found him?

Keeping his shoulders bowed, Watters mingled with the crowd that boarded the train. He watched Ted board the carriage ahead; the other two must be elsewhere on board. Watters knew he could either remain on the train or leave and find another means of transport. Travel by sea? That would be too slow, even if he could find a vessel that was sailing to Dundee. Horseback? Again, slower than the train, and he was not an expert horseman. He had no choice but to sit tight. With luck, he could still warn Beaumont before Ted reached him.

The journey across Fife seemed interminable, with the train stopping at a score of stations. At each halt, Watters expected Ted or one of his colleagues to appear at his carriage door. Each time the train restarted with a hiss of steam, he felt relief surge through him. Without a weapon, all he could do was sit in hope, but the train reached the crossing at Ferryport-on-Tay without incident. Again there was the confusion of crowding into the ferry, *Thane of Fife*, but this time, Watters shuffled along with the mob, keeping his head ducked down.

The passage was short, so Watters told himself that all he had to do was stay hidden until they reached Broughty Ferry.

Only twenty minutes and I'll be in my own territory. Once there, Ted can whistle for all I care.

Finding a seat near the starboard paddle-box, Watters pulled up his collar as far as he could. From here, he could see Mount Pleasant with its flanking Italianate tower from where Beaumont observed his vessels sailing into the Tay. Watters wondered if Beaumont was watching him now, and then thought of Marie and how she would view his return. Thinking of Marie relaxed him; he closed his eyes as tiredness overcame him.

'There's our man!'

Dear Lord!

A pair of powerful army hauled Watters bodily backwards onto the deck before he could retaliate. Ted and Niner stood in front of him, hard-eyed, both dressed in smarter clothes than they had ever worn at sea.

'Keep still you bluebottle bastard,' Scouse breathed in Watters's ear without relaxing the grip around his neck.

'Dundee Police!' Ted shouted. 'Stand back! This man is attempting to escape from justice!'

When Watters tried to speak, Scouse increased the pressure on his throat, so the words came out as a strangled croak.

Niner pushed a small revolver against Watters's temple until Ted snarled, 'Don't be stupid, constable; we'll need his evidence at the trial!'

'It's all right, sir,' Scouse said. 'I've got him secure.'

'Gag him and keep him still!' Ted ordered as Watters struggled to escape.

The crowd watched with interest as Watters fought back, but their sympathy was all with the respectably-dressed attackers rather than the travel-stained man in his sea clothes. A middle-aged, middle-class matron murmured approval as Scouse squeezed harder, at the same time banging Watters's head against the rail.

'That's the way, constable! Give the scoundrel what for!'

Her words distracted Scouse for barely a second but sufficient time for Watters to ram his straight fingers into Scouse's throat. He twisted away as the garrotter's grip slackened.

'You villain!' The matron stepped quickly back from Watters. A heavily whiskered businessman held a rolled-up newspaper like a club while putting a protective arm around the matron's shoulders.

Watters had a flash of satisfaction to see that Scouse's face was severely bruised, while a fresh bandage adorned one wrist. He wondered briefly if Katy's customers in the Ratcliffe Road had given him those decorations, but there was no time to gloat as Niner slashed at him with what appeared to be an official police baton.

'I'll take him.'

'Give him toco!' The matron was pressing against her protector, watching intently. She slid a hat pin free and held it before her, jabbing threateningly towards Watters. 'Go on! Hit the blackguard! Wallop him hard!'

Watters had only landed a single punch when something slammed into his kidneys. He grunted in agony, reeling away. Ted slipped a blackjack from up his sleeve and aimed a blow that Watters managed to avoid just as the ferry gave a lurch; water churned from the paddle boxes.

'Is he one of these garrotters?' The matron answered her own question. 'Yes, he is. It's in the eyes you know.' She turned to the whiskered man who held her. 'I can always tell. He's one of these garrotters.'

Unarmed and against three iron-hard men, Watters knew that he could not win. As the police baton descended again, he rolled away, hoping to give the impression that he was severely hurt. He sheltered in the space between the crowd and the white-painted paddle box, trying to gain time, but the passengers were urging his attackers on, seeking blood to assuage the boredom of their existence.

'Hit him again!' the matron shouted. 'Go on! Wallop the garrotter again!'

The movement of the boat upset Ted's swing, but the blackjack still landed with enough force to numb Watters's shoulder. He grunted, swung a wild kick, overbalanced as the ferry rose to a wave, and fell against the low guard-rail. The Tay was grey and choppy, with a vicious current, but it offered more chance than he had here.

After a last glance over the unsympathetic faces, Watters threw himself over the side. He allowed the cold water to close above his head, kicking to gain distance from the ferry. Surfacing with a rush, Watters struck out for the shore. Niner took quick aim with his revolver and fired, but the shot went wide, then the wash of the paddles pushed Watters back under; the current carried him away from *Thane of Fife,* scraped him against a sandbank, and thrust him further out to sea. He swallowed water, heard that horribly memorable roaring in his head, attempted another couple of strokes towards land, and winced when something struck him hard on the head.

For a moment, Watters was back off of the Sisters, drowning. 'Grab hold, mister!' The voice was not unfriendly, and Watters obeyed, finding himself holding onto a rope that somebody was pulling. 'What are you doing, falling off the passage boat like that?'

The face was familiar, the words pleasant as Curly John pulled him aboard the fishing boat. 'Oh, it's you, Sergeant Watters! We heard that you had drowned.'

'Not yet.' Watters slumped to the bottom of the boat. 'Not yet.'

The entire episode had only taken a few minutes, but already *Thane of Fife* was docking at Broughty Ferry, the crowd was waiting to surge ashore, and Curly John was steering for land.

'There's a life at stake,' Watters announced, deliberately dramatic as he felt his various aches and pains, 'and I have to get to Dundee.'

'Dundee?' Curly John shook his head. 'We're not going there. We're taking you to Nesshaven, so lie quiet now, Sergeant Watters.'

Perhaps it was the result of the repeated blows from blackjack and baton or the strain of the past few days, but Watters could not resist as the fishermen steered for their home. Somebody placed a bottle in his mouth, but it was water, not reviving spirits that eased down his throat. After three swallows, Watters spewed it up again.

'That's the way, Sergeant, get rid of all that salty sea. You lie easy now. We'll soon have you safe.'

CHAPTER TWENTY-THREE
NESSHAVEN AND DUNDEE: DECEMBER 1862

By some instinct that she had, Marie had arrived at Nesshaven. She was waiting with the women, staring at Watters through moist eyes. 'I thought you were dead,' she said.

He looked at her for a long minute before replying. 'No,' he said, 'I'm alive.'

She helped him out of the boat, her hands warm and secure on his arm. 'I thought you were dead,' she repeated. 'I was told you were drowned.'

Watters winced as the blows from blackjack and baton took painful effect. 'Not quite. How are you?'

'I'm all right. How did you get here? What happened?' As Marie became more used to his company, her voice raised. 'You disappear for days, and then step out of a fishing boat as if nothing had happened!' Sudden anger had replaced Marie's concern, but Watters could not spare time for explanations.

Stooping, he planted a quick kiss on Marie's forehead. He desperately wanted to hold her close. He knew he could not. 'I'll have to warn Mr Beaumont. He's in danger, great danger!'

'Do you think I care a fig for Mr Beaumont or a hundred Mr Beaumonts?' Marie glared at him with her expression slowly calming. 'Danger from what?'

'I'll have to get to his office', Watters said. 'Now.'

'He's at Mount Pleasant.' Marie was already moving toward the village, her skirt snapping against her legs with every stride. 'I've got a hired chaise.' She glanced at Watters. 'You look shattered, George. I'll drive.'

'You don't know how to,' Watters said.

'You muffin! How do you think I got to Nesshaven? Sit tight; you look awful.'

Watters had never known anybody drive so fast and with such recklessness as Marie did on the road to Mount Pleasant. She hurtled out of the fishing village, forded the burn in a cascade of spray, and splashed along the muddy track with a careless disregard for her appearance or comfort. 'Hold on George,' she said, taking a bend so sharply that Watters thought she would overturn. People stared as the chaise rattled through Broughty Ferry, crashing over the potholed road and showering passers-by with mud from the many puddles, but Marie was in no mood to listen to complaints. When a carter raised a fist in anger, she lashed at him with her whip.

'Stupid man!' Marie said, pushing the horse even faster to the quieter West Ferry.

By the time she reached the drive of Mount Pleasant, Marie, Watters, and the chaise were filthy.

'I rather enjoyed that drive,' Marie said. Jumping from the chaise, she threw the reins over the horse. 'I'm coming too!' She followed Watters up the broad steps to the front door. The footman had difficulty masking his astonishment at these two apparitions.

'Mr Beaumont is busy. You cannot go in just now.'

'Busy? Damn it, James, this is a matter of life and death!' Watters pushed past the man. 'Where is he?'

'Why, in his study, sir, with Cattanach, Mrs Caskie, and an American gentleman.'

An American gentleman? Dammit, Ted has got here first. 'Don't come up, Marie,' Watters said. 'It might be dangerous.'

'Try to stop me,' Marie said. 'Just try!'

Despite being hampered by her long skirt, Marie was only three steps behind Watters as he launched himself up the stairs. She was at his heels when he reached the carved door of Beaumont's office. Watters heard the voices coming from inside the room, lifted his foot, and booted the door open. It slammed back on its hinges as he threw himself inside.

'Good God, man! What the devil do you mean by that?!' Beaumont rose from his chair. He stared at Watters. 'Sergeant Watters! I heard that you were dead!'

Holderby and Mary Caskie also rose, staring as Marie crashed in behind Watters, her hair dishevelled and skirt spattered with mud from her hectic ride. She still held her riding whip in her hand. Cattanach took a step back from the desk as though in fear.

Mary Caskie pointed at Watters. 'How dare you act so?'

'There's a plot on your life, Mr Beaumont,' said Watters. He felt suddenly foolish with his dramatic entrance into what had evidently been a civilised discussion.

Only the heavy ticking of a long case clock broke the silence of the next few seconds, then Beaumont invited Watters to sit down and explain. Raising his eyebrows, Holderby rose from his seat.

'Cattanach,' Beaumont said, 'fetch a decanter of brandy and some glasses. Sergeant Watters seems distraught.'

Watters jerked a thumb at Holderby. 'I think it would be better for us to be alone, Mr Beaumont.'

'You are very direct, Sergeant Watters.' Holderby rose from the chair. 'I can appreciate that in a man, but perhaps Mrs Caskie would prefer a more gentlemanly approach.'

'Please sit down, Mr Holderby,' Beaumont said quietly. 'Sergeant Watters, I appreciate your concern, but I trust Mr Holderby implicitly.'

Smiling, Holderby bowed to Marie. 'Your servant, ma'am.'

Watters dragged across a chair and held it until Marie sat down. 'Whether or not you trust Mr Holderby, Mr Beaumont, your connections with the Southern States have created problems. With your permission, sir?' Without waiting for a reply, Watters crossed to the door, pushed it shut, and propped the single remaining chair against the handle.

'He's dressed like one of these gypsies.' Mrs Caskie produced a fine ivory fan and wafted it before her face. 'Is the man mad?'

'No, Mrs Caskie. I am merely concerned. Now listen.' Remaining on his feet, Watters paced across the room to check the windows while quickly relating what he had heard on the Federal paddle steamer.

'I see,' Beaumont said when Watters had finished. 'Thank you for telling me this.' He sat for a moment. 'So what do you advise, Sergeant Watters?'

'Inform the police, arm yourself, and warn each of your factory managers to be extra vigilant.' Watters had spent his time on the long train journey from London devising countermeasures. He glanced again at Holderby, who had listened with an expression of incredulity on his face. 'There is more, sir, which you may prefer to hear alone.'

'Continue,' Beaumont ordered. 'I do not need to repeat that I trust the present company with my life.'

'You may have to, sir, but if you insist.' Watters took a deep breath. 'For your own safety, and that of your family and workers, I advise you to break all contact with the Southern States of America and publicly announce your disapproval of their peculiar practices.' He was aware of the growing tension in the room. Marie was watching him intently.

'Mr Beaumont has no intention of obeying the orders of such as you,' Mrs Caskie interrupted. 'So please leave.' Snapping shut her fan, she pointed it at Watters. 'I am sure that this whole affair is exaggerated, or you have misheard. It is all stuff and nonsense. I wonder at you men sometimes; I really do.'

'Sergeant Watters has been correct in the past,' Beaumont said. 'I have never had any reason to doubt his word.'

Mrs Caskie snorted. 'Don't you indeed. Well, I do. Mr Holderby, pray forgive this impertinence. I am sure that Mr Beaumont will order these people removed from his property.'

Mr Holderby shook his head. 'I agree with Sergeant Watters that you, Mr Beaumont, should break all contact with the slave states. However, I can assure you that the United States government has not, and never will, sanction your assassination, or the assassination of anybody else.' Holderby looked at Watters. 'The idea is not only ludicrous, Sergeant, but it is also downright insulting.'

When Beaumont looked at Watters, there was strain in his eyes. 'In this case, I agree with Mr Holderby. It would be better if you left now, Sergeant Watters.'

'Mr Beaumont,' Watters began, 'there are three men presently in Dundee who plan to kill you.'

'That may well be true, but I am sure they are not in any way associated with the government of the United States.' Beaumont exchanged a quiet nod with Holderby. 'I will pass on your warning to your superiors, Watters, who will doubtless look into it. Really, Sergeant, I am sure that you speak with the best intentions, but I am only a businessman. I'm hardly a target for the United States government.' He led the laughter in which Mrs Caskie and Holderby dutifully joined.

'George,' Marie took hold of Watters's arm. 'It's time we were leaving. We're doing no good here.' She lowered her tone. 'George!'

Watters nodded. After his adventures on *Alexander MacGillivray* and his mad dash from the Dogger Bank to London to Dundee, all his efforts were wasted. Waves of intense weariness engulfed him.

'Come on, George.' Marie led the way to the door, which Cattanach opened with a small bow.

'Thank you for your time, gentlemen. My regards, Mrs Caskie.' Watters managed to remember his manners. 'I do hope you reconsider your position, Mr Beaumont.' He stepped outside.

'He's not worth it, George,' Marie told him as they boarded the chaise. She drove away at a sedate pace. 'Let's get you home.'

'No.' Watters struggled to free himself from his exhaustion. 'Even if Beaumont does not believe me, the girls at his mills are still in danger. Take me to the police office.' He took a deep breath. 'I think I'd better drive.'

'In your condition?' Marie shook her head. 'You're not fit to walk, let alone drive, George.'

* * *

'Watters! Good God man, I heard you were dead!' Mackay stared at Watters across the width of his desk. 'How the devil...?'

'Never mind that, sir,' Watters said. 'I have to warn you that Mr Beaumont and his mills are in grave danger.'

'We've been through all this before, Watters,' Mackay said. 'Neither Mr Beaumont or I consider that there is any further danger.'

'I know, sir. Bear with me for a moment.' Watters gave Mackay a brief description of the past few days.

'Your life gets ever more interesting, Watters.' Mackay's fingers drummed on his desk. 'Are you sure of your facts?'

'I saw these men,' Watters said. 'They murdered a telegraph operator in London. One, the man who called himself Ted Houghton, is the leader. The other two I only know as Niner and Scouse.' He gave a brief description of all three.

Mackay frowned. 'I have one hundred officers to cover all of Dundee, including eighty-seven constables. I shall send a couple to protect Mr Beaumont. I shall also order the harbour police to be extra vigilant, but like Mr Beaumont, I cannot think that the United States authorities would sanction assassination.' He looked at Watters. 'Now I suggest that you return home, Watters, sleep, wash, change, and maybe get something to eat. You look like a packet sailor rather than a sergeant of the Dundee Police!'

'Yes, sir.' Watters saw that he was not making any impression on Mackay.

'I will take what action I can, Sergeant,' Mackay spoke kindly. 'I also have to police the weekly market at Fairmuir and, as you know, at present, Dundee is plagued by illicit shebeens, which means a rise in drunkenness and petty assaults.'

'Yes, sir.'

'Now off you go.' Mackay's voice was nearly benign. 'You've done your duty and all you can do. It's time to let somebody else take the strain.'

As he returned home, Watters's sense of failure was overwhelming. He had tried to warn Mr Beaumont but failed; he was only a sergeant of police, a man without power. Worse, he was now a man who engaged in actions not compatible with respectability, for no honest man would consort with women like Katy or roll stupid youths for their pocket-book.

'Come on, George.' Marie managed him. 'Eat, wash, and sleep.'

Watters allowed Marie to bully him.

'You've done your best. It'll all seem better after some sleep.'

Watters's bed was welcoming amidst all the familiar surroundings of the room, from Marie's clothes hanging up to the golf clubs sitting in the corner waiting for him. He closed his eyes to be immediately transported to the golf course, where Ted Houghton stood at the first tee with a pistol in his hand as a train rumbled through an explosion halfway across the rough. Ragina's face came to him, with Katy smiling as she stripped that unfortunate young man, while bearded fishermen tried to drag him across a crowded train in a net.

Watters woke with a start as the messages scrambled through his brain. What had he left undone? He rummaged through his memory, from *Alexander MacGillivray* to Katy and Ted Houghton. There was something he had forgotten. What was it?

That cylindrical fire-making device! He had told Beaumont about it, but in the confusion, he had forgotten that he still had it in his inside breast pocket. Swearing, Watters rose to his feet, for he knew that he had to show the thing to all Beaumont's factory managers, or they would not know what to look for.

'Damn it all to buggery!' Watters poured cold water from the pitcher into the ewer for a brisk wash. He was still unshaven, but that could not be helped. Ignoring the seaman's canvas, Watters dressed as respectably as he could, slipped the cylinder into his left breast pocket, Marie's seawater-stained New Testament into the right, and opened the sea chest that sat under his window. For a second, he considered Beaumont's four-barrelled Sharps revolver but returned to his Tranter Dragoon despite its longer barrel.

He knew that, whatever Beaumont or Mackay believed, Ted Houghton was not yet finished. Ted had resolved to kill Beaumont and seemed sufficiently professional to carry out his intention. While dealing with such killers, it was better to stick with what was familiar. Fastening on a shoulder holster, Watters slipped in the Dragoon, tore a hunk from the loaf of bread that Marie had in the pantry, and hurried to greet the morning.

Dundee woke early to go to work, and although it was not yet six, already the streets were busy. Cold December rain dampened the shawl-shrouded heads of women that thronged towards the mills while men moved towards the shipyards, forges, and warehouses around the docks. With the omnibus service not starting until 8:45, even the mill clerks, artisans, and square-backed businessmen had to walk. Watters hailed an early-rising Hackney.

'Where to, mate?'

Watters told him, listing the mills and factories individually while the driver raised his eyes in disbelief. 'That's half the mills in Dundee!'

'No, it's only Mr Beaumont's mills. On you go, driver!'

One by one, Watters visited the mill managers, from Mr Fairfax in Brown's Street to Mr Cosgrove in distant Lochee, while the Hackney driver mentally toted his fare with every call. Watters explained to the managers precisely what they were to look for, showing them his example.

'This little thing!' Mr Cosgrove lifted the cylinder.

'This little thing can destroy your mill,' Watters said. 'Watch for it.'

It was after eleven when Watters left the Bon Vista Mill. 'One last stop, driver, and then you'll have to find another fare.'

The driver, head bowed to the near-freezing rain, shrugged. 'Where to this time, mate?'

'Dock Street. The offices of Beaumont's Mount Pleasant Company.'

There was a hold up at the old Toll House near Logie House lodge, and another opposite Dudhope Free Church, so Watters, impatient as ever, ordered the driver to take the Scouring Burn route. Only when the driver turned his horses did Watters see what had caused the trouble. A horse pulling a jute cart had slipped on the greasy road, spilling some of the bales of jute, which impeded the passage of a Hackney. One of the passengers had left the cab to complain, his tall-crowned hat glistening in the rain. Even at this distance, Ted's false London accent cut thinly through the rougher growl of the carter's reply.

'Use the whip, driver!' Watters was suddenly urgent. 'Get down this road as fast as you can.'

'I'll lose my license if I do,' the driver began.

'You'll lose your teeth if you don't,' Watters assured him, and one glance at his level eyes was enough to convince the driver to whip up his horses.

It was a mad dash down to the Scouring Burn, but then the cab's speed ebbed as they again encountered heavy traffic. Carts of jute and wagons of coal clattered over the road, with carters jockeying for position against a background of the incessant racket of the mills.

More prof*it*; more prof*it*; more prof*it*.

'Move past them, man!' Watters swore, but the driver gestured ahead with his whip.

'How should I do that? Go through the mills? You'll have to have patience!'

Watters glared ahead at the congested street, dark with tall buildings, crowded with wagons, its atmosphere thick with smoke. He could either wait or go on foot. Wastefully throwing the driver a sovereign, Watters leapt from the Hackney cab and began to run, hoping that the Lochee Road was equally busy to delay Ted's cab.

Dodging between the carts, Watters ran down the middle of the road, ignoring the jeers of the carters. Panting with effort, he hurried from the Scouring Burn, past the West Port and into the thickly populated Overgate with its old houses, corbie-stepped gables and crazy windows. Ahead of him, toward the narrow eastern end of the Overgate, a Hackney manoeuvred around a static water cart.

'Halloa! Cabbie!' Watters shouted, waving his hand to attract the driver's attention.

Ignoring him, the driver eased free, cracking his whip, but Watters put his head down and spurted with the thought of Ted gloating over the bloody corpse of Beaumont spurring him on. He drew level with the cab as it reached the narrows of the Overgate.

'Hey! Open up!' Running alongside, Watters hammered at the wooden cab door. 'Ease up, cabbie!'

'Bugger off, you! I've already got a fare.' Glancing over his shoulder, the driver swung his whip in a vicious backwards sweep that cracked off the door an inch from Watters's hands. A man's face appeared at the window of the cab, his mouth working frantically, and then the door slammed open, nearly throwing Watters back into the street.

'It's bloody Watters!' Niner leaned out, his face still swollen and bruised.

'Push him off.' That was Ted's voice but now graced with his Western American accent.

The whip swung again, slashing against Watters's shoulder so he gasped with pain. The driver shouted: 'Shut that damned door, somebody! I can't drive like this.' The cab swayed from side to side as it rattled over the cobbles of the High Street, with the pillared Town Hall on the right and Reform Street opening to the left.

Ted leaned out, his face calm. 'You again, Watters? I thought we had got rid of you.' Pulling a Colt from inside his jacket, he levelled it, only to replace the weapon quickly as curious passers-by stopped to stare.

There was a sharp right-hand turn down the slope of Castle Street, with the Exchange Meeting Rooms looming at the bottom and the masts and spars of shipping thrusting from the docks just beyond. 'You'll keep,' Ted said, nodding grimly.

'Hey! You! Let go of that cab!' Tall in his blue coat, Constable Mackenzie pointed to Watters. Ted slammed shut the door, agonisingly trapping Watters's fingers. Pulling his hand back, Watters lost his balance, fell, grazed his knees and elbows on the granite cobbles, banged his head against the tall wheels of a stationary phaeton, and lay still for a second, recovering his senses as the cab clattered downhill.

Somebody was walking toward him. 'Are you all right, mister? That was quite a tumble you took.'

A horse was nuzzling Watters curiously as he struggled upright, swaying. He saw Ted's Hackney turn sharp left onto Dock Street, where Beaumont had his shipping offices. Watters followed, limping at first but picking up speed as the urgency of the situation chased away the sting of his injuries.

'Mackenzie!' Watters yelled. 'Come with me!'

Without waiting to see if Mackenzie obeyed, Watters ran onto Dock Street, where the great Royal Arch dripped rainwater onto the fish wives sheltering below. The Hackney rattled to a halt outside Beaumont's offices a hundred yards ahead. Ted looked quite casual as he left the cab, paid the driver, and slid through the open door of the Mount Pleasant Company, with Niner following close behind. Scouse remained on the street. Standing with legs apart in the company's doorway, Scouse looked as formidable as a guardsman.

There was no time to work out tactics. Watters ran along the street, swerved around a group of seamen who swarmed from a collier brig, and threw himself at Scouse. Aware that Scouse was probably his match in a fair fight, Watters did not hesitate. Feinting for Scouse's eyes with the forked fingers of his left hand, Watters jerked up his knee into the man's groin, followed by a smashing right hook to his jaw. He felt the snap of breaking bone, heard the shout of Constable Mackenzie somewhere behind him, followed through with two swift and savage kicks to Scouse's kidneys, and thrust through the door.

Niner was waiting immediately inside the doorway. His swung blackjack grazed Watters's forehead, opening a shallow cut. Temporarily blinded with the blood flowing into his eyes, Watters reeled back as Niner smashed down the blackjack a second time. Blocking the blow with an instinctively raised forearm, Watters countered with a feeble punch that glanced off Niner's bicep. The cosh swept upward, aiming for Watters's groin, but he jerked backwards, legs apart and arms crossed in front of him. The blackjack struck his left hand, numbing his thumb. He grunted, sensed the figure behind him, and turned to defend himself.

'What's happening here?' Constable Mackenzie was broad and fair with eyes that had seen twenty years of dockside brawls. He produced his truncheon with a flourish and moved in. 'Drop that blackjack, you!'

Nursing his injured hand, Watters leaned against the wood panelled wall. He noticed the reception clerk lying across his desk with blood seeping from a cut in his head.

Niner lowered the blackjack. 'It's a personal thing, officer.' He attempted a Dundee accent. 'It's a continuation from an earlier argument. This man has followed me all across Dundee.' His sudden smile took them both by surprise. 'Look, officer, I'll show you.'

Reaching inside his jacket, Niner pulled out a .32 pocket Adams. The first shot took Constable Mackenzie high in the chest, sending him staggering against the wall. The second slammed between Mackenzie's eyes, killing him instantly. However, the few moments' diversion had given Watters time to clear the blood from his eyes. Even before the sound of the shots faded, Watters was moving.

With no time to pull his own gun, Watters threw himself forward, grabbing for Niner's arm. Niner dropped the Adams at once, jabbed an elbow into Watters's face, and leaned forward to bite deep into Watters's already injured hand.

Yelling, Watters jerked backwards as Niner thrust two fingers toward his eyes. Watters snapped his teeth at the fingers, missed, and reeled as a knee smashed against the outside of his thigh. He staggered, grunting in agony as Niner's iron-shod boot raked down his shin. As Watters fell against the wall, Niner scooped up his Adams.

'I'll take him, Sergeant!' Duff's voice was welcome as the stocky criminal officer smashed his staff against Niner's wrist. The crack of breaking bone was audible as Duff followed up with an underhand swing to Niner's groin and a savage blow on the back of his head. Niner fell without a word. After a single step toward the polished stairs that led to Beaumont's office, the accumulated pain of Watters's injuries hit him. For a long moment, he leaned against the wall, fighting to control the agony.

'Take a deep breath,' Watters told himself. 'Fight the pain.'

He tried again, grunting as he limped up the stairs, ignoring the staring faces of Beaumont's office staff.

'Call the police!' Watters said. 'Tell them that Sergeant Watters needs help!'

Beaumont's door was shut, but Watters smashed through, staggering to regain his balance as he reeled into the room. Beaumont was sitting upright in his chair, both hands to his neck, around which Ted had a length of thin cord.

'Let him go, Ted,' Watters said. 'It's over.' He pulled the Tranter from his shoulder holster, but Ted ducked behind Beaumont, still pulling on the cord. Beaumont waved one hand in a gesture that could have meant anything.

As Watters tried to aim, Ted hauled Beaumont from the chair, using him as a human shield as he gradually backed toward the open window.

'We're two stories up,' Watters said, 'and you're alone in a strange city. The gunshots will have alerted the police. You've no chance, Ted. Give up now, let Mr Beaumont free, and you will get a fair trial. You might not get the rope.'

'What's the rope to me, Watters?' The Western accent was pleasant, despite the circumstances. 'I'm fighting for the cause of freedom. You're fighting to retain slavery. If I die, I go to heaven; when you die, it's an eternity of brimstone and pitch!' Still retaining his hold on Beaumont, Ted took another backwards step.

Watters followed slowly, looking for an opening to fire. 'I'm fighting to maintain law and order in Dundee, Ted, if that's your name. Was it you who killed that poor fellow in Calcutta as well? Or was it one of your paid assassins? Niner or Scouse or some other hireling?' Watters spoke desperately, grasping for time as he tried to think what best to do. 'They're both under arrest by the way.'

'I've no idea what you're talking about.' Ted shifted even further back until he balanced on the window ledge. 'I know nothing about a killing in Calcutta.'

Watters realised that Ted was a fanatic, a man prepared to die for his cause. There was no point in trying to reason with him. Watters met Ted's gaze, saw his eyes widen slightly, and guessed that something was happening behind him.

Instinct made Watters duck and spin in time to see the bloodied and battered Scouse stagger into the room with Niner's Adams revolver in his fist. Almost immediately, Scouse fired. Watters never knew where the bullet went, for he squeezed the Tranter's trigger in the same movement. He saw his bullet strike Scouse's chest, cocked, and fired again. Scouse crumpled, staring at the blood that spurted from his chest. The incident had taken less than fifteen seconds.

Noticing that Ted was staring at his fallen comrade, Watters tried to outflank him. He moved sideways, only for his injured leg to drag, knocking down a pile of Beaumont's files. Watters instinctively tried to catch them, with that slight movement saving his life as Ted fired the Colt he flicked from his shoulder holster. Afraid to return fire with Beaumont so close, Watters fell to the ground, rolled, slithered on the files, and slammed against the legs of the desk. He looked up to see Ted levelling the revolver.

'No, you don't!'

Reaching up, Watters grabbed the barrel, so the shot slammed against the far wall. Using the barrel as a lever, he bent Ted's wrist backwards, forcing him to drop the revolver. Ted countered by dropping on top of him with a broad-bladed knife in his right hand.

'Sergeant!' That was Duff's voice. 'I'm coming! Watch the knife!'

As lamplight flickered on the steel, Watters twisted aside. The knife blade rammed into the floorboards. Watters jabbed straight fingers into Ted's throat, saw Ted's mouth open as he gasped for air, and pulled at his tongue.

Ted gargled but still managed to land a shrewd punch into Watters's kidneys. Watters jerked in agony with the metal cylinder falling from his pocket. Again Ted moved forward, wrenching the knife from the floor. His slash would have cut Watters's throat had Duff not blocked the blow with his staff.

'Sergeant Watters!' Beaumont's warning shout sounded surprisingly strong for a man who had just been strangled. Ignoring Beaumont, Watters snatched up the cylinder. Pressing the button, he thrust the device inside Ted's shirt.

Ted screamed with a mixture of fear and frustration. He tried to slash with the knife again, only for Duff to dash forward and push him through the open window. Ted's scream only ended when the explosion of the cylinder tore a hole in his chest. After that, there was silence except for the sound of hurrying feet as people ran to see what had happened.

Watters took a deep breath. 'Thank you, Duff. I think you saved my life there.'

'I think you both saved my life.' Beaumont looked shaken as he slumped behind his desk.

CHAPTER TWENTY-FOUR
DUNDEE: DECEMBER 1862

Morag handed the cup to Watters. 'There you are Sergeant Watters, a nice cup of tea.'

The ticking of the longcase clock was soft against the crackle of the fire and the hiss of the gas lighting. Lighting the cigarette on the end of his ivory holder, Beaumont sat back in his winged armchair. 'It was as well that I bought a steel anti-garrotter collar after all your warnings,' he said. 'That American fellow could never have strangled me with that thing around my neck.'

'He could have shot you though,' Watters reminded, but Beaumont shook his head.

'Not with you there, Sergeant. I knew that you would not let me down.' Beaumont's eyes were suddenly terribly wise. 'Of course, I have informed Mr Holderby. He was so frightfully upset about the whole thing that he could not apologise enough.'

'Mr Mackay and Sir John Ogilvy have been busy at the United States Consulate,' Watters said, 'and between us, we've worked out the sequence of events. The fellow we threw out of the window, the man I knew as Ted Houghton, was a rogue Federal agent posing as a Confederate while passing information to the North. He was the fellow that bribed the local abolitionists to set fire to your mills as well.'

Beaumont nodded. 'Houghton was a dangerous man.'

'As you can imagine,' Watters said, 'Sir John Ogilvy and Mr Mackay asked many questions of Mr Holderby. He assured us that the United States government was not connected with these outrages. Houghton used his official position to further his extreme ideas of murder and fire-raising.'

Beaumont pulled at his cigarette. 'That is what Mr Holderby told me.'

'Ted Houghton was also a bit of a chameleon, able to alter his accent and his attitude depending on whom he was with. I suspect he may even have worked in Rogers' Yard for a while for he told the Federals all about *Alexander MacGillivray* even before it was launched. The other two, Niner and Scouse, were mid-level maritime toughs who would do anything for a few sovereigns.'

'I don't like to think about foreign spies loose around Dundee,' Beaumont said.

'Yes, sir,' Watters agreed. About to say that it would not have happened if Beaumont had not sought money at the expense of morality, he remembered Marie's opinion of his diplomacy. 'It seems that Mr William Caskie was keeping secrets from you, Mr Beaumont.'

Beaumont did not reply directly. He smiled. 'I spoke with Sir John about using the Volunteers to search for the incendiaries. I consider Sir John as a friend. He listens to me.'

'Yes, Mr Beaumont. As long as the explosive devices, if any, are located, I do not care who finds them.'

Beaumont looked up as his clerk entered. 'Here, Cattanach. Deal with this lot, would you?' He handed over a batch of files.

Cattanach gave a little bow. 'Right away, sir.' He scurried away with the swallowtails of his coat flapping over his lean backside.

'It seems, however, that the Volunteers were not necessary.' Beaumont drew deeply on his ivory cigarette holder. 'You had already warned the mill managers.' He walked toward the fire, turned his back, and surveyed Watters through clear eyes. 'They did not find any of these fire-raising devices in the mills.'

'No, Mr Beaumont. However, my colleagues Constables Duff and Scuddamore found six in Houghton's luggage.'

Beaumont raised his eyebrows. 'In that case, Watters, you probably saved hundreds or even thousands of pounds worth of damage and subsequent higher insurance premiums and loss of profit.'

'Possibly some lives as well,' Watters said quietly. 'If the mill hands had been inside the mills when these fire-raising things went off, God only knows how many might have been hurt or killed.'

Raised voices sounded from downstairs as Amy argued with Elizabeth about whose turn it was to use the piano. Beaumont shook his head in paternal condemnation.

'Sir John advised that we should not make an official complaint about this matter to the American authorities. He says the least said, soonest mentioned. That's it, ended now. However, you did save my life, Sergeant, and I won't forget it. I do not know where my son-in-law is.'

'France,' Watters said bluntly. 'He broke no law, despite all his actions.' He remembered Caskie's callousness and resolved to investigate every section of his business interests until he found cause to arrest him. 'We did not find the seaman, Jones,' Watters reminded. 'Nor did I solve the murder on *Lady of Blackness*.' These two failures rankled.

Beaumont shook his head. 'I don't think anybody ever could solve that murder, Sergeant, not considering the time and distance involved.' He reached for a sealed packet that lay on the table. 'Here's a small gift for you, Sergeant. Open it when you get home. It's not much, but please accept it as a token of my gratitude.'

Watters shook his head, smiling as he pushed the packet back. 'I was only doing my duty, sir. I cannot accept any reward.'

'As you wish, Sergeant.' Beaumont held out his hand. 'I hope you will accept my handshake instead.'

'I will do that with pleasure, sir.'

Watters felt vaguely dissatisfied as he walked out of the building. Mackay had set him three tasks: solve the murder on *Lady of Blackness*, protect Beaumont, and find out who had planned the fire-raising at Beaumont's mills. He had completed the third and second task. The Dundee and Forfarshire Anti-slavery Alliance had set the initial fires, with the US government, officially or unofficially, behind the operation, yet he had not located the mysterious woman that Ted Houghton believed headed the Alliance. With Ted Houghton out of the way, the threat to Beaumont's life had eased, and Watters had been assured that he could rely on Sir John to pressurise the US government to end any possible intimidation from that quarter.

Watters swung his cane. He had not solved the murder on *Lady of Blackness.* When Ted's conspiracy had come to light, Watters had supposed there to be a connection. Yet Ted had twice denied any knowledge. Something nagged at Watters's mind. The moment he reached the police office, he called over Scuddamore and Duff and explained his worries.

'Things are not as clear-cut as I like,' Watters said. 'I like order; I like reasons for things happening.'

'They are criminals, Sergeant,' Duff said. 'They don't think like normal people. Houghton was probably lying.'

'Houghton was more than a common criminal,' Watters said. 'As well as a fanatic, he may have been an agent of a foreign government. I agree his mind was coloured by his beliefs, so to him everything was black and white.' Watters shook his head. 'In that case, why should he deny something of which he would ordinarily be proud?'

'Maybe he forgot?' Scuddamore said.

'No.' Watters adopted Mackay's habit of drumming his fingers on the desk. 'Houghton was too dedicated for that. I am well aware that most assaults are stupid, casual affairs fuelled by drink or quick temper, while poverty or simple greed drives petty theft. More major crimes are different. A man does not suddenly decide to destroy a ship with the explosives he happens to have in his possession.'

'Yes, Sergeant.' Scuddamore and Duff exchanged glances. Watters realised that they now believed he was as obsessed as Ted Houghton had been.

'Something is not right,' Watters said. 'And I mean to get to the bottom of it. This enquiry is not completed until every last I is dotted, and every last T is crossed. Get back to work, gentlemen. I want every lead followed again. I want to find the woman who paid Varthley, I want Seaman Jones, and I want the murderer of that unfortunate fire-raiser in Calcutta.' *I also want William Caskie, but that is now personal.*

'How, Sergeant?' Duff asked.

'I'll start by interviewing Varthley again.'

'He's in prison, sir,' Duff said.

'Then that's where I will go.' Grabbing his hat and cane, Watters rose. 'I'm not happy, gentlemen. When I'm not happy, it means that you two are not happy because I will make you work until I am smiling again. Duff, scour the shipping companies for this Jones fellow. I want to know the whereabouts of every seaman on the day of the murder on *Lady of Blackness*.'

'There are thousands, Sergeant!'

'Then you had better get busy, hadn't you?'

'I'll help him, Sergeant,' Scuddamore said.

'No, Scuddamore.' Watters put a hand on his shoulder. 'I want you to find the name and address of every woman in the Dundee area who supports anti-slavery. Find every woman who makes a donation, who attends meetings, who even speak to them.'

'Yes, Sergeant.'

'Every single one, Scuddamore.' Watters strode out of the police office. He had set his men work to do. Now he must justify his decision.

It was fortunate that Varthley was held in Dundee Prison, only a few yards from the police office. Limping from his various cuts and bruises, Watters followed the turnkey to Varthley's cell.

'Don't be too hard on him,' the turnkey said as he opened the door. 'He's a poor soul; he spends his time either crying like a baby or spouting his abolitionist nonsense.' He shook his head. 'I agree with his sentiments, mind, if not his methods.'

Watters raised his voice to enable Varthley to hear. 'I don't find the poor fellow's abolitionist views offensive,' he said. 'In fact, I agree entirely that the slaves should be freed.'

'Do you, Sergeant?' Varthley looked up from the thin straw mattress on which he had been lying.

'Of course, I do,' Watters said honestly. 'No decent person can agree with slavery. It is a filthy thing to do to any human being.'

'So you agree with us.'

'I always did,' Watters sat on the bed at Varthley's side. 'It is the attempts to burn down factories and endanger lives I am against.' He shook his head. 'I did not like the attack on poor Amy Beaumont either. You could have really hurt her, Varthley.'

'No, Sergeant Watters.' Varthley sat up, shaking his head. 'That wasn't the idea. I was only to slap her the one time, or maybe twice at most, and say the things against slavery.'

'You did not say that before,' Watters pointed out.

'You never asked that before,' Varthley said.

'Now, Mr Varthley,' Watters employed his gentlest tone, 'I need you to help me now. Think hard, think as hard as you can. Tell me about this woman who paid you.'

'Yes, Sergeant Watters.' Varthley looked at Watters much as a rabbit might stare at a predatory stoat.

'What was she like?'

'I don't know,' Varthley said.

'You spoke to her; you saw her.' Watters retained his patience as best he could.

'I never saw her,' Varthley shook his head. 'She was all covered up with a scarf.'

Watters sighed. He should have expected that the main instigator had hidden her identity. 'Was she tall? Short? Slender? Plump?'

'Oh, she was tall,' Varthley said. 'Tall for a woman. She was nearly as tall as a man, Sergeant Watters. And a nice shape.' He moved his hands to illustrate a woman's curves. 'Like that. Lots to hold on to, you know?'

'I can imagine,' Watters said. For a second, he had wondered if the woman had in fact been a man in disguise, but Varthley's description of her charms disposed of that idea.

'A tall woman then,' Watters noted. 'Was she intelligent? Educated?'

'Yes,' Varthley said at once. 'She was a gentlewoman.'

'And what did she say. Tell me as accurately as you can remember.'

Varthley thought for a long moment. 'She said I was to run up to Miss Amy Beaumont, say "creatures like you should not be allowed to walk, not when your father is encouraging so much suffering in the world," give her a good slap on the face, and then run away. She said I had to do it in the most public place in Newport. I was to give her one or two hard slaps and then run away.'

Watters frowned. 'How did you know where to find Miss Beaumont?'

'I just said.' Varthley frowned. 'The lady told me. She told me that Miss Amy Beaumont and Miss Elizabeth Caskie would be in Newport Pleasure Gardens.'

How the devil did she know that?

'Thank you,' Watters said. 'I have one more question before I leave you in peace.' He chose his words carefully. 'Would you recognise her voice again, even if you could not see her face?'

Varthley nodded eagerly. 'Yes, yes I would. It was very clear.'

'Thank you, Mr Varthley.'

Watters's mind was in turmoil as he walked away. He was a step further forward. The instigator was a tall, educated woman who was fully aware of Amy's movements. She had told Varthley what to say and wanted only one or at most two slaps. *Why stop at two? If the woman intended to hurt Amy and by implication, Beaumont, why did she not order a more serious attack? As assaults go, it was minor;* indeed, Watters remembered, Elizabeth had slapped Amy quite hard at the dance. Watters frowned again. *What had Amy said then? "Oh, what we suffer for fashion and beliefs."*

Why had she added 'beliefs' then? Watters grunted. There had been no reason to mention beliefs for a fashion statement. Women were strange creatures indeed. However, he was making progress. Now he had to find out who else would know about Amy's movements.

The servants? They were not present when Amy and Elizabeth discussed Newport.

Twirling his cane, Watters marched from the prison toward Dock Street. No matter what happened, he would solve this case, even if he had to work unpaid overtime to do it. Watters knew the answers were there, nagging at the corners of his mind. He felt as if the chess master was laughing at him, allowing him to know just so much before pulling agonisingly away again.

Well, that could not be allowed. He was Sergeant Watters of the Dundee Police, not some Johnny Raw recruit with squeaky boots not yet adequately broken in.

As always, factory smoke tainted the street air of Dundee, despite the bite from the Tay. Watters stood outside Beaumont's Dock Street offices, adjusted his new hat, and twirled his cane. He nodded to Cattanach as the clerk scurried past.

'Morning, Cattanach.'

'Good morning, sir.' Cattanach gave his usual little bow.

'Is Mr Beaumont in the office?' Watters asked.

'No, sir,' Cattanach bowed again, smiling. 'Mr Beaumont is in Mount Pleasant House, sir. He is with Mr and Mrs Caskie.'

Damn. 'Thank you, Cattanach. I will call on him there.' Watters turned around to find a cab as Cattanach withdrew into the building.

Overshadowed by the ship's spars that overlapped one side of the street, seamen hurried on various errands while dock workers wheeled carts and rolled barrels. Watters saw a cab parked further up the road with the driver engaged in conversation with a familiar figure.

'Good morning, Captain Bremner.' Watters tapped the brim of his hat with his cane. 'How are you today? And is this cab free?'

'I am very well, thank you, Sergeant, and the cab is all yours.' Although Bremner looked as harassed as any ship's captain preparing to cast anchor, he spared time to talk to Watters. 'I see you found Jones, then, Sergeant.'

'No, Captain.' Watters shook his head. 'We have not given up yet, though.'

Bremner frowned. 'I saw you talking to him a moment ago, Sergeant.' The captain nodded across the road. 'Outside Beaumont's shipping office.'

'You must be mistaken, sir,' Watters said. 'The only man I was talking to was Cattanach, Mr Beaumont's clerk.'

Bremner's frown deepened. 'You were with the man I knew as Jones, Sergeant. I don't care a tuppeny damn what he calls himself now, but that was Jones. You have my word on it!'

Jones! Watters took a deep breath. 'Thank you, Captain. I am very much obliged to you.'

Watters fought his surge of excitement. *So Cattanach is Jones. That opens up a whole new can of worms. Does Beaumont know? He must know that his clerk was on a voyage to Calcutta. Why the secrecy?*

Watters had to think. Touching his hat once more, he strode away from the confused cab driver. He always thought with more clarity when he walked or played golf. Marching along Dock Street with his mind working and his cane swinging, Watters tried to slot things into some sort of logical order.

Cattanach was Jones. Cattanach the servile clerk, always bowing and scraping, was Jones, the nondescript, average-built and average-looking seaman that nobody could describe or find. Why? Why did Beaumont hide him? Was Cattanach responsible for the murder in Calcutta? Watters knew he had no proof except the coincidence of place and the fact that Cattanach disguised his name. *Why should he do that unless he has something to hide?*

Even more important than that: why had Beaumont not informed him? Watters looked up. His thinking walk had taken him to the western side of Magdalene Yard Road. Turning abruptly, he strode back. There was no rush to pick up Cattanach; he knew where the man was. *By God, I'll crack this case yet!*

* * *

'Duff, do you have that list of women for me?' Watters strode into the police office. 'Duff! Where are you?'

'Here, Sergeant!' Duff was at Watters's desk.

'Get off my seat.' Watters hauled Duff away. 'Do you have that list of women connected to the abolitionist movement?'

'Yes, Sergeant.'

Watters scanned the names. 'There are twenty women here. How many do you know by sight?'

Duff hesitated. 'Some of them, Sergeant. Not all. Not many.'

'Right, fetch me Scuddamore. He'll know them all, I wager.' Watters looked up. 'Well move, Duff! I haven't got all day!'

'Yes, Sergeant.' Duff nearly ran away as Watters reread the names.

'You want me, Sergeant?' Scuddamore hurried up. 'I'm still working on the list of seamen...'

'Forget Jones. You're a ladies' man, Scuddamore. Tell me what these women are like.' Watters handed over the list.

Scuddamore smiled. 'Alicia Hepworth is a stunner,' he said.

'Tall or short?' Watters asked.

'Short, she's about...'

'Score her off the list. Score anybody off the list who is not tall.' Watters handed over his pen and watched as Scuddamore removed half the names. 'How many are left?'

'Nine, Sergeant.'

'Right, our woman also sounds well-educated. That argues for at least a middling background.'

'Yes, Sergeant,' Scuddamore said. 'Should I remove any mill hands and the like?'

'Yes,' Watters said after a minute's consideration. 'Unless they are tall and well-educated.'

'That only leaves six women,' Scuddamore said. 'We have Mrs Jacqueline Foreman, Mrs Charlotte Caskie, Mrs Mary Caskie, Miss Elizabeth Caskie, and Miss Anna MacKechnie.'

Watters leaned back in his chair. 'By our rough process of elimination, gentlemen, one of these women might be our suspect.' Realising that he was again drumming his fingers on the desk, he stopped. 'What do we know about Miss Anna MacKechnie?'

'She is a school teacher.' Trust Scuddamore to know about Dundee's female population. 'She is reasonably tall for a woman.' Scuddamore's glance at Watters killed his incipient smile. 'She's about five foot five, maybe five foot six, with auburn hair and a temper!' Despite Watters's frown, Scuddamore could not control his grin. 'What a temper that woman has on her! I pity her pupils; I really do!'

'So in height and class, she could be a suspect. In your opinion, would Miss MacKechnie be liable to bribe a man to attack Amy Beaumont?'

Scuddamore nodded. 'Yes, Sergeant. She is an evil bitch. Sorry, Sergeant, I mean, she can be aggressive to anybody who disagrees with her.'

Watters guessed that Scuddamore had once been the victim of Miss MacKechnie's temper. 'What do you know about the others?'

'Mrs Foreman.' Scuddamore screwed up his face. 'She's as ugly as sin, tall as a man, and dedicated to the abolitionist's cause.'

Watters nodded and said nothing. He did not agree with Scuddamore's description of Mrs Foreman. On the other hand, he had never been prone to judging women by their looks. 'Is she liable to advocate violence?'

'I don't know,' Scuddamore said frankly. 'I think you have spoken to her more often than I have. We don't move in the same circles.'

'Keep her on the list,' Watters said. 'Who does that leave?'

'Just the Caskie women,' Duff said, 'Mrs Charlotte Caskie, Miss Elizabeth, and Mrs Mary Caskie.'

About to discount all three, Watters closed his mouth. He already knew his opinion. He wanted Scuddamore's thoughts.

'We all know how Mrs Mary Caskie feels about Beaumont,' Scuddamore said.

'No, we don't,' Watters contradicted at once. 'How does Mrs Mary Caskie feel about Beaumont?'

'Don't you know?' Scuddamore sounded amused. 'The two of them were walking out together before Beaumont met Mrs Beaumont.'

'I did not know that,' Watters said.

'Common knowledge in Dundee,' Scuddamore said.

'Not to me.' Watters's fingers were now automatically drumming on the desk. 'That must be twenty-odd years ago.'

'That was.' Scuddamore evidently enjoyed having information that Watters did not know. 'When first Mrs Beaumont died, and then Mr Caskie senior, Mrs Mary Caskie tried to rekindle her relationship with Mr Beaumont.'

'How do you know all this tittle-tattle?' Watters asked.

'Some I heard in the publics, other bits were in the society columns of the papers,' Scuddamore said. 'You should read them, Sergeant.'

'I'll leave that sort of muck-raking, scandal-seeking nonsense to you,' Watters said. 'All the same, maybe we should have a word with Mrs Mary Caskie. That leaves the other Caskie women.'

'Miss Elizabeth and Mrs Charlotte Caskie, nee Beaumont,' Scuddamore said.

'Yes,' Watters said. 'I know young Elizabeth. Tell me about Mrs Charlotte. Does she also have dark secrets?'

Scuddamore shrugged. 'Not that I know of, Sergeant. She's not the most attractive of women, so I have no interest in her.'

'All right. We have four possible suspects to interview: Mrs Mary Caskie, Mrs Foreman, Miss Elizabeth Caskie, and Miss MacKechnie.'

'Is that Miss MacKechnie the skelp-doup you're looking for?' Sergeant Murdoch's heavy tread shook the fittings as he stomped across the room.

'Aye, that's her.' Watters smiled at Murdoch's description of a school teacher.

'Well, you'll not find her in Dundee,' Murdoch said. 'She Jimmy Granted to Canada about six weeks ago.'

'I wondered why I hadn't seen her,' Scuddamore said. 'She immigrated to Canada, did she? Poor Canada. What has it done to deserve a demon like her?'

'Six weeks ago.' Watters did a quick calculation. 'That was before all this nonsense started, so she's out of the picture.' He stood up. 'Before you go, Murdoch, what do you know about these other women?'

Murdoch shrugged. 'Nothing much, Watters; I've had no occasion to arrest either of them. I only know about the MacKechnie woman because she taught our wee Alice.'

'Do you know anything about Beaumont's clerk?' Watters pushed for any information he could get. 'That's the fellow who calls himself Cattanach. He might go under the name Jones.'

'I don't know him either,' Murdoch said. 'Why?' He grunted when Watters explained. 'I never did trust Big Man Beaumont. He was too much of a preacher to be true blue. I don't believe people who appear white as the driven snow. Is Cattanach your murderer?'

'He might be,' Watters said. 'I know where he is, and I think he believes he's got away with his deception. He can wait.'

'You're working on something,' Murdoch said.

'I do have a bit of a plan,' Watters agreed, motioning Duff and Scuddamore closer. 'It might work, and it might not. Now listen carefully, you gentlemen. This might be a complete waste of time, or it might crack the case. If it fails, it will land me in a lot of trouble, but it will eliminate our prime suspect, leaving only two.'

'How about us?' Scuddamore asked.

'You will be obeying my orders,' Watters said. 'You have no choice in the matter.' He grinned. 'That's not quite true. I will give you the opportunity to back out now if you wish. Are you with me?'

Duff shrugged and said nothing while Scuddamore grunted. Taking these responses for assents, Watters explained what he wished to do.

'You're taking a risk,' Scuddamore said when Watters finished.

'You might be completely wrong.' Duff evidently agreed with Scuddamore.

'When we tried to trap the woman who bribed wee Willie,' Watters said, 'I thought it was Navarino. It wasn't, but when I tackled Navarino, Mrs Foreman was there, in the crowd near the steps. She is also a recognised abolitionist.' Watters frowned. 'I should have put two and two together earlier.'

Duff and Scuddamore glanced at each other, saying nothing.

Watters continued. 'I want her to confront Beaumont face to face. I want to see her reaction, and I want Willie and Varthley to hear her voice.'

'Do you think she's the woman?' Duff asked.

'I don't know,' Watters said. 'I think she might be.' He thought of the occasions when Mrs Foreman came to him in friendship. She had often asked about the case. At the time, he had felt her irritating. Now, he wondered if she had been squeezing information from him.

'Will Mrs Foreman come to Mount Pleasant?' Scuddamore asked.

'She might if Mr Beaumont sends her his card with an invitation to discuss his withdrawal from any Confederate connections,' Watters said. 'Beaumont gave me his card some weeks ago.' He produced it from a drawer of his desk.

'That's surely illegal,' Scuddamore said.

'I know,' Watters agreed calmly. 'I also know a scribe who can copy Beaumont's handwriting perfectly, which will be a blatant forgery and equally illegal.'

'You could certainly land in major trouble,' Scuddamore pointed out. 'Anyway, young Willie said the woman who spoke to him was a foreigner. Mrs Foreman is as Scottish as I am.'

'That concerns me,' Watters admitted. 'Varthley said the woman was educated. Willie said she was foreign. I wonder if there were two women.' He sighed. 'I want to finally wrap this case up. This experiment might go badly wrong.' He forced a smile he hoped looked confident. 'Or it could trap Mrs Foreman and finish things off. We're setting the cat among the pigeons in no uncertain manner.' He nodded to Duff. 'Are you sure that neither Mr Beaumont nor Cattanach have ever met you?'

'Never,' Duff said. 'And they won't think I'm a police officer. I only managed to sneak in by standing on my toes, stretching, and pushing up the measuring tape.' His laugh drew the attention of everyone in the room. 'That was a blatant forgery as well.'

* * *

A light flurry of early snow blurred the outline of Mount Pleasant as Watters and Duff drew up in the hansom cab. Watters felt the nerves biting at him as he ordered the driver to wait.

'We could be some time,' Watters said. 'So find a dry spot and catch some sleep. We'll pay for your time.' *Mr Mackay will surely love the expenses I am causing him.*

Nodding, the cabbie cracked the reins. Watters watched him drive the cab around the side of the building.

'Here we go.' Watters checked for the Tranter inside his coat as he headed for the front door. James, the footman, immediately ushered him towards Beaumont's study at the top of the house.

'Go right up, Sergeant.'

Dressed in a canvas shirt and trousers, with a battered cap on his head, Duff followed, his footsteps sounding hollow on the thick carpets.

'Oh, James,' Watters tried to sound casual. 'I have taken the liberty of inviting Mrs Foreman over to talk to Mr Beaumont. Please show her up to the study when she arrives.'

'Very good, Sergeant Watters.' James nodded.

'Come in,' Beaumont called in response to Watters's knock. He looked surprised as Watters and Duff entered. 'Sergeant Watters. I was not informed you were coming.'

'No, sir.' Watters stepped in with Duff a pace behind. 'I have some new information about the murder on *Lady of Blackness*, which I would wish to share with you.' He saw Cattanach look up from his position beside the desk.

'Indeed?' Beaumont hardly blinked. 'I thought that was all done and dusted, Sergeant. Were the Americans not behind it all? I reasoned that a Confederate agent stopped a Federal supporter, possibly that Houghton fellow, from destroying that vessel.'

'That was one of my theories, Mr Beaumont. However...' Watters indicated Duff. 'This gentleman was a seaman on board *Lady of Blackness*.' The lie did not come easily. 'He can identify the man Jones who is our prime suspect for the murder.'

Duff snatched off his cap and held it respectfully in front of him as he shuffled forward. 'Begging your pardon, Mr Beaumont, sir, I was on *Lady of Blackness* on her voyage from Calcutta.'

Watters inwardly cringed at Duff's overacting. 'This is Alexander Duff, sir.'

'There was no Duff on that vessel,' Cattanach said at once.

'Come along now, Jonesy,' Duff countered Cattanach's words with a grin. 'You and me were side by side in the foc'sle. Don't you remember that storm off the Cape when we had to go aloft and furl the topmast? We were on the same yardarm when the old *Lady* nearly tossed us out, remember? You said your cousin Davy Jones was waiting for us.'

Cattanach shook his head. 'You're talking nonsense, man.'

Beaumont half rose from his desk. 'This is Cattanach, my clerk, Duff. You must be mistaken.'

Watters tried to appear confident. He was acting on the word of a ship's captain who had glimpsed Cattanach across a busy street. 'There is no mistake, I'm afraid, sir. Your man Cattanach was on that ship under the name of Jones.' Watters took a deep breath. 'I am placing him under arrest, sir, on suspicion of murder and will take him away for further questioning.'

'The devil you are.' Beaumont stood up, his face red with fury. 'Get out of my office, Sergeant.'

'I will leave your office, sir,' Watters said, 'and I will leave with Cattanach. He can come willingly, or I can have him restrained.' He produced his handcuffs. 'We will question him at the police office and find out the truth.' Watters's pause was significant. 'The whole truth.'

'Your superiors will hear about this.' Beaumont had regained control of himself. 'Now leave. Cattanach remains where he is. I won't permit you to take away my clerk.'

'It's all right, sir.' Cattanach had been examining Duff. 'I know the manifests of your ships. There was no seaman named Duff on *Lady of Blackness*. That man,' he pointed to Duff, 'is the imposter, not me.'

Beaumont reverted to the charming gentleman that Watters knew so well. 'I believe you have made an honest mistake, Sergeant Watters. I do appreciate your zeal, however, so on consideration, I will not take this matter any further. My clerk will fetch the crew manifest for *Lady of Blackness*; if there is no seaman named Duff on the list, then we will call this matter closed.'

Watters knew his bluff had been called. He had hoped for a more extreme reaction from Cattanach. 'Where is the manifest located, sir?'

'In the shipping office on Dock Street,' Cattanach replied for Beaumont. 'If Mr Beaumont allows me to take a cab, I can be there and back within the hour.'

'No.' Watters had to force the issue. If Cattanach left Mount Pleasant, he might never return. 'You're coming with me.' He held out the handcuffs. 'Come along, Cattanach, Jones, or whatever your name is.'

A knock at the door interrupted them. 'Not now!' Beaumont roared. 'God damn it, can a man not have peace in his own house?'

The knock sounded a second time, louder than before.

'Not now!' Beaumont shouted again.

Watters glanced at Duff. 'That will be the lady,' he said quietly, opening the door. Rather than Mrs Foreman as he had hoped, Scuddamore stood there with young Willie at one side, washed, neat, and in handcuffs that seemed larger than his hands. Varthley stood at the other side, bow-shouldered and shaking.

Watters cursed. He had planned for Mrs Foreman to arrive first. *Oh well, the best-laid plans of mice and men aft gang agley.* He thought quickly. 'Wait in the hall downstairs, Scuddamore. We are not ready for you yet.'

'Yes, Sergeant,' Scuddamore said. 'Come on, you two.'

'What's this?' Beaumont was red-faced with anger. 'How dare you treat my home in this fashion?'

'What's all the commotion, Father?' Amy enquired as she ran up the stairs as fast as her commodious skirt would allow, with Elizabeth standing on the landing. Halfway up, Amy stopped, stared at Varthley and gave a small scream. 'You!'

Watters swore again. He had never intended that Amy should come face to face with the man who had attacked her. His plan was collapsing into chaos.

Elizabeth turned away. 'Amy! Don't take on so. Come back down.' Turning quickly, she skipped back towards the lower floor.

'That's her!' Varthley shouted, rattling his handcuffs as he tried to point. 'That's the woman who paid me!'

Watters was unsure which emotion was uppermost, relief or confusion. He stepped outside the office door, expecting to see that Mrs Foreman had arrived, but instead, Varthley was pointing at Elizabeth.

'I remember her voice,' Varthley was shouting. 'That's the woman. That's the one!'

'It's her!' Young Willie joined Varthley. 'She done it!' He grabbed hold of Scuddamore's coat with both manacled hands. 'She still owes me five shillings.' He also pointed directly at Elizabeth.

'What the devil is the meaning of this?' Beaumont stood at his doorway, staring at the turmoil in his usually well-ordered house.

'Well, I'm blessed if I know,' Watters said to Duff. 'I think we'd better take them all along for questioning. We'll straighten this up at the police office.'

Cattanach broke first. Leaping from his position beside the desk, he dived for the stairs to find Duff blocking his passage.

'Not so fast.' Duff had drawn his baton from under his coat.

Watters preferred actions to words. Reversing his cane, he lashed out with the lead-weighted end, catching Cattanach across the back of the right knee. Staggering against the ornate bannister, Cattanach dropped a long spike from up his sleeve into his fist. 'Right then, you bluebottle bastard!'

Watters stepped back, remembering the deep hole in the neck of the murdered man on *Lady of Blackness*.

'He's mine, Sergeant.' Without hesitation, Duff smashed his baton onto Cattanach's wrist. The crack of broken bones was quite audible as Cattanach gasped. The spike thumped onto the deep Axminster carpet. Duff hit him again, laying him flat on the floor.

'It's the noose for you, boy!' Duff said.

'I was just obeying orders!' Cattanach clutched his bleeding head.

'Whose orders?' Watters threatened with the weighted end of his cane.

'Mr Beaumont's.' Cattanach cowered away. 'He said he'd look after me. He said there was a plot to sink *Lady of Blackness,* and I was to guard it and he'd look after me. If I'm for the noose then so is he.' He spat at Duff. 'Did you think he was the saint that everybody said he was?'

'Guard Cattanach,' Watters said. 'Put Mr Beaumont under arrest as well.' Watters turned his attention to Varthley and Willie. 'Right you two, what's all this nonsense about? You know these two ladies were not involved...'

'That's her.' Willie was nearly frantic as he rattled the handcuffs. 'That's the woman. I told you she was foreign!'

'Miss Caskie is no more foreign than I am.' Scuddamore shook him. 'You're a lying little tyke.'

'You're foreign too,' Willie said. 'You're as foreign as a Frog. You're no' from Dundee!'

Watters breathed out slowly as realisation dawned. To Willie, trapped by poverty in the hell's kitchen of Dundee's slums, any outsider would be a foreigner. It was a new concept to Watters, and one he blamed himself for not recognising. Willie had no idea of national or international boundaries; to him, his own sordid corner of Dundee was the world. He would see even the countryside round about as alien and therefore foreign. 'Hold her, Scuddamore!'

'Why?' Watters directed his question at Elizabeth. 'Why pay somebody to attack your special friend? Why pay somebody to burn down Mr Beaumont's mill?' He no longer wished to speculate. 'Not that it matters; you'll be in jail for a long time for instigating fire-raising.'

'It would be about the slave question,' Scuddamore said.

Elizabeth's laughter mocked them all. 'Slaves! You really don't know anything, do you? You know nothing and understand even less! It's nothing to do with slaves.' She jabbed a finger toward Beaumont. 'It's all to do with him! It's that manipulative tyrant!'

'We'll talk about all this in the police office.' Watters looked up. He had not heard Mrs Foreman arrive. She smiled at him.

'Oh, Sergeant Watters,' Mrs Foreman said. 'Isn't this exciting?'

CHAPTER TWENTY-FIVE
DUNDEE: DECEMBER 1862

If Mackay's fingers had danced the polka before, now they performed a Highland jig as both hands drummed on his desk. 'This has been a most confusing case, Watters. It has been most confusing indeed. I confess that I am nearly as much at a loss now as I was when the events occurred.'

'Yes, sir,' Watters said.

Mackay stilled his fingers, sighed, and leaned back on his seat. 'Tell me what's happened, Watters. Start with Mr Beaumont.'

'Yes, sir. Mr Beaumont was aware that somebody was targeting his business without knowing who it was. He heard about the threat to destroy *Lady of Blackness*, so hired an ex-Royal Navy steward, Cattanach, to infiltrate the crew under the name of Jones. When they were in Calcutta, Cattanach saw the fellow in the hold with gunpowder and fuses, crept up, and killed him with this.' Watters placed Cattanach's spike on the desk.

Mackay nodded slowly. 'We can't charge Mr Beaumont with protecting his own ship.'

'No, sir, but we can charge him with concealing a crime by not handing Cattanach over to us when he knew he was guilty of murder.'

Mackay grunted. 'That will ruin his business credentials, which will be the worst punishment possible for such a man. Now, let's look at

Cattanach. As the murder was on board a British ship, he was techni-cally on British soil, so he'll be charged with murder or at least culpable homicide.'

'Yes, sir,' Watters agreed.

'Do we know who the murdered man was?'

Watters consulted the notes he had made during his interrogation of Elizabeth Caskie. 'I believe so, sir. Do you recall the case of the Hon-ourable Peter Turnbull?'

Mackay nodded. 'I recall Turnbull, the aristocrat who went missing owing thousands of pounds.'

'That's the fellow. I doubt he'll ever pay his debtors.' Watters permit-ted himself a small smile. 'Elizabeth Caskie was quite talkative once we got her into the interview room.'

'Was she indeed? What the devil did Turnbull have to do with anything? How the devil did Elizabeth Caskie contact him?' Mackay stilled his fingers. 'And why did he agree to act the incendiary?'

'The world of the minor landowners is small, sir,' Watters said. 'Turnbull had gambling debts; he owed two thousand to Caskie. Eliz-abeth arranged for him to ship out to India with a hundred pounds to start a new life and his debts to Caskie quashed in exchange for destroying *Lady of Blackness*. That's her story anyway.'

Mackay's fingers rapped on the desk again. 'We'll contact Turnbull's family for identification. Now, Elizabeth Caskie. Tell me about her.'

'On her own admission, sir, she was the prime instigator.'

'For God's sake, why?' Mackay shook his head. 'She is a close friend of Beaumont's younger daughter; she had everything anybody could possibly want. Why go against Mr Beaumont?'

Watters consulted his notes. 'Two reasons, sir. Firstly, The Caskies were in financial difficulties, while Beaumont was a major commercial rival. William Caskie was a gambler, as we know. That was one reason he agreed to build a ship for the South; he would recoup his losses.'

'Foolish fellow.' Mackay's fingers were drumming again.

'Yes, sir. If William Caskie's business failed, then Elizabeth would face relative poverty, which she could not stand.'

'She would still be comfortably off.'

'Yes, sir, but her sort needs wealth, not mere comfort.'

Mackay's fingers increased their dancing. 'And the second reason?'

'She is an evil, unprincipled woman, sir.' Watters waited for condemnation.

'Explain further,' Mackay demanded.

'The less business that Beaumont got, the more could go to Caskie, so Elizabeth disrupted the mills with fires, tried to sink Beaumont's ships, and made the world, and us, believe that there was a conspiracy against Beaumont. It was pure coincidence that the Federal agents had a similar notion. It was Elizabeth who suggested that Amy should go to Newport. She planned the attack.'

'That's very cold-blooded,' Mackay said.

Watters nodded. 'Amy endured worse at the dance when she mentioned suffering for fashion and beliefs. I wondered at her choice of words at the time and thought she might be involved in some way. I was wrong about her.'

'I suppose that Elizabeth also put the mannequin in Beaumont's bed,' Mackay said.

'Elizabeth was staying at Mount Pleasant at the time,' Watters confirmed.

Mackay took a deep breath. 'You mentioned Amy. Was she involved in this blasted case?'

'I think Amy was unaware of anything,' Watters said.

Mackay sighed. 'So you completed your case, Watters. Or rather, your cases, for it seems two ran side by side.'

'Yes, sir.' Watters did not mention his suspicions about Mrs Foreman and Mrs Caskie. Mrs Foreman evidently did not like Mrs Caskie, with her hints at poisoning, but that had not been his case.

'The thing is,' Watters said, 'if they had kept their cool, even then, they could all have got off with it. We had nothing concrete, only speculation combined with vague theories. The word of young Willie or Varthley would never have stood up in court against respectable people such as Beaumont and Elizabeth Caskie.'

'It just goes to show,' Mackay said. 'These supposedly respectable people are only actors. Behind the façade, they can be as crooked, devious, and downright unpleasant as any garrotter from Couttie's Wynd.' He sighed. 'And if you tell anybody that I said that, I will deny it.'

'Yes, sir.'

'There remains William Caskie,' Watters said.

'William Caskie did not break the law,' Mackay said. 'But you can rest assured that he did not get off scot-free. He is deep in debt and nobody will lend him money now. Mr Caskie faces a future of poverty. If he is lucky, he may find a job as a before-the-mast seaman.' Mackay's smile was bleak. 'Well done, Watters.'

'Just one more thing, sir.' Watters took a deep breath. 'Why did you give the case to me, a mere sergeant, rather than to an inspector?'

Mackay's fingers began another dance. 'There was nothing sinister, Watters. One of my inspectors may be retiring soon. I may need a good man.' His smile lit up the bright Highland eyes. 'I would not tell Marie that yet. Now dismiss.'

'Yes, sir.' Lifting his hat and cane, Watters left the room. If he hurried, he could grab a few holes at the golf course. He swung his cane, smiling.

HISTORICAL NOTES

The American Civil War divided public opinion in Great Britain. While many of the working classes despised the slave system, there was respect for the bravery of the Confederate soldiers. The sometimes high-handed attitude of the Federal Navy also created resentment among some people.

Scottish fishermen lived perilous lives with many casualties, often due to the open boats they used in the treacherous waters off the Scottish coast. Until 1883, there was no obligation to report the death of a fisherman at sea. From that year, any death at sea had to be reported to the Board of Trade.

The ship name *Alexander MacGillivray* was the son of an exiled Jacobite and a Cree Indian. In the eighteenth century, he became chief of the entire Cree nation. History claims that he commanded over 30,000 warriors and at one time held the balance of power in the American South when Great Britain, Spain, and the United States competed for control.

Uniforms: the Confederate Navy found it difficult to obtain sufficient uniforms, so often used whatever they could, charging the poorly paid recruits for the privilege.

Men: perennially short of men, the Confederate Navy filled its ships from whatever sources it could. Attempts to draft from the army often failed as commanders refused to part with soldiers who were precious when facing a numerically superior enemy. Confederate naval commanders often asked for volunteers from the ships they captured, so the sailors who manned Federal merchant vessels would often change allegiance to avoid imprisonment.

Ratcliffe Highway – was a famous or notorious seaman's haunt in the nineteenth century. A street of bright shops and shady pubs, at night it teemed with prostitutes and sailors. Well-known for its sudden violence, the Highway was backed by a network of horrible lanes and alleys, into which it was not advisable to stray. The White Swan or Paddy's Goose was perhaps the most famous seaman's pub in the Highway.

Leviathan – the first train ferry in the world, opened between Granton, near Edinburgh, and Burntisland in Fife in 1850. The ferry was designed by Thomas Grainger and built by Thomas Napier in Govan. The arrangements for loading were designed by Sir Thomas Bouch, who later designed the ill-fated first Tay Bridge that collapsed in 1879. The opening of the Forth Bridge in 1890 ended this rail ferry across the Forth.

Malcolm Archibald

Dear reader,

We hope you enjoyed reading *The Fireraisers*. Please take a moment to leave a review, even if it's a short one. Your opinion is important to us.

Discover more books by Malcolm Archibald at
https://www.nextchapter.pub/authors/malcolm-archibald

Want to know when one of our books is free or discounted for Kindle? Join the newsletter at http://eepurl.com/bqqB3H

Best regards,

Malcolm Archibald and the Next Chapter Team

The story continues in:

The Atlantic Street Murder by Malcolm Archibald

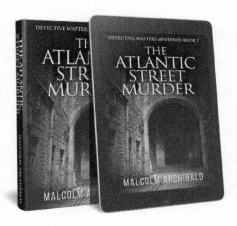

To read first chapter for free, head to:
https://www.nextchapter.pub/books/the-atlantic-street-murder

AUTHOR BIOGRAPHY

Born and raised in Edinburgh, Malcolm Archibald was educated at the University of Dundee, a city to which he has a strong attachment. He has experience in many fields and writes about the Scottish whaling industry as well as historical fiction and fantasy.

Books by the Author

- Jack Windrush -Series
    - Windrush
    - Windrush: Crimea
    - Windrush: Blood Price
    - Windrush: Cry Havelock
    - Windrush: Jayanti's Pawns
- A Wild Rough Lot
- Dance If Ye Can: A Dictionary of Scottish Battles
- Fireraisers
- Like The Thistle Seed: The Scots Abroad
- Our Land of Palestine
- Shadow of the Wolf
- The Swordswoman
- The Shining One (The Swordswoman Book 2)
- Falcon Warrior (The Swordswoman Book 3)
- Melcorka of Alba (The Swordswoman Book 4)

Made in the USA
Monee, IL
10 January 2021